1
2
3
4
5
6
7
8
9
10
11
12
Iacobus Magnæ Britanniæ Rex
Solwey Fyrth
Lancaſter
Lincoln
LINCOLNIA
Coventre
Gloceſter
WARWIC
CANTIUM
Le pas de Calais
BRIT
NICVS

The KING'S MESSENGER

Also by Susanna Kearley

The Vanished Days
Bellewether
A Desperate Fortune
The Firebird
The Rose Garden
The Winter Sea
Every Secret Thing
Season of Storms
Named of the Dragon
The Shadowy Horses
The Splendour Falls
Mariana

SUSANNA KEARSLEY

The KING'S MESSENGER

SIMON & SCHUSTER

London · New York · Sydney · Toronto · New Delhi

First published in Great Britain by Simon & Schuster UK Ltd, 2024

1 3 5 7 9 10 8 6 4 2

Simon & Schuster UK Ltd
1st Floor
222 Gray's Inn Road
London WC1X 8HB

Simon & Schuster: Celebrating 100 Years of Publishing in 2024

Simon & Schuster Australia, Sydney
Simon & Schuster India, New Delhi

www.simonandschuster.co.uk
www.simonandschuster.com.au
www.simonandschuster.co.in

A CIP catalogue record for this book
is available from the British Library

Hardback ISBN: 978-1-3985-1436-2
Trade Paperback ISBN: 978-1-3985-1437-9
eBook ISBN: 978-1-3985-1438-6
Audio ISBN: 978-1-3985-2988-5

Typeset in Arno by M Rules
Printed and Bound in the UK using 100% Renewable
Electricity at CPI Group (UK) Ltd

FSC
www.fsc.org
MIX
Paper | Supporting
responsible forestry
FSC® C171272

This book is dedicated to my readers. Whether you've just joined me on this road, or have been walking with me for a while, you bring me joy and help to make my days a grand adventure, and I'm grateful for your company.

I hold this for a generall Maxime good,
True honor comes from virtue as from blood.

SIR DAVID MORAY
'Epitaph on the death of his deare cousin, M. David Murray'

The Players

*(*fictional)*

LAURENCE WESTAWAY, writing master and scrivener*
PHOEBE WESTAWAY, his daughter*
ANDREW LOGAN, King's Messenger*
ANDREW'S MOTHER AND SISTERS*
OWEN GILROY* } Andrew's friends, grooms in the service of Queen Anna
ROGER PETERS* } Andrew's friends, grooms in the service of Queen Anna
VALENTINE FOX, a courtier*
HECTOR REID, a stable lad*
Robert Carr, VISCOUNT ROCHESTER (later Earl of Somerset), favourite of King James
Henry Howard, 1st EARL OF NORTHAMPTON
KING JAMES VI of Scotland and I of England, son of Mary, Queen of Scots
ANNA OF DENMARK, Queen of Britain, wife of King James
HENRY, PRINCE OF WALES, eldest son of King James
SIR WILLIAM MORAY of Abercairney, childhood companion of King James, now in service to Queen Anna
SIR DAVID MORAY, brother to Sir William Moray and formerly Gentleman of the Robes to Prince Henry
PATRICK GRAEME, 4th Laird of Inchbrakie and cousin to the Morays
ESTHER INGLIS, scrivener and writer in miniature

Phoebe

Great St Bartholomew's, London, 22nd April (St George's Eve) 1613

THE STARS WERE HIDDEN at my birth. There was no moon. A tempest rising in the west sent clouds that settled like a veil of black across the night sky, and my father feared this total darkness was a sign of trouble.

The doctor of astrology he summoned reassured him that my future would be fortunate. My stars, although unseen, would serve me well.

Through all that followed after, and with all we lost, my father held those words so closely to his heart they might have been a rope tossed out upon the water to a drowning man. 'Whatever happens in your life,' he'd often tell me, 'you'll be guided by the planets and their motions. They will lead you to your destiny.'

I let him keep his fancies.

But this morning, as I stormed across the grass still wet with dew, I felt convinced that any planets guiding me were misaligned. They'd started this day poorly, and since there was truth in the old saying that an ill beginning led to an ill end, I knew my morning would do nothing but get worse.

The front door of our house, though heavy, gave way to my forceful push.

'He is the most infuriating man.'

I spoke those words to no one but myself as I was entering the kitchen, yet my father and his elder sister – my aunt Agnes – heard me notwithstanding and immediately knew which man I meant.

My father, fitting on his doublet, asked, 'What has he done to sour thy mood this morning, with the sun so newly up?'

The truth was, Andrew Logan had to do no more than stand within my sight to sour my mood. He'd been our neighbour ten years, since the death of Queen Elizabeth had passed her crown to Scotland's King James, binding both the courts in one and bringing Logan's family south to London in his service. And in all that time I could not think of once my path had crossed with Logan's when he hadn't left me irritated. Nor when I'd been granted the last word.

It was that final point, in truth, that had me most annoyed this morning, because having put the distance of the courtyard between myself and Logan now, my mind could rapidly frame several sharp replies to his last comment, any one of which would have done better than the gaping silence in which I'd watched the big Scotsman's back retreating from my view.

I had been unprepared. I did not often see him at the conduit – most days one of his sisters fetched the water – and hearing the old gardener who came there every morning fawn and laugh and praise him for his drunken misdeeds of the night before had made my temper flare.

I freed my shoulders from the hard yoke with a force that made the pails thump to the floor and told my father all the details, as I'd gleaned them from the gardener's talk, of Logan's violence. Then I said, 'I merely asked him if, by daylight, he did not feel shame for his attack upon a better man.'

My father's eyebrows lifted. 'And what did young Logan say to that?'

'That he would feel no shame for having done what needed doing, and if I stood in defence of Valentine I had his pity.' His contempt, he might have said, for it showed plainly in his eyes while he was speaking, and for one weak moment I had been confused enough to want to ask him why, but then he'd wheeled away abruptly and eventually I'd turned my own back, too, and we had neither of us wasted any further breath in argument.

Aunt Agnes disliked conflict. She brushed the subject away with a move of her hand, as she might wave aside rising smoke from the fire at the hearth where she sat with the linens and hose she was patiently mending. ''Tis but words,' she reminded me. 'Valentine Fox can defend himself.'

'I know he can,' I said, and trusted my voice sounded confident.

Privately, I was less sure. I'd seen Valentine give a display of his swordsmanship, and with his height and lean form he would make an impressive opponent, but Andrew Logan was built like a great, brainless ox, and in a fight with fists – as it apparently had been last night – the odds fell in his favour.

It was plain he had my father's favour also. 'Perhaps Valentine provoked him.'

I thought it hardly likely. 'Pray, when has Andrew Logan needed provocation to begin a fight?'

'When it would make an enemy of someone who could see him lose his place at court, that's when,' my father said. 'It is a rare honour to be a King's Messenger, one that no man would lose lightly, and only a very great insult indeed could have made him take such a risk.'

I raised one shoulder in a half-shrug. 'I'm sure Valentine told him no more than the truth.'

In his place, I'd have thought of a great many things to tell Logan – that he was a bully, for one, and uncultured, and—

'You think too harshly of the lad,' Aunt Agnes said in her mild tone that held the firmer edge designed to shape my manners into something more polite.

I said nothing, though I might have pointed out that Andrew Logan was a lad no longer. The sullen sixteen-year-old who had come here from Scotland was a grown man now with two more years beneath his belt than my own twenty-four, and at the conduit he had fair towered above me, or so it had seemed. I'd been forced to look up, all the daggers of my own gaze being deflected by his stubborn chin.

Plainly my aunt and father had not faced that side of Logan yet, else I would have more of their sympathy.

My father, for his part, was fully focused now on dressing in a way I had not seen him do in some days, and that fact diverted me from my small inconveniences and minor squabbles.

As he fitted on his hat, the one with the fine feather and the polished gilded clip shaped like a rose, I said, 'You are called to the palace.'

'I am.'

'Then the king has returned?'

'He has.'

My aunt said, 'But the Princess Elizabeth has not yet sailed for the continent. You would think her own father might wish to stay by her till her ship leaves, so she's given a proper farewell.'

With one glance, *my* father reminded his sister the king was not someone to criticize.

Returning his attention to the angle of his hat brim, he asked, 'What would he gain by standing on the shore and weeping while the ship sails off? It would not make their parting any easier. The king owes no one any such display of his emotions, for it is in truth a private pain, to lose the ones we love.'

Aunt Agnes had no argument to offer, knowing well my father knew that pain himself, and deeply. As did I.

The king had also suffered loss. Of his seven children, only three survived their infancy, and one of those had fallen just this past winter – handsome Prince Henry, the Prince of Wales, pride of our nation – struck down by an illness so sudden the gossips still crouched in their corners and whispered strange theories.

So yes, the king might be forgiven for turning his face from another loss.

Except, 'The princess has not died,' I told them. 'She has only married.'

My aunt said idly she saw little difference between death and marriage. 'I've observed some women wish for death the longer they are married.' She was teasing, but it drew another sidelong look of warning from my father.

'Agnes,' he rebuked her. 'Do not fill my daughter's head with nonsense. She will marry a fine man of a good family, who will give her healthy children and—'

'—a life of ease at court.' I spoke those words with him in unison, an easy thing to do when I had heard them said so frequently. I did not share my father's faith in almanacs and stars, nor in the doctor of astrology who'd cast a figure of the hour of my birth and made that bold prediction.

But I hoped.

For, after all, there *was* a man to whom I'd given my affection, and he was a fine man of good family, who had risen now so high at court that he could give his wife a life of ease there, if he chose to marry.

As though he had read my thoughts, my father asked, 'Have you seen Valentine this morning?'

'No, I've had no reason to.'

My aunt piped in, 'Besides, 'tis barely six o'clock, he will be sleeping, surely.'

'Not this morning,' said my father. 'He has business at court also, and he promised I may ride there with him in his coach. Phoebe, would you go across and tell him, please, that I am nearly ready?'

I suspected that my father, in reply to my remark that I'd no reason to see Valentine, was trying now to give me one. I smiled. 'Of course.'

I might have wished my hair was not arranged so plainly, nor that I had laced my stays so loosely underneath my long-sleeved bodice in a style two seasons out of fashion. But I could at least draw comfort from the knowledge that my fray with Logan would have brought some colour to my cheeks.

'You're very pretty when you're angry,' Valentine had teased me once.

To his credit, *he* rarely made me angry.

We'd grown up together, here in St Bartholomew's, within this close community that sat outside the city walls of London, on what once had been the grounds of an old monastery. Nearly fifty years before my birth, when Great King Henry broke with Rome and founded our own Protestant religion here in England, he declared an end to nunneries and monasteries, claimed those buildings for the crown, and gave or sold them into private hands. Thus St Bartholomew's had been transformed.

The church itself remained – its bells still tolled the quarters of our waking hours – but the buildings that the monks had used were fashioned into mansions, and new houses had been built within the walls of the great inner courtyard that we called the Close, with yet more houses built upon the field where every August's end the fair of St Bartholomew brought people thronging, as they had time out of mind, to sell their wares and see the spectacle.

It was a fine address to have. When we'd first come to live here I had scarce believed our fortune. Even then, though I'd been small, the Close had seemed a sanctuary, beautiful and privileged, where several of our neighbours, like my father, worked at court, while others had no need to work at all by virtue of their birth and status.

Valentine's father was such a man. His family owned estates in Wiltshire but he rarely saw them, having argued with his brothers as a younger man and hardened as he aged so he continued unforgiving. That always made me sad, for could I have had my brothers back again I'd not have wasted any moments left to us in arguing, so glad would I have been to have their company.

But Valentine's father never changed his course, once set. There was an order to his life, and to his days. I knew at this hour he would be outdoors patrolling in his gardens, as a military leader might inspect the boundaries of his headquarters.

His mansion was well situated for this purpose, being in what had been designed to be the frater – or great dining hall – for the use of the long-departed monks. A long building of grand proportions, it shielded the church behind it and butted up at right angles to the equally impressive former dormitory, which had also been converted to a mansion of great beauty that formed the far angle at this north end of the Close.

To the other side of the Foxes' mansion, and a stone's throw to the south of it, as though aware it ought to keep itself below its betters and not seek to share their level, lay our own house, less impressive. Yet the bricks still had a solid look and all the shutters had been newly painted and the window glass was catching the new rays of rising sunlight, and as always when I stepped into the Close, I felt a sense of pride.

'Up early,' Valentine's father said as I came across the green to greet him, which I judged the closest he had come in weeks to giving me a compliment.

I often marvelled he could be so like his son to look at, and yet so completely unlike him in character.

He said, 'You'll be wanting my son, I expect.' Then, with great disapproval, 'He's been in a fight.'

I didn't reveal that I'd already heard. Valentine's father disliked gossip as much as Aunt Agnes. Still, I couldn't help but defend Valentine. 'Then he must have been greatly provoked.'

If I hadn't known better, I might have thought Valentine's father eyed me with something approaching amusement before he collected himself and corrected me. 'Gentlemen are not provoked by their lessers.'

He glanced past my shoulder, along the green length of the Close, and although I did not turn to follow his gaze I knew where he was looking.

The Logans' house lay, like our own, on the long western edge of Bartholomew's Close, only more to the south, near the conduit. I made a point of not giving it notice.

'My son's with his friends, in the stables,' said Valentine's father. ''Tis not the kindest of company for a young lady, but stop up your ears and you ought to survive.'

And *that*, I thought, was humour, or his rare attempt at it. I smiled and said, 'Yes, sir.'

The stables were reached by a passageway hugging the mansion. Built broad enough to take a coach, it opened to the square enclosure of what, in the monastery's time, had been the cloisters. Here the walls and spire of the church loomed high and cast their shadows as though frowning down upon the fate that had befallen the once prayerful, silent walks and archways, turned to use as horses' stalls.

No doubt the church was frowning harder still this morning, I thought, with the language Valentine's close friends were using freely with each other.

There were three of them today. Their numbers changed from time to time, but from the day I had first met him, Valentine had always drawn a following.

It was no more than natural. He looked like every gallant knight I'd seen in tapestries and paintings – tall and sure of step, his golden hair a little wayward with its waves, his beard somehow managing, even when he trimmed it to a close and tidy point, to remain distinctly roguish.

And his eyes – those eyes that made me feel I was the only person in his view – were like the eyes of every hero who, when moved to action, had called men to come along with him, and found a sudden army at his back.

Except this morning, underneath one of those eyes there was faint bruising.

'Phoebe!' Valentine had noticed my arrival. 'You look very pretty this morning.' His eyebrows raised as I came close. 'And very irritated.'

'Not at you,' I promised. 'I do think of Andrew Logan.'

'Why does he deserve your thoughts?'

'Because of this.' I raised my hand to lightly touch the bruise beneath his left eye. 'Does it hurt?'

'I feel it not at all, when you do that.' He smiled, then asked, 'What makes you think that it is Logan's work?'

'Because I heard him talking at the conduit this morning to the gardener, who was praising him for last night's fighting.'

'Then you know what happened?'

'Only that you were attacked by Logan and his companions, and that your friends bravely took your part.'

Looking at his friends now, it appeared they'd paid a price

for that decision. One, much bruised, was leaning heavily against the coach while waiting for the groom to finish harnessing the horses, while another held a bandaged arm close-cradled to his chest, and the third was already within the coach, where shadows only half concealed his lounging and defeated pose and bandaged hands.

Turning my attention back to Valentine, I said, 'I'm sorry you were made to fight. Could it not be avoided?'

'Not by me. Did not the gardener touch on how the fight began, when he was talking at the conduit?'

'The gardener took Logan's part, and seemed glad you'd been challenged.'

'Oh? What did the gardener say, exactly?'

All the words were clear and stinging in my mind, and easy to recall. 'He said that Logan had just done the Close a service, because you'd long needed to be taken down a peg.' I frowned. 'Why did it start? The fight, I mean.'

''Tis not for gentle ears to hear the insult that began it.' Over the years, Valentine had often regaled me with tales of the ungentlemanly brawls he'd witnessed Logan fight in. That this latest one was too heinous for Valentine to describe told me much. He smiled slightly. 'But I've not been taken down, as you can see. I am yet standing.' Glancing from me to his friends, he added, 'And I'm late to court.'

That nudged my memory. 'I am sent to tell you that my father's nearly ready.' Then, because his face remained uncomprehending, I said, 'You did say that he could ride to court this morning in your coach.'

'I did.' His turn to frown.

He knew as well as I did that my father's health had faltered these past months. It was not common knowledge, but I'd shared with Valentine how I had seen my father several times appear to lose his breath while walking, and once stumble in the road, and once drop in a near faint after a long day of business, which he blamed upon a want of sleep.

I could feel my temper rising for the second time this morning. 'You promised him.' I let the sharper edges of my tone show through. 'A promise is a promise.'

'So it is. But thanks to Logan, we've no room, the coach is full. My friends are injured and must ride within. They are the sons of noblemen,' he told me.

'But my father does not merit your attention.' I did not try to hide the sarcasm that edged my tone.

'I've angered you.'

'You are not often selfish. Nor did the favour of noblemen's sons used to make you forget your word.'

'Phoebe.' His eyes asked for my understanding. 'They are also friends of my lord Rochester, my patron. I would lose my place at court were I to leave them unattended. And if I lose my place at court, what future could there be for us?' He bent to kiss my cheek but I was turning from him, so the touch was brief. He told me, 'Give your father my regrets. He'll understand.'

He did, of course. My father was an understanding man.

He stood with me outside our door and watched the coach departing, having heard it pass. It travelled down the Close, past Logan's house, and out the gate into the labyrinth of lanes and streets that lay beyond.

'Ah, well,' my father told me, 'I've no doubt your uncle at St Paul's will have room in his coach for me. I have time left to catch him, and 'tis not so far to walk.'

Too far, still, for my comfort.

Pushing down my disappointment in what Valentine had done, I said, 'I'll come with you.' And when my father looked at me as though I were proposing to run off to the New World, I added, 'Only to St Paul's. It has been too long since I've seen my uncle.'

'And how will you get safely home?'

'He has so many servants, one of them can be my escort.'

He agreed to this, to my relief, but only after he took from his pocket the crisp copy of his almanac. My aunt considered almanacs a needless waste of pennies, but my father bought a new one every year, to guide his actions. At the stationer's, he'd carefully survey the different almanacs, each named for their compiler. His favourites were those of one Mr Parker, whose predictions for the year were drawn more closely from astrology and who, beside the listing for each month, with all its days of feasts and festivals and forecasts of the weather, left a blank page for the user's daily notes and jottings. Mr Parker's almanac provided tables of the tides, the time each day of sunrise, and the aspects of the moon. But to my father, the most useful feature of the little book was that it warned him in advance which dates would bring him luck, and which he should approach with caution.

'No,' my father said, 'there is no "D" for danger marked beside this day, so we may safely walk abroad.'

I made no reply at first, because I'd been distracted by a black and white bird settling on the tiles of the roof directly opposite. A magpie.

My Aunt Agnes, had she been here, would have thrown a stone to chase it off, and then she'd have recited prayers to counteract its evil.

As I met the bird's unblinking eyes, I understood that impulse. But it was only a bird, and to imagine it as more than that – to think it truly might be an ill omen – would be like thinking Mr Parker's almanac was accurate.

My father nudged me. 'Phoebe? Did you hear me? Mr Parker says today will bring us no misfortune.'

'Good.' I smiled, and linked my arm with his, as much to steady him as from affection.

But as we walked on, I couldn't help but feel the black eyes of that lurking magpie watching us, as steady as a stone.

Andrew

The Strand, London, the same day

'Be grateful ye were born a man,' my younger sister Margaret said to me.

She was the dreaming sort, and not inclined to notice things that did not touch on her directly, and admittedly I had arranged my hat to hide the worst part of the bruising round my eye from last night's brawl, but I could not keep from smiling at her comment, which was all at once divided from the truth of life as I had lived it, and yet still exactly what I needed most to hear this morning to restore my humour. Looking down at her, I asked, 'And why is that?'

I had to put my arm out as I spoke to draw her back a moment while a cart horse lumbered by, its great hooves landing in the very place her smaller feet had lately been. My own horse, Brutus, tossed his head against the reins held in my other hand, indignant he was being led instead of ridden, but since he had cast a shoe a short while back, I had no choice but to endure his silent wrath and lead him, for to bear the weight of both of us would have done his hoof damage.

With a lethal glare at me, he fell in step as we walked on.

Margaret hadn't noticed, as her whole attention was still focused on explaining why I was so fortunate to be a man. 'Because,' she said, 'if ye did have a mind to marry, ye could do it as ye pleased, while I can't seek a match myself till Jeannie weds, and she and Roger have been waiting so long for the queen's approval that I fear it never will be given, and I'll die a maid.'

I was about to reassure her that she had no need to worry – that the queen, in her own time, would give her blessing to our sister's marriage – but it struck me she seemed over-interested, and glancing down more piercingly, I asked, 'Who is it ye would haste to marry?'

Frowning, she reproved me, 'Andrew Logan, I am not one of your criminals, ye needn't turn Inquisitor. There is no man. And even if there was a man – which there is not – it would not be your business.'

Meaning that there definitely was a man, then.

Her deep sigh confirmed it. 'But 'tis an outdated rule that the younger must wait till the elder is wed. I'll be eighteen soon, Andrew. And Jeannie,' she added, her tone pitched to sound like a warning, 'is twenty-two.'

'Ancient,' I said. Four years younger than me, and I felt every day of my age as my shoulder protested the sharp movement I made to hold back my sister a second time out of the way of disaster. 'If ye don't mind how ye go, ye'll have no need to worry over weddings.'

I might as well have told a skylark not to sing.

Margaret was a lively lass, and as we came through together into the stableyard of the queen's palace of Somerset House she was still oblivious to everything around us, and still brightly talking.

My height and size rarely allowed me to pass through a place without notice – less still when I was with Brutus, for he was giant himself – and I was fair impossible to overlook when wearing my full livery as I was now. This scarlet doublet, slashed with blue and trimmed with gold, and with the king's own coat of arms emblazoned on my chest, its quartered shield combining all four nations of our kingdom underneath his golden crown, at either side supported by the lion and the unicorn, marked me as a King's Messenger in service of the crown. I wore it proudly.

But even if Brutus and I had been as stealthy as shadows, there was no hope of moving discreetly when I had my sister beside me. Her laughter and chatter rang out in that cobbled, enclosed space so musically that all the heads of the horses came over the posts as if they, too, would listen.

The scents of this stable stirred bittersweet memories. I'd worked here, afore I'd been raised to the Messengers' ranks. I'd spent long, happy hours here, and each time I came through the stable doors part of me wanted to turn time's hands backwards, and then stop the clock altogether.

My friend Owen Gilroy, who sat on a bench near the stable door bent to his work on a saddle, glanced over and nodded at me, and then flashed a smile full of charm. 'Good morrow, Margaret.'

She blushed and returned him the greeting, and rising on tiptoe she kissed me and thanked me and wished me a good day and scurried along to her work in the kitchens and left me with no chance to make a reply.

But as I turned back to Owen, I mimicked his gallant voice. '"Good morrow, Margaret"? What is that, exactly?'

He stood and grinned. 'Nothing you need be concerned about.'

I had my next question framed in my mind but it faded to nothing as the scene I was looking at started to waver and blur. As I focused on Owen, he no longer seemed to stand here in the stables, but in a strange church, at the side of a baptismal font, with the light coming in from a window behind. At his right side stood Margaret, her hair in a style I could not recall seeing her wearing, her eyes bright with pride. In her arms she was holding a bairn, newly born. 'We'll be naming him Donald,' she told me. Our father's name.

And then as swiftly as they had appeared, Margaret and the bairn vanished again, leaving Owen alone and the stables as they'd always been.

He'd stopped what he was doing with the saddle and was watching me. 'What?'

I ignored him, not from rudeness, but because it was the simplest way to manage things. I'd learned this lesson young, when I had realized that not everybody had this gift – or curse – of Second Sight that gave unbidden glimpses of the things that were to come. My mother, a Macdougall from the Western Isles, had warned me I should hide it well, for while the Sight was commonplace among her people, elsewhere it was nothing but a danger to possess, viewed as the Devil's work and witchcraft.

But Owen persisted. 'Are you feeling well?'

I knew the change was slight when I was Seeing – a loss of focus in my gaze, a blankness of expression brief enough to make most think I was distracted, nothing more. But that distraction had been great enough, this time, for me to miss the entrance of the man who was now standing close beside me.

Roger Peters was a fixture in these stables, being one of the queen's favourite grooms. His father had been one of the African servants Her Majesty brought with her from Denmark to Edinburgh, where I'd met Roger as a lad. Then, he'd seemed quiet. Now a man of my own age, he had a quick laugh and a quicker wit, and since I'd come to London he and Owen had become my closest friends. With Roger waiting for the queen's consent to wed my sister Jeannie, it appeared both men were destined to become my brothers, also.

But this morning, Roger's first thought was for Brutus. 'He has cast a shoe.'

'Aye, I noticed as we came across Fleet Bridge.'

'You did not ride him after that, I hope?'

'Ye take me for a fool?'

The white of Roger's grin flashed suddenly against his darker skin as he tipped up my hat brim. 'I had best reserve my judgement till you tell me who did give you those?'

He'd seen my bruises.

I hedged and did not answer him directly. 'I was in the Star last night, and helped a lad who needed helping, that is all. He was young, and in his cups, and rashly found himself outnumbered in a fight. I took his part to make the odds more even.'

Owen, from his corner, said, 'A noble cause, I'll grant you.' But he knew me far too well, and with his keen eyes on my face he asked, 'Who was on the other side?'

I shrugged. 'Three men whose names I could not tell ye.'

Owen waited. 'And?'

He would not leave it alone, I knew, so I relented. 'And Valentine Fox.'

They both made the same noise, turned away from me briefly, and Roger said, 'You *are* a fool! Did you strike him?'

I shook my head. 'The lad did. That's how it began. Had I not been there, he might have been killed.'

'Better his death than yours,' Roger told me. 'You might try remembering Valentine Fox is the favourite of Viscount Rochester, and Rochester is *the* favourite of King James, and a ruthless man like Rochester who has the king's ear only needs to whisper it was you, and not the lad, who did strike Valentine, and who will dare to call him liar? You could find yourself arrested for assault. And who would guard your mother and your sisters then?'

He seemed about to carry on but, thinking better of it, took the reins from my hand with the promise, 'I will have him shod for you when you return from Whitehall.' He eyed me very soberly, and added, 'If you *do* return.'

When I went out to the street again and started towards Whitehall, people moved aside respectfully, their gazes touching briefly on the leather bag I carried at my belt as though wondering if it held royal letters or a warrant of arrest.

Had I been in a mood to indulge their curiosity, I could have told them it was empty, and that it would likely remain so if Valentine's powerful patron decided to punish me for what I'd done last night at the Star Tavern.

Not that I would have done anything differently. There'd been no question which course was the right one. The lad had been out of his depth. He'd been drinking too long and too heavily, searching for courage, and when he staggered across the Star's floor I'd known no good would come of it, even afore he had flung out his fierce accusation – his sister defiled and abandoned by Valentine.

Valentine, arching his eyebrows, had smoothly replied, 'I apologize.' Then, taking out his purse, he'd tossed two coins upon the table. 'There, that is the going rate, I do believe, for whores.'

Of course, the lad had swung for him, as any brother would. He'd struck a lucky, glancing blow that gave me one small moment's satisfaction. But then Valentine had touched the place beneath his eye, and turning to his friends had told them, 'Make him pay for that.'

I'd seen the lad's fear. There were three of them against him. And I could not stand aside.

No, I did not regret the action I had taken, but I did not wish to lose my scarlet doublet for it. Not every man could work as a King's Messenger. My father strove for years to be promoted to their ranks, and called in every favour possible, afore his death, to smooth my path so I might take his place. Losing that position as the price for crossing Valentine would sting badly enough, but not till Roger's lecture had I reckoned there could be a price to pay yet more severe.

And Valentine was vengeful. These past years living in the Close had taught me that much, and his nature showed itself to me so plainly that I marvelled anybody could be blind to it.

I thought of Phoebe Westaway, this morning at the conduit, the water from the wellhead spilling over in her bucket as she stared at me with bold contempt.

She had not always looked at me that way. When first I'd come to St Bartholomew's, she'd merely been dismissive. Kept her distance. She had stumbled on the walk one morning when she'd passed our house and I had offered her my hand and she'd ignored it as though I had been invisible.

Thus it continued, although I'd done nothing to give her offence. She avoided me, crossing the Close if she saw me approaching, her haughtiness freezing out all my attempts to be kind. So I stopped being kind.

And her disregard turned to dislike.

That she wished she were Valentine's lass had been plain from the start. I could see how she looked at him. See how she followed him. See how he led her along in the dance. Had she been more agreeable, I could have warned her and spared her the heartache and grief that would come in the end from her taking that road, but I reasoned the two of them likely were well suited to one another and kept my thoughts private.

This morning, though, when she stood close afore me at the

conduit, her upturned face so angry and accusing, I could no more hold my silence.

I felt no regret for having done *that*, either – having spoken truth. And there was satisfaction to be had, however small, in having won the last word in our argument. In fact, when I replayed our brief exchange now in my mind, I gained still further satisfaction from the realization Phoebe's words, designed to wound me, had in fact provided me a perfect line to add to the apology that I could give the king if I were summoned – the apology that I was counting on to save not only my position, but my freedom.

'I'm ashamed,' I said, beneath my breath, 'that I attacked a better man.'

No, I could not deliver that convincingly.

'I do regret . . .' There, that was more believable. 'I do regret that I attacked a better man.' I carried on from there, and had run through the whole apology three times when I caught sight of Charing Cross and took the turning into King Street, where the wide approach to Whitehall began.

Whitehall was unique, not a centralized palace with everything under one roof, but a sprawling community unto itself – different buildings and halls and a chapel, and galleries three storeys tall that connected one part to another – with views across St James's Park or the lush privy gardens and, always, the Thames that ran majestically aside the longest gallery, from where the king's pier commanded the river.

When we'd first arrived in London, when I'd been a lad of sixteen years, my favourite part of Whitehall had been the long tiltyard that lay behind the wall I was now passing. There'd been something of the taste of legend in that tiltyard – boyhood tales of knights and quests and bold adventure, things that had been lost to progress in our modern world, and that had lived again in my imagination when I'd watched Prince Henry, younger than myself, run at the ring on horseback with his lance, like any knight of old might do, afore the cheering crowd.

But now the prince was dead, and all the cheering had died with him, and the tiltyard was a quiet space of dust and empty dreams, and I could no more bear to look at it.

Instead I aimed my eyes ahead to Holbein's Gate, the grand, four-turreted gatehouse guarding the inner precincts of the court. Elaborately built of brick, its leaded windows turned to mirrors in the morning sun, its height and form minded me of the great Netherbow I had walked under so often in Edinburgh, and raised the memory of home.

Today, its tall central archway was already busy with coaches all waiting their turn to pass through to deposit their passengers. Word travelled fast that the king had returned, and he never did stay long at Whitehall. Those seeking his favour would have to move quickly.

I kept myself clear of their path and instead used the court gate that lay at the corner of the new Banqueting House. Here, too, it was crowded. Along the broad walk leading down to the king's lodgings, men stood singly or huddled in close conversations.

Near the doorway to the guard chamber, a larger group stood clustered round a man whose clothing, of the latest fashion and in brightly coloured silk, was likely more expensive than the rent I yearly paid to lease our house. There were a few at court who dressed like that, but chief among them was the Viscount Rochester, who seemed to own more doublets in more fabrics than the queen had gowns. As I drew closer, I saw his features, deliberately charming, until he saw me – then they took on a measure of canniness.

Valentine, close by his side, had the look of a sleek cat observing its prey.

But I did not break stride.

At my shoulder, a black shadow fell into step with me. The blood rose swiftly pounding in my ears afore a calm voice said, 'You're late,' and, turning, I saw that the man was not a guard come to arrest me, but my lord Northampton.

He wore black like a uniform, day after day. I'd not seen him in anything else. I'd been told that he'd done the same as a young man when he'd first come to court, back in the time of Queen Elizabeth. Some said it was because he was a sober man and a scholar; others thought it more likely he wore perpetual mourning since his family, the Howards, though not lacking power, had weathered so many misfortunes.

His father and brother had both been beheaded. That my lord Northampton had survived his life at court and reached the age of seventy-odd with his head still firmly on his shoulders was a testament to the wisdom of the mind within that head – or at least, to its ability to guess the moves of his opponents on the board, and keep one play ahead of them.

He said, 'You are nearly an hour past your usual time.'

'Forgive me, my lord. It could not be avoided. My horse cast a shoe, and—'

'No matter. I only hope he's as forgiving. He does not like being kept waiting.'

I dreaded asking, 'Who does not, my lord?'

'The king, of course. Now come, he asked for you expressly. You'd do well,' he said, 'to ready an apology.'

I did not need to steal an upward glance at sky and sunlight as we neared the looming guard chamber to know that I might not see either for some space of time. Nor did I need to waste a glance at Valentine as we swept by to feel his gaze of triumph.

I stood tall, and strode with ease, for I'd not have him thinking I felt worried.

Yet my worries found me, all the same.

We Messengers were often made to wait. I'd learned to seem unbothered by it, even when, as now, the waiting tested all my nerves. The trick of it lay in distraction, though here in this small room that course appeared limited.

It was the first time I had been within one of the king's closets, and while it was furnished with fine things, it held not the grandeur of the formal chambers. Instead it was homely, if such could be said of a room in a palace. A private retreat for a king who was rarely allowed time alone.

On a table set next to the window were papers and pens and ink laid out for writing, with books stacked haphazardly everywhere. A Turkish carpet silenced footsteps, and the panelled walls were hung with tapestries of bright design.

I counted the books: fifty-seven. The diamond-shaped panes in the tall window: ninety-four. And when the king had not yet come, I turned to the tapestries. These were of Biblical scenes, richly done, but the one that held my eye showed Jacob, asleep in a pastoral wilderness, while behind him, his dreams revealed angels descending and climbing the ladder to heaven, and God Himself at its top, pronouncing His prophecy of Jacob's future.

Northampton, who had taken up a place beside the writing table while we waited, remarked, 'How must it feel when God does favour you so greatly that he gives you such a perfect sleep as he gave Jacob?'

'No perfect sleep, my lord, but one disturbed by dreams and visions.'

Though he was behind me, I could hear the dry amusement in Northampton's voice. 'I take it, then, you would not wish for such a gift yourself?'

Another man's voice asked, 'What gift is that?'

I had not heard the room's door open. Neither had Northampton, evidently, but when I turned from the tapestry to face the king and bow my knee, Northampton, too, was kneeling. When he rose, I stayed where I was, head bent.

'Stand, Logan,' said the king. 'Ye are too tall to hold that pose so long.'

The king was tall himself, with deep set eyes that at first glance seemed languid but concealed a sharp intelligence. They took note of the bruising on my face but when I'd straightened, he said only, 'Now, what is this gift ye would not wish to have?'

Northampton spared me the need to reply by telling the king what we'd been speaking of, and so the king, with interest, made a study of the tapestry of Jacob's ladder.

'Jacob was most fortunate to have his dream and know it came from God,' the king said, 'for prophecies come often from a darker place. In Scotland, my mother's death was spoken of before it happened by those men whose power of Sight showed them a bloody head dancing in the air. When I learned this, I sought out of certain books a way to attain this knowledge, for it is tempting to imagine that men might foretell what horse shall win at match-running, what side shall win in battle, and what way and at what age a man shall die. But all my studies led me to the sure belief such prophecies in our time are the Devil's doing, and cannot be trusted.'

I kept silent. I knew well the king's views on witchcraft. I'd witnessed the trials and torture and burnings of poor wretches who were accused of it, knowing that could have been me.

The king's gaze was still upon the tapestry. 'This always pleased me for another reason. I'm surprised ye do not see it, Logan.' When I looked at him, he smiled, and I began to relax. 'The angels on the ladder,' he explained. 'They mind me God relies upon His Messengers. And so do I.'

He was the sort of man who liked to walk while he was thinking, although the confines of this room prevented him from pacing more than several steps together. He crossed to the writing table. 'Your father served me very loyally. How long now since he died?'

I said, 'Five years, Your Majesty.'

'I trust your mother and your sisters are all well?'

It honoured me that he would ask. 'They're very well, Your Majesty.'

The king strolled back to me. 'Your elder sister is betrothed, I understand, to my wife's groom – the African. Ye do approve?'

I might have pointed out that Roger had been born in Edinburgh, and so was Scottish, just as I was, but one should not contradict the king, and so I simply said, 'With all my heart, Your Majesty.'

'Then we must see what we can do to speed their marriage,' said the king. 'I have a mission for ye.' He appeared about to carry on, but stopped as one who, wanting entrance to a room, finds one door barred and seeks another. Moving to the window, he said, 'Ye'll have heard the rumours, I don't doubt, about Prince Henry's death.'

I knew not how to answer that. Of course I'd heard the talk. One could not work at Whitehall and not hear it, but I took the neutral path. 'Forgive me. There's aye gossip in the palace, but I pay it little heed.'

Northampton seemed approving of my answer.

The king said, 'People whisper that my son's death was

unnatural. That he was poisoned. This upsets the queen. *She* pays them heed, and she would see the matter properly investigated.'

I assured him, 'I stand ready at your service.'

'And I am grateful for it.' He paused again, returning to the subject of my mission by a sideways route. 'There is one man who was much closer to my son than any other.'

I knew what name he'd say afore he spoke it. Everyone had seen that one man sitting as the lone attendant in the prince's funeral chariot beside the black-draped effigy, and looking as though it were his own son who had been lost.

'Sir David Moray,' said the king, 'will hold the answers we do need, if any man has knowledge of the truth.'

Northampton said, 'I wrote to him requesting his co-operation, but his only answer was to travel into France. I fear that shows a guilty conscience.'

'Aye.' The king looked grim, and turned to me. 'I need ye to arrest him and return him here to London where he can be well examined on the things he knows.'

I frowned. 'Am I to go to France?'

Northampton told me that there was no need. 'Sir David's currently in Paris but is soon to be returning to his family's home at Abercairney. We have men in place who'll give us timely notice before he sets out for Scotland. In the meantime, you should haste you north to Edinburgh, to wait for our instruction.'

This would be the farthest distance I'd been made to travel for my work, and mentally I tallied up how many days I'd need to travel north and then return, more slowly, with a prisoner. My mother and my sisters would need somebody to guard them in my absence, and—

The king had more to say. 'When ye have Moray in your

custody, I wish for ye to keep a written record of whatever he might tell ye of my son. In case some accident befalls him, we at least will have that testimony.'

I felt I'd stepped from solid and familiar ground to something more uncertain. 'I can promise ye, Your Majesty, if he is in my charge, I'll see he does not come to harm.'

'Nevertheless.' The king's smile, this time, was but slight. 'My lord Northampton will be sure to give you all the paper and supplies ye need. Here, take one of my pens.'

The king liked giving gifts. He chose a pen from those laid on his desk, and I accepted it and thanked him.

He said, 'Your hands, at least, escaped unharmed from your adventures last night at the tavern.'

My heart dropped. I had been too quick to think I'd been reprieved. I cleared my throat. 'Your Majesty, I do regret—'

''Tis nothing.' My apology was waved aside. The king gave me his hand and once again I knelt and bowed my head. 'I pray you, Logan, do me justice in your service and report, and I'll not fail to see ye – and your sisters – well rewarded.'

That was all. He left us there alone, Northampton and myself.

Northampton met my eyes and said, 'I'd imagine that went rather better than you'd feared.' And then, more practically, 'You should be on the road as soon as possible tomorrow morning. Once we have discussed your warrant, you may go make your arrangements. For the writing, I will hire you a scrivener, to travel with you.'

Now there would be three of us – myself, Sir David Moray, and a scrivener, all travelling together. It would make the journey slower, but I did not raise an argument.

I had a different thought, now that my heart had settled back into its normal pace. 'Why did he ask for me?'

Northampton's eyebrows lifted. 'What?'

'The king. You said he asked for me expressly. Why?'

'I cannot claim to know the king's mind,' said Northampton. 'But I should imagine he desired a Scottish Messenger to carry out this mission, since your travel takes you into Scotland.'

'But I'm not the only Scottish Messenger.'

'Well, then, I have no certain answer for you.' His tone did not change at all as he went on, 'Why did you choose to leave your horse at the queen's stables, and not bring it to one of our farriers here?'

Carefully, I schooled my face. Even though I knew Northampton, having lived so long at court, had eyes and ears at work for him in many places, it still caught me off my guard to hear him casually let slip that he'd been watching *me*. I shrugged. 'My horse is most particular whom he allows to hold his feet. He trusts the queen's groom.'

'Ah.' Northampton nodded. 'Then perhaps you'll understand me when I tell you that the king, too, is particular in whom he puts his trust.' He levelled his keen gaze upon me. 'You'll also understand, I'm sure, that nothing must be said of this to anyone?'

'Of course.' I was surprised he'd ask. He knew, as I did, that my oaths and duty bound me to keep all the details of my service secret, even from my closest friends and family. 'Ye have my word.'

'Not anyone,' he stressed again. 'This court is like a hive of bees that swarms about the slightest scent of gossip, and it would be most unfortunate if any mention of your mission were to reach the queen.'

I frowned. 'Forgive me, but I thought the king was doing this to ease the queen's misgivings.'

'He is,' Northampton said.

I must have still been frowning, for he added the reminder, 'What does pass between the king and queen is not your business, Logan. Keep your focus. Mind your orders. And remember,' he said gravely, 'every wall has ears.'

'I do not like it,' Roger said. He'd come to stand with me while I ran a questing hand down Brutus's near foreleg, testing that his tendons remained sound after this morning's misadventure. If we were to make a journey of this length, I would not see him injured.

Roger asked, 'Why now? And to a distant place?'

I glanced at him. 'I did not say that it was somewhere distant.' I'd not told him anything at all about where I was sent, or why.

'It is somewhere far enough away that you've asked us to watch your family while you're gone,' he pointed out.

'And will ye do it?'

'Yes, of course. The queen will any day now start her progress towards Bath, and I will keep watch over Jeannie while we travel with her.'

Owen, who'd been sitting by in his good-natured way, said, 'And I'll happily bed down within your house to see that Margaret and your mother are protected.'

It did cross my mind to tell him he should have a care where he did make his bed within my house, my sister being young and inexperienced, but I bit hard to hold my tongue for I would not insult him so. The vision I had seen of him and Margaret told me that, whatever passed between them, he would treat her honourably.

Straightening, I thanked them both.

'But still, it strikes me wrong,' said Roger. 'Somewhere far. The road, alone. Who will be there at your right hand, to offer you protection?'

'Brutus,' I replied. My horse, on hearing his name, turned his head within the stall to look at me with an expectant eye, and reaching up I scratched the place behind his ear, beneath his mane, known only to himself and me. 'He is a brave companion.'

Owen thought him fierce enough. 'He nearly bit me, earlier this afternoon. 'Twas fortunate that Roger talked him out of it.'

Roger commented, 'I would I could do likewise with his master.'

Impatience surged and made me turn. 'What would ye have me do? Refuse the king? Did not ye warn me just this morn my fight with Valentine might put me in the Tower, and now ye wish to put me in the grave? One does not,' I finished, very sure, 'refuse the king.'

I had not raised my voice. When I was angered, to be honest, I more often did the opposite, and spoke more low and levelly. But Roger had stepped back a pace, as though acknowledging he'd come too near the line.

We did not need apologies between us. We stood on equal ground, for I had lost my temper with a friend, and although he had prodded me I knew he was but worried for my welfare. Our exchange of looks acknowledged this, and Owen played the peacemaker by telling us a joke so bawdy that our laughter masked the noise of anyone approaching, so the voice behind us caught us unprepared.

A man's voice, dry. 'I thought tomorrow was the holiday. Or has St George's Day begun already, before sundown, so ye've laid your work aside?'

Sir William Moray, Laird of Abercairney, was a man of middle age, near fifty, like the king. He'd been the king's companion from the time when they'd been lads together, and had served him closely since, though now his work was in Queen Anna's household. Formerly in Scotland he had been her Master of the Horse, until the ever changing fortunes of the court had seen him shuffled to a new place of high favour.

He commanded great respect, and did it easily, with a decided swagger that suggested his had been a life of action.

His few words had been enough to dislodge Owen from his seat and spur him to recall a sudden need to be elsewhere, while Roger touched his hat and nodded and then melted with efficiency into some shadowed corner. I'd have done the same – this was the brother of the man the king was sending me to apprehend, and being near him while I had this knowledge was uncomfortable – but I had Brutus to saddle.

Head down, I kept on with that, while Sir William approached. 'Your horse is most handsome,' he said.

'I do thank ye, but don't let him hear ye. He's vain as it is.'

Brutus twitched an ear, rolling his eye back at me in what could only be described as an indulgent look, as if he knew I didn't truly mean it. He *was* vain, but he had every right to be. He was a bonny beast.

Sir William remarked there were few breeds could equal the courser of Naples, and there we agreed.

All the finest features of the courser showed in Brutus, from his size and strength and clean proportions to his telltale regal head that curved its hawk-like line from eyes to nostrils. Brutus was a dapple-grey, his mane and tail the shade of smoke.

Sir William said, 'This cannot be the same horse that the king did give ye . . . what, four years ago?'

'Five years. And aye, the very same.' And then, because I knew my words would likely be transmitted to the king, I said, 'It was a generous gift.'

'Indeed. Although I did not think the king was being generous to ye at the time, not in exchange for what you'd done.'

Once again I bent my head and concentrated on the saddle's girth. ''Twas nothing.'

'Most young Messengers, surprised by thieves as ye were and in danger of their lives, might well have done what the thieves ordered, given up what they were carrying, to save their skin.'

'What I carry, as a Messenger, is not my own to give.' I did not tell him that I had not been surprised. I'd Seen the brigands in a vision on the night afore that ride, I knew they would be lying there in wait for me, and it had taken all my courage to start down that road. But I had learned in life that what I Saw could never be avoided. Fortunate or foul, it was my destiny. What saved me was that I had been forewarned, that I was on my guard, and knew from which direction they'd attack.

Sir William said, 'Ye need not be so falsely modest. All of London knows your bravery, lad, and would do even had the thief ye left alive not cursed ye from the gallows so that everyone could hear. Such deeds do cry to be revealed. 'Tis why they're well rewarded.' He was close enough now that I saw the gold glint of his earring as he tipped his head to study Brutus. 'And 'tis why I thought the king should give ye something better than a stubborn, reckless three-year-old that wouldn't heed any fool trying to ride him. This horse was difficult then.'

'Merely headstrong,' I defended him, and Brutus angled back his ears again to catch my voice as I tightened his girth to the next hole, giving him time to adjust to the pressure. I did not say what I suspected – that he had been ill used as a colt by someone who did not appreciate his nature – but we understood each other well, and he confirmed this now by turning his head round to take my cape's edge in his mouth and tug, a show of his affection.

'I can see he chose his master,' said Sir William. 'But obedience can also have its dangers.'

Cautiously, I drew the girth one notch tighter.

He said, 'I know ye have your orders, and I would not interfere. But ye should not be sent north blind. I will speak plainly.'

It were better if he did not speak at all, since I could not discuss the matter. But his rank made it impossible for me to say as much.

'Ye have a reputation, Logan, as a man of honour. So ye need to know that what they mean to do to David, to my brother, is dishonourable.' Anger raised a roughness in his voice. He paused, and smoothed it like a wrinkle in fine fabric, and went on, 'I do not hold the king responsible. He grieves the prince, the rumours rise of poisoning, he wants to put an end to them. But of those rumours, none accuse my brother. None. And those the rumours name would seek a whipping boy to stand and take their punishment.'

I glanced at him in silence. He had steady eyes.

He said, 'He has done nothing wrong. Ye must obey your orders, this I know, but hold that in your mind. You'll bring my brother here to London and they'll force him to stand trial for the prince's murder, and they'll judge him as they please, but he is innocent. How well will honour serve ye then?' The pause was longer this time, and it did not clear the roughness. 'David grieves the prince as well. He should be given space to do so.'

There was nothing I could say to that, if I could have said anything.

He cleared his throat. Lifting a hand, he gave Brutus a firm pat on the rump. 'Such a magnificent animal.'

Brutus forgave him the touch for the sake of the compliment.

Sir William observed, 'He's been newly shod?'

'Aye.'

'Well, that's good for a long journey. Have a care, Logan,' was his final piece of advice, lightly given, as he turned away from me. 'Keep a watch out for my kinsmen. They're thick on the ground where you're going.'

ANNA, QUEEN OF BRITAIN

Somerset House, London, the same day

'IS THAT THE MAN they're sending?' Looking down from where she stood by the tall windows of the gallery, she could not claim the best of views, but to her eyes he looked too large, and in his scarlet livery, beside his massive horse, much too intimidating.

Standing at her side, Sir William Moray also glanced down at the young man in the stableyard and told her, 'Aye, that's Andrew Logan.'

'What do you know of him?'

'If someone must be sent, he is a better man than most.' The queen had known Sir William long enough to know he would be smiling when he added, 'He's a Scotsman.'

Anna said, 'Then I do wonder he would do the deed at all.' But even as she said the words, she knew that they were foolish. Of course he had no choice, this Scottish Messenger. They none of them had any choice but to do what the king commanded.

'I am very sorry,' she said softly, to Sir William, 'that it came to this.'

''Tis not your fault, Your Majesty.'

A gracious thing for him to say, but Anna knew the wheels of this whole venture had been set in motion by her actions.

Two weeks had passed, and yet she could recall each detail of that walk at Whitehall down the river steps to meet the barge that would bear all of them to Greenwich.

It had been a tedious procession, and a painful one for Anna, still recovering from an attack of gout that left her ankle swollen, but James had insisted. 'A king should be seen by his subjects,' he'd told her. 'Besides, 'tis the last time most of them will see Elizabeth. They'll wish to say farewell to her and her new husband.'

Anna cared not what the people wished. Not with her son, her Henry, barely five months in his grave, and now this second loss to bear. She had endured the wedding of her daughter to the young Prince Palatine, and smiled through the festivities, but now that their departure to the continent was days away, those smiles came with difficulty.

Walking stiffly behind James that day, she had no smile to show the crowd. She kept her gaze fixed straight ahead, and did not pause. Until she saw the old man kneeling by the river steps.

He had a kindly face, lined deeply from his years of labour, and his eyes were blind. They stared upwards, unseeing, at the guardsman who was trying to persuade the man to rise and move along.

Anna stopped. 'What is this?'

With apologies, the guardsman turned. 'He claims that he must speak with you, Your Majesty.'

The king, already halfway down the steps, would not have stood for this delay. Still, if her guards moved the old man, they'd do it roughly.

Anna told the guardsman, 'If he be unarmed, let him approach, and I will hear him.'

For a moment, when the old man was first brought before her, she regretted her decision. Looking at those eyes, fixed so unerringly upon her face, it seemed impossible they could not see. She found their clouded gaze unsettling.

The man bowed deeply, greeting her, 'Your Majesty. God save and keep you. I do bear a message from the prince, your son.'

She glanced in some confusion at the river steps, where

she could see her son, Prince Charles – the one son left alive to her – now talking to his sister and her husband as they all prepared to board the royal barge under the king's direction.

The old man, although blind, appeared aware of Anna's action. 'Not Prince Charles.' He shook his head. 'Your other son, Your Majesty. Prince Henry.'

Anna brought her head around. The cold she felt owed nothing to the April wind. It curled its fist around her from within and stole her voice. She said, 'My other son is dead. You are mistaken.'

The guardsman moved as though to drag the old man from her presence, seemingly aware of her distress.

The old man quickly said, 'He bids you speak to David.'

Anna held her hand up in a gesture that would stop the guardsman. 'David?'

With a nod, the old man told her, 'That is what he said. This David, he does hold the answers that you seek.'

She met the blind eyes with a feeling of unease. She nearly said that she was looking for no answers, that she had no questions, but she sensed this man would know that was untrue. Instead she asked him, in a cautious tone, 'And is that all?'

'He said to tell you that he kept his promise. That his flames of truth and justice are yet burning, as you wished. They burn so brightly that even a blind man like myself can see them.'

Anna stared, although he could not see her. 'How did you . . . ' She recognized the promise, and remembered Henry making it, but they had been alone then – there'd been no one else within the room to hear. How then could this old man speak almost Henry's exact words?

She nearly asked him, 'Was it poison?' But she knew. She *knew*.

His face creased slightly in a smile, and yet she barely saw it, for her eyes were flooded suddenly with unshed tears.

She sharply turned her face to hide them, and to her shock met the too-perceptive gaze of James. He must have wondered why she'd been detained, for he'd retraced his progress up the river steps and now stood half a stride away from her.

James eyed her closely, and demanded, 'What is wrong? What did this man say to upset ye?'

'Nothing.' Anna knew that nothing good would come of telling James the truth. He dealt harshly with all those who spoke of Henry, even more so now that some claimed James himself had ordered Henry's death. It wasn't true, of course. A thing so terrible could not be true. But James, impatient with the rumours, sought to silence them, and cared not how he shut the gossips' mouths.

Anna tried to shield the old man. Turning back, she told him, 'I do thank you for your kind good wishes.'

Once again he bowed and said, 'God save and keep you, Majesty.'

And Anna saw two children take his arms and start to walk away with him, as if they sensed that leaving him so close to James was dangerous.

Breathing more easily, Anna reminded James, 'We must not miss the tide.' Head high, she walked on before him.

But she had forgotten the guardsman, who'd been near enough to overhear at least a part of what the old man said.

From the quayside, Anna watched while James stood several moments longer on the river steps, his dark head bent in thoughtful conversation with that guardsman. Then James nodded and came down the final steps in silence.

Settling on his cushioned seat beside her in the barge, James looked across at Anna. He could imitate a smile so that it nearly reached his eyes, but not entirely.

She knew exactly what that smile was saying. James was

telling her that she could have no secrets; that he'd learned the old man's message.

They both knew which David the old man had meant for her to speak to, for there only ever was one David in the confidence and heart of their Prince Henry.

James disliked Sir David Moray.

Anna felt the cold wrap slowly round her chest and grip it tightly. She should not have stopped to hear the blind man. Now, that single action could have consequences beyond her control.

She briefly closed her eyes and prayed for strength and guidance, as the barge, freed from its moorings, caught the current of the sparkling Thames and started downstream, towards Greenwich.

That had been two weeks ago. Elizabeth and her new husband were now gone, and after the farewells were said, both James and Anna had returned by separate ways to London.

Anna hoped the old blind man had made it safely home that day, and not been intercepted by the king's guards. When he questioned someone, James was ruthless. And relentless.

She had known he would not let the matter lie.

So she had sought Sir William.

True, he'd been raised with James since they were in their nursery days, and he was loyal to his king, but blood was blood. Sir David was his brother.

'I am sorry,' she had told him then. 'The king's advisers will not tell me anything. But you . . .'

Sir William doubted he'd have better luck. 'They may not tell *me* anything, if it concerns my brother. But I do have other avenues of information.'

Which was how they'd learned of James's plan to send the Messenger.

Now, standing at the window looking down at the young giant dressed in scarlet in her stableyard, the queen had doubts about their own plans, which were very different from the king's.

While James intended to arrest Sir David and arrange to have him punished for a crime he'd had no hand in, Anna wanted no more than to talk to him in private, as the old man had advised her.

I do bear a message from the prince, your son ... he bids you speak to David.

The cold she'd felt upon the river steps gripped her as fiercely as it had that day. 'What if my letter does not reach him?' Anna asked.

Sir William said, 'I sent it by a man I trust completely. It will reach him.'

'But what if he is taken, all the same?'

'We have our friends in France. And if he heads for Scotland, well, I've warned our cousin Patrick there to do all in his power to see that David does not come to London.'

Anna frowned, still looking down upon the young man in the stableyard. 'And the Messenger?'

'I've spoken to him, privately. I've called his conscience into play. He has a strong one. It may serve us well.'

'And if it doesn't?' Anna could not help but ask the question. 'If it comes to bloodshed?'

She was aware of silence at her back, as though the answer wanted some consideration. But the answer, when it came, was unconcerned.

'Look at the size of him,' Sir William said. 'He's a braw lad, who can take a little bruising. And,' he promised her, 'there's no one else will come to harm.'

Andrew

Fleet Street, London, the same day

MARGARET HAD NOT PAUSED for breath. Most evenings on our rides home she was far too weary from her work in the queen's kitchen to do more than comment now and then on something we were passing, but she seemed determined now to talk the length of Fleet Street without stopping.

'... and I'm sure I stood there staring, but what else was I to do? I couldn't help it, I was that astonished. I always thought Cook hated me, for she gave every sign of it, but when she got the order that she was to go along to Bath, she said she could not do it without me, because I was her right hand. Her right hand, Andrew!' Margaret rode behind me on the pillion affixed to the back of my saddle so I could not see her face, but I could hear her pride.

I made the sort of sound I'd learned was all she needed from me to confirm that I was listening, and Margaret carried on explaining every minor point of her good fortune.

I was happy for her. Both my sisters worked hard and deserved such recognition. And to have them both included in Queen Anna's entourage as the queen made her progress soon to Bath, to take the waters, would be fortunate for *me*. Far better that my sisters be together, under Roger's watchful eye.

My mother would have Owen. And we did have some good neighbours.

Phoebe Westaway aside, her aunt was kind, as was her father. Laurence Westaway, in fact, had been one of the first men in the Close to pay us his condolences the week my father died.

'If you need anything,' he'd told my mother. 'Anything at all.'

I knew he'd aid her if she asked, while I was gone.

At first I thought it was because I had his face in mind that I imagined now, as we approached Fleet Bridge, that one man walking in amongst the others near us looked like him. He had the same slow, measured walk. The same slope to his shoulders.

It was not till we drew level with him and he stepped aside to give us room upon the road that I saw it *was* Laurence Westaway. I greeted him, and he looked up.

His face looked pale, and weary, but he found a pleasant smile.

'Why, Logan! Mistress Margaret. You are heartily well met. Well met, indeed.' He swept his hat off in his gallant way for Margaret, but the action seemed to throw him off his balance, and he stumbled. And then, to my horror, fell.

Dismounting, I was first to reach his side. He'd landed with his face half turned towards the ground. His eyes had closed. I told those who had gathered, 'Leave him. Give him air.'

As they withdrew, the scene that I was looking at began to blur and alter. Laurence Westaway no longer wore his ordinary clothing. He lay shrouded in a winding sheet, as though he'd been prepared for his own burial. It had been knotted at his feet, but did not fully reach his head – it stopped below his shoulders. Then it vanished altogether and he lay there as afore.

His eyes came open. Blinked. And focused. 'Logan?'

'Aye.'

I saw him realize what had happened. Saw the shame.

And Margaret must have seen it, too. She thought more quickly. Pointing to a stone near where I crouched, she said, 'I swear that is the same stone that made Brutus cast his shoe this morning. It is wreaking havoc, tripping everybody up.'

'You're very kind,' he told her, 'but 'twas not a stone.' He levered himself upright so that he was seated on the ground, still with my hand to hold him steady at his back. 'It was the heat,' he said. 'I will recover once I've rested here awhile.'

'Ye cannot stay here in the road,' I said. 'Nor will I leave ye here to walk. I'll see ye safely home.'

Margaret, again, was quick to think. She knew I would let Phoebe's father take my place on Brutus. Meaning Margaret could not ride. A woman riding pillion behind a man, sitting sideways on the horse, held onto both the handle at the back edge of the pillion and to the man himself – or to the belt he wore, designed for just that purpose. If the horse baulked, or changed gait, or lost its footing, she depended on the strength of the man's seat to keep her in her own. And it was plain to see that Laurence Westaway was not in a condition to keep anyone protected.

Margaret did not wait for me to help her to dismount, but slipped down neatly from her seat upon the pillion. 'I have a mind to walk.' Her tone was cheerful. 'Will it trouble ye if I go on ahead a little, Andrew?'

I shook my head. 'Just keep where ye can call me if ye need me.'

'Come, help me stand,' said Westaway, and watching Margaret leave us he remarked, 'Your sister is a gracious girl. She knows that no man likes to let a woman see his weakness.'

'Aye, she's spent a lifetime watching me hide mine, no doubt that's why.' I wasn't sure he had recovered well enough to hoist himself into the saddle, even if I gave him a leg up, but near the bridge there was a block of stone that would do as a mounting block, so I manoeuvred us towards it, being mindful of the watching eyes of people passing on the road, and those who might be peering from the windows of the houses that surrounded us, and any who might be below in boats upon the murky waters of what once had been the River Fleet until long years of use and mud and filth had so reduced it to the less grand name of the Fleet Ditch.

A man as proud as Westaway would never wish to have his weakness seen by anyone at all, and after the indignity he had just suffered in the street, the least that I could do was let him mount my horse unaided.

Once in the saddle, he looked sturdier, if still too pale. This would have worried me far less had I not had the vision of him wrapped within his winding sheet.

The first time I had Seen a man like that, when I was but a lad, my mother reassured me it was commonplace for those like me, who had the Sight. ''Tis how God shows ye someone's life is coming to its end,' she'd said. Then, 'How high had it climbed, the sheet? His knees? His shoulders?'

'Just below his waist.'

'Well, then,' she'd said, 'he has a good while yet. When it has reached his neck, ye'll ken his time is very close and can be counted then in days.'

I'd watched that man over the next months with a feeling of foreboding. 'Tis a curse to see what other men cannot, and be unable to give warning of events that are to come. I knew that, had I tried, I'd have been brought up on charges of sorcery, and so I held my tongue and watched the white linen rise higher round the man until at last it reached his neck. And then I counted. Five days, that was all, until they laid him finally in his grave.

He'd been the first I'd Seen. There had been others since. Strangers, more often than not. Some much closer. When I'd Seen the winding sheet first start to rise on my father's legs, I'd thought my heart would crack open and stay that way, broken forever.

Five years had gathered up its pieces into something like its former shape.

But now I knew the summer would be difficult, for I liked Laurence Westaway.

He said, 'I have not ridden in a long while. Not since the last time we worked together, you and I. Where did we go then? Into Kent, was it not?'

'Down to Margate, aye.' I took care shortening his stirrups, since his legs were not so long as mine.

He took the reins in hand and told me, 'Scotland is a fair ways farther than that, but I am ready for the journey.'

My hands stopped their work on the stirrup until I reminded them not to reveal when a piece of news caught me off guard. Cautiously, I continued to buckle the strap, and said, 'Scotland?'

'Yes. I'm sorry, Logan. Did my lord Northampton not tell you? I'm to be your scrivener for this . . . shall we say this latest venture? And we'd best not say much more than that,' he warned me, 'for here comes your sister.'

Margaret was indeed returning. She did not like to walk these streets alone, so I had not expected her to wish to keep ahead of us for long, but clearly she had seen that I had Westaway now safely seated in the saddle and that he was talking normally, so she had judged this to be a good moment to rejoin us.

''Tis far too dull, to keep to my own company,' was her excuse. 'There is no one to talk to.'

So on we walked, the three of us, with Margaret at the other side of Brutus, and her lively talk kept Westaway well entertained, and gave me space to think.

The trip to Edinburgh and back could take a month if all went well, and more than that if it did not. And it was not an easy road. It would be taxing for a younger man, and Laurence Westaway was not young. His death was near, his health was failing, and his last days should not be spent labouring so far from home. It troubled me.

I stayed in silent thought until we came into the Close. And when we reached our house and Margaret took her leave of us and Westaway would have dismounted, I said, 'Nay, I've brought ye this far. Let me take ye to your door.'

The green was deserted except for the long shadows cast by the sun dying low in the west. The sound of Brutus's great hooves would doubtless make some of our neighbours look out of their windows, but there were none close enough to overhear a quiet conversation. I had a scant few minutes now to speak, or not at all.

I could be clumsy with my words. I tried to choose these ones with care. 'Sir, I'm not certain it is wise for ye to make this journey up to Scotland.'

Turning sharply to look down at me, he said, with a strong edge of desperation, 'But I must.' Then he collected himself, and more calmly added, 'I do also have my orders, Logan. Like you, I must go where I am sent.'

'My lord Northampton is a reasonable man,' I said. 'I think he trusts my judgement, and if I explain the matter of your health—'

'That won't be necessary.'

'Aye, it is,' I said. 'I've no wish to offend ye, but we both ken it was not the heat that made ye fall. Ye need to rest, not ride the length of Britain.'

He looked stricken. ''Tis essential that I do this, Logan, for my daughter's happiness.'

A strange response, for surely she could have no stake in our affairs, but such a fall as Westaway had suffered sometimes left the mind confused. I said, 'I think she would be happier to have ye with her.'

We had reached his house. Brutus stood as still as any statue to let Westaway dismount, as though he knew the older man was yet unsteady in his movements. I stood by, but being mindful of his pride did not rush in to aid where I had not been asked.

Still, it was plain to see that even that small effort left him drained.

I told him, gently, 'Bide at home, be with the ones who love ye. I will find another scrivener.'

And I would have left it there. But as my hand closed round Brutus's bridle, the door of the house opened and Phoebe Westaway stood on the threshold, her face flushed from running downstairs, eyes afire.

If a glance could have killed a man, I'd have been slain on the spot.

That one glance was all she spared me, then she raced straight for her father.

'What's happened?' she asked him.

'Nothing of importance. I am fine,' he reassured her.

She did not seem reassured. She wheeled on me. 'Why aren't you helping him? You see he is unwell.'

Her father answered forcefully, 'I tell you I am well!'

It was the first time I had heard him use that tone of voice to her, although in truth I knew he spoke those words to both of us. He straightened, and with slow, deliberate steps brushed past his daughter and went into the house.

Phoebe tried again to slay me with a look, and once again she failed.

I said, 'It would appear he does not need my help.'

And, taking up my horse's reins, I left her standing, speechless, on her doorstep.

Phoebe

Great St Bartholomew's, London, the same day

The Logans' house, unlike the ones that pressed to either side of it, had stables built beneath – three arching stalls that had once held, so I'd been told, the horses of a former Messenger who'd served the eighth King Henry. No doubt that was why this house had been assigned to Logan's father when the family had arrived here and the lease arranged. It was a larger house than ours, and I imagined somewhat grander on the inside, though I'd never seen it.

Just now, I was only seeing Logan.

He stood solidly within the nearer stall, brushing the broad flanks of his horse – a dappled beast so massive it made Logan seem a man of ordinary height.

He would not make a gentleman, like Valentine. His hair was close-cropped to his head and nondescriptly brown. His eyes – I knew from holding his gaze once too long in argument – were undecided between grey and something even more devoid of colour; something like a frozen northern stream into which I had no desire to step.

Yet step I must.

The grey eyes briefly slanted downwards and dismissed me as I came towards him. Logan shifted so his shoulder shut me out, and went on with his measured brushing of the horse. 'How is your father?'

'Much improved.' I swallowed. Spoke the words that stung like acid: 'Thank you.'

It didn't help that he wore his court livery – the scarlet

doublet with its royal badge of office, the uncompromising collar showing hardly any lace, and the high boots whose folded tops came to his knees. It made him look still more imposing.

I said, 'I believe I owe you an apology. My father told me how you helped him when he . . . fell.' I hoped he would not catch my hesitation on the word. 'I'm in your debt.'

'The debt would be your father's, surely?'

'Either way.' He did not make it easy.

Logan shrugged. 'I'll take it, then.'

'Take what?'

Those grey eyes touched mine. 'Your apology.'

I could feel my temper rising, but I pushed it down. I needed to stay calm. 'I'm sorry.'

Logan gave a nod. 'Accepted. Thank ye.' When I did not leave, he glanced towards me once again in silent enquiry.

I said, 'My father also told me that you said he could not go to Scotland with you.'

I'd surprised him there. He took care not to show it, but I saw the slight break in the rhythm of his brushing motions. And his momentary frown.

'Mayhap your father speaks too much.'

'Mayhap my father trusts me.'

Logan said, ''Tis naught to do with trust. We take an oath to keep our business secret.'

'And he does. He tells me nothing of the details.'

'Just to ken the place he's going is to ken more than ye should.'

I could not help it. 'Yet you stride around in scarlet? Pray, how do you plan to keep your movements on the road a secret? I should think within two days a fool would know which way you're bound.'

His mouth compressed into a thin line. 'There's a point to all this, is there?'

'Yes. My father needs to go to Scotland.' There it was, I'd said it. 'He won't tell me why he needs to, but he does.'

'He cannot go.'

'Why not?'

'Ye ken why not.' He stopped his brushing and faced me directly. 'How often does your father fall?'

I could not lie to eyes like that. 'Not often.'

'But this was not the first time. And it is not an easy road to Scotland. He would find it taxing. And I cannot be responsible—'

'I will come with him.'

This time Logan did not bother to hide his surprise. 'What?'

'I will come with him,' I said again. '*I'll* be responsible for him. I'll care for him.'

I saw the change in his features – a slight loss of focus, as though he were lost in deep thought.

I said, 'Please, Logan.'

That cost me more than he knew, saying those two words, but he just looked at me blankly a moment and went back to brushing his horse.

'I will think on it,' was all he said. Which meant no.

I had humbled myself enough. I'd not beg further.

And since Logan seemed always determined to have the last word in our arguments, I let him have it, and hoped he would choke on it.

Andrew

Great St Bartholomew's, London, the same day

In all the houses we had lived in from the time I'd been a lad, the room I liked best was the kitchen. 'Twas my mother's fault – she kept a tidy, homely hearth and always sang to please herself while she was working, so the room was ever filled with warmth and music.

And with food.

This narrow table set against the wall between the back stairs and the larder door was where we ate most meals, leaving our dining room above the hall unused.

My mother pushed aside the plate of bread and cheese she'd set between myself and Margaret that I'd barely touched, and handed me a bowl of steaming broth. 'There,' she said, 'get that inside ye. I've put herbs in that to make your head ache less.'

I probed the deep brown surface with my spoon. 'I didn't say I had a headache.'

'I'm your mother, and ye'll aye be my wee lad,' she said. 'Ye'll never grow so large that I can't see when something ails ye.' She had lit the evening candles. Their light always made her face look young, and gave her eyes a glint of mischief. 'And there are not many things that make ye disagreeable.'

'When was I—?'

Margaret interjected, 'Ye telt me to hold my whisht.'

I did admit I'd been unfair to ask my sister to keep quiet, even if her talking had been making my head rattle. 'Aye, well, I'm sorry for that.' She did have every right to be excited. 'I'm fair proud of ye.'

That earned me her forgiveness. With a smile, my sister said, 'Mayhap I'll catch the queen's eye as our Jeannie did and find myself a better place at court.'

My mother thought it possible. 'But mind, that's a blade with two edges. We haven't seen Jeannie at all these past days, the queen's kept her so hard at her work.'

'I will see her,' said Margaret, 'in Bath.'

'Aye, that ye will.' My mother looked at her with fondness. 'Thoughtless lass to go and chase your fun and leave me here with none but this unpleasant lad to give me conversation.' She was teasing, but her eyes became more serious when she saw my expression. She could read me as though I were a child's book writ in bold lettering. 'And will ye then be leaving, too?'

I told her, though she knew the answer, 'Aye. I must away the morn. I ken not for how long.' Neither of them asked where I was bound to, for my father's years in this same service had well trained us all. 'But Owen will be coming here to stay, to keep ye guarded. And he likes to talk.'

My mother smiled. 'Indeed.'

'Owen is coming here?' That broke from Margaret, who looked so distraught that if I'd wondered at her feelings afore this, I knew them now. 'But surely he will join the rest of us in the queen's household on her progress west to Bath?'

My head hurt when I tried to shake it, so I only moved it slightly. 'No. He's not like Roger, nor like Jeannie, who do always travel with the queen. He travels at her pleasure, and it pleases her this time to let him bide at home in London.'

Margaret blinked back sudden tears that we were not supposed to see, and stood, excused herself, and left us. When we were younger, she would seek me out when she was sad and weep upon my shoulder, but these days she kept her sorrows private, so I did not try to follow her, for all I would have wished to give her comfort.

It was always a hard lesson to be learned: that service to a royal master oft meant putting your own heart aside.

I looked at my mother, and knew from her keen eyes that she had just strung a new thread between Margaret and Owen. She asked, 'Is there aught I should ken about, there?'

'Only that it all ends well.'

She thought a moment, then she nodded. 'Ye've been Seeing things. I'm sure that has not helped your head. It often tired my father when he used his Gift.'

It usually had no effect upon me, and I said as much. 'But neither would I count my Sight a gift,' I told her. 'Not today.'

'Why? What have ye been Seeing?'

The best course, I had learned, when I had no wish to discuss a subject, was to lead the talk along a different path. 'I paid the rent last month,' I said, 'at Lady Day, so it will not come due now till Midsummer. There is money in the kist for that.'

'Midsummer is a long way off. Ye surely will be home by then?'

'I cannot say for certain. If ye find yourself in want of funds, tell Owen, and he'll ask my lord Northampton. Ye can draw upon my wages.' Though I tried to keep my voice as normal as I could, my mother was not fooled.

She said, 'There's danger in whatever they are asking ye to do.'

'No more than any other mission.' But I did not meet her gaze. If I had hopes of hiding any of my thoughts, I'd rather face the king's most merciless inquisitor than face my mother.

Again she asked me, 'What have ye been Seeing?'

Even my shrug set my head throbbing. 'Naught that affects ye directly. And naught I can change.'

She accepted that fact. She knew better than I how our lives were already cast, having been raised in the Isles where foretellings were not only common, but where her own family were likely to make them.

I looked like my grandfather, she had once told me. And, like him, I'd had to learn my size and strength could not turn events from their course. A stronger will than mine had set their wheels in motion, and would not be stopped.

My mother did not press the matter. Taking up my empty bowl and Margaret's trencher, she carried them across to the bench beneath the window where she kept the tub of washing-water. With her back to me, she asked, 'Did I see that Westaway lass leaving the stables?'

'Aye.'

'And is there aught I should ken about *there*?'

'No.' *Decidedly not*, I'd have added, except with my mother, least said was the best, else she'd not let the matter lie. She would keep—

''Tis a shame,' she said, 'for she's a bonny lass.'

It was a fact, and did not need me to confirm it. When we'd come to live at St Bartholomew's, I had been half bewitched at my first sight of her. In fairness, it was not her face alone, although her face was pretty. Nor was it her hair, so nearly black that, with her large, brown eyes, it made her look a little foreign, as though she, like me, did not belong within the Close. It was, more simply, everything – the way she moved, the way she laughed, the way the sunlight touched her when she turned her head. I saw these from a distance.

Then I offered her my hand in help, she shunned it, and my senses cleared.

And now I knew a bonny lass could have a cold and careless

heart. I knew her laughter could be swiftly turned to words that cut a man. I bore the marks as proof.

'And she is clever,' said my mother. 'Did ye ken she reads and writes as well as does her father? Her Aunt Agnes telt me that. Imagine. 'Tis a rare and fine accomplishment.'

Again, a point of fact. I would have let it pass without reply, had not something occurred to me. 'How often do ye talk to Agnes Westaway?'

'Often enough.'

'Ye're friends?'

'We're friendly, aye.' She glanced at me over her shoulder. 'Is that not allowed?' She was teasing again, but whatever she read in my face made her instantly sober. 'What's wrong, Andrew?'

'Nothing.' But that was a lie.

She would know that it was, but I could not explain. Could not tell her that something about this new mission unsettled me, nor that the man I was sent to arrest might be innocent and being played for political purpose, nor that I constantly heard Roger's voice in my ear saying, 'It strikes me wrong.'

More than that, I could not tell my mother of the vision I'd had not an hour ago, when Phoebe had stood in defence of her father and argued that she could come north with him.

'*I'll* be responsible for him,' she'd offered. 'I'll care for him.'

I should have said there and then such a thing was impossible, but at that moment the stable had wavered and blurred and become a straight road under skies chased with swift-running clouds. I'd been riding at a walking pace among companions – one was cloaked, and one was Laurence Westaway, who looked at me and, smiling, said, 'Did I not say you were worried for nothing?' while past him, across the wide slope of an unknown field, I saw riders on horseback approaching at speed.

And then someone had moved at my back, pressing close

from their position on the pillion, behind my saddle. Hands – a woman's hands – had gripped my waist, and Phoebe Westaway had asked, 'Can we outrun them?'

I had Seen no more than that.

My visions lasted only briefly, she'd have likely noticed nothing when it happened, and indeed she showed no sign of any change when I returned to an awareness of her standing with me in the stables.

Granted, she had asked me 'Please,' which was itself remarkable, and I might have remarked upon it more had I not been sorting through what I'd just witnessed and what it all meant. I'd told her I would think on it, when I knew there was nothing that required thought. The things I Saw were destined, they were set, and they could not be changed.

She and her father would be coming with me, whether I wished it or not.

I said to my mother, 'Ye should ask Agnes Westaway if she would like to come stay with ye here at the house while I'm away. It would give ye both company while Owen's off at his work.'

My mother turned fully from the window bench, her eyes too keen to be fooled. 'Andrew,' she asked me a third time, 'what have ye been Seeing?'

Leaning back, I passed a weary hand across my eyes, and told her. 'Trouble.'

Phoebe

Port of Leith, Scotland, 3rd May 1613

I'D NEVER BEEN SO grateful to step down to solid ground.

When Logan had said I could come on this journey, I'd grudgingly thought he was generous. When he'd delayed his ride north till he found a ship able to carry my father and me up the coast into Scotland, sparing us the need to keep pace with him on the road and letting my father conserve his strength, I'd even thought him helpful.

But my thoughts towards him since had been less kind.

Our voyage had taken nine days and I'd enjoyed none of them, my head and stomach clearly not designed for travel on the seas, especially not in high gales of wind chased by a violent storm.

Now, when I let go the ladder's ropes with my two feet firmly planted on the wharf, my back turned to the looming, great hull of the ship that creaked and bobbed still at its moorings, the sick sensation vanished with a suddenness that left me feeling slightly weak, but thankful.

Our ship had come into the harbour on the high tide, early in the dark hours before sunrise, and now that it was fully light I saw the town more clearly. It was not what I'd expected.

Valentine had been here once. The evening of St George's Day, as I'd prepared to start this journey, Valentine had sought me out, in private.

He'd said nothing till he'd led me by the hand into a shadowed corner of the cloistered courtyard of his house. There, with my back pressed to the ancient wall, and his turned so it shielded us from prying eyes, he'd asked me, 'Were you going to leave me without bidding me farewell?'

How Valentine had known that I was leaving was a mystery, since my father and my aunt and I had closely held the secret. My confusion must have shown, because he smiled.

'You do forget I have the trust of those who write your father's orders,' he said. 'I am well aware you're bound for Scotland, and with whom, and why.'

I warned him, 'No one is to know.'

'I'm fully capable of keeping things in confidence.' He placed a hand against the stone wall near my head and leaned in closer. 'I might wish you had a better guide than Logan, and that you were going to a better place than Edinburgh.'

For the first I could not argue with him, but, 'What's wrong,' I asked, 'with Edinburgh?'

'I've been there. 'Tis a filthy place, with houses built of wood, and rude inhabitants who are unmannered and unclean. You'll smell the town before you see it.'

'Oh.' I touched the little pomander that always hung from its fine chain suspended at my waist and hoped that it would counter any stench. It was but small – a nutmeg bound by filigree of silver with a knot of seed pearls at the bottom – but it had long protected me from plague.

Valentine had seen my gesture. From the bag at his own belt he drew a handkerchief of fine, white lawn all edged in ivory silk, with his initials at one corner worked in thread of silver gilt. It was scented with a perfume unfamiliar to me, no doubt something rare and, knowing Valentine, expensive.

He said, 'This will serve you better than your pomander.'

'You know I can't accept it.'

'Why? What other man would you accept a token from?'

He'd pressed the handkerchief into my fingers, and closed his around mine firmly. 'Take it. Mayhap when you come home, I'll have a gift for you of greater worth. And in return, I'll take your pledge that, whenever you're able to along the road, you'll write to send me word that you are safe.'

I held that handkerchief within my hand this morning, ready to be used if needed, but nothing – apart from a freshening sea breeze – assaulted my senses. In fact, all I'd imagined of Edinburgh seemed to be wrong.

This was a smaller town than I had pictured in my mind, but all the houses here were built of stone, not wood as Valentine had claimed. They hugged the long curve of the stone wharf that stretched into the sea, while on the far side of the narrow harbour there were more stone buildings and long wooden piers, providing space for ships to seek their berths.

Despite the early hour, the harbour was alive with men and motion. Sea-birds cried and called and sailed with wings spread wide upon the wind, in search of any opportunity for theft as decks were cleaned and smaller boats brought cargoes in to shore.

The shore, too, was a busy place, but those who bustled past us did not seem unmannered, merely unfamiliar, and I put that down in large part to the manner of their dress.

While many of the women were in petticoats and waistcoats just like me, others wore long mantles drawn up over their heads like hoods and wrapped around their bodies, just as Logan's mother often did on wet or wintry days. Like hers, these mantles had been woven of light wool in different colours, their variation of pattern matched only by the diverse fashions worn by the Scottish men, which ranged from austerely severe to flamboyantly French in appearance.

But the most remarkable costume of all was that worn by the boy who'd been watching us since we arrived.

He was young, perhaps ten, with a shock of bright, copper-red hair, and a freckled face, neither of which was set off to their best advantage by his shirt, that looked to be made of the same stuff as my own red petticoat. He wore this red shirt long and belted over narrow breeks that left him barefoot, with a dagger hanging at his waist. And over all he wore a cloak in the style of the men at court, tied on a diagonal across the chest and slung over the left shoulder only. The cloak would have reached past the waist of a grown man. It just brushed the pavement when worn by this boy, and it gave him the air of a stage actor playing a part.

He had stood for all this time within a shadowed lane across from where our ship had docked, content to wait while others passed between us on the wharf. When he stepped forward to address my father, I expected an appeal for money, but instead he made an expertly respectful bow and asked, 'Beg pardon, sir, are ye the scrivener?'

If that surprised my father half as much as it did me, he did not let it show, but he did drop his guard enough to smile. My father had a tender place within his heart for children. I scarcely could recall my eldest brother, who'd been near this boy's age when he died, but I knew from the wistful light within my father's eyes that he was chasing memories.

'Yes,' he told the boy, 'I am.'

'Then ye're tae come wi' me.' He turned, and started up the curving wharf that was part shoreline and part street, the ships docked all along the one side and the tall stone buildings rising at the other, with the sea now at our backs.

My father took our portmanteau in hand and followed him, unquestioning.

I kept my place beside him, but I touched my father's sleeve and asked him, low, 'How do you know he can be trusted?'

In surprise, my father answered it was obvious. 'Cannot you see it?'

'No.'

'My dear, his clothes.'

I might have asked my father to elaborate, but he'd already taken out his almanac and turned to Mr Parker's calculations of the tides. At any rate, I had become distracted, too, by the square, ancient tower looming now in front of us. It rose above its neighbours, being several storeys tall and built of stone and buttressed at its upper corners, with a high, peaked roof.

It seemed to have been built to be a citadel or watchtower, commanding a clear view of all who might approach the shore. But I could see no soldiers, and when the boy pushed open the nail-studded oaken door and led us through the shadowed entry, I soon found myself within the sunlight of a courtyard, where I saw only four people: to my right, two masons deep in some discussion over several piles of dressed stone that was evidently stacked there for their use; ahead, a woman in a broidered waistcoat and red petticoat, both finer than my own. And Andrew Logan.

Truth be told, I saw him first, but not wishing to stare, I forced my mind to notice all the others in their turn before I gave him my attention. Having done so, it became clear why my father had been quick to trust the boy who'd led us, from his clothes alone. There could be no mistaking the intentional resemblance of the costume, now that I was faced with Logan in his livery – the scarlet tunic of his office, and the cloak he wore when he was travelling, tied across his broad chest on a diagonal and slung over his left shoulder, leaving his right arm free to draw his sword for fighting.

Plainly the boy idolized him. Standing before him now, the boy drew himself up sharply and announced, 'I found them for ye, sir. The scrivener and your lady.'

It was almost worth the irritation of being called Logan's lady to see his own discomfort at the thought. But he did not correct the boy.

Instead he gave a nod such as he might have given any colleague, and said, 'Well done, lad. I'm in your debt.' And then he smiled, and turned that smile on my father, and it so transformed his face that for a moment I could only blink.

He said, ''Tis good to see ye. I'd expected ye afore this. Were the winds not fair?'

'Not very,' said my father. Holding up his almanac, he said, 'But Mr Parker did predict the storms, so I was well prepared for rough seas.'

I was glad my father did not look at me, and gladder still that Logan let it pass, for I would not have wished to have him know my weakness. No doubt *he* could weather any gale, and do it standing on the ship's deck in defiance of the rain and rolling water, like a rock.

The woman next to him was looking at me quizzically, but when our glances met, hers softened. She was in her middle years, still lovely, with blue eyes set off by hair nearly as dark as mine, though streaked with ivory strands that almost matched the fine, starched linen of her cap.

Aunt Agnes always said that you could tell a lady from her posture, and this woman stood so very perfectly that I was not surprised by Logan's introduction.

He said, 'Lady Lindsay, pray allow me to present my neighbour, Master Laurence Westaway, and Mistress Phoebe Westaway, his daughter.'

Lady Lindsay offered her hand to my father in a graceful

gesture and he bowed low over it as I paid my honours, too, with my best curtsey.

Her accent, when she spoke, was more refined than Logan's. 'I do greet you well, and bid you welcome to the King's Wark. I'm sorry my husband is not here, but his lands in the king's Irish plantation needed his attention. Is this all your baggage?' she asked, looking at my father's portmanteau.

He said, 'Our orders were to travel lightly.'

We had done exactly that. My father's clothes and mine, together with our tools for writing, had been somehow stuffed into the single leather bag, shaped like a cylinder that could be strapped across a horse's hindquarters, behind the saddle.

Lady Lindsay was impressed, and told us so. Then, turning to the red-haired boy, who all this time had stood beside us, she said, 'Hector, will you carry up their things, please?'

He appeared to hesitate, and sent a pleading look to Logan, who was on the brink of saying something when my father took a firmer hold on the strap of the portmanteau.

'No need of that,' my father said, 'I'd rather carry it myself.' And, 'Hector, is it?' to the boy, who faced him.

'Aye, sir. Hector Reid.'

'Well, Hector Reid, I don't doubt you have more important things to do than carrying my bag.'

'Aye, sir. I'm meant to watch the harbour.'

'Important work indeed,' my father agreed. 'And very fitting for a Messenger. Do not let us detain you.'

'Aye, sir. No, sir.' Hector swelled with pride, and gave a short bow. 'Thank ye, sir.' And wheeling, raced off back towards the wharf.

The look on Logan's face was half-indulgence, half-appreciation as he reached to take the portmanteau's strap from my father's hand and lift the bag to his own shoulder.

'That was kind of ye. I thank ye. He's a good lad, Hector, and he's fairly made himself my deputy since I arrived.'

My father smiled. 'I knew him by his livery.'

That brought a laugh from Lady Lindsay. 'Och, the trouble we had finding him a red shirt! You would scarce believe it. And my groom has been beside himself these past days, without Hector helping in the stables. But Andrew needed him, so how could I refuse?'

The easy familiarity between her and Logan baffled me until we sat to dinner in the hall – a grand, square room on the ground floor – and she began to speak first of her husband, Sir Bernard Lindsay, one of the gentlemen of the chamber to the king, who had granted him the keeping of this tower house.

'Oh yes,' she said, in answer to my father's question about the building's age, 'very ancient. The King's Wark was built two centuries ago by our first King James, for a warehouse and arsenal, and when my husband was put in charge, it showed the wear of all those years of storing cannon within while being battered by them from without. But he soon put things right. When our own king first fetched Queen Anna home to Scotland as his new bride, they stayed here, in the chambers just below your own.'

'Imagine,' said my father, who loved all things that touched royalty.

'Indeed.' Lady Lindsay dipped salt with the tip of her knife to season the stewed beef on her trencher. 'Of course, Andrew, you'd not remember that, for you'd have been but a wean.'

'I was three.' Logan calmly spoke over the rim of his wine cup. 'And I recall it plainly, for the crowds were thick and I was small and had no view of anything. My father lifted me onto his shoulders, so that I could see the king.'

I tried to picture Logan being small, and failed. He drank,

and as though he could sense my gaze he met my eyes above the wine cup, and I looked away.

But from the talk that followed, I learned to my surprise that Lady Lindsay had been born a Logan, and that Andrew Logan was her kinsman, and that this town was his birthplace.

My father's frowns across the table let me know me my silence was becoming something noticeable, so I searched for something I could say. Into the next brief lull, I said to Logan, 'I was unaware you came from Edinburgh.'

'I don't,' he told me, bluntly. 'This is Leith.'

Lady Lindsay's eyebrows lifted slightly as she smoothly said, 'It is a common misconception, for those new to Scotland. Edinburgh does rule our town, 'tis true, and we serve as its harbour, but we Leithers have a character and pride that's all our own.'

'Lady Lindsay, I assure you, if your kinsman is the model of a Leither,' I replied, 'then I'm already well acquainted with their character.' My tone was sweet, deliberately. I should have known that Logan would not let me have the final word.

He said, 'She means we're faithful, honest and reliable.'

'I wouldn't choose those words.'

His grey eyes were a challenge. 'Pray, what would your own words be, then?'

I could feel my father's futile efforts to attract my gaze, but I ignored him and instead met Logan's eyes. 'The foremost, surely,' I said, 'would be stubborn?'

I liked the sound of Lady Lindsay's laugh. 'You know us well indeed! What else?'

It was a careful line to walk, to needle Logan and not give offence to Lady Lindsay. 'Proud,' I said. 'You mentioned pride yourself, my lady, and I've seen it.'

Logan waited. 'And the last? I offered three words. Ye've returned but two. Ye owe me one.'

I was determined not to be the first to look away. He would not win this time. 'I have not yet discovered it.'

He shrugged, and said, 'Then ye are in my debt until ye do.'

Then he did something most unfair. He grinned.

I had not ever felt the force of Andrew Logan's smile. One autumn I'd been walking in the street when unexpectedly a gust of wind had struck me hard, and robbed my lungs of breath. This felt like that. It stole my concentration for the moment that I might have used to frame an answer.

It was most unwise, I knew, to be in debt to such a man as Logan.

Stubborn, proud, and . . .

Doggedly, I chased that third word through my mind, and let the conversation pass me by. But at each turning, it escaped me, and would not be caught.

Anna, Queen of Britain

Bath, Somerset, the same day

Her thoughts would not be still. They mocked her body's lack of movement as she sat back in her chair, her feet raised on a cushioned footstool for the comfort of her legs. A week of travel had increased their swelling, and a painful ulcer had erupted on the inner side of her left ankle. Her doctor had wrapped both her legs in plasters mixed with rose oil, so the scent of roses filled the chamber, offering a sense of peace.

But Anna's thoughts were active.

She'd heard nothing from Sir William, and the silence set her nerves on edge, because she knew firsthand how very ruthless James could be when he was trying to protect his reputation.

Anna's fingers found an errant thread that hung loose on her gown's embroidery. She pulled at it, unthinking, and a tiny section of a flowered vine unravelled, lifting from the fabric as though it had never been there. It was futile wishing years could be that easy to unravel. Wishing time could be turned back with such a simple act as pulling on a thread.

And yet her mind turned backwards anyway, three years and a few months to that cold Christmas court at Thetford, when she'd sought out James in private, in his study.

It was evening. He'd been reading.

Without setting down his book, he asked, 'What is it?'

Anna had made very sure the door was closed. 'I come to speak with you about Lord Balmerino.'

James sighed. He laid his book aside. 'What of him?'

'He's been sentenced,' Anna said, 'to die a traitor's death.'

'The courts decide his punishment.'

'At your persuasion.'

It had been a great embarrassment to James, this whole affair. A friendly letter to the Pope, sent years ago and signed by James, before he was made King of England. Having lately surfaced, it caused difficulties, and the blame had fallen squarely on the Scottish nobleman Lord Balmerino.

Anna held in her frustration. 'He is innocent.'

'He has confessed.'

'At your suggestion. James, you know you signed that letter.'

James raised his eyebrows. 'If I did, I could hardly admit to it. Not since Guy Fawkes and his conspirators set fire to any chance I had of showing tolerance to Catholics.' As though certain she would understand, he added, 'Balmerino is a loyal man.'

'And loyalty must have a price, is that it? You would watch him die a brutal death, you'd let him hang and then be taken down and drawn and quartered in his blood upon the gallows, just to spare your reputation?'

He looked back at her, unmoved.

Anna controlled her breath, and caught the taut reins of her temper. 'It would be unfortunate if people were to learn about the letters that you had *me* write on your behalf to Rome, before we came to England.' She met James's gaze. 'Those people might begin to see a pattern in your contact with the Pope.'

His gaze grew narrow. 'Anna. Have a care. I will not stand for threats.'

'And I'll not stand and watch you kill a man who's never done you harm. Where is your conscience? Do you even have one anymore?' she asked him. 'Did you ever?'

'Anna.' He paused then, and his tone changed in the way a room's light altered when the sky was filled with shifting clouds. Idly, he asked, 'If you believe I'm so unprincipled, why don't you live in fear of me? A little poison in a cup, 'tis such a simple thing.'

She told herself it was a test, and not a threat.

'Because,' she said, 'apart from any love you may still feel for me, my brother is the King of Denmark, and you would not have him as your enemy.'

She turned her back to him, and made to leave the room.

He said, 'I do love ye.'

'Yes, so you often say. I'd rather you did show it.' Anna reached the door, and turned. 'Lord Balmerino keeps his life,' she told him, 'or believe me, James, I will make very certain that the whole world knows he's innocent.'

Her hands shook very slightly as she closed the door behind her. She walked past the guards in the gallery outside the study and into the small chamber just beyond, which was deserted. Or so she thought.

Until she saw Henry, sprawled in a chair in the corner, a book in his hand. He glanced up as she entered. He was nearly sixteen then. Already a young man, with eyes that missed little.

He studied her. 'You've been with Father.' Then he smiled. 'Will I have to play peacemaker between you?'

Anna shook her head. ''Tis not your place to mend our quarrels. They will pass.' *A little poison in a cup* ... She pushed the thought aside, and looked more closely at the book Henry was reading, recognizing it as that which he had carried with him since his childhood.

With indulgence, she remarked, 'You like that book.'

'Yes, very much.'

'I read it also, when I lived in Denmark.'

Henry seemed surprised by this. He asked her, 'Did you like it?'

Anna said, 'Yes, very much.' On the table at her side, a row of candles had been set alight to cast their dancing shadows on the wall. 'Some parts I still remember. Like the part about the candle flame that does not lose its brilliance till the moment it's extinguished, and how, like that candle, we all carry flames of truth within us, and of justice, which should only be extinguished by our deaths. Yet, see how easily a candle is put out.' She took the pewter snuffer in her hand and killed a flame. 'And so it is with truth, and justice,' Anna said. 'Especially with justice.'

Henry watched her, saying nothing, as though knowing there was more behind her quiet words than she could say. She would not tell him what the king had done. There would be time enough for him to learn that side of James, though she suspected Henry had already glimpsed it.

She only told him, 'You must always let those flames shine brightly, Henry, for as long as you do live. More brightly still when you are king.'

'I promise you,' said Henry, very solemnly, 'my flames will burn so brightly that the blind will see them. And, if God allows me, they will burn beyond my death.'

The small, embroidered vine upon her gown was nearly all unravelled. Anna stilled her fingers. Smoothed the fabric.

Time was in its place.

Lord Balmerino had not died.

And only weeks ago, a blind man on the river steps at

Whitehall had repeated Henry's words to her – the words that none but she and Henry had been in the room to hear – and told her, *I do bear a message from the prince, your son. He bids you speak to David.*

Anna had said nothing of the old man in her letter to Sir David Moray, only told him it was vital that they meet, if he could do it safely.

Now, she could do nothing more than hope her letter found Sir David before James's Messenger.

PHOEBE

The King's Wark, Port of Leith, Scotland, the same day

THAT NIGHT, AS I'D promised, I started my letter to Valentine. Finding a moment to write had proved challenging. Not because there was no space for me to sit – our lodgings here took up the whole of the square tower's third floor. I hadn't relished climbing all those weathered steps that circled up the turnpike staircase, with its damp scent of old stone and its sensation of confinement, Logan's cloak brushing my face once as he led the way, my father pressing close behind. I'd had to breathe, and focus on more pleasant things.

The rooms were worth the climb. The stairs, set in the tower's corner, brought us to a door, which opened first into the parlour. It was wainscotted in rich, dark wood that matched the floorboards, softened by a woven carpet. Two windows looked towards the waters of the harbour, letting in the light. Both windows were so deeply set into the thick stone walls that they formed private nooks, with benches built to either side – the sort of seats where, as a child, I might have curled myself for hours to watch the ships.

But there were also proper chairs here, and a small, round table, and a hearth.

And from the parlour, two more doors that opened to the bedchambers.

These rooms were designed for the comfort of someone who travelled with servants. While the larger chamber had a lovely bed with broidered hangings, there was also a rough pallet bed set on the floor nearby.

''Tis not a parliament,' was Logan's answer when my father raised a protest. 'There'll be no debates. Ye'll take the bed, I'll have the pallet. I'll be fine.' And that had been the end of that.

I was given the smaller bedchamber. Although it had a soft bed and a small basin of fresh water I could wash with, it was darkly panelled all around, its one small window set too high to be of help, and when the door was closed the room felt airless.

And when darkness came, it brought the fearful dream.

Apparently, I never made a sound when it did visit me. My father said I sometimes stirred or frowned, but never cried out. Never called my mother's name. Not even when I reached the moment where I rolled upon the bed and saw my brother lying there beside me, dead.

I wakened suddenly, adjusting to the strangeness of the room, the sheet so tightly tucked about me that I panicked for a moment from the fear I, too, might be a corpse wrapped in a shroud – until I heard my father snoring through the wall, and the familiar sound relaxed me.

Sleep, I knew, would not return. It never did, after the dream. But I would never have a better time to finally write my letter.

I had tried to write it earlier, within the confines of my chamber, but it proved impossible. And Logan and my father had been sitting talking in the parlour, making it impractical for me to use the table there. But now they were both shut up in their chamber, and the parlour was my own, in all its solitude.

Outside the sheets, the air bit sharply through my linen shift. Had I been home, I could have donned my loose gown, but that useful garment was one of the things I'd had to sacrifice when packing for this journey. In its place, I took the finely woven blanket from the bed and wrapped it round me in the manner of the women I'd seen earlier upon the wharf, so that it made a kind of mantle, leaving my head bare. My feet were bare as well, but that could not be helped. At least they made no noise as I slipped out into the parlour, crossing the soft carpet to the hearth, where last night's coals had been banked well to leave the faintest glow beneath the heaps of ash.

By stirring deeply, I drew flame enough upon a thin wax taper from the box that hung nearby to light the candle at the table, where my father's writing tools and paper still lay where he'd left them.

He'd brought *so* much paper. I could not think why.

There was one full quire of five-and-twenty sheets stacked on the table, and I knew three more quires had been rolled to line our portmanteau, so there were plenty to be shared. I took one, folded it to write my letter, chose a sharpened quill, and drew the ink pot near while settling in the chair that faced the door of the large bedchamber, so I would have some warning if it opened.

Valentine had only asked for word that I was safe, but after giving that, I told him of our voyage north, although when I began describing Leith I paused, because my own impressions of this town were so different from Valentine's unpleasant memories of Scotland. I compromised by writing mostly of the King's Wark, and of Lady Lindsay, saying: *She is such a gracious hostess and so pleasant in her manner I confess I find it difficult to yet believe she sprang from the same line as Andrew Logan. He is here, and—*

There, again, I paused.

And . . . what? What could be written about Logan without spoiling the letter?

I was staring at the candle flame and thinking when the object of my thoughts spoke from the darkness, near the far wall.

'Are ye foundered still upon the final word that would define a Leither?'

Logan's voice was quiet, but he must have found the way I jumped amusing.

My heartbeat leapt, and raced, and settled as my irritation rose. I saw his outline now. He sat within one of the window nooks, his white shirt showing pale against the stone wall in the shadows.

'Have you been there all this time?' I asked.

'Aye.'

I'd have gone straight past him, walking from my chamber to the hearth, and he had let me pass without a word. 'A gentleman,' I told him, 'would have made his presence known.'

'Ye ken I'm here the now.'

I could not argue that.

He asked, 'Why are ye not abed?'

To my surprise, I answered honestly. 'I had a dream. It wakened me. Yourself?'

His movement might have been a shrug. 'Your father snores.'

I bristled. 'He can't help that.'

'I was not complaining. My own father did the same.'

His father, too, had been a Messenger – a smaller man than Logan, and more friendly, who had whistled in the Close and found a cheerful word for everyone. He'd seemed well loved by all his family, and his death was unexpected, from some wound that spread a poison in his blood. Four years ago, that would have been, or five. Not long enough to make it any easier for Logan.

He had turned his head away, to look out of the window at the darkness of the harbour. I'd have told him I was sorry for his loss, but I suspected Logan did not want my pity.

And he killed my sympathy with his next words.

He said, 'I'll take that letter.'

'What?'

'I cannot let ye send it.'

'Why not?'

He rose from his seat. He was half dressed, in shirt and breeks and boots, and cast so dark a shadow on the wall behind him that I nearly did not see the red edge of his scarlet doublet in the dim light, hanging from a wall hook by the window. He took something from its pocket, and approached me.

'This is why not.'

Holding out a narrow, folded document, he all but dared me to accept it from his hand. I did.

He told me, 'Read it,' so I did that, too.

An open warrant, it began, *to Andrew Logan, one of the Messengers of His Majesty's Chamber.*

I stopped, and glanced up at him. 'Surely this is private?'

'Read it.'

Whereas Sir David Moray, knight, was lately called to answer questions touching on the death of our beloved Prince, and instead departed out of the kingdom without permission, therefore in His Majesty's name you are to make your speedy repair to Scotland, there to apprehend the said Sir David Moray upon his return, and to bring him hither to us for his examination; in the execution whereof you are not to permit him to speak to any other person but in your hearing, and if there be any papers or books upon his person you will seize and seal those up and bring those hither also, with all speed. You may freely call upon the aid and assistance of all His Majesty's public officers, but forasmuch as this business is of a most special nature, we command you to use all secrecy, and to charge those whom you employ in this service to do likewise.

When I looked up this time, I'm sure the shock showed plainly on my face. 'Sir David Moray?'

'Aye.'

'But of Prince Henry's men, he was the most . . . the most . . .'

'Aye.' Logan's tone was curt. 'Ye see why this does call for care, and secrecy.'

It all seemed strange. 'I can't believe Sir David Moray could have ever harmed the prince. There must be some mistake.'

''Tis not for ye nor I to judge. Our task is to deliver him to London, and while keeping to these orders.' He took the warrant back from me, and with his hand outstretched, he said again, 'I'll take that letter.'

'But I am writing to Valentine.'

He didn't follow my argument. 'Why should that matter?'

'Because,' I replied, using Valentine's words, 'he has the trust of those who write my father's orders, and your own. He knows of all of this already.'

'Did he tell ye so himself?'

I nodded. 'On St George's Day, before we sailed.'

'What did he say?'

'He knew that we were coming up to Edinburgh to meet you, and he said that he knew why.'

Logan's frown looked darker by the candlelight. His tone was absent as he told me, 'This is Leith.' Then, 'But he said nothing of Sir David Moray?'

'No.'

'Then I would not assume that he knows all, no matter how he sought to charm ye.'

'He did not—' I bit my words back with an effort, trying to maintain my temper. 'He is a gentleman.'

'Unlike myself. I understand. But even so, I cannot have ye writing to him. As the warrant says—'

'I'm only writing to him,' I explained, 'because he wished to know that I was safe.'

That made him slant a long look down at me, his eyebrows raised. 'Ye're travelling with me. That makes ye safe.'

The ego of the man! I longed to raise a further protest, but we'd reached an impasse, and I knew it. Logan never let me have the last word, and he was not going to let me keep this letter. I admitted I could see his point – the warrant *was* specific in its wording, and it bound him and those working with him to obey its rules. 'We take an oath,' he'd told me, in the stables at his house, 'to keep our business secret.'

He was right, but I would yield on my own terms.

Ignoring his outstretched and waiting hand, I rose and rolled the letter tightly. Crossing to the hearth, I pushed it deep into the embers I had stirred, until the letter caught the flame and burned.

While I knelt and watched it, Logan offered me an olive branch. 'When this is done,' he said, 'and we are all come home again to St Bartholomew's, ye can tell Fox that ye tried, and I prevented it. I've no doubt he'll forgive ye. Ye can say I was a tyrant. He'll believe it.'

'Anybody would believe it.' I could tell, the instant I had said the words, that I had gone a step too far, but words, once spoken, could not be called back again. They hung there, ugly, in the air between us.

Straightening, I slowly turned to face him.

Logan stood, as always, square and solid, his eyes level on my own. 'I'd not say anybody,' he replied. 'There may be some among my friends whose views are not so prejudiced. But they are common men, like me, and such as ye and Fox would never ken the views of common folk, now, would ye?'

Somehow he could always tie my tongue with his disdain.

I should have told him I was sorry. Should have told him I was common, too. I should have told him anything, but I could only stand and meet his gaze with helpless eyes, until a firm knock sounded at the main door to the stairs and Logan turned his back to me and went to answer it.

The boy, young Hector, did not step into the parlour, but stayed on the threshold, looking hesitantly from myself to Logan. 'Beg pardon, sir, but ye did say to tell ye if I saw a French ship in the harbour. One is coming in the now.'

'Good lad,' said Logan. He took his doublet from its peg and shrugged it on and fastened it. 'Ye wouldn't ken the name?'

'I couldnae read it in the dark. Shall I go have another look?'

'No need. I'm coming with ye.' Logan had his sword belt fastened on now, much to Hector's fascination.

Hector glanced at me again. 'Forgive me, mistress, if I interrupted—'

Logan cut him off. 'Ye interrupted nothing.' As he took the cape that had been hanging underneath his doublet from the peg and tied it carelessly across his shoulder, he asked me, 'We are finished, are we not?' And daring me to tell him otherwise, he sent me a dismissive nod and followed Hector out.

Dawn came creeping faintly in its first pale streaks low in the eastern sky so shortly after Logan left that it seemed his departure had removed the darkness and allowed the light to shine.

My father, when he wakened, found me sitting in the

window nook where Logan had been sitting, with my blanket-mantle gathered round my shoulders as I watched the sunrise spread across the waters of the harbour.

'You are up before the birds, I see, as usual.' He smiled, and looked around the parlour. 'Where is Logan?'

The full answer, of course, was that Hector had come to fetch him because of the French ship, and Logan had gone alone down to the wharf and was waiting there still. I could see him from here. He'd forgotten his hat in his hurry to leave, and he'd drawn his cape fully around him so none of his livery showed, though his size made him easy to spot.

But I felt too weary to give the full answer, so I simply said, 'He went out.'

My father nodded sagely. 'Chased him off already, did you? Ah, well, it was bound to happen. Shall we wait for his return before we call for breakfast?'

His acceptance of the situation stirred me to reply, 'Are you not curious?'

'About what?'

'I am sitting in my nightclothes, I've been talking with a man, in private, and you're not demanding to know every detail?'

'If it were another man, perhaps. But Logan is a man of honour.' As though it were obvious, my father added, 'If I believed otherwise, I never would have let you join us.'

I'm not sure which rankled me more – that my father thought so highly of Logan, or that he felt he'd allowed me to join them, when in truth I'd been the one who had arranged things. 'You seem very sure of his character.'

'I am.' His face altered. 'Why? Did he behave in any way that—?'

'No.' My conscience pricked me for upsetting him. 'Of course not.'

'Well, then. As I said, a man of honour. Anyway, you may be in your nightclothes, but you're not indecently attired. Which reminds me, Logan brought you a present.'

I decided I couldn't have heard that correctly. 'A present? For me?'

My father didn't hear me. He'd already disappeared into his bedchamber, returning with a folded length of light wool cloth of varied colours, woven in a geometric pattern. I knew what it was – I'd seen it many times at St Bartholomew's – but still I scarce believed it till my father said, 'His mother sent it, actually. Apparently she worried for you riding all day in the open weather, with your face exposed to sun, or in the wind, and when she asked him whether you were well prepared, he did not know, and so she sent you this.' He handed it to me, and I allowed the fabric to unfold into the garment I knew it to be. My father carried on, 'He says it's called a plaid.'

It took a moment for me to absorb the impact of the gift. My father cared for me and loved me, as did my Aunt Agnes, but I had been motherless for so long that it struck me in a tender, painful place to have a woman so concerned about my comfort in the weather that she'd wish to wrap me in her own clothes.

When I found my voice, it sounded small. ''Twas very kind of her to think of me.'

'The Logans are a kind and thoughtful family.'

I nearly said, *Not all of them*. Instead, I only asked my father, 'Why did Logan not give this to me himself?'

My father sent me the same look he always did when I was asking a question whose answer I already knew. 'I'd imagine he thought you would better accept it from my hands than his.'

Logan was not wrong. But he had made the effort, notwithstanding. It felt petulant, on my part, given that we would be bottled up together for who knew how long, to not begin to make an effort, too.

I began with a small step. 'Was it four years ago or five that Logan's father died?'

My father looked surprised. 'Five. Surely you recall. It was the very summer Logan nearly died, as well. Why do you ask?'

'I had forgotten,' I confessed. I turned my head away, to look out of the window at the stoic figure on the wharf. 'I thought it was a thing that I should know.'

ANDREW

Port of Leith, Scotland, 4th May 1613

I DID NOT ALWAYS SEE the dead.

That would have been a special curse, to ever see the wraiths that walk among us. But from time to time, on battlefields, I spied those who had fallen there and never found their peace. They looked to me like living men, till they came close enough for me to see there was a light unnatural in their eyes.

I noticed the man next to me because his clothes were out of fashion and because, like me, his focus seemed to be on the French ship that, having stood off in the road outside the harbour for some time, had just now finished docking at the wharfside here in front of us. The man, of middle age and armed with pistols and a sword, was doing me no harm. I stepped aside to give him space. That no else did should have warned me.

A younger man, sleekit – most likely a merchant awaiting his cargo – passed so closely by the other man he all but trod on his shoes.

I said, 'Mind how ye go!'

Which had little effect on the younger man, who merely shot me a questioning glance, but the man with the pistols and sword turned his head to me. Nodded.

I saw his eyes, then. And I knew.

It still struck me to silence, each time that it happened, although by now I realized wraiths could not touch me. The thought of them did something cold to my blood. And I couldn't help wondering who they imagined *I* was. They were not of our world, but neither were they walking wholly in the world they'd lived in, and yet clearly when they looked at me they saw – or thought they saw – a face they recognized.

This wraith was French. At least, that was the language he was speaking when he gestured to his head and mine and laughed as if to share a joke about the fact I wore no hat. Had my own French been more accomplished, I'd have telt him that the fault lay at the feet of Phoebe Westaway, who'd distracted me enough that I had left our lodgings with my hat forgotten on its peg behind me.

But all the French I knew went little beyond how to count, and how to bargain, and the way to say good morrow and good evening, having learned that much from dealing with the doctor who had tried to cure my father, and whose ministries had left us an account I'd only last year finished paying.

To the wraith, I gave a brief smile and returned his nod, and hoped that none who stood with us along the Shore would see and think it strange.

Given his clothing and his nation, he had likely died here in the siege of Leith in the last century, when our king's mother, Mary, Queen of Scots, still lived in France, and with her mother ruling here as regent, thousands of French soldiers came to fortify this town against the Protestants and English. They fought bravely and fought long, but they of course could not hold Leith for ever.

In the end, as with all battles, one side had to yield. A truce was called. The French went home again. At least, most did.

The wraith said something else, and sighed. Then, brightening, he motioned to the French ship, and said something in which I caught the words, 'Nos amis'. *Our friends.*

Again, I nodded.

There was little point, I'd learned, in telling him his friends were dead, or that he was. Wraiths never took it well. Instead I turned my full attention back towards the ship, and to the men who were now disembarking – in particular, to the tall, weary-looking man in black with clipped red hair and beard, his eyes downturned towards the wharf.

I stepped in front of him. 'Sir David Moray?'

It was only a formality. I'd seen him often enough with Prince Henry to know that I had the right man. He was younger by a few years than his brother and had nothing of Sir William's swagger, but he had a quiet presence all his own. He raised his head and with a sharp eye took my measure.

'Aye?'

I did not wish to make a scene, but I allowed my cape to part so he could see my scarlet doublet with its royal coat of arms. 'I have a warrant, sir, by order of His Majesty, to take ye in my custody and see ye safe to London.'

I expected him to ask me what the charge was, but he didn't. At least, not directly.

He asked, 'May I see this warrant?'

I produced it, knowing he'd learn nothing by it that should be concealed. Besides, while he stood reading, with his focus on the paper held between his two hands, it gave me the perfect opportunity to fit him with the manacles I'd taken from my belt.

He made no resistance. He simply looked down at his wrists, now bound together with the narrow iron bands linked by their chain, and while I finished with the second lock, he asked me, 'Is this absolutely necessary?'

'Aye, sir. I'm afraid so.' I'd come a long way to find him. I wasn't about to risk having him run.

Sir David studied me. 'If you are fearing I'd try to escape, I could give you my word as a gentleman.'

I said, 'I'll take that as well, sir. But till we reach London, I'll trust to these.' With the keys to the manacles still in my hand, I recovered the warrant and tucked it all safely back into my pockets.

We were starting to attract attention. Where the wraith had gone, I knew not, but its place was taken now by someone else – a living man who showed too great an interest in my conversation with Sir David Moray for my liking.

'Come,' I said, and steered him with as much respect as possible along the Shore. I tried not to lay hands on him, but only kept a half a pace behind and to the side, to see he did not leave my keeping.

'Are you not supposed to search me?' he asked. 'By your warrant, you are charged to seize my books and papers, are you not? How can you be sure I'll not throw them into the water?'

There were several points at play. His tone was lightly dry, so I felt reasonably certain he was joking. He had so far been compliant with my orders. And he was, by several levels, my superior in social rank. But still, experience had taught me that it was important, from the start, for me to let him know I was in charge, or else I would have naught but trouble later.

I said, 'Because ye have given me your word, sir, as a gentleman. And because if ye tried, ye would be going straight into the water after them, to fetch them back.'

His head turned, and he looked at me for a moment over his shoulder. 'I shall keep that in mind.' A pause. Then, 'Do you have a name?'

'Logan, sir.'

I watched him thinking. 'Andrew Logan?'

'Aye, sir.'

With a nod, he faced front again. 'Where are we going?'

'Just there. The King's Wark.'

I hadn't told my cousin who I'd come here to arrest. All walls had ears, and though she was my kin, she, too, was of that higher rank that sometimes sheltered their own kind from justice.

More than that, her husband and Sir William Moray had both served the king together for so long they'd know each other well, and thus my cousin, too, would know the family. I was proved right when I came into the Wark's hall with my prisoner beside me, and my cousin's face showed shock and recognition.

But she tempered it, and crossed to greet us.

'Lady Lindsay,' said Sir David, as he took her offered hand within his bound ones, bowing gallantly. ''Tis a pleasure to see you again, whatever the circumstances.'

She returned the honour, and asked after his kin, and these pleasantries continued for some minutes while I stood aside, impatient. But at length my cousin turned and asked me, 'So now, Andrew, what will you be needing for your journey south?'

And from her gaze I knew I had her loyalty.

I said, 'Two horses from your stables, to accompany my own. And food, if ye can spare it.' There was one more thing that would be better done by her than me. Her husband was the Searcher for the port of Leith, and in his absence she fulfilled that office, giving her authority to board and search and seize the cargo of all ships that anchored here. 'Ye'll see Sir David does not have his baggage with him. I am sure he'd wish to have it brought here, for his use.'

Sir David said, 'That's very kind,' though with his eyes he let me know he knew my motivation was not kindness. 'I'd arranged to have my things sent on to Abercairney, but if we are going to London, it would be most useful to be able to at least have some clean shirts to take along.'

My cousin smiled her graceful smile. 'Then let me go now to your ship, and see what I can find.'

She found one wooden chest, bound well with iron straps and locked. And a fine leather portmanteau of better workmanship than mine.

When both had been carried upstairs to our lodgings, I sat with Laurence Westaway while Phoebe and Sir David watched, and sorted through the items to prepare a proper inventory. There was nothing that concerned me – only clothing, and a tall hat with a turned-up brim, which on its own took up nearly a third part of the chest. I'd feared that Sir David, being a learned man, would have been weighted down with books that I'd have had to seize and drag along to London, as my orders did demand. But in the end, the only books I found were on his person, in the pocket of his coat.

Two books, both small, and both with leather bindings worn to smoothness by repeated readings.

Westaway, examining the first, pronounced it, 'Xylander's translation of the Emperor Marcus Aurelius Antoninus's philosophical thoughts upon life, in Latin and Greek,' and noted it down in the inventory. The second book appeared to hold him fascinated.

Calling Phoebe over, he said, 'Read this page, and let me have your thoughts.'

She bent her head above the book that he held open, no doubt glad it gave her an excuse to carry on pretending that I wasn't in the room. I didn't mind. I had work to attend to, and it was more peaceful when Phoebe ignored me than when we were arguing.

'I don't see ... wait, this is ... this is not printed.' Her tone blended awe and the joy of discovery. 'Somebody has done this by hand, very cleverly, so it appears printed.'

'It had me fooled, too,' said Westaway. 'But that's hardly surprising, considering who held the pen.' He turned the pages back to show her.

Phoebe's eyes grew wider. 'Esther Inglis!'

'Indeed.' Looking across to Sir David, who'd drawn his chair close to the wall as though trying to detach from all of us, Westaway said, 'You're a fortunate man, sir, to own such a book. Esther Inglis is a talented scribe.'

Sir David agreed. 'It's not my only work by her, but that was a special gift and I value it greatly.'

'"A Treatise of preparation to the Holy Supper of our only Saviour and Redeemer,"' Westaway read the title out while writing it with care into the inventory.

Phoebe watched him, stunned, then took the book carefully up in her hands as though it were a treasure and held it closely to her chest. She looked at me. 'You cannot take this from him.'

Westaway said, 'Phoebe, don't be foolish. Logan has his orders.'

She did not give way, her gaze fierce upon mine. 'Our king owns books by Esther Inglis, as do people of the best quality at court, and nothing she produces is in any way objectionable.' Dismissively, she said, 'I don't expect a man like you to understand. Books wouldn't mean as much to you. But when you care for them, to have them taken from you causes pain. What would you gain by confiscating this apart from being cruel?'

That was what she thought of me, I knew. That I was cruel.

I briefly looked down at the book she held. Then, seeking space to think, I reached beyond her to the table and took up the other book – the one in Greek and Latin – and although I knew I wouldn't understand the words inside, I leafed through a few of the pages. Somebody had written short notes in the margins, in pencil.

'Are these your notes?' I asked Sir David.

'No,' he said. 'Those were Prince Henry's.'

His voice hadn't changed. He still sat the same way in his chair. But I thought I saw something pass over his face like a shadow that made me remember his brother's words, back in the stables of Somerset House: *David grieves the prince as well. He should be given space to do so.*

Grief was a shadow whose shape was familiar. And orders or no, I knew Phoebe was right. If I took this book from Sir David, I'd hurt him, and I couldn't do that. I handed it to Phoebe, met the challenge in her eyes just long enough to have the satisfaction of seeing it change to confusion, told her, 'Give him both,' and, turning, put a few paces of distance between us, crossing to the window that overlooked the harbour.

Westaway said, 'Are you sure?'

I told him, 'Aye. Your daughter's right. There's nothing seditious in either of those.'

'But your orders—'

'—are to seize any books and papers and bring them safely to London.' I was well aware. 'I've seized *him*, haven't I? And I can seize what he's carrying while it's in his pockets as easily as I can when it's out of them. He's not likely to throw either of those books in the ditch on our way to London, and if anyone wants to see them once we're there, then I'll take them in hand. Right?' I answered myself with, 'Right.' Then took a deep breath, having no wish to show my short temper to Westaway.

He seemed unbothered. 'You'd best keep hold of this, though,' he advised me, and when I looked I saw he held the final item needing to be inventoried – a small, folded letter I had taken from Sir David's pocket with the books. Westaway, unfolding it, said, 'Letters, I know well from my experience, can oft hold hidden messages.'

At any other time I might have asked him what experience he'd had of hidden messages, but once again I'd been distracted by what I believed to be a swift change in Sir David's keen expression. That intrigued me, so I fixed my gaze upon Sir David, and asked Westaway, 'What does it say?'

He read the letter aloud. It was brief, and had no salutation. 'I am in receipt of yours from Paris. I shall meet your ship at Leith, and bring a horse for you. Safe voyage and Godspeed, Your devoted et cetera, Inchbrakie.'

I fought the urge to curse. No hidden message, but one every bit as ominous.

Sir David's clear eyes met my own.

I kept my voice calm. 'That would be your cousin, Patrick Graeme of Inchbrakie?'

He was very good at hiding his reactions, but a trace of his surprise showed through. 'I am impressed,' he said. 'You know my family.'

Have a care. Sir William's words rang once more in my memory. *Keep a watch out for my kinsmen. They're thick on the ground where you're going.* Now, too late, I understood that final warning.

'Aye, I ken your family.' Crossing back to Laurence, I took the letter from him and secured it in my own pocket. 'See that your papers are safe. Get your portmanteau ready while I help Sir David pack.' His upward glance showed that he'd not yet caught up with my reasoning.

'We need to leave,' I said. 'Now.'

My haste surprised my cousin, but she did not try to change my mind. She had our horses waiting in the courtyard for us, with one small addition that surprised me in my turn.

'A Garron?' I could feel my eyebrows lifting at the sight of the small, sturdy Highland horse, more like a pony, standing with the taller dark bay gelding and black mare in company with Brutus. 'What do I need with a Garron?'

''Tis a present for the king,' my cousin said. 'He asked my husband some months past to send him a Garron to carry the game for this season's hunt. Besides, it will give Hector something to ride.'

'Hector?'

'Naturally. He'll be a help to you in caring for the horses.'

She did not *look* as though she'd lost her sanity, yet I could not be sure. I asked, 'What will his mother say to that?'

The answer came, not from my cousin, but from Hector, who moved past us with a saddle that he hoisted onto the Garron's back, atop the blanket already in place. 'She'll say naught,' he told me, certain, 'for I have no mother.'

As I watched the expert way his young hands made adjustments to the saddle's girth, my cousin said, ''Tis not as though I have a choice. Were I to keep him here, he'd only follow you, and I know you'd not have the heart to send him back alone.'

She had me there. And it was true that I could use an extra pair of hands to help me with the horses. 'Right,' I said. 'Sir David, take the mare. The gelding is for Westaway. And Hector, ride behind them, if ye will, and be my eyes. If ye see anybody following us, shout so I will hear ye.'

Hector seemed excited at the prospect. 'Do ye think that anyone *will* follow us?'

Sir David, who had managed to swing neatly to his saddle

even with his hands still manacled, looked down to meet my eyes. His were unreadable.

I said, to Hector, 'Aye, I do.'

I understood the thrill my answer gave the lad. I'd been a lad myself, once, and I'd craved adventure. Now I was a man who must deliver this young lad, a dying scrivener, a lass who didn't like me, and my prisoner to London. All I craved now was a safe road, and a quiet one. I knew that I'd find neither. Our portmanteaus were strapped to the backs of the saddles. I'd originally thought Westaway would have to carry two, but with the Garron it made one apiece for every horse but mine. Mine had the pillion, which Phoebe, who had stayed some distance off from us, was staring at with mingled horror and dismay.

She said, 'We came by ship. Cannot we travel back to London the same way?'

'The wind has changed. The ships here will be held within in the harbour till the wind turns, and we cannot wait.' Which was the truth, although I did not add that, from the vision I had Seen at St Bartholomew's, when we were in the stables at my house, I'd been forewarned our way from here would be on horseback. Though I'd spared her father what exertion I could on their journey north, it was plain that, from here on—

'I ride with you?' asked Phoebe.

'Aye.'

'But I thought …' She looked towards her father, as a drowning person looks towards the land, but he was already astride his horse and paying her no heed.

I guessed her thoughts, but I couldn't explain why riding pillion with her father was impossible without drawing attention to Westaway's weakness, and that was a thing I'd never do in front of others. I knew she would have rather ridden with the Devil than with me, but, 'This is the arrangement. I've no time to waste in argument,' I told her. 'Either come along or bide here. Make your choice, but make it now.'

She lifted her chin in the way that she did when accepting a challenge, but I saw the fear in her eyes.

I knew the cause of that, too. Leading Brutus a few steps away from the others, I gave her the space to be brave.

And she was. With her head high, she crossed to us. 'How do I do this?' she asked.

'Come to this side, the near side.'

She wore my mother's plaid wrapped round her – incorrectly, but I dared not show her how it should be done, and she'd be glad of it, regardless, when the sun rose higher. Between that, and the firm stays she'd trussed herself with underneath her jacket, I felt nothing of her heartbeat when I took her waist in my two hands and lifted her. But I could see the pulse beat strongly in her throat, and knew that she was nervous.

Helping her settle herself in her new sideways pose on the cushioned seat strapped to the back of my saddle, I tried to speak patiently. 'Ye see this handle that's close by his tail? Take hold of it, that's right. Now, place your feet here, and I'll adjust it. Tell me when it's comfortable.'

Not every pillion had a platform, like a single stirrup, for the lady's feet to rest upon. Margaret, when we rode in London, liked for me to leave it off, to let her legs hang freely. But since Phoebe would be riding with me on a longer journey, and was new to riding pillion, I'd reattached the platform for her.

'It's fine,' she said, though her face told me otherwise.

Still, she clung onto the pillion's handle, white-faced as she was.

Well done, I wanted to tell her, but she'd not have welcomed my praise. Instead, I gave a quick word to Brutus, who lowered his head so that I could vault into the saddle by swinging my leg up and over his neck. Brutus shifted his position as I did so, and I heard a sharp intake of breath behind me.

Looking back over my shoulder, I said, 'Take hold of my belt.'

She did not move.

I said, more sharply, 'Phoebe!'

In response, I felt her right hand clutch at my belt, and hang on tightly.

'That's the way,' I reassured her, as we moved into the lead of the unlikely chain of travellers abandoning the safety of the King's Wark for the dangers of the road to London. 'I'll not let ye fall.'

PHOEBE

The Middle Shires of the Scottish Borders, 5th May 1613

WE WEREN'T BEING FOLLOWED.

The first day, I'd caught the contagion that seemed to have Logan and Hector and even my father held fast in its grip. Three times Hector called out to warn he'd seen motion behind on the road that might be a pursuer, and thrice we'd moved into the trees at the roadside, to wait in the shadows, not daring to breathe lest we make a betraying sound.

Each time, my heart raced with the fear every hunted thing feels.

And each time, we'd watched innocent merchants or wayfarers pass on the road, unaware and in no degree threatening.

When, in the evening, we came to a village called Stow, Logan hadn't allowed us to stop there. Instead he had taken us off the road up a long lane to a farmhouse where we'd taken lodgings that, if I were kind, might have suited a fieldworker. I had been careful, though, not to complain.

Partly because I knew Logan expected me to, and I'd not give him that satisfaction. And partly because I knew it was the best that the farmwife, our hostess, could offer, and she was a good woman, cheerful and welcoming, and to repay her by being ungrateful would have been unspeakably rude.

But I was stiff from riding sideways all day on the horse, adjusting to its constant motion, trying not to fall. And I was stiffer still this morning, after sleeping on the thin pallet bed with its uneven stuffing of straw that made lumps in some places and let me feel through to the floor in some others.

When Logan had lifted me onto the pillion this morning, I'd flinched, even though I'd tried not to. I'd brushed off his hands.

As his grey eyes met mine, I'd explained, 'My back hurts.'

He said nothing at first, merely swung himself into the saddle, fitting his long legs behind the pistol holsters that hung down at either side from hooks by the front pommel. Valentine's pistol holsters, like his saddle, were covered in velvet, ornately embroidered in silver thread, and edged with silver braid and gilt brass nails. Logan's were workmanlike, of unembellished leather made to match his saddle, capped below with plain brass as a guard. His sword hung just before the near one, in its scabbard, and if we *were* being followed, any villain would have found it hard to come through him.

But we weren't being followed.

The whole of this second day we had been looking behind us for whatever Logan imagined was there, and again there'd been nothing to see but the road, on which we were most often the only ones travelling.

That was understandable. The way was narrow, closely pressed by forests, and in some spots crossed by rivulets and streams that had no bridge, so we were forced to urge the horses through them at a fording-place.

In fairness, we passed farmhouses from time to time, and even villages, and at midday we came upon a market town with huddled roofs, a steeple, and the scent of woodsmoke hanging in the air. I heard the sound of children laughing at a game, and clanging iron from what might have been a forge, but Logan did not let us pause.

He drew his cloak about his doublet, hiding any trace of scarlet, and he spoke a word to his great horse and led our party onwards, and we did not stop until the town was far enough behind us that we could no longer hear the sounds of people, only birdsong. There, in the shelter of the trees beside another stream that chased over smooth stones, we ate our dinner – a cold meal of oaten cakes and eggs cooked in their shells, wrapped up in packets for us by the farmwife who last night had been our hostess, and washed down with ale. I was thankful my father, who'd travelled like this before, had thought to bring us two small wooden tumblers from home, for it saved me the indignity of swilling ale from the communal jug.

My father marked a note into the pages of his almanac. 'I have not seen that bird before.' He stood to see it better, and then quickly sat again, as though his legs had lost their strength and failed him.

I forgot my food. 'Are you unwell?'

My father shook his head. 'I stood with too much haste, is all. My muscles were not ready.' But his face was pale.

The bird, as if in understanding, flew to perch upon a lower branch. My father took his notes. His face regained its colour. And the bird at last came fluttering to hunt the crumbs we'd left upon the ground, to Hector's great delight.

Hector faced our day as though it were a grand adventure. I wished I could do the same, but it was difficult while trying not to topple from the pillion or lean too close to Logan's broad, unyielding back for what seemed endless hours of discomfort.

In the waning hours of the afternoon we came upon another town, and Logan drew his cloak about him once again as we approached a crossroads that would lead us off away along the riverbank, and I could no more bear it.

'Logan?' Without letting go of his belt, I nudged my hand into the small of his back.

His head angled sideways. 'Aye?'

'We should stop here for the night.'

'The horses can go further.'

'I cannot,' I said. 'Nor can my father.'

Logan glanced back at the others, and I thought perhaps he might be feeling the effects of our day's ride more deeply than he would admit, for his gaze lost its focus a moment. He said, 'Very well. But say nothing to anyone, understand? Not without looking to me. I will speak for us.'

His head stayed half turned when I did not reply, and he asked, 'What, no arguments?'

Had we been friends, I'd have said he was teasing me, but we weren't friends, so his comment could only be mocking.

In truth, I'd been forming the words of debate in my mind, but discarded them now. I'd not give him that victory. I'd happily hold my tongue if it meant I could get down from his horse, and away from *him*. Archly, I told him, 'No arguments.'

'Well.' Logan sounded amused. 'There's a first time for everything.'

Reining the horse to a halt, he lifted his arm to gather the others around us on the road. My father did look tired, but otherwise was bearing up well, and gave me a small smile of encouragement. Sir David made a stoic figure, all in black upon the black mare, with his red hair hidden by the hooded cloak whose folds he kept around his wrists to hide the chains and manacles so no one passing on the road would notice them. A man with pride, then. Younger than my father, perhaps in his middle forties, he still had an air of weariness about him, though he sat upright and easy in the saddle. Last came Hector, on his Highland pony, still looking like a miniature Logan, his cloak drawn around him to hide any trace of his red shirt, his young face determined. He only wanted the boots and the arrogance.

Logan told them, as if it had been his own idea, 'We'll be

stopping here. Heads up, mouths shut, eyes open. And keep close. We are not out of danger.'

We started on again, and though I was still unconvinced, I cast one furtive look behind, to reassure myself the road was truly empty.

It was a pretty town. The broader river met a smaller, brighter, dancing stream here, and there was a mill, and all the houses' roofs were freshly thatched. The bustle of activity around the well and market cross led me to hope the town might have a tavern or an inn that offered rooms and meals to travellers, but such things seemed a rarity in Scotland.

Instead, Logan asked a man, 'Where would we find the bailie?'

What a bailie was I did not know and could not ask, since I was bound to silence, but from having seen how closely some Scots words resembled English ones, I guessed it might be something like a bailiff, so a person of authority.

My guess was proved right when we were directed to the man himself – the bailie of the town, who introduced himself as Robert Scott, and was warden of a tower house set near the banks of the swift-flowing stream, beside an ancient bridge whose arches seemed as fixed and timeless as the old church on the other side, its steeple rising from the hill like an all-seeing guardian.

This tower house was very like the King's Wark, both outside and in – its sturdy, square walls built of stone to keep out all intruders – yet Logan clearly questioned its security.

He stationed Hector in the stables, with instructions to observe the care the tower's groom gave to the horses. 'See that they're fed and watered well, and not handled by strangers.'

When the rest of us were shown upstairs, he left us sitting in the parlour and strode through the few rooms of our lodgings, making an inspection, while the bailie sought to reassure him, 'You're as safe here as you would be at my own estate at Alton. Why, this tower stood when all the town was burnt, in our king's mother's time, and it will stand a good while longer, mark my words, against whatever comes.'

Logan said, 'That may be so, but I would have ye set a man to watch at every entry to the town. And post another in the steeple of the kirk. Tell them to shout if they see riders.'

The bailie nodded, but he also glanced towards Sir David, who had chosen not to sit and was now making his own circuit of the parlour, pausing now and then to look out of a window or examine some small item on a table.

As discreetly as he could, the bailie leaned in close to Logan. 'Is that not Sir David Moray?'

From the far side of the room, the answer came directly from Sir David, who without turning his head or pausing in his study of the room, replied, 'It is indeed.'

The bailie coughed, and begged his pardon. He himself, from what I gathered, was a member of the local gentry, not unlike Sir David's father in his social standing. From his expression I could see that dealing with such men as prisoners made him feel uncomfortable.

I sympathized.

Since leaving Leith, Sir David had behaved in every way towards us as a perfect gentleman. That Logan made him wear those wretched manacles was not only unnecessary, but an insult to his station.

I'd have said as much, but I had promised Logan I would hold my tongue, so I said nothing, keeping to my corner in my chair beside a tapestry that smelled of heavy dust no years of beating could dislodge.

The bailie, though, could speak his mind. 'Our doors here all have sturdy locks, you'll find them quite secure, so you'll have no need for those manacles while you're within our tower.'

Logan's grey eyes narrowed slightly in a look I'd seen so many times before I could have told the bailie he could save his breath, for he would never win the argument, but once again it was Sir David who replied.

He lightly said, 'I thank you, but in truth I find them useful. I have taken little exercise of late, and my arms sorely needed strengthening.' He demonstrated, raising his arms on a level before him, his wrists held by the two iron bracelets and connected by the iron chain between. 'You see? I shall be lifting all manner of heavy things by the time we reach London.' He started to smile, but it froze on his features, then fell away altogether.

His eyes were fixed upon a point beside the bailie's head. The bailie twisted round to look, and in a tone of understanding said, 'It is a faithful likeness, is it not?'

I looked, as well. I'd somehow missed the portrait earlier – it was not large, and hung beside one of the windows where a shadow slanted over half its frame. But even from my corner, I could recognize the serious and watchful eyes of the painting's subject.

'Yes,' Sir David said. 'A faithful likeness.'

'That was painted when Prince Henry was not yet two years of age,' the bailie told him. 'And you see how nobly he does hold himself.'

I saw an infant weighted down with coronet and heavy robes, a rattle clutched within his hand as though it were a sceptre. And his face was far too grave for one so small.

The bailie said, 'It is a copy, naturally. The original was a gift from good Queen Anna to Sir Walter Scott, my kinsman. She fought hard, the queen did, for Sir Walter to be made the governor of the young prince, but the king, as always, had his way.'

My father could not bear to hear the king be criticized. He asked, 'You think that is unnatural, sir, that the king should rule his wife?'

The bailie looked suddenly uncertain. 'No, of course not.' His gaze flashed to Logan. 'I meant no disrespect, you understand. I'd be most grateful if you would not mention—'

This time Logan reacted as though the suggestion offended him. 'I serve the king,' he reminded the bailie. 'I'm not his spy.'

The bailie, nodding understanding, deftly switched the subject. 'You'll be wanting supper. I will have a meal sent up for you, and see that food is sent out to the stables for your lad.'

'The lad will eat with us,' said Logan. 'I'd be grateful if ye'd post one of your men to guard our horses in his place.'

'It shall be done. If there is nothing else . . .'

'Fresh water, if ye have it.' Logan's gaze brushed me impassively. 'I've no doubt Mistress Westaway would thank ye for the chance to wash. Our ride has been a long one.'

It was thoughtful of him, asking that, and I'd not learned the way to deal with Logan when he did things that were thoughtful.

It wasn't until we had finished our meal and dispersed to our various evening activities that I worked up enough courage to try to approach him. He'd taken a chair by the hearth and was cleaning his boots. Somehow, when he was focused on such a small, everyday task, with his head bent, relaxed, it was harder to know what to say.

I strolled past him three times before stopping. He glanced up.

I said, 'Asking the bailie for water was very kind. Thank you.'

'Aye, well. I'll try not to make a habit of it. I'd not wish to ruin your ill opinion of me.' But he was smiling slightly as he said it, and his eyes held an almost friendly warmth, and I might have ventured to say something further if my father, who had settled at the table to write his official record of our day, hadn't asked, 'What is the name of this town?'

Logan replied, but I couldn't decide whether I had heard HAW-eek or HOY-eek or something between the two, spoken so quickly it all but slid into one syllable.

'How is it spelled?' I asked.

Logan said, 'As it sounds.'

My father's pen hovered uncertainly over the paper.

Sir David took pity upon him. ''Tis H-a-w-i-c-k.' He had taken the tall chair at the other side of the hearth, not far from where I stood beside Logan, and was leaning back into it, his own booted feet stretched out before him as he watched the flames of the fire dance across the coals.

Since supper he had held himself apart from us, remaining quiet.

Logan studied him a moment, then half turned and called to Hector, who had been exploring in the room.

The boy was frowning at the portrait of Prince Henry. 'Aye?'

'Ye wanted to learn how to be a good Messenger. This would be part of it,' he said, and lifted the boot he was polishing. 'My appearance must always reflect well upon my king. Since ye've no boots of your own, ye might come clean Sir David's, for the practice.'

Sir David said, 'He need not be my servant.'

Logan countered, 'I'm but teaching him a skill that any man might find of use, and if the lesson does ye service, where's the harm?'

Hector was willing, but he had a question of his own, first. 'Who would put a bairn in clothes like these?' he asked, still looking at the portrait of the infant prince. 'He's weighted down so much with frills and finery he cannae move.'

My father looked up sharply from his writing. 'Hector, Logan asked you to—'

'See his face, though?' Hector carried on, oblivious to our discomfort, or to how we were all stealing glances at Sir David. 'This wee man looks like he's telling ayebody exactly what he thinks of them, as well he should. That hat's too tall for him, it's pure ridiculous.'

Logan's mouth tightened. 'The boots, lad.'

Hector dutifully came and pulled a stool beside the hearth and sat upon it between Logan and Sir David, who, no longer sombre, sat smiling faintly as though at a joke that the rest of us couldn't share.

Relinquishing his boots to Hector, Sir David told the boy, 'You're right. He hated to be overdressed, and always let us know it.'

Hector looked up, wide-eyed. 'Ye kent him, then? The bairn who's in the painting?'

'Aye.' Sir David's voice grew soft. 'For nearly all his life, I knew him. And if you think what he wears in that portrait is ridiculous, you should have been there on the day of his baptism.'

My father, always keen for any bit of royal news, asked, 'You were present when the king's son was baptized?'

'Oh, aye,' Sir David said. 'Most of my family had that honour.'

Hector frowned. 'The king's son?' Then his face changed as he grasped the truth. 'That bairn – is that Prince Henry?'

The awe in his voice clearly touched Sir David, who answered him, 'Aye, lad.'

'And ye actually kent him?'

My father said, 'Sir David served the prince twelve years, my boy, as his closest companion. No man knew him better.'

To think any man knew the prince was intriguing. Prince Henry had always seemed more like a myth than a living young man, shifting shape to become what the people expected to see. Some loved him for his handsome face, while others praised him for his faith, or for his bold, adventure-seeking nature that set ships upon the sea. But for younger boys, like Hector, the prince stood for all the manly skills they prized and wished to master.

Hitching his stool round to face Sir David more completely, Hector took up a boot and polished it with newfound care. 'They say that none could ever best the prince when he was jousting.'

'He was very good,' Sir David owned. 'And there was jousting, now I think of it, upon the field at Stirling Castle, in the days that led up to his baptism – although the prince was only six months old and very likely slept through most of it.' Again the small smile, such as men got when they were remembering. 'Sir Walter Scott, the Laird of Buccleuch – the kinsman of our host – he took part in those jousts, to help to entertain all the ambassadors who'd come from foreign lands, while they were waiting.'

'Waiting for what?' Hector wanted to know.

'For the English ambassador to arrive. He took his time,' Sir David said, 'and came last of all, to be sure we'd all know he was very important.'

I'd heard that dry humour before in his tone, but this time it was gentler, as though Hector sitting in front of him stirred memories of when another young boy had once sat with him, wanting a tale to be told.

'Then what happened?' asked Hector.

'Well, this was in August, mind, so it was very warm, and every kingdom on the continent had sent its representatives to join our Scottish noblemen and gentry in the chapel that the king had newly built at Stirling Castle, meaning there was scarcely room to move. Which was just as well, for had I not been pressed between my brothers, I'd have fallen on my face from standing in that heat.'

Hector accused him of exaggerating.

'Aye, mayhap I am. It may not have been from the heat, but from the boredom of the Bishop's preaching, which he gave twice over, first in ordinary speech and then a second time in Latin – for the benefit, presumably, of any ancient Romans in our midst.'

My father laughed. 'Come now, Sir David. Surely you understand Latin.'

'Aye, but I regret the prince at that young age did not. He was then fast asleep, and who could blame him, being wrapped in robes even more stifling than those—' He nodded at the portrait. 'They were styled of purple velvet, weighted down with pearls, and fashioned with a train so long it took two noble lords to hold it and carry it between them. 'Tis most fortunate the prince but slept, and was not suffocated.' His mouth quirked. 'But he wakened when they blew the trumpets, and he gave us all that same look as ye see there in that portrait, lad, and aye, he let us know exactly what he thought then of his situation.'

Logan kept his head bent to his work, but asked, 'And were ye at the banquet also?'

'Aye.'

'Then ye would have seen the ship they wheeled into the great hall. My father telt us how he saw them building it, although he was not there for the festivities. He said it was a full-sized ship, with sails of silk, a silver anchor, galleries of blue and gold, and thirty-six brass guns.'

Sir David nodded. 'Aye, and bearing Neptune and his minions and a party of musicians, sailing on an artificial sea. It made a great impression when it entered, I recall, although my own attention was elsewhere.'

Hector could not imagine anything that would distract someone's attention from a sight like that.

Sir David said, 'One day you'll find, lad, that a woman's face does oft have that effect. And I was seated with the most fair woman in the room, which has, I fear, blurred all my memories of the details of the banquet.' Sir David settled his shoulders against the chair, fixing his gaze on the changeable flames of the fire. 'Or perhaps what happened later drove all other memories from my mind as being less important.'

It surprised me that my father had kept writing through this storytelling. I could hear his pen still scratching as he asked Sir David, 'Why is that?'

Sir David paused, and faintly smiled.

I didn't think he'd answer.

I was wrong.

DAVID

Hawick, Roxburghshire, Scotland, the same day

THE OLDER MAN, WESTAWAY, was taking notes. David knew what that meant, he was nobody's fool. They'd be taking down all that he told them, to use it against him in trial, if what King James was planning could be called a trial.

His brother had given him warning. 'For God's sake,' he'd written to David from London, 'do not come home. Nor should you linger in Paris. They know where you are. Travel anywhere else, but stay safely abroad, for your life is in danger.'

And yet, that was no way to live – being hunted. He'd not found the peace that he'd hoped for in France, and he doubted he'd find it by travelling farther.

Besides, his brother's letter had enclosed another, sealed by the queen's hand, and in her writing, echoing his brother's warnings, finishing with, *Come not now, but when the way is safe, come speak with me, for there are questions I must ask you.*

David wasn't sure he had the answers. He had questions, too. But he'd burned both letters, packed his things, and headed home.

Dead must to dead, the living to the living,
The grave cannot be capable of love,
It ill beseems thy youth to be thus grieving;
Must thou a mourner restless ever prove?

He'd written those words bravely once within a poem and published them, but that had been before ... They were but words now, without meaning. Hollow. Written by a man he barely recognized.

In front of him, the young lad, Hector, sat and waited hopefully for David to explain what happened on the night the prince was christened that could have been more important than the banquet and its spectacle. The knowledge of Westaway's writing gave David pause, but then he knew he need not tell them everything. He could decide what to share, and how, and what he wished to keep private.

But for himself, he could remember everything. As David gazed now at the fire, he saw the shapes of people move within it, dancing back to life. And always, always, he saw her.

Stirling Castle, Scotland, 30th August 1594

He did not know the hour, but they'd left midnight long behind. The banquet would be drawing to an end and all the guests departing, and he'd lose this time to talk with her. That knowledge should have made him speak more clearly of the way he felt. Instead, it made him silent.

Celia did not seem to mind. She'd been the one who'd looked around at all the frenzy of the banquet, met his eyes, and smiled, and told him, 'Take me somewhere there is peace.'

And here they were.

In all his twenty-seven years, he'd found no place where he felt more relaxed than on this narrow terrace sheltered midway up the castle's southern face.

The stonemasons who worked upon this terrace had outdone themselves and wrought a fantasy of twisting columns, arches, tangled leaves and vines, and painted gargoyles. Of all these, David's favourite was the little dragon, perched above one window with its gilded wings furled tightly to its back, still shining even by the moonlight.

Celia had not seen the dragon. She appeared to be absorbing what he'd told her about why this place was special to him, because when she finally spoke, her voice, with its faintly French accent, was incredulous.

'But surely, they could not have let you play up here as children?'

''Tis the perfect place for play.' The terrace ended at a strong, square tower, standing guardian, backed securely by the tall windows and elaborate stonework of the limewashed castle walls. At its front, a crenellated, waist-high wall allowed young boys to make believe they stood upon the battlements, and gave a view across the valley of imagined armies and invaders.

David said, 'By daylight, you can see the battlefield of Bannockburn, just there.' He pointed to the place, framed by the blacker rise of the Touch and Gargunnock hills. He knew each crag and contour of those hills, and knew the green depths of the forests that swept down the valley folds between. 'And over there's the battlefield of Sauchieburn, with noble deeds and tragedy enough in that one scene to keep a schoolboy from his studies.'

'You were sent to school here, then, at Stirling?'

'On occasion, aye. The king and William had their classroom there, within the tower. There were other lads as well who came and went, as I did. We did share good times, at play upon this terrace.'

High above them rode the half-moon on its field of stars, and all around the landscape lay in shadows, with the huddled rooftops of the town of Stirling sleeping now beneath them.

The view he loved was masked by darkness, but Celia came to look anyway, over the low wall. 'You might have fallen to your deaths.'

'We'd not have dared. My aunt ran a very strict household, and falling to one's death was not allowed.'

He liked to hear her laugh. It turned the head of the fierce guardsman who stood further down the terrace, and who, recognizing David, had allowed them up here, grudgingly.

'Your aunt is very frightening. I would not guess she was your mother's sister, for your mother is so sweet.'

He smiled. 'My aunt's been forced by life to shield her softer side in order to survive. The court can be a jealous place, and dangerous to those who rise too high, and when my uncle was made Earl of Mar and keeper of this castle by Queen Mary, it brought out the sharpened knives. So aye, she shows her frightening side more often than her friendly one, but not without good reason.'

Celia watched his face with eyes that by now had learned all his expressions. 'You're fond of her.'

'I am. And she is tolerant of me.'

She laughed again. 'You give yourself too little credit.'

'Some would say I give myself too much.' He strove to make a joke of it, but she looked unconvinced, so David said, ''Tis true. My brothers have set their course in life, while I'm adrift in Edinburgh with nothing but my wits to steer by.'

As second born, his wits would be his sole inheritance. The family estate would go to William, as the eldest, which was why his other brothers had secured their own support – one in the army in the Low Countries, one in a study of the law, one in the church. A life of service to the church held definite appeal to him, as well. A quiet living, perhaps somewhere in the country, with a wife, and bairns, and books.

But something deep within him warned him that was not his path, and so he waited.

'Anyway,' he told her, 'William is the charming one.'

'I'd rather be steered by your wits than by your brother's charm.' Her hand seemed closer to his own, unless he had imagined it. 'And were you not in Edinburgh, I never would have met you. That would be a loss indeed.'

He smiled. 'Your parents would think otherwise.'

'They like you.'

He knew better, but he held his tongue.

Her sleeve now brushed his own. She wore a gown he had not seen before, of pale blue silk embroidered with small fleurs-de-lis in golden thread that matched the colour of her hair, with a lace ruff so fine and delicate about her neck it seemed the work of faeries. In the great hall, in the light, her gown had sparkled. Here it caught the softer moonbeams and became a thing of beauty.

He thought then that she was right. This place held dangers. He could fall so far and fast it might prove fatal.

'David?'

'Aye?'

'They wish to see me wed, my parents. I have heard them speaking. I am three and twenty now, they think it is past time.'

He looked to where the woods lay, out there in the darkness of the night. 'And what do you think?'

'I think I would have to love the man who asked me. But for such a man,' she said, 'I do believe I might be ready.'

David wanted to reply, *You could love me*. But the words failed him. If she spurned him, he would lose her, and the thought of losing Celia brought an emptiness he did not want to contemplate.

Still, he was unprepared for the warm clasp of Celia's hand upon his own.

He turned his head and met her upturned gaze, and while he realized that the moon gave an uncertain light, he thought her eyes looked hopeful.

He took a deep breath and was about to speak when he became aware of someone's footsteps drawing near them on the terrace, at his back.

His brother William's voice said, 'How can you see anything out here? 'Tis dark as Hades.'

And he knew that, once again, he'd lost his chance.

Celia turned, lifting her hand clear of David's so gracefully that the small motion might have gone unnoticed. Except David knew, from the shuttered concern in his brother's expression, that William had seen and missed nothing.

Elder brothers seemed designed to torment and protect in equal measure, and just at the moment William's whole demeanour was protective.

Celia seemed to sense it, too, and lightly said, 'He was showing me where you played your games.'

'Ah.'

David said, 'She thinks it was a miracle we did not plummet to our deaths.'

His brother's grin flashed briefly in the dim light. 'Aye, well, there was never any fear of that, not with me here to guard your back. I'd never let you fall.'

The hand he clapped on David's shoulder was intended both as reassurance and a soft reminder that it was not fitting to bring Celia here alone unless he wished to ruin both their reputations.

But however disapproving William was of David, he showed only charm to Celia. 'I would catch you, too, of course, though

I suspect you'd not be fool enough to venture near the edge. You're like my wife, you're far too practical.' Then, in a tone that held a faint apology, he said, 'Your father asks for you.'

'Oh.' Celia's face fell, only slightly, but enough that David noticed.

Turning from the wall he offered her his hand, for here on these uneven stones and in the dark, that much would be permitted – nay, expected of a gentleman. 'I'll take you back.'

But William said, 'He isn't with the other guests. He's here, within the palace. Follow me.'

The king and queen each had their own suite of rooms in this part of the castle of Stirling. The windows of the queen's apartment overlooked the terrace and the schoolroom tower to the south, while to the north the king's rooms had a fine view of the chapel and great hall. Their bedchambers connected with each other in the east wing, though of course most people entering the palace never made it that far, since the palace itself – built on a square plan around an inner courtyard called the Lyon's Den – was laid out in the formal manner of most royal residences.

Those wishing to see queen or king were first admitted into that monarch's outer hall, and in that great room with its soaring ceiling they must wait, admiring the tapestries and painted decorations, passing time until they were allowed to pass into the presence chamber. Here, the monarch came to take their seat of estate and speak with any who'd been granted an audience.

The king's presence chamber, where William had brought them, was an impressive room, not only from its size but from its ceiling, which had been completely covered by some forty or so fair-sized roundels of wood with the carved heads and shoulders of various people made famous by history or by their relation to the kings of Scots. These heads, in profile, painted in bright colours, drew the eye upwards.

The room was empty but for them and for the guards who stood discreetly placed along the walls. Their purpose was to shield the king from any threat, though David thought they might have missed their moment, since the sound of voices raised in bitter argument – the king's among them – could not be contained by the closed door of the king's bedchamber.

William met his eyes, and said, 'There's some discussion still, I gather, about where the prince will live.' He turned to Celia and included her with, 'That is why your father has been called upon, to serve as an interpreter.'

A little furrow drove between her brows the way it always did when she found anything incomprehensible. 'My father is in *there*?'

They all three looked across the presence chamber to the closed door that seemed sure to break and fall beneath the angry battery of words within.

A shrug from William. 'That's where I delivered him, as ordered, after fetching him from the Great Hall.' Drily, he added, 'I must be uncommonly gifted at seeking out people and bringing them back, because everyone wants me to do it this evening.'

Celia asked, 'But why summon my father?'

'They needed someone who speaks French.' With his head slightly tipped to one side, William said, 'There, you can hear him if you listen closely. He's the only one not shouting.'

David frowned. 'The king and queen speak French.' It was, in fact, the language they had largely used these few years since they'd married, while the Danish-born Queen Anna gained more use of Scots and English. David knew his brother, being close to King James, would know this, but he felt the need to add, 'They speak it perfectly.'

'Aye,' William said, 'but you can't say the same of all those in the chamber with them. And although the king could translate what the queen says for the others, 'tis my understanding that the queen is not inclined to trust the king to speak for her. Not in this matter.'

David glanced with what he hoped was nonchalance towards the nearest guards, to see if they had overheard, and warned his brother, 'You should mind your tongue.'

But William grinned. 'It is no secret. Faith, these very walls ken that the queen would rather leave her right arm here at Stirling than the prince.' He looked directly at the nearest of the guards and asked him, 'Am I wrong?'

Exasperated, David said to William, 'Tread with care.'

'You worry overmuch. We are not ruled by tyrants. I'm the Master of the Queen's Horse, and the king's lifelong companion. I do pledge them both my loyalty and love, as well they know. Though in this instance, I confess I take the king's part.'

Celia took the queen's. 'You cannot blame her, that she wants to keep her own child near. Why should she not?'

'Because it's a tradition,' William said, 'for royal children to be raised at Stirling Castle.'

He might well have said more, but from inside the king's bedchamber the sharply sudden wailing of the infant prince rose over all the voices, and almost immediately the door to the chamber opened and the Dowager Countess of Mar burst out, the crying bairn held in her arms, her face a storm about to break.

No one meeting her at that moment would have guessed

she was approaching sixty years of age. Her face was firm, her back was straight, her eyes held fire. 'Impossible,' she said, addressing all of them. 'God save me from a stubborn woman.'

David had to work to hold his face straight at the irony of that, but his aunt's gaze had focused onto Celia.

'Good, they found you. Here.' She thrust the bawling prince, wrapped in his blanket, into Celia's arms. 'Stay here, and give him comfort. William, come with me. We have to find my son, the earl. Perhaps he can persuade the queen where I cannot.'

The gold of William's earring flashed as he tossed back his head. 'Why me?' he asked, the way a lad resists a chore. 'Why not ask David?'

Celia said sweetly, 'Because you're uncommonly gifted at seeking out people and bringing them back.'

William glanced at her drily. 'That's very good.'

'Thank you.'

To David, he said, 'Tread with care.' But he smiled as he left them.

Celia did her very best to soothe the prince. She joggled him and sang to him, but nothing stopped his sobs.

'Here,' David offered, stretching out his own arms. 'Let me try.'

She looked at him with doubt. 'You'll drop him.'

'I will not. I've held a fair few bairns.' Then, second-thinking how that might sound to her, he added, 'The advantage of being an uncle. William's eldest lad thought sleep was for the faint-hearted. We all took turns walking him.'

Softening, Celia allowed him to gather the prince into his arms.

There was no weight at all to him, really – this lad who would one day be king. David shifted him carefully into the curve of his left arm and shoulder, and with his right hand started freeing the bairn from his tangle of blankets.

'There, now,' David said, looking down at the miserable, red, tear-stained face, 'you've had too long a day, and with too many people, aye? But now I've got you, so you can stop weeping. You're safe.'

As if a spell had just been cast, the prince stopped crying. There was no way that a bairn of seven months could have caught all the sense of David's words, but little Henry seemed distracted by the deeper tones of David's voice, and calmer now the blankets weren't confining him.

The sobs subsided into tiny hiccups, and the prince's gaze – too serious – locked onto David's.

Nothing had prepared him for the fierce rush of protectiveness.

It overcame him so completely that he briefly lost awareness of the others in the room. It took the touch of Celia's hand upon his sleeve to make him notice that Queen Anna had now entered from the bedchamber, and was approaching.

David turned to face her, bowing, and the infant prince in protest scrambled round to clutch his doublet, clinging to him tightly with his small face pressed to David's shoulder. David held him close, aware of Celia in a deep, respectful curtsey at his side.

Queen Anna bid them rise. She was a stately woman for her young age – tall and slender, very fair, and only twenty, but with eyes that showed intelligence and, usually, a lively humour. Now, they were red-rimmed, the tracks of tears still visible upon her too-thin face, as though she had been under strain of late.

But she had been a princess of Denmark from birth, and so was accustomed to showing a braver face to the world, and putting protocol ahead of all things personal. She spoke to Celia first, in French, and recognized her as the daughter of the man translating for them in the bedchamber. 'I'm grateful for his help, and for your patience,' said the queen. 'We will not keep you waiting too much longer.'

Turning then to David, she looked at her son and frowned faintly. Still in French, she said, 'You stopped him from crying. How did you manage it?'

'He wished to be free of his blankets, Your Grace.'

'But it's more than that, surely. He cried in the king's chamber when there were no blankets yet wrapped around him.'

'Then I cannot say,' David truthfully told her. 'Perhaps he was weary of crying.'

Queen Anna stepped closer and studied him as if they'd met in the mist of a battlefield and she was unsure if he were a friend or a foe. 'I was raised in Denmark for my first years by my grandparents,' she said, 'and then by my own mother. Who raised you?'

He could not lie. 'My mother.'

The queen nodded. 'That is as it should be.' She took in their surroundings, all the grandeur of the presence chamber with its great stone fireplace, and the carved heads on the ceiling, looking down and watching. 'The king rarely speaks of his mother. He cannot remember her. Your aunt has taken that place in his heart.'

David, with his eyes upon Queen Anna's face, saw the betraying tremble of her lip before she stilled it, and he knew the thing she feared.

He said, 'Those circumstances were unique. The king could not have seen his mother, for she was in England, and in prison. And his regents were all ruthless men. 'Twas natural he would prefer my aunt. What other softness was he offered?' David saw the queen's attention had refocused on the prince, who, from the soft weight of his head on David's shoulder and the warmly rapid rhythm of his breaths on David's neck seemed to have drifted off to sleep. 'But you will be at Edinburgh,' David told the queen, 'and close enough to visit often.'

'She will not allow it. *He* will not allow it. You will see.' Queen Anna's eyes were deeply sad. 'If I permit this, I will lose my son.' She lifted one hand and reached out to stroke the prince's hair.

He was not sleeping after all, for at her touch he turned away and burrowed deeper into David's shoulder.

'There, you see?' Queen Anna said. 'Already he does take your part.'

She sounded so forlorn that David sought to reassure her in the only way he could, by giving back the bairn – except the prince resisted, and the more that David tried to gently prise the tiny fingers from his doublet, the more tightly they took hold.

He looked to Celia for assistance, but she shook her head once, slowly, as if saying that she would not interfere. He could not fault her for it. No matter what William believed, there was danger in catching the wrath of a king or a queen.

But Queen Anna, to David, did not appear wrathful. Her eyes, when they met his, were bright with emotion. She glanced one last time at Prince Henry, contentedly curled against David and holding him fast, then she tearfully said, 'Keep him, then.'

And in one regal swirl of silk she turned and left them, her back very straight and her head very high, and whatever her face looked like just at that moment, none saw but the carved heads above on the ceiling, and they – like the guards standing silent along the walls – spoke not a word.

In the end, all David told the others sitting in the tower house at Hawick was what happened in the presence chamber, and he did not tell them all of that. He'd thought of leaving Celia out of it, but found she crept in anyways, however much he tried to keep her hidden.

Gone and lost, those days. *The grave cannot be capable of love…*

He watched the fire, and knew he'd never written words more false.

PHOEBE

Hawick, Roxburghshire, Scotland, still 5th May 1613

I HADN'T THOUGHT SIR DAVID would say anything, but in the end he told his tale the way most men told tales – in plain words, without sentiment. He was a private man, and so he did not share his private thoughts, nor tell us any details of the woman, Celia, who had waited with him and his brother in the presence chamber, and who I imagined – from the fact he had included her at all – must be the 'fairest woman in the room' who'd so distracted him that evening from the banquet. He was too much of a gentleman. And yet, with only facts, he drew for us a picture of that night – the castle, and the queen, and infant prince – and it was not so difficult for me to go a step beyond the words that he had shared with us and see the younger man he must have been, and to imagine how he'd felt.

When he had finished speaking, all of us stayed quiet. There was no sound but the measured scraping of my father's pen across the paper on which he'd kept writing, all throughout the telling of the tale. I had settled on the bench beside him at the table, from which I could see the others in their tableau by the hearth – Sir David, thoughtful in his chair, his gaze still fixed upon the fire, and Logan, finished now with polishing his boots, but sitting restlessly and not relaxed. It fell to Hector, on his stool between them with his chin cupped in his hands, to break the silence.

Hector, frowning, asked, 'How did ye get the prince to let ye go?'

I could not see Sir David's face in full from where I sat, but I could see the corner of his mouth twist upwards in the shadow of a hollow smile. 'He never did.' His eyes stayed steady on the flames. 'He never did let go.'

Which threw us into silence once again – Hector because he did not understand; the rest of us because we did.

I expected that my father, who'd lost sons himself and knew that pain, would offer words of comfort, but to my surprise he went on writing. It was Logan who rose first and poured a cup of wine and passed it to Sir David, and then stood and watched him drink it in the manner of a doctor watching someone take his medicine.

Sir David told him, 'Thank you.'

Hector watched Sir David, too – less from concern than from his efforts to make sense of what he'd just been listening to. 'I thought there would be more about the jousting, like.'

This time Sir David's smile, though small, was genuine. 'Aye, well, if it's jousting you wish, I have stories aplenty.'

'Mayhap he'll tell those tales to ye,' said Logan, 'while we're seeing to the horses.'

I could see Sir David's features fall to blankness for a moment. 'While we're . . . ? Ah yes, I see.' His face cleared and he nodded. 'Now?'

He didn't wait for Logan's answer. Finishing his drink, he put his boots on and stood stiffly.

For of course, wherever Logan went, Sir David had to go, being his prisoner and under his close guard. And Logan, as I'd learned during my time in Scotland, never went to bed without first seeing to the horses in the stables.

He might just this once have left Sir David here, when it was plain to see the man was walking every step with grief.

As Logan passed, his grey eyes glanced my way and I was not afraid to let him see my thoughts, making it feel in that brief moment as though we'd crossed blades. But then, that's how it almost always felt with him – if we weren't arguing, we were preparing for a fight.

I watched him leave with Hector and Sir David, and I realized that my hands were both clenched into fists. Relaxing them, I said, 'He has no heart.'

My father looked up from his writing, 'Who?'

'Is it not obvious?' I motioned to the closed door. 'Logan. Dragging poor Sir David to the stables when it's clear he is no threat to us. A kinder man would let him stay and drink his wine beside the fire.'

My father inked his pen and gave this thought. 'The thing with wine, my dear, is one cup washes down your sorrows, but too many cups will flood your mind and float your demons up from their dark prisons to torment you.' He applied the pen to paper with the effortless precision of a man who'd done this for a living nearly all his life. 'If you would throw a man awash in grief a rope to save him, Phoebe, give him work to occupy him. Any task will do, however small, if it be honest. No doubt Logan knows that well. And if you think he has no heart, you know him not at all.'

It was a soft rebuke, and yet it stung. I tried pretending that I didn't care, and looked instead at what my father had been writing. Only that was a mistake.

The angle of the papers meant I could read but a part of it, but that was all I needed to be sure. 'Why are you taking notes of what Sir David said?'

All my life, my father had retreated into silence when he sensed a coming argument. He didn't answer now.

I said, 'His words were meant for us, they weren't intended to be public. You can't do this.'

Very patiently, my father finished his last sentence and he

set his pen aside. From his perforated pouncet-box he sprinkled sandy pounce across the page to dry the ink, and shook it clear. And then he raised his eyes to meet the accusation in my own. 'I'm doing what I was sent here to do,' he said. ''Tis not your business. And we will not speak of it again.'

I'd been afraid of horses nearly all my life. It didn't help that Logan's horse seemed bred for waging war, and not for ambling round the countryside. It was too large – its hooves, its head, the whole of it. I almost didn't mind when Logan did his customary move as I approached and turned his back towards me. He was tall enough that his broad shoulders blocked most of the huge horse from my view, and since he stood between the horse and me, I gained a little confidence.

'Good morrow,' I said, speaking past him to Sir David, standing not far off awaiting Hector, who appeared to still be in the stables. 'I am sorry that we overslept.'

'By half an hour.' Sir David smiled. 'It is no great transgression.'

Logan said, 'Your father was in need of rest.' He glanced around. 'Where is he?'

'Coming presently,' I said curtly.

'Ye've had your breakfast?'

'Yes.' The baillie must have sent more food, for we'd awakened to a plate of oaten cakes that tasted fresh, and ale to wash them down with. And Hector, who'd been left behind to give us our instructions, which he'd done all in a rush before escaping back to Logan and the more compelling duties of a Messenger.

As Logan nodded now and turned away, I noticed he was

holding up a pail of water for the horse to drink. At least, it looked like water, till I sniffed the air, and, 'Is that ale?' I asked in disbelief.

'Aye.'

Sir David said, 'He's put a magic powder in it.'

Logan's voice was dry. 'Hardly magic. Only plain ale and a cordial powder, to prepare the horses for their travel. We've a full day's ride ahead, and they'll need to be ready to run at the sign of a rider behind us.'

My patience was not at its highest this morning. 'There's no one behind us.'

He faced me with eyes that knew better. 'We had the advantage of time when we came out of Leith, but we'll not keep it long. Afore he gets to Berwick on the main road he'll have figured out we didn't go that way, and doubled back again. That leaves him two more paths towards the border – this one, and the more well-travelled road through Glasgow. If he chooses this one, we'll be looking at his face the day. And if he takes the Glasgow road, he'll not go far on *that* afore he kens we didn't take it. I can't see—' He stopped, and set his jaw, correcting what he meant to say. 'I cannot guess at his intent, but we must ride and hold the lead we have, if we hope to outwit him.'

I already felt half dizzy just from following his thoughts. 'And pray, who is this mastermind who follows us?'

Sir David smiled, and answered me, 'He speaks of Patrick Graeme, Laird of Inchbrakie. My cousin.'

I thought back to the letter that my father read aloud in Leith. 'The one who promised he would meet your ship?'

'The very same.'

That letter had seemed innocent enough. I turned again to Logan. 'And this is the man you fear?'

'I didn't say I feared him.'

'If the Devil and his full army of witches were all chasing us, you could not be more cautious.'

Logan slid me the sidelong glance that meant I'd struck a nerve while at the same letting me know he found me ridiculous.

'Caution,' he said, 'is what keeps me alive.'

'But so much of it for one man?'

'He'll not be alone.'

I challenged that, thinking again of the letter, which mentioned no companions. 'Why are you so sure?'

'Because the last time someone took one of the Graemes' own and held them captive, Patrick Graeme of Inchbrakie took to horse with forty armed and mounted men and rode as if to war, and stopped for nothing till they took the lassie back, that's why.'

'The lass – it was a girl?'

'Aye. But they'll do the same for him.' He nodded at Sir David, who did not dispute the charge.

My father chose that moment to arrive, and when he bid a friendly greeting to Sir David, I could not contain my frown. And while I tried to keep my feelings to myself, I must have done it poorly, for when Logan came to help me mount his horse, he looked the way men did when they were weighing whether it was wise to speak.

The others were close by, but not so close that they could overhear us. Hector held the bridle of my father's horse to help him mount. Sir David was already in the saddle of the elegant black mare, ready to ride.

Logan put both hands on my waist and lifted me up to the pillion as though I were a fragile thing that needed gentle handling. Glancing up, he met my eyes. 'I'm well accustomed to receiving your disdain,' he said, 'but 'tis unlike ye to extend it to your father. What could he do to so deserve your coldness?'

He surprised me. Not his question – I was used to Logan being bold. But in his eyes was something different, something new, as though I'd glimpsed a door standing half open where I'd always thought it locked. And then I realized it must be a trick, for Logan would not make himself so vulnerable.

I told him what my father had told me. ''Tis not your business.' And whatever I had seen – or thought I'd seen – was gone. The door slammed shut. I found, to my dismay, that I regretted speaking so abruptly, and I tried to make amends. 'But since you ask, I'm angry – no, I'm disappointed – at what he is doing to Sir David.'

Logan's eyebrows lifted slightly. 'Oh, aye? And what is he doing?'

'Writing an account of everything Sir David says.'

'But that's his job.' Standing beneath me, he still made me feel the smaller person. 'Why did ye think they sent a scrivener along with me?'

I hadn't thought that through. But even so, 'It isn't kind.'

'Kind is not a piece of what we do. Ye're angry at me, too, for how I keep Sir David fettered.' It was not a question.

I looked down at him with what I hoped was calmness, but I wasn't sure I managed it. The horse was moving under me, and that most likely filled my eyes with fear. 'It is unnecessary, surely. He's a gentleman.'

'And gentlemen are always to be trusted, are they?'

I was not entirely naïve. I knew all men could break their word, but I was in a battle now with Logan. I had claimed my ground, and so I held it. 'Yes.'

'Like Valentine.'

'I . . . yes.' I might have said that with more strength if I had not been picturing my father's face, crestfallen, as the coach with Valentine and all his wealthy friends rolled past us in the Close that morning. Still, it was the first time Valentine had failed to keep a promise, and he'd tried to make amends. I said again, more strongly, 'Yes.'

Logan attended to my stirrup. 'My experience with gentlemen,' he said, 'has taught me differently. And I've a scar just here' – he tapped a spot below his left shoulder, above his heart – 'to mind me of the last time that I took the fetters off a man upon his word alone. I'll have to bide a while longer with your anger.'

I couldn't tell if he was joking, in this mood. I didn't think he was. There was a tightness to his jaw, and when he looked at me again his gaze was level.

'But your father should be spared it. He does think the world of ye, and ye should show him understanding. Ye can't fault a man for doing what the king has ordered.' For the briefest instant I believed I saw it once again – that tiny opening to something . . . unexpected.

Logan turned away, and taking up a handful of his horse's mane he vaulted to the saddle, settling in his place before me, so again I faced his solid back. An end to our discussion. Almost.

'Anyway,' he said, 'you asked to come.'

I could not argue that.

Just once, I would have liked to win the last word, but I realized Logan was not ever going to let me have that satisfaction. Had he been of higher birth, he might have made his living in the law or stood for parliament. Nobody would survive him in debate.

I knew he was right about my father – I *was* judging him too harshly – but to have that pointed out to me by Logan, of all people, didn't help my mood. Nor did the fact that, when he'd said my father thought the world of me, I'd found myself, for that one small, unlikely moment, wondering what Logan thought of me.

A foolish notion. He disliked me just as much as I did him. Of course he did. And more than that, it did not matter. Why the question crossed my mind, I didn't know. I pushed it firmly to the side, and gathered up the folds of Logan's mother's woollen plaid, and brought them up around my face to shield me from the morning sun.

I hadn't learned to wear the garment properly. I could not tuck it into place the way the Scottish women could, but wore it like a mantel, loosely wrapped. It did the necessary service – kept me warm, and blocked the wind and rain, and kept the sun from burning me, but I knew I fooled no one. I looked nothing like a Scotswoman.

Most people would have said that I looked nothing like an Englishwoman, either, for I had my mother's colouring. *Her* father came from Portugal – part of the entourage of an ambassador who travelled to the court of Queen Elizabeth. He never did return to Lisbon. Having met my grandmother in London, he abandoned his position and his Catholic religion and became a writing master, who in time employed my father, which was how my parents met.

I had no memory of my grandfather – both of my mother's parents died before my birth – but his blood ran strongly through my family, for my mother and my brothers, too, had shared the dark eyes and dark hair that marked us out as different from our neighbours in the Close at St Bartholomew's.

That bloodline only ran in me, now. Everybody else was gone.

I didn't often feel the prick of tears when thinking of such things. I'd lost my mother and my brothers twenty years ago, and weeping would not bring them back. If I felt more emotional this morning, it must be because I was so far from home, away from all that felt familiar, fighting hard to keep my balance on this horse I feared, behind a man who wished me elsewhere.

Which was probably the only thing we had in common. I, too, wished that I were someplace else.

You asked to come.

But only to assist my father, who today appeared to be in perfect health, engaged in cheerful talk with Hector while they rode behind us on the rough, uneven track that here took the place of a road. Sir David kept much closer to us, but his head was down and he was busy with his own thoughts, and I'd not disturb them.

I sat straighter on the pillion, blinked back the unshed tears, and told myself that, while I might be lonely, I was not alone. Someone was thinking of me, and I had the proof.

When I dressed every day, I tucked Valentine's handkerchief into my bodice, just under the curve of the neckline, where no one could see. I drew it out now. Held it up to my face. Closed my eyes as I breathed the scent.

Sir David's voice said, 'That is a fine handkerchief.'

I lowered it to find him smiling at me, riding close beside us on the trampled grass that edged the track. His black mare was not as tall as Logan's horse, but still I kept my focus on Sir David as I thanked him. 'I do prize it greatly.'

'Yes, I can imagine that you would, since from its monogram I see it was a gift from Viscount Fairfax. He's a dashing fellow, I have met him, but I'll warn you that his wife may not take kindly to the competition.'

'Oh, but it is not from—' I began, before I saw that he was

teasing, and knew very well I didn't know the viscount. But I liked to see him in good spirits, so I took the opening he offered me and played along. 'I thank you for the warning, for I'd not want any trouble.'

'No indeed.' He made a masterful attempt at looking serious. 'But love does often bring it, all the same. What say you, Messenger?'

Logan half turned in the saddle to look back at me. His gaze dropped briefly to the handkerchief I held, then moved on to Sir David. 'What say I to what?'

Sir David said, 'We speak of matters of the heart. The lady says she wishes for no trouble in them. I say love brings trouble. What is your opinion?'

Logan shrugged and turned again to face the hills before us. 'I have no opinion.'

He truly was a Leither – stubborn, proud, and … and … I searched in vain for that third word, then giving up, I told Sir David, 'This is a rare privilege for us both, sir, to be present at the first and perhaps only moment Andrew Logan offers no opinion.'

Sir David's grin flashed pleasantly through his red beard. ''Tis rare, then, is it?'

'Very. I expect it was because you asked his thoughts on love, and not on fighting or some other rough pursuit that is more suited to his interest.'

Where my hand held onto Logan's belt, I felt the muscles of his back flex as he sighed, but he continued to ignore us.

In an offhand tone, Sir David said, 'You should not count a quiet man incapable of understanding love. Oft times his feelings run the deepest.'

I had never thought of Logan as particularly quiet. I imagined that Sir David spoke more of himself than anyone.

I wondered what had happened to the woman, Celia, who kept him company at Stirling Castle. He'd told us very little of her, but his voice had softened at her name. I could not ask him, that would be a great intrusion, so instead I tried to settle more decidedly upon the pillion. 'Tell me about the lass,' I said. 'The one your cousin rode to save.'

Another sigh from Logan, who asked, 'Will we then be talking *all* the way to the border?'

I told him, 'Very likely. It does help the time to pass.'

'From where I sit,' he said, 'it does the opposite.'

Sir David chose my side. 'She was his brother's lass. His brother George, who's ages with myself, and is now Bishop of Dunblane. In those days, George was a young minister in charge of his first parish, where he first met his fair Marion.'

I asked, 'And fell in love?'

'With all the heat and heart of youth. And as I told you, it brought trouble.'

'Why?'

'She was an heiress, and wherever there is property, a woman's hand becomes a thing of value to be bartered. And George – a simple minister – had little he could offer. He was a younger son, you see. We younger sons have little that can recommend us to the world when we set forth in it. The eldest will inherit the estate, so all the rest of us must find our own path, be it to the army or to court or to the law or to the church, or by some wilder way. My cousin George's path was most respectable, but—'

'Not enough for Marion?'

He shook his head. 'Marion would not have cared if he had been a pauper. No, it was her mother who disapproved. When Marion's father died, her mother remarried, and Marion's new in-laws wished to keep her dowry in the family, so they sent her to their own great house and kept her there, away from George.'

'How cruel,' I said.

'Yes, separating those who love each other is most cruel.' Sir David fell to silence for a moment, but he roused himself, continuing, 'But fortunately Marion's brother liked George, and was keen to see her freed. So her brother joined my cousin Patrick, and they raised their band of forty men, and armed us well, and off we rode to that great house, where we demanded Marion.'

'We?' I felt my eyes grow wider. 'You rode with them? You were there?'

'I was more reckless in those days. They were my cousins. George was hopelessly in love, and I am hopelessly romantic. Aye, I rode with Patrick and his men. But George did not. It would not have been fitting for a minister to take part in a raid.'

'But he and Marion were reunited?'

'Oh, aye. Patrick always gets his way. He always wins. We freed the lass. She rode with us as bravely as a clansman, too.' He smiled a little at the memory.

'And did she wed your cousin George?'

'Most happily. They're married still, and I keep losing track of all their children. They must now have five or six, at least.'

I said, 'Then that's a tale with a happy ending.'

Sir David nodded. 'Yes, it is.'

Logan, who'd listened in silence to all of this, half turned his head to look back at Sir David. 'Each tale has two sides to the telling. Ye say ye demanded the lass be brought out to ye. I heard it said that your cousin and his men broke into the house and made off with her, and with a good many valuable things that belonged to the family. I heard an older lady of the house was injured,' he said. 'There was violence done.'

Even though I could see only the side view of Logan's hard gaze, I was very familiar with how it felt to be receiving the full, cold, grey force of it.

'Am I wrong?' he asked Sir David.

'No.' Sir David, to his credit, met that gaze honestly. 'No, you're not wrong.'

'Then ye ken why I'm keeping ahead of your cousin the now,' Logan said. As the rough and narrow track carried us deeper between hills rising so steeply to each side of us that someone could be even now approaching and we'd not have known, he looked back briefly. 'Happy endings are of little comfort,' Logan told me, very sure, 'to characters who die afore the tale is done.'

Andrew

The valley of the River Esk, Scotland, 6th May 1613

I'D HOPED TO BE close to the border by nightfall, but Brutus was wearying. Not that he would have allowed me to see it – he held his head proudly, still setting his feet as precisely as any foot soldier who'd march till his officer told him to halt. But I noticed the change in his gait.

We Messengers could, by the king's authority, lay claim to any horse we wished. Ride one horse hard for a short distance and exchange it for a fresher one, to travel farther faster. And yet horses were not things, they were as varied as ourselves, each with their limits and their habits, and not all of them reliable. I much preferred to ride the one horse I knew well and guard his health along the road.

Besides, it wasn't speed I needed now from Brutus, it was strength. He had to carry two of us.

In London, he was only called to carry Margaret's weight upon the pillion for half an hour in the morning and the same again home in the evening, which he seemed to view as no great burden. Here, he did not gain the same relief, and I had noticed that he walked with greater care when he had Phoebe on his back, the way he'd once walked when I'd let a young lad ride behind me – as though he feared she might fall off, and he was seeking to look after her.

A horse that sensed a rider's inexperience would alter its behaviour to adapt to it. Some horses, prone to mischief, took advantage of such riders. Brutus treated them like glass. It was his nature, I was glad of it, but I knew that it cost him, always paying such attention to his movements.

As we came in view now of a little settlement, I felt his interest quicken. His great head lifted higher to catch the faint new sounds – a hammer strike on metal, and men's voices rising over the bright running of the water in the burn beside us – then his ears swivelled back hopefully, waiting for some word from me.

'Aye,' I reassured him. 'We'll try stopping here.'

Forward the ears went again and he snorted to show satisfaction and nodded, and I told myself for the thousandth time that any man who thought horses were creatures without sense or feelings had never spent time with them.

For me, horses were easier to understand than people. 'Twas certain they were easier to understand than women, and a hundred times easier to understand than the lass seated behind me. This morning, with her words and looks, she'd made it plain she'd rather not be near me. Yet for some time now she'd been leaning on my back, asleep, her hand tucked underneath my belt, her head a gentle weight between my shoulder blades.

Like Brutus, I was careful not to jostle her, and riding in this way raised feelings of protectiveness within me, though she'd not have welcomed them. It helped me to remember whose initials marked that handkerchief she held so tightly. Mayhap she'd let go of it while sleeping, and with luck it lay an hour behind us on some thorn bush, torn and soon to be forgotten, as it well deserved to be. If so, we'd not be turning back to find it.

'Where . . . ?'

She'd wakened with no sudden movement, quietly, her head still resting on my back. She raised it now, as though aware whose back it was, and levered herself upright. With that motion came the wafting scent of that infernal handkerchief – a scent that was not hers, but his. The cloyingly expensive smell of indolence.

She said, 'I do apologize. Did I sleep long?'

I briefly thought of lying, but there wasn't any point to it. 'Aye, but ye've missed nothing.'

She seemed unconvinced. She must have caught sight of the settlement. 'Where are we?'

I'd have telt her, if I could. Truth was, I didn't know. I'd been this way but the one time, with my father, and in honesty I'd been dead bored myself then as well, I'd been so young. I'd paid no proper mind to the way we were passing. I wished that I had. I only knew this was the way that went to the border and then to Carlisle, where we could safely pick up the road that would lead us to London – not by the route I took more commonly, but by the ways in the west.

I had knowledge enough of those roads, once we reached them, to help us evade Patrick Graeme of Inchbrakie's men. But we weren't yet at Carlisle.

And as to where we *were*, I answered Phoebe with the one thing I was sure of.

'Armstrong country.'

Being English, she'd know nothing of the Armstrongs, nor the Elliots, nor any of the Border families so notorious for leading raids upon their neighbours in this lawless region that the king had finally brought his boot down hard upon them all, so they had grumbled into peace.

If I told Phoebe we were riding through the land of Reivers, she'd not be familiar with the word, nor would she understand the risks of being here, and I did not enlighten her. Why tell a lass that you had brought her to the lair of thieves?

Besides, there might not be a problem. While the glory of

the Reivers was behind them and they weren't as fearsome as they once had been, their pride remained, and even among thieves, there still was honour.

I'd wait to judge our welcome.

The rough trail we had been riding on became more recognizable as something like a road, and Brutus perked up even more, his big feet fairly dancing on the rutted dirt as though he sensed an ending to the day was close at hand.

The sound of metal striking upon metal came much closer now, and I could see it came from a small forge set aside one of the houses at the near edge of the settlement. Besides the stone mill, there were only three houses in all, and this nearest one a bastle house – a kind of farmhouse common in the Borders, designed to stand like a small fort against the Reivers' raids. Two storeys tall and built of stone, it had a slate roof to repel attack by fire, and thick walls to stand battering, and only tiny windows on the upper floor, to keep out all intruders but allow a stout defence.

The forge abutting it was built of stone as well, and its inhabitant stopped work as we approached. He had the rough look of a man who earned his living with his hands, fair-haired and in his middle-thirties with the leather apron of his trade tied over homespun clothing, and his sleeves rolled up to show impressive forearms. I thought he stared at me a little overlong, but as I brought our party to a stop outside his open forge he dragged his gaze instead to Brutus, who was then demanding all attention.

The blacksmith gave it to him. 'That's a rare, fine beast. Pure courser of Naples, is he?'

'Aye.'

'I've not seen his equal.' Setting down his hammer, he bravely stepped forwards, and Brutus – as he did with all men who praised him – permitted the touch, even letting the blacksmith take one of his great forefeet into his hands and examine it. 'Recently shod, I see.'

'Aye.'

'A pity, that. To shoe a horse like this would be a privilege.'

Brutus gazed down at the blacksmith with what I can only call fondness, then angled his ears back towards me, expectantly. I had no fears of forgetting he'd been bred at court, for his head was so easily turned by a wee bit of flattery. But just the now, I agreed with his instincts.

The mill might be larger, and farther beyond was a castle that no doubt could offer more comfort, but this was a strong enough house that could offer protection, and those who pursued us weren't likely to look for us here.

I said, 'We may not need the horses shod, but we do need to stable them the night, if ye have room.'

Again he favoured me with that peculiar stare, then said, 'Aye, I have room enough. And beds, too, for yourselves.'

I thanked him. But I had a question, first. 'Have ye a family?'

'Aye. Two lads,' he told me, 'and my mother. Why?'

'I serve the king, and in his name I hold this man a prisoner.' I nodded at Sir David, who had halted his mare close enough behind that he could hear all we were saying. 'We are followed now by men who seek to set him free by force. I would not wish to put your family in harm's way.'

The blacksmith studied me. 'Who are these men?'

I told him, and he nodded. 'They are fierce, the Graemes.'

He'd know from experience. While there seemed little binding the Graemes in Perthshire with their distant cousins who'd settled years past in the Borders, they sprang from the same source and shared the same blood.

'But they are none of my kin,' he assured me, 'so ye'll have no trouble beneath my roof.' He was less certain, though, when it came to Sir David. 'Will *he* be dangerous? What was his crime?'

The question, though fair, wasn't one I could answer. Not only because of my oath, but because I was not altogether convinced that Sir David was guilty of anything. He held himself in all ways with such dignity I could not help but hear his brother telling me, 'He has done nothing wrong' with such conviction I was half inclined to take Sir William's part and feel Sir David must be innocent.

Not that my feelings changed the mission. I was but the Messenger. Yet if I were to guard the man, I surely ought to guard his reputation, since like life, if lost, it could not be restored.

I gave the blacksmith no specific crime, but said, ''Tis nothing that need worry ye. Your family will have naught to fear from him, he is a gentleman.'

I had no doubt that Phoebe, at my back, would raise an eyebrow at my reference, after all the words we had exchanged this morning about gentlemen, but thankfully, she held her tongue.

'And yet ye keep him fettered.'

'I do fetter all my prisoners. The law requires it.' I prayed the blacksmith did not have the education that would let him catch my twisting of the truth.

The dice fell in my favour. He gave a short nod of acceptance. 'Then stay and be welcome.' He offered his hand. 'Sandy Armstrong. Round here, I'm Hob's Sandy.'

A pattern of naming that helped to keep everyone organized when they all had the same surname – it meant that his father was Hob. Returning the blacksmith's firm handclasp, I gave him my name, but didn't introduce the others. This was still uncertain country, and the best protection was to guard your privacy.

The blacksmith didn't seem to mind. Turning, he crossed to open the broad, wooden door centred in the stone front of his bastle house and swung it wide. 'There ye go.'

Houses like this were built to defend not the family alone, but its livestock as well. Cattle, horses, and chickens – whatever you owned – could be safely shut in for the night behind thick walls and a stout wooden door on the ground floor, while you and your family slept one floor above. An ingenious design.

Phoebe had not yet discovered the plan of it. When I dismounted and lifted her down from the pillion I saw her look of dismay and I realized she thought we'd be sleeping the night in a barn. And God help me, I couldn't resist. 'Were ye wanting the stall on the left or the right?' I asked.

Her look of horror was well beyond price. 'What?'

'The manger appears to be already taken . . .'

'You cannot be serious.'

I couldn't hold back my grin any longer, which spoiled it. 'Of course I'm not serious. I ken this is like to surprise ye, but we're not all uncouth in Scotland. We do ken what beds are for.' I'd not planned that to have a double meaning, but when her cheeks suddenly reddened I reasoned it might just be better for me to stop talking.

The blacksmith – Hob's Sandy – had fitted the ladder in place to the trap door that led to the upper floor. I let him take Phoebe and Westaway up with him while I stayed back with the others to see to the horses.

This work had a rhythm that calmed me. The bridles and saddles and blankets removed, and the brushes and combs all applied in their order, removing the sweat and the dust and the dirt of the day so the horses could rest. The wee Garron was not over fond of the curry comb, but the black mare would have stood all the day for it, arching her neck to the feel of its strokes.

'They should have named ye Princess and not Charger,' I informed her, 'for ye like a life of softness, do ye not? And here ye are, stuck on this road with us, poor lass.' I tapped her offside foreleg. 'Up.' She raised it daintily, so I could take her foot into my hands and pick the muck and gravel from her hoof.

Sir David, leaning on a nearby post to watch me, said, 'I think you've missed your calling.'

I was dealing with a stubborn stone. I didn't raise my head. 'How so?'

'Not to disparage your work as a Messenger, but I can well understand why my brother was sorry to lose you as one of his stablehands.'

Hector looked over at that. He'd been cleaning a saddle, but now his attention was wholly on me. 'Ye were a stable lad, like me?'

'Aye, for a time.'

Sir David said, 'He was a very famous stable lad. He—'

But I cut him off then with a glance, a frown, a swift shake of my head.

'He what?' asked Hector.

I could see Sir David thinking. He recovered with, 'He polished twenty saddles in an hour.'

Hector, impressed by this, redoubled his own efforts, and I let my eyes roll at Sir David, who responded with a shrug, as if to say, 'What else was I to do?'

In tones more serious, he said, 'That was a kind thing you said earlier to the blacksmith.'

'What was?'

'When you told him that I could be trusted. That I was a gentlemen.' He sounded moved by it. 'Thank you.'

The stone in the mare's hoof shot free finally and I released her foot, straightening. 'Aye, well,' I said to him, 'see ye don't make me regret it.'

There was some strategy involved in getting all of us upstairs. Sir David climbed the ladder first, which took more effort with his manacles. Then Hector followed, carrying one portmanteau, and me, with the remaining two. The ladder protested my weight, but held until I'd reached the upper floor. Hauling up the ladder after me, I let the trap door fall and made sure it was closed securely.

Only then did I turn round, to find myself facing a woman who stared at me as though she'd just seen the dead.

'Christ defend us,' she said, as the bowl she held slipped from her hands to the floor. Thankfully it was a wooden bowl, empty, and so fell undamaged, although it spun noisily. Cursing beneath her breath, she picked it up while the blacksmith remarked, 'I did warn ye.'

The woman was clearly his mother. They had the same colouring, and the same eyes, and just now she was gaping at me in the same way her son had when I'd first approached him.

The blacksmith explained, to me, 'Ye have the look of my father. He was a large man, like yourself.'

From how they'd both reacted to me, plainly the resemblance was a strong one. I made light of it. 'Mayhap I have an Armstrong hiding somewhere in my pedigree.'

The blacksmith laughed. 'Mayhap ye do. We could be cousins. Anyhow, that's what we're telling the neighbours, so they'll say naught if anyone asks after ye. We take care of our own here at Langholm.'

So that was the castle then – Langholm. And these were the few houses built round its mill. And I'd made a good choice by not carrying on to the castle itself, for Langholm Castle was held by the Lieutenant of the Borders, who while loyal to the king was hard and ruthless. Had he been at home, Sir David would be sleeping in the dungeon this night, and not sitting now beside the fire with Phoebe's father.

Phoebe wasn't in my view, but then the room itself was dim. There were no windows, and the only light came from the fire upon the hearth and from the candles scattered round that gave a homely warmth.

The blacksmith's mother had retrieved the fallen bowl. She took my arm. 'Come, I'll see ye fed afore I go.'

I looked a question at the blacksmith, who said, 'She's taking my lads to my brother. As groundskeeper up at the castle he has his own lodgings with plenty of room for them all.'

My relief likely showed. He had taken my warning to heart. It was hard enough being responsible for the one lad in my care without having to fret about somebody else's. My relief was the greater when I saw his lads, for the elder could not have been twelve, and the younger was smaller than Hector.

Their grandmother brought me a supper of broth thick with barley and pieces of chicken. 'Sit ye there,' she said, meaning the elbow chair set near the wall. It was high-backed and sturdy, the broadly carved wooden arms worn and well loved. ''Twas my husband's chair, built for a big man.'

I found it comfortable, and told her so, with thanks.

With a broad smile of pleasure, she replied that I was welcome to whatever little they might have. 'I telt yer wife the pair o' ye could take my bed the night, and close the curtains for some privacy.'

I nearly choked upon my broth at that suggestion. I tried not to look at Westaway, who'd quickly turned his head as if preparing to defend his daughter's honour. Not that there was any need, since she could do it for herself. I bore the scars from years of Phoebe's words. I knew if I were ever fool enough to try to touch her, she would slay me where I stood.

Westaway stayed silent, wisely, and I thanked the blacksmith's mother. Her hand settled on my shoulder, very likely in a gesture she'd used often with her husband, and she looked past me and said, ''Tis a good man ye've married, lass. Just like my Hob. Bigger men have the biggest hearts. See that ye don't let him go.'

I braced myself for Phoebe's answer, but none came. The blacksmith's mother gave my shoulder one last pat before she moved to gather up her grandsons. Lighter footsteps trod the floor behind me, and to my astonishment I felt another hand rest on my shoulder in a touch that felt affectionate.

I froze. Phoebe's father looked just as surprised, though they seemed to share some sort of private glance over my head that left Westaway satisfied, for once again he said nothing.

I followed his lead. Phoebe baffled me daily. Whatever her game was, I wasn't aware of the rules and was probably safer not knowing. I finished my broth.

'Let me take that,' she said. She removed my bowl, then returned, seating herself on the stool at my side.

For the moment, the blacksmith was busy with setting the ladder in place again at the trap door so his mother and two lads could be on their way.

I turned my head to look at Phoebe. Low, I asked her, 'Are ye well?'

She flushed a little, but she tipped her chin up bravely. Met my eyes. 'Yes, thank you.'

'Ye've not hit your head on anything?'

'Not that I'm aware of. Why?'

'No reason.'

I could say no more, because the blacksmith had returned

to take the chair across from us. The fire had a pleasant, earthy scent that I'd not breathed in years, and Hector, in the unreserved way of the young, asked, 'Are ye burning mud?'

I chuckled. 'No, lad. Those are peats. There'll be a moss nearby.'

The blacksmith nodded. 'Aye. The Tarras Moss.'

Politely, Westaway said, 'Do excuse my ignorance, but what's a moss?'

I hadn't known it was a Scottish word. There were so many differences between our native languages. I tried to think of what the English knew it by. 'A bog, ye'd call it.'

'Aye,' the blacksmith said again. 'A place where what ye think is ground deceives ye, and the peat floats on pools deep enough that they'll swallow ye whole and the Devil will take ye and ye'll nae more be seen. Not in this lifetime, anyways.' He placed another dried brick of peat onto the fire, watching as the flames slowly took hold. 'It saved the Armstrongs more than once, the Tarras Moss, for none but us ken where the ground is safe to tread, and when the English came for us, we'd only to retreat into the moss and bide our time to get the better of them.' His mouth curved in a smile of reminiscence. 'Back in eighty-eight, the Earl of Angus thought he had us cornered, so he did. He was Lieutenant of the Borders then, and we were outlawed thieves, and when he moved against us and we took our refuge in the Tarras Moss, he thought he would outwit us. He found a spy who took some of his men to wait at the far side of the moss, while he and his other men flushed us out from the other, but we were not to be fooled, we escaped him, and in our retreat nearly captured his kinsman.' His smile broadened briefly, then faded. 'A victory, it would hae been, but for the loss of a few. My own grandfather, Ringan, was killed in the skirmish. He never came home from the moss.'

A foul place to die, I imagined. I told him, 'I'm sorry.'

He shrugged. 'There's not been a man of my family who died in his bed. I doubt that I'll be any different.'

Sir David attempted to cheer him. 'But you're not a Reiver.'

The blacksmith's glance knew better. 'Nor was my father. He did honest work, he looked after his family, it didnae change anything. He was an Armstrong, and we're not allowed to be honest in all men's eyes.'

I saw the pain that passed over his features, and knew it for what it was because I shared it. The loss of a father you loved was a hard thing.

I asked, 'What became of him?'

'Someone accused him of stealing a horse. There was doubt, mind. The Border commissioners weren't all convinced, and the horse's owner said he wisnae sure, but still, my father was an Armstrong, so they drowned him in the drowning-place, the Grieve, just up the Ewes water.' One more brick of peat went onto the fire, this time more forcefully. 'So no, I dinnae think I'll die abed. But if I live to see my lads grown, that will be enough.'

I wished I could work my Gift at will – that I could look forwards in time and See for certain whether he would sit beside that fire with grandsons of his own upon his knee, but I could not. I only knew that by our coming here, we'd put him and his family in danger.

I pushed back my chair and said, 'I need to see to the horses.'

Sir David said, 'Surely not yet. You just—'

'Saddles need cleaning,' I cut him off.

And to his credit he held back his protests and lifted an eyebrow and only said, 'Ah.' Then stood with me and motioned to Hector to join us while Phoebe looked at me as though I were mad.

'Don't wait up,' I advised her.

She didn't.

When I returned she was already asleep, or pretending to be, in the bed with the curtains drawn round in the corner. The small bed that must have been shared by the blacksmith's lads was filled by Westaway, stretched out and snoring. The rest of us made our own beds on the floor where we could with the blankets provided.

I'd readied two excuses why I'd not be sleeping with my 'wife' in case the blacksmith asked me, but he did not interfere.

He did, though, waken me afore the sun was up. His hand upon my shoulder was insistent, and his voice held urgency. 'Ye must rise. There are riders.'

I was on my feet. 'Here?'

'At the castle. They've stopped there to rest their horses, but they'll soon be coming on. My eldest lad ran home to give us warning.'

'Graemes?'

'Aye.'

'How many?'

'Five and thirty. Maybe more.'

Sir David was awake now, too, and starting to sit up, eyes wary.

'Dress yourself,' I told him. 'We are leaving.' I was doing likewise when the blacksmith shook his head.

'Ye cannae wear the scarlet.'

'I've a cloak to cover it.'

'That will not be enough. The Graemes are claiming they're hunting a fugitive of the king's justice who's wearing the garb of a Messenger.'

I was forced to admit Patrick Graeme was not only crafty but clever. I wasn't well known in this part of the country, so his tactic made it my word against his, meaning in any town I would be jailed while the magistrates dealt with the matter, and he would be free to ride off with my prisoner.

He'd taken my badge of authority and made it something that marked us for capture.

The blacksmith said, 'Wear this instead.' And he offered a doublet of plain, homespun wool, dyed a warm, wheaten colour, with breeches to match, and a jerkin of well-weathered leather. 'They'll fit ye, I think,' he said. 'They were my father's.'

I hesitated, looking at his face. 'I cannot take your father's clothes.'

'Who else can wear them? Ye can see I'm not his size.'

'One of your lads may yet—'

'The Graemes mean to kill ye, do they not?' His jaw set stubbornly. He pushed the clothes into my hands. 'I'll not be having that upon my conscience.'

While I strove to think of words of thanks that would not seem inadequate, he turned from me, saying, 'Make haste now, and waken the others. My lad and I will see your horses are ready.'

Sir David had dressed and was watching me while, having fastened the old doublet over my shirt, I shrugged into the worn, sleeveless jerkin, with care.

He remarked, 'Those clothes might have been made for you. Mayhap you do have an Armstrong or two in your pedigree.'

I could have told him that I owed my height and size and colour of eyes all to my mother's family from the Western Isles, who'd passed their Sight to me as well, but I said only, 'I think not.' And went across to waken Westaway.

Phoebe had wrapped the plaid in the wrong way again, but I'd no time to correct her. We'd already wasted enough time in packing, and now I'd discovered the blacksmith's lad had put the pillion on the wrong horse, so I'd have to remove it, and—

Sir David said, 'You should leave that, and let Mistress Westaway ride with me.' He'd come to stand at the side of the black mare while I worked to unhook the pillion.

'Why would I do that?' I asked him.

'For her safety.'

That stopped my hands, and I could feel the rush of blood I sometimes felt afore a fight as I looked up to meet his steady eyes. My voice, even to my ears, sounded challenging. 'And how would ye keep her safe where I could not?'

Sir David, clearly not a man for fighting, told me, 'Use your reason, not your pride. Who is my cousin attempting to save?' When he saw that I'd answered that within my mind, he carried on, 'His men will not harm *me*. They will not fire upon me. Faith, I doubt they'd dare to chase me, for if I were injured, they would have to deal with Patrick.'

He was right. It would be safer to let Phoebe ride with him. Reversing what I'd done, I made sure the pillion was firmly fastened. We were by ourselves, with no one near us who could overhear, but still when I stepped closer to Sir David to fasten the belt for the pillion round his waist, I kept my voice low, deliberately. 'It may be they'll not harm ye,' I said. 'But if Phoebe's harmed, or even frighted, then your cousin Patrick and his men will have to deal with *me*. And they should ken that I'll not stop until I have my justice. Understand?'

The fierceness of my tone had taken him aback, but now he gathered calm again and faced me. 'Yes, I think I do.'

He did not need my help to mount. He was a fine, accomplished rider. But I waited till he'd settled in the saddle afore calling Phoebe over.

She was worried, I could see it in the tight lines of her face, so I tried smiling, though I wasn't sure I managed it convincingly. 'Ye'll have your wish the day. I'll let ye ride with a more amiable companion.'

Phoebe, knowing we were in a hurry, moved to let me lift her to the pillion, but her eyes met mine knowingly. 'You think the men who chase us will be gentler with Sir David, so there is less danger to me if I ride with him.'

I didn't look away. 'The men who chase us,' I said, 'will not catch us.'

I lifted her onto the horse. The black mare was more spirited than Brutus, and danced sideways a little. I held Phoebe's waist till she had a firm hold of Sir David's belt, and then I told him, 'She's nervous of horses, so keep the mare calm.'

He held up his fettered wrists. 'I could do that more effectively without these.'

I didn't trust him. But I knew that he was right. 'I would have your word, first, that ye will not run.'

'You have it.'

Such an easy promise – one I should have been too canny to relax my guard for now, but it was more important to ensure that Phoebe would be safe. As I unlocked the fetters and removed them, I reminded him, 'My horse is faster than the mare. My pistols are kept loaded. And my aim is true.'

The prospect of a chase had Hector restless with excitement. His red shirt, like my scarlet livery, had been tucked into one of the portmanteaus, and in its place he wore a shirt of Westaway's under a jerkin cast off from the blacksmith's lad, so he was once again a smaller version of me.

From the saddle of the Garron he looked over at me, hopeful. 'Should I have a pistol, too?'

'No,' I said. We were all ready now.

The blacksmith had mounted his horse as well to lead us out. 'Single file,' he cautioned us. 'That way our tracks will not betray our numbers.'

He might not be a Reiver, but his Armstrong blood ran in him strongly enough that his grandfather, Ringan, who'd died in the raid on the Tarras Moss, would have been proud.

He kent a place to cross the river where the banks were stony so our horses' hooves left no impressions. By a winding path he led us up the hill beyond and brought us out onto the moorland, where the waking earth had breathed a mist that hovered low above the ground and lent the lonely view a strangeness.

This was no ordinary moor, for while it had the common things – the coarse, wheat-coloured grasses and the darkly spreading clumps of heather overlaying the new green of spring – I also smelled the peat, and Brutus was already on his guard, great nostrils flaring as he caught the scent of hidden pools of stagnant water. We were on the moss, and looking down into a rugged, thickly wooded glen that stretched between ourselves and the smooth rise of hills on the horizon.

More trees had climbed the slopes and clung to them in ways unnatural, so here and there a stand of rowan mixed with stunted birken trees bent stubbornly against the wind, like armies of old men who would not fall afore the enemy.

A whaup – or curlew, as the English called it – passed above us with its piercing cry. My mother's people of the Western Isles would have believed that to be an ill omen for our journey, but I did not hold such superstitions. I was riding at the back, where I could keep an eye on everyone and guard them from behind, but when we reached a level place, the blacksmith motioned us to stop, then wheeled his horse around and came back down the line to have a word with me.

'I'll have to leave ye here,' he said. 'I must get back in case the riders come. It wouldnae do for them to find my lad alone.'

I understood, and told him so.

Relief showed in his eyes. 'We'll tell the Graemes that ye left us yestere'en, along the road to Carlisle. If they think ye ride that far ahead of them, they'll not stop long, they'll be too keen to follow.'

'And your neighbours?'

'Are all Armstrongs,' he said proudly. 'Not a man among them will betray ye.' He seemed very certain, and I hoped his faith was justified.

I shook his hand, and thanked him, pressing coins into his palm – more than I'd ordinarily give for a night's lodging, but these circumstances were exceptional.

''Tis too much,' he said.

'Ye've given me your father's clothes,' I pointed out.

Acknowledging this with a nod, he returned the thanks gruffly and turned my attention to the hills on the horizon. 'Ye'll be heading there, just where that spear of light has touched the land, ye see?'

I saw.

He said, 'Keep to this high ground and out of the glen, aim your horse's nose towards that spot, and ye'll come through the moss like ye were born to it. I'll send a guide to help ye if I'm able.'

He left us then, and I moved up to take the lead. Passing Sir David, I drew up straighter in the saddle, levelled one more warning look upon him, and said, 'Mind ye keep your place, now.'

As we ventured on, a low, familiar warbling filled the air around us, growing ever louder.

Phoebe asked, 'What *is* that noise?'

Sir David answered first. ''Tis but the blackcocks at their haunt, my dear. They gather in the mornings at this time of year to strut and jump and fight off all the other males to win themselves the favour of the greyhens.'

I caught the dry note of amusement in his voice and knew he'd aimed a barb a me, but when I half turned to look back his eyes were wholly innocent, so all I said was, 'We are being tracked. Best to keep silent.'

Truth be told, I needed silence just to concentrate. It was no easy task to find the safe path on the moss, even with Brutus's keen instincts, and our progress, although steady, left us too exposed for comfort.

I was focused so entirely upon the ground beneath me that I didn't hear the man approaching till he came alongside, walking swiftly and with ease, well muffled, wearing clothes much like the blacksmith's in their colour and their cut, his hat drawn low.

He said, 'They're close ahind. Come, follow me, I'll take ye where it's safe.'

When I didn't turn immediately, he urged me, 'None but Armstrongs ken this way. Come. There's nae time tae waste.'

I'll send a guide to help ye if I'm able. Bless the blacksmith, I thought. Thanking our new guide, I followed where he led, and motioned to the others to do likewise.

It was not a simple route, but I kept Brutus in the footsteps of the guide, and looked back often to make sure that all the others safely managed it as well. When we were halfway down the glen, Sir David looked as though he would have asked a question, but I raised a hand to hold him silent, knowing our pursuers might be close enough to hear.

We were within the woods now, moving ever deeper into the dark tangle of the birken trees and rowan, and the stunted oaks that bound their branches overhead and cast an eerie shade that broke the dawning light into uncertain fragments.

Nearby I heard water running, rapid like a river, and with each breath I inhaled the strong, cloying scent of dampness rising from the ground.

Brutus baulked, and I reined him in, and our guide turned and told me, ''Tis perfectly safe, Hob.'

I saw his eyes, then. And I knew.

He was no man, but a wraith.

I had followed a dead man away from the safe path and into the depths of the Tarras Moss, where there were pools that could swallow ye whole so ye'd no more be seen, and now we were all of us going to be dead.

The wraith wanted me to dismount. I weighed the wisdom of this for a moment and finally decided that it might be best to converse on the ground and look less like a madman. If I kept my voice low, the others would, with luck, assume I was talking to Brutus, a thing they often saw me do.

Once down from the saddle, I moved to make show of checking the fit of Brutus's bridle, and told the wraith, quietly, 'Will ye take us up again to where ye found us?'

'Nay, lad, I telt ye. The English hae their watchmen set tae follow ye, and will by now hae all our southern entries guarded also. Ye must bide here, as I taught ye.' I saw something close to kindness in the wraith's expression. 'I ken well ye wanted nae part of this life, Hob, but life disnae allus allow ye tae choose.'

He took no notice of the others. Perhaps he did not see them, or, since they could not see *him*, he counted them inconsequential. But for once, I did not have to guess who he imagined I was. He had called me Hob, which meant that clearly he believed I was the blacksmith's father, from my size and clothing.

And I had a strong suspicion from the way the wraith was talking to me that he was Hob Armstrong's father, Ringan, who had died here in the Tarras Moss during the battle with the English.

I tested my theory. 'Father—'

He grinned. 'Are we living in the castle, now? Father, is it? I'm yer da, my lad. Now, keep yer heid well doon, and mind what ye were taught, and dinnae shift yerself from here until it's safe.'

Sir David called, 'Is something wrong?'

Impatiently, I looked up, and at the sharpness of my action Brutus jerked his head against my hold and I gave his neck a reassuring pat, and when I turned my head the wraith had vanished.

Tight-lipped, I held back what I wished to say, and instead answered, 'All is well.'

Sir David said, 'I'm glad to hear it. I thought we were meant to keep to the higher ground.'

I said, 'It didn't feel safe.'

I allowed Sir David some credit for making no comment when he surveyed our current surroundings, which I had to admit appeared anything but safe, but he held his tongue admirably when I announced we would be stopping here awhile, 'here' being a nondescript clearing of sorts with a handful of rocks and fallen trees for seating, nearly lost in the densely green undergrowth.

Sir David merely halted and continued to say nothing when I came back to lift Phoebe from the pillion and escort her to a seat upon a stone across the clearing, where at least some light broke through. But when young Hector, who by now had dutifully dismounted the Garron and come forwards to assist Sir David, raised a hand to the mare's bridle, then Sir David told him sharply, 'Hector, do not move.'

I turned. My pistols were still in their holsters on my saddle, fully fifteen feet away, but even as I registered that fact, Sir David reached his own hand down and, in one swift motion, took a firm hold of the back of Hector's jerkin and lifted the lad to sit afore him on the mare.

I would have cursed aloud, if not for Phoebe, but I thought the words with feeling. Reaching for my knife, I started for him, but already he had walked the mare back several paces.

'Logan, stop,' he told me. 'You misunderstand.'

I understood he had the lad between us as a shield and was attempting an escape, but when I would have told him this, he shook his head and pointed at the ground where Hector had been standing.

'There's an adder.'

He had halted for a second time, and seemed now to be waiting. Just behind him, Westaway, yet on his horse, was waiting, too. I stopped, and watched the place he'd pointed to, and sure enough, the leaves began to move. And then the snake emerged, its markings jagged black like saw's teeth on its long, grey body as it slowly made its way across the clearing and slipped silently into the tangled roots and leaves and grasses on the other side.

Hector's eyes had gone wide, and Sir David gave him a reassuring pat on the shoulder. 'He was a sound sleeper, that one. Like you, my lad. Else he'd have wakened when he heard our horses approaching, and made himself scarce.'

'Was he not hunting me, then?'

'Never. Adders won't harm you if you let them be. They're retiring, peaceable creatures who wish to live quietly, bothering no one, removed from the world and its noise. But if they're attacked . . .' He looked over the lad's head then, his eyes keeping level on mine. 'Well, they've no choice then but to defend themselves with what defences God gave them.'

I was well aware that speech had naught to do with the adder, but Hector took all at face value, and asked him, 'If it *did* bite me, would I have died?'

From where the lad sat, he could not see the moment of conflict that showed on Sir David's face as he weighed whether to tell him the truth.

I spared him by stepping in, cheerfully telling the lad, 'Hector, I promise ye, lad, ye've got no chance of dying while I'm here to guard ye.'

The lad looked fair pleased. 'No?'

I shook my head. 'No chance at all.'

Hector grinned and jumped down from the mare's back and went to help Westaway, who after all of this drama was stiffly dismounting.

Sir David did likewise in his calm and elegant way, and held out his wrists to be manacled, patiently.

I met his gaze without words. Then leaving him unbound, I turned and went back to where Brutus was standing, aware of the weight of the eyes that were watching me, waiting for me to announce our next move.

In my life, never once had I wished for a wraith to appear, but I wished for it now. Ringan Armstrong, if he had in truth been the wraith who had led us down here to our probable doom, opted not to oblige me by showing his face again. I saw no movement at all in the trees, and heard no sounds but those made by us or by nature.

And then, very faintly, I heard the sure rhythm of hoofbeats. One rider, alone. Coming nearer.

The others heard it, too, and I motioned them to get behind me as I drew my pistols from their holsters on my saddle and stepped forwards to confront whoever was approaching.

I expected he'd come cautiously. He didn't.

With my pistols levelled at him, I called out, 'That's far enough.'

He halted his horse, but seemed otherwise unconcerned. Not the response I'd expect from an ordinary country man who'd stumbled onto a party of armed strangers deep in the woods of the Tarras Moss. And this man – middle-aged, roughly dressed, looked in all ways like an ordinary country man.

'My God, he telt nae lies. Ye hae the look of Hob.' He gave his head a half-shake. Then he grinned, and dismounted, and led his horse forwards, ignoring my weapons. 'How in the Devil did ye end up down here? He said he had telt ye tae go by the high ground.'

So *this*, then, was our guide. I took a keen look at his eyes and slowly lowered both my pistols, and my guard.

Sir David answered for me. 'Logan felt the high ground was no longer safe.'

The man, who so resembled both the blacksmith and the wraith that I assumed he was an Armstrong, looked me over with respect. 'Your feelings serve ye well. I wasnae the only rider coming ontae the moss tae follow ye. There were twa others, who came up just ahind me.'

I didn't need to ask the question. 'Graemes?'

'Aye. They overtook me. Asked me if I'd seen three men, a lassie and a lad, and one man all in scarlet.'

It was not the lack of sunlight in the woods that drove the

swift chill down my spine. *They're close ahind,* the wraith had warned me. And they had been. Very close.

'Indeed, says I,' the Armstrong carried on, 'they set off on the road tae Carlisle, yestere'en.'

I frowned. 'And they believed ye?'

'Well, they turned right quick and headed back the way they'd come. As anyone could see, ye were nae on the moss. And even Graemes ken well none but Armstrongs could survive here in the woods.' He grinned again and clapped my arm with an approving hand. 'Ye mind those feelings, lad, and allus listen tae them well.' Then, to make sure the others understood, he said to them, 'He saved your life.'

I couldn't take the credit, but I couldn't have explained why not. I let the matter pass. And I was more than ready to allow our Armstrong guide to lead us from those woods, with their uncertain light and smell of dead and dying things, where any step might take you onto ground that wasn't ground at all, but dark, unholy mire that dragged you down into a living grave from which you'd not return.

As we came out into the open air once more, I deeply breathed to fill my lungs and bring some order to my thoughts.

I tried to think a step ahead of Patrick Graeme. We'd escaped him this time, but the next time we might not, and I knew well he'd come at us again. I'd Seen it on that day in London, in the stables of my own house, when I'd looked at Phoebe and I'd suddenly been elsewhere, with her sitting on the pillion behind me, and strange men on horseback riding down upon us.

She had asked me in my vision then, *Can we outrun them?* I'd have given much to know the answer. But as I looked around me now, I reassured myself this landscape was not what I'd Seen – not fields divided by a road, but trackless moors and hills. And while I didn't fully trust Sir David, letting Phoebe ride with him instead of me meant I'd be fairly sure this day was not the same day from my vision.

Not that any plan was foolproof, as life had taught me to my cost, but being cautious did no harm. The Graemes had gone by the road to Carlisle. We'd go east instead, drawing them into a landscape more foreign to them, more familiar to me. I had ridden the great road from London to Newcastle more times than I cared to count. There, I'd have the advantage.

The getting there, *that* was the problem.

The towns close by us now were too exposed and would not offer safety. There was but one way I thought we might manage it, though it would prove a rougher path for Phoebe and her father.

Urging Brutus forwards, I drew level with our Armstrong guide.

'Which way is it from here,' I asked him, 'to the Roman wall?'

DAVID

Cawfields, Northumberland, England, 7th May 1613

THE LAD WAS NERVOUS. Understandably enough, since they had ridden more than thirty miles, and darkness was now drawing in to steal the last of the day's sun and leave instead uncertain shadows. A grown man, being weary from such travel over difficult terrain, might be forgiven if he conjured ghosts within his mind at every sound or breath of wind that stirred the long grass in the fading light.

And Hector, for his cloak of borrowed bravery, was not a man.

The Messenger had shown uncommon patience, even kindness. When they had stopped an hour ago to make another meal of the provisions that their Armstrong guide had given them before they'd parted ways, the Messenger had watched the lad a moment, then divided his own portion into thirds. One part he gave to Westaway, who protested half-heartedly, but being tired and hungry and presumably not used to riding so long in one day, accepted it and ate it.

For the second part, the Messenger had crossed to Hector. 'Here, lad. Get this down ye. I am full enough, and ye are growing still.'

As always, the presence of the Messenger brought new life to the lad, who'd wolfed the food and asked, 'D'ye think I will ever grow as big as you?'

The Messenger, thought David, had a pleasant laugh. ''Tis possible,' the young man had replied. 'Although your horse will never thank ye for it.'

Hector said, 'Then I will have to get a horse as big as Brutus.'

'Aye.' They'd looked together at the massive beast, who with the other horses was content to stand and graze within the limits of his tether alongside the shallow rivulet whose waters swiftly ran and chased across its stony bed. 'We'll let him and the others drink and rest for a few minutes more, and then we'll carry on.'

Hector had sagged. 'Why cannae we bide here the night?'

Some men might have returned, 'Because we can't.' Instead, the Messenger had taken time to give his reasons. 'Here, we're too exposed. Ye see the way the land is? Low, with all the hills around us?'

'Aye.'

'Well, anyone might be up on those hills now, watching us, and we'd not ken it. And if they attacked us, we'd be at a disadvantage. Ye should always seek the higher ground.'

Hector had thought about this. 'Like those crags, there?'

With a smile, the Messenger had said, 'Exactly like those crags. Good lad. That's where we're headed.'

Hector had seemed briefly cheered to know their long day's journey would soon end. But when they reached the steep rise of the cliffs that stretched to either side of them in an unyielding line, Hector lost confidence.

The climb proved a fair challenge, and the Messenger had everyone dismount to climb on foot and lead their horses riderless, to ease their load. Which was how David came to be now walking side by side with Hector, who was looking all around them with unease.

David sought to reassure him. 'We are not the first who sought these heights for safety. See that wall, or what remains of it? The Romans built that for protection, centuries ago. It was the great frontier, and ran from sea to sea, to guard the towns of Roman Britain from the Picts who ruled the north.'

'The who?'

'Well, us,' admitted David, with a smile. 'The Scots. The Romans looked upon us as their fiercest enemies, for we would not be conquered.'

Labouring behind them, Westaway put in, ''Twould be more accurate, I think, to call the Picts your distant ancestors. They were not Scots.'

'They harboured the same sentiments,' said David, proudly. 'Rome could not defeat them.'

Westaway appeared amused. 'You had best sleep with one eye open, then,' he said, 'lest any of the Romans left their ghosts behind to settle that old score.'

They'd reached the top. The ground was level here, if slightly sloped to face the south, and close against the remnants of the Roman wall a large, rough square of tumbled stones and turf lay open to the wind and weather, overgrown with blowing grass.

The Messenger, well satisfied, saw to it that the horses were securely tethered in one corner of this square of stones before he loosed their girths and started to unstrap the portmanteaus they carried.

Hector asked him, 'Are there truly ghosts here?'

'No,' the Messenger replied.

The wind struck Hector and he shivered. 'Are ye sure?'

The Messenger glanced over. While his hands kept up the movements of his work, uninterrupted, he looked all around and said, 'I'm very sure. There's none but us.'

David, who'd confirmed this fact by studying the view in all directions from the crag, found it of little comfort. All day he'd been forced to run from those who might have saved him, and unlike the others, he'd have been relieved to see his cousin Patrick's men approaching.

He had known the king too long to harbour any doubts about what lay in store for him in London. *For God's sake, do not come home,* William had warned him. *Your life is in danger.* As if he'd not already known that he'd never be granted the peace he desired, for the king could not ever allow him to live.

Phoebe Westaway said, 'I feel half dead, myself.' She passed close beside David, her pretty face showing the strain of the day. ''Tis a good thing there aren't any ghosts here, for after that ride, I have no strength to face one.' She sat on the nearest stone, stretching her feet out in front of her.

David said, 'Nor I. Although in perfect honesty, I would not mind so much to meet a ghost, if it were Roman. Think of all that I could ask, and learn?'

This puzzled Hector. 'But I thought ye said they were our enemies?'

'Time marches onwards. Those who were your enemies one day become your allies, or your friends. And apart from waging war, which they were very highly skilled at, the Romans had many good qualities. They were fine statesmen, and philosophers and builders of important things. This wall, for example.' He took some moments then and tried to reconstruct it with his words for Hector, so the lad might see the great wall as it had been, with its watchtowers and roads. 'The wall had forts at either end and in the middle, but along it there were towers built at every Roman mile to house the soldiers who were stationed here to watch the north and stand on guard.' He gestured to the open square surrounding them, of tumbled stones and turf, and added, 'Mayhap this was one of those. It sheltered them,' he said, 'when they had need of it. And now its ruins shelter us.'

'They might have left a roof,' said Phoebe, with a rueful smile.

Her father's gaze found David's, and he lightly said, 'The young Prince Henry did admire the Romans greatly, I believe.'

David looked away. 'Aye, so he did.'

He was not reconciled yet to his grief. It caught him unprepared, as always, but he pushed it firmly down into the hollow place where once his heart had been.

The wind rose like a thing alive, and David heard a voice upon it.

'Everything that happens,' said Prince Henry, 'happens as it should. That's what the Emperor Marcus Aurelius says.'

And David knew then that the Messenger had been mistaken.

For there was at least one ghost now walking with them, here upon this hill.

Stirling Castle, Scotland, 13th May 1599

'But why me?' David asked his aunt, still trying to make sense of it. She'd met him at the gate and they had crossed the inner court together. Now, as they came in from the outdoors to the dim passageway that opened to the king's guard hall, he paused to let his eyes – and thoughts – adjust. 'I'm hardly qualified.'

His aunt found that amusing. 'If it were required that those at court be qualified to do the work assigned to them, I daresay every post would be unfilled.'

He shared her smile. 'Except yours.'

'Naturally.'

His aunt had always been a force of nature. Even though the

management of Stirling Castle had technically passed years ago to her son the Earl of Mar and his wife, who had become the new countess, David's aunt had continued, in her role as Dowager Countess of Mar, to counsel and direct as she had always done, and one had but to see the way the guards all drew themselves up to attention when she entered the king's guard hall, like a row of bairns seeking approval, to know who was truly in command here.

'I am old,' his aunt said. 'That is what they call me – the old countess. Never to my face, mind, for I'd make them pay, and well they know it. But 'tis true, my body is now wasting from my years of service, and I cannot say how long God will allow me to remain before he takes me to him. In that time, I have one purpose, and that is to see my family settled comfortably.' The look she sent to David bordered on defiance. 'I have managed to find places for your mother and your brothers.'

'Leaving only me.'

'You've always been a challenge, David.' In the centre of the room, his aunt stopped walking. Faced him with a look of fondness. 'We do share that aspect of our character.'

'You flatter me,' he told her.

'No, I mean it. From your cradle, you have never sought the easy path. But choosing the less-travelled one,' she said, 'can leave you lonely, and that's not a fate I wish for you.'

'I am not lonely.'

'Neither are you happy.' She seemed certain of the fact. 'You're not still pining for that girl, the French one?'

'Celia? No.' The lie came easily.

It satisfied his aunt. 'Good. It's been three years. Time you were married, too. You need to find another woman.'

David could not help but point out, 'I'm hardly likely to do that here.' To his aunt's raised eyebrows, he explained, 'Did you not say yourself that all these changes are now taking place because the king has ordered that Prince Henry be removed completely from the care of women, so that he's surrounded by the influence of men?'

'Yes, but—'

'Then if you would seek to match me with a future wife, you should not have proposed me for a place within the prince's household, for I will not find one here. Your plan,' he said, 'does have a flaw.'

'My plans are never flawed,' his aunt assured him, not allowing him the point. 'And I did not propose you for the place. You were requested.'

David looked at her. 'By whom?'

'By Queen Anna herself.'

David couldn't think why. 'I have met her but once, on the night of the christening.'

'Well, you apparently made an impression.' His aunt's weathered features, if just for a moment, showed something like pride. 'She wishes for you to take care of her son, David. 'Tis a great honour. You would be the first gentleman of his bedchamber. Sleep at his bedside, and dress him and tend to his needs. There's no man who'd be closer than you to the prince.'

David felt a frown tighten his brow as he thought those words through. 'Then it should be his choice.'

His aunt stared as though she'd not heard him correctly. 'What?'

David made it clear. 'The prince should have some say in choosing who will be that near to him.'

'He's a child.'

'He's a prince. Let him meet me and judge me, and if he approves of me, I will accept the position.'

His aunt said, 'You cannot say no to the queen.'

David told her again, very calm, 'Let him meet me, and judge me.'

The sigh his aunt gave was identical to those he'd heard all his life from his mother. 'You'll get on well, you and the prince,' she decided. 'You're each of you as stubborn as the other. Come.' She started walking again, towards the door that led into the presence chamber. 'He is not like his father. When I raised the king, when he was small, it was no easy thing to see his mind at work. This lad is different. All he feels is plainly writ upon his face, and it will cost him dearly if he cannot learn to hide it.'

'Surely honesty is something to be fostered in this world?'

They'd reached the door. His aunt looked back at him, her eyes both wise and pitying. 'In this world? 'Tis a weakness.'

The young prince was in the presence chamber, waiting for them.

Slender for a lad of five, and serious, he had been dressed for the occasion in a suit of velvet that was too warm for the day. His cheeks, though pale, were lightly flushed. But his large eyes were clear and steady, watching David bow and staying fixed on him with interest through the introductions following.

David could not help but be reminded of the night he'd held the prince five summers past in this same chamber, when the prince had ceased his weeping and looked up at him with much the same expression.

David's aunt said, 'I shall leave you two alone, to get acquainted.'

They weren't entirely alone, of course. A prince could never be alone. The guards remained, one each against the four walls of the presence chamber, standing at attention. They were silent and discreet, but ever present.

Young Prince Henry took no notice of them.

David watched the war of curiosity and shyness wage across the prince's face, and understood then what his aunt meant by her claim that the prince hid not his feelings. Curiosity emerged triumphant.

'I am told,' the prince said, 'this is not the first time we have met.'

'No, it is not, Your Highness. Though you'd not recall our first meeting, as it was at your christening.'

'I'm told you made me cease my crying when none else could.'

'I performed no magic,' David told him. 'I suspect you were astonished by my beard.'

The prince considered this as though it were a serious suggestion, not a joke. 'You have red hair, like me.'

'I do, Your Highness.'

That earned little but a nod. And then, in one of those blunt, sideways turns of conversation common to the young, the prince asked, 'Do you like this chamber?'

David wasn't sure if there were a right answer to the question, but he chose to answer honestly. 'I do, Your Highness, very much. It is, in truth, my favourite in the castle.'

'Mine as well.' The prince's smile transformed his face. 'I like the faces on the ceiling.'

David agreed that the carved and painted faces were the room's best feature. He craned his neck to look at them, then said, 'They're best observed another way, if you'll permit me?' When the prince's nod allowed him leave to do so, David lay upon the floor, stretched at his full length, on his back, his hands linked casually beneath his head.

The prince, after a moment's hesitation, joined him, and they lay together, looking up at the rows of brightly painted profiles.

David felt the quiet disapproval of the guardsmen at their posts, but he ignored them. To the prince, he said, 'I did spend many hours here with my brothers in this manner, trying to decide what sorts of lives these people led.'

Prince Henry asked, 'Who was your favourite?'

'I don't know that I ever had one. Who is yours?'

There was no hesitation. 'Him.' The prince's small hand pointed to a Roman with curled hair and beard, his commander's cloak pinned with the head of a lion. 'He has red hair, too.' In a tone of discovery, the prince added, 'He looks like you.'

David said, 'I am flattered you think so, Your Highness, for that is a great man.'

'I know.'

'Do you, now?'

'Aye, that's Marcus Aurelius Antoninus Augustus,' the prince told him, carefully. 'He was an emperor, and a victorious general.'

'That's so, Your Highness. But with respect, there were many men who ruled in Rome and won battles. What made this man great is how he lived his life while he was doing it, for he was good and virtuous, and left behind his writings so that we might learn from them how to be likewise. His book is a fine guide for life.'

The prince lay a moment and looked up in silence at Marcus Aurelius. Then he said, 'You've read this book?'

'Aye,' said David. 'In Edinburgh, there is a gentleman I know who owns a copy of it, and he gives me free use of his library.'

The prince asked, 'Would he sell it to me, do you think?'

'If Your Highness desired it, I do not doubt he'd gift it to you, gladly.'

But the young prince shook his head with firmness. 'I will pay him for it. It would not be right to take a person's book from them and not give payment. It would not be virtuous.' He said the word so solemnly that David's heart was touched.

'Then I'll arrange the terms, Your Highness,' David promised.

'Thank you. David? I would call you David – this does not displease you?'

Once again, that unexpected tug upon his heartstrings. 'No, Your Highness.'

'When you have the book, you'll bring it to me?'

'Aye, of course.'

'And read it with me?'

'Aye.'

There was a pause, and David had the strong impression that Prince Henry held his breath. 'Will you be staying here?'

He answered plainly. 'I've been asked to serve you as the first gentleman of your bedchamber, but I'll not say yes unless you'd like me to.'

'What does a first gentleman of the bedchamber do?'

David explained, and the prince brightened. 'Then you would be with me all the time?'

'Aye.'

The shyness had returned, and with it hope. Until he saw the blend of both emotions cross the prince's features, David hadn't fully seen the loneliness they masked. 'Then I should like that very much,' Prince Henry said, and with the first trace of his father's blood within him showing, added, 'You will tell them yes.'

He hadn't thought about that day for what seemed ages. Maybe it was Hector that was stirring up old memories, or the fact they were now lying on their backs, within the toppled walls of what had likely been a Roman tower at the Roman wall within the wilderness, beneath the stars, and looking up, in much the same way he had lain upon his back beside the prince those years ago.

'Marcus Aurelius Antoninus Augustus.' Hector tried the name upon his tongue.

'Well done,' said David.

'And he was the prince's favourite?'

'All his life. And this book' – David took the small book from his pocket, even though the moonlight did not give them light enough to see the words by – 'was the very book the prince did ask me to obtain for him.'

Hector asked him, 'Could I hold it?'

'Certainly, if you are careful.'

Hector held the book as if it were a pane of window-glass. 'Could I read it?'

David was about to answer him when Westaway, who'd come to sit beside them, cut into the conversation with the question, 'Can you read?'

Hector looked hurt. 'Of course I can. The mistress had me schooled in Leith.'

The older man said, 'Very good. An education is a useful thing to have.'

But Hector was not finished. 'I can read *and* write. I'm not a fool.'

The Messenger through all this had been sitting to the side upon a tumbled fall of stone, working to mend a bit of harness, but the lad's tone made him lift his head. 'There's no one saying that you are,' he said. 'But lads who might be minded to be Messengers must keep a watch upon their tempers and be aye respectful to their elders.'

The effect was immediate. Hector, in a quieter voice, said, 'I beg your forgiveness, Master Westaway. I was very mismanerit.'

Westaway assured him there was no harm done, and took some of the blame upon himself. 'For even I might be ill mannered if somebody were to question my intelligence.'

David said, 'They're not the same, though, are they? Education and intelligence. A learned man can yet be witless in all other aspects of his life, while an uneducated man who's never set foot in a classroom can possess a fine and gifted mind. In that book, Marcus Aurelius says we ought to look at things below the surface, and not let their quality nor worth escape us.' Which in fact might be advice David would give Westaway's daughter, were he in a mood to give advice. But then again, her troubles with the Messenger were not his business, and he had enough to occupy his mind. 'Sadly, the book isn't written in English, it's only in Latin and Greek.'

Hector passed the book back to him, ruefully. 'I cannae read the Latin or the Greek.'

David looked a moment at the boy, thinking how life could sometimes work in circles. 'No matter,' he said. 'I'll read it with you.'

The silence held a moment, and then Westaway lay back until he, too, was stretched beside them on the turf and gazing upwards at the bowl of the night sky. 'What does your Roman say,' he asked, 'about the stars?'

Phoebe

Cawfields, Northumberland, the same night

The stones against my back blocked some part of the wind, but not enough. I drew the folds of Logan's mother's plaid around me tightly as I sat there in the moonlight, wishing we could have a fire. I understood why Logan had forbidden it – a fire was too great a risk, if we were being followed. On these heights, we might as well have lit a beacon. But I still felt cold.

I seemed to be alone in my discomfort. Logan sat a little distance from me, uncomplaining, diligently working on a broken bit of horse harness. The others were all lying on their backs upon the rough ground, in a contemplation of the stars.

That was my father's doing. Had I been a better daughter, I would no doubt have reminded him that he was far too old to lie directly on the ground. It did his health no good. But earlier this evening, when we'd climbed the steep path up this hill, he'd brushed my hands aside when I had offered him support to hold him steady. 'I am not an invalid,' he'd told me then. And now, he looked so happy that I held my tongue.

It was a revelation how the boy coaxed from each man a different aspect of their character. Logan, when he dealt with Hector, showed uncommon patience. It was plain the boy considered him the next thing to a god and wanted only to be near him, and while some men might consider that a burden, Logan seemed unbothered by it, taking time to answer every question Hector asked. Sir David dropped his careful guard, allowing his dry wit to slide through, as it no doubt did when he was with his friends. And my father was again the teacher, as he'd been for all the years when he'd worked as a writing master, and as he'd have been with both my brothers, had they lived.

He was in full cry now upon the subject he loved best. 'See there, my boy, those stars that sit above Orion form the charioteer. And that bright star—'

'Who was he?' Hector asked.

'I beg your pardon?'

'Well, ye telt me that Orion was the sea god's son and the best hunter in the world.'

My father smiled. 'That he was.'

'So the charioteer must have been someone special,' Hector reasoned, 'to have been turned into stars.'

'Ah.' I could see my father thinking, but the day had been a long one and his memory, although strong, seemed to be failing him on this one point, so I stepped in.

I raised my voice so that I would be heard above the wind, and said, 'In ancient Greece, they thought the charioteer was Phaeton, son of Helios, the sun god. Every day the sun god had to drive his chariot of flames across the sky, to bring the daylight, and one day his own son, Phaeton, begged to do it in his place.' I'd heard this tale told countless times. I kept it to the bare essentials. 'But Phaeton, in the chariot, could not control the horses, so they flew too low above the earth and set it all aflame. And Zeus – the highest god of all the gods – was angry, and struck Phaeton with a thunderbolt and killed him. But in the end Zeus set him in the sky, among the stars.'

Logan had fixed the harness. Setting it aside, he went across to lie beside the others, so that now there were the four of them stretched out like toppled logs upon the turf, with blowing grasses at their heads and feet.

I was half tempted to leave my cold, lonely seat and join

them, but my father, at the furthest end, lay close against a ridge of stone and earth, which left no open space except that beside Logan.

Hector, with Sir David on one side and Logan on the other, let his hero-worship show. When Logan put one hand behind his head and let the other rest upon his stomach, Hector did the same. He even crossed his ankles just as Logan's were, which made me smile, because it was exactly like the children's game in which you tried to mirror your opponent's every move, only Logan did not know he was a player in the game.

My father said, 'The stars have a great influence upon our lives. For instance, Hector, that star high upon the shoulder of the charioteer, the brightest one, is called Capella, and it is a most auspicious star, but sadly, Mercury did shadow it too closely at the moment of my birth, which has resulted in much difficulty in my life.' I could barely see his features, but I knew he turned his head and looked across to where I sat. 'My Phoebe, now, she'll have a better life than I had, for the stars that did attend her birth were fortunate. She'll marry a fine man of—'

For some reason, I did not want him to finish the whole prophecy. Not here, in front of everyone. And Logan.

I cut in with, 'Do you put faith in astrology, Sir David?'

'Very little, I confess. Though I'll allow that there are things in life we may not understand.'

My father said, 'But it is proven science, practised by respected doctors.'

Hector asked, 'How do they ken which stars were where when ye were born?'

My father summarized the way a doctor of astrology might cast a figure for the hour of someone's birth, and Hector asked, 'But how would they find out the hour?'

'You tell them,' said my father.

Hector said, a little sadly, 'Then I'll never learn what stars were in my sky, for no one kens when I was born.'

'Your mother surely knows,' my father said.

'I have no mother,' Hector reminded him. 'Nor a father, either.'

Logan did not let the silence last. 'Then ye may freely choose your own star. 'Tis the rule.'

'It is?' Hector was dubious.

'Aye. Just ask Master Westaway.'

My father, for the softness of his heart, did not dispute the claim. 'It is indeed.'

'Ye see?' said Logan. 'Look up in the heavens, lad, choose any star ye like, and ye can have it for your own, to guide your destiny.'

Hector looked long and hard and searchingly into all corners of the sky, and then at last he pointed upwards and said, 'That one, there.'

My father praised his choice. 'That is the brightest star in Leo, or the constellation of the lion, and that star is called by some the lion's heart.'

Sir David said, 'Its proper name is Regulus, which means "the little king".'

My father turned his head. 'I thought you said that you believed not in astrology.'

'That doesn't mean I wasn't made to study it,' Sir David told him. And, to Hector, 'Regulus is truly the most fortunate of all the stars, and it will bring you honesty, nobility of spirit, and great courage.'

'All good qualities,' said Logan, 'for a Messenger.'

'A good star,' Sir David said.

But there was something in the way he said it, and the way he fell to silence for a moment after, that made me think that maybe looking at a star known as 'the little king' had raised sad memories of the prince he had so lately lost.

Hector remarked, 'It's very bright.'

Sir David murmured, 'Aye. Some say the brighter stars do faster fall, but I've observed the brightest of them steal the light from all the others in the sky, which makes those lesser beacons envious.'

This time, his silence held, and he remained lost in his private thoughts.

Hector's own thoughts had travelled down another road. He looked around at the dark ruins of the Roman wall, now overgrown by grass and turf, and turned to Logan. 'And ye're sure there are no wraiths here?'

'Aye, lad. Very sure.'

But Hector inched a little closer to the side of Logan anyway, before he fell asleep. And once again, I found I envied him, because my own sleep, when it came, was full of dreams and fitful, and it did not last.

I spent a long time in the darkness, lying lonely by myself and looking upwards at the lion's heart that stole the light from all the lesser stars.

I was awake when Logan rose. The sun had barely shown itself above the hills, and even with its efforts the damp air still had a chilling bite, but Logan stood bareheaded and without a coat for so long at the wall's edge, with his gaze fixed on the line of the horizon in the west, that it intrigued me. Rising too, I hastily restored some order to my hair and clothing, took the plaid that I'd been using as a blanket and re-wrapped it round me as a mantel, and made my way over the rough ground to join him.

It wasn't a silent approach and I thought he would hear me, but his whole attention was still on the far hills when I came to stand at his shoulder. His eyes had the unfocused look that I'd witnessed before, when he looked at my father, or on that day when I had gone to his house, to his stables, and asked him to let me come north with them. Maybe it was the way Logan looked when he was worried.

I tried not to startle him, keeping my voice calm. 'Good morrow.'

The unfocused look disappeared in an instant. His head turned towards me. 'Good morrow.'

I never could hold his gaze long, but for some reason I found it harder this morning. My own attention wandered to the way his brows were drawn together and the hard set of his jaw. I asked, 'Is something wrong?'

'Aye, there is.' He said it bluntly. 'They are coming – Patrick Graeme and his men. We have to go.'

I looked where he had just been looking, to the west. 'But I see nothing.'

Logan was sure. 'They'll be here by midday.' He was already moving away from the wall. 'We'll have no time to waste. Wake your father.'

'My father,' I told him, 'has yet to recover from yesterday's ride. You cannot be forcing him into the saddle again before he's had a chance to find his strength.'

'He'll have to find it on the road,' said Logan, but he briefly met my eyes with something touching sympathy. 'We'll break the journey when we can. I promise.'

There was little point in arguing, I knew, especially since my own father would not take my part.

My father, being wakened, stretched his weary limbs to cure their stiffness, and remarked, 'Well, I for one will trust to

Logan's feelings, since they served him well when he did bring us safely through the Tarras Moss.' He did not even change his mind when, opening his almanac, he found a red 'D' marked beside this day.

I told him, 'There you are. Your Mr Parker thinks you should not travel.'

Hector asked, 'What is the "D" for?'

'Danger,' I said.

But my father qualified, 'I think, my boy, that Mr Parker's warning us there will be danger for us if we linger here, so we should lose no time in leaving.'

Hector seized upon the chance to try persuading Logan once again to let him have a pistol. 'I'd not need to carry it. I'd hang it in a holster on my saddle, same as ye do.'

'No,' said Logan.

'But ye telt us that the Graemes were fair deadly.'

'So they are. But I've no doubt Sir David will persuade them not to shoot ye.' Logan's face was serious, yet when he came to lift me to the pillion, I saw the effort he was taking to conceal his smile. He hadn't fully managed it within his eyes, and when they met my own, I noticed for the first time they weren't purely grey, but were instead shot through with unexpected flecks of pale brown – tiny glints of bronze against the silver.

'What?' he asked me.

'It is nothing.'

But as we started southwards I was thinking of those eyes. They rose unbidden in my mind.

'You seem distracted,' said Sir David.

Sharing a horse with Sir David was different from riding with Logan. For one thing, Sir David talked often and pleasantly. And whether from his own nature or from his long years spent at court, he was finely attuned to the minor moods of those around him, and his eyes missed nothing.

I told him, 'I slept poorly, that is all. I'm over tired.'

He sympathized. 'But I implore you to not fall asleep in the saddle. I know that you managed it on the way down into Langholm, but I can assure you my shoulders aren't nearly as broad as the Messenger's, and if you fall while you're riding with me, he'll not let me reach London alive.' He glanced at me over his shoulder. 'I'll sing to you, if that helps keep you awake.'

'Would that not be more likely to lull me to sleep?'

'Not my singing.'

I laughed. 'And you're wrong about Logan. If I were to fall and be lost on the journey, I doubt he would care at all.'

'Then you'd be gravely mistaken.'

'We have a long history,' I said, 'Andrew Logan and I, and there is little love lost between us.'

'Forgive me,' said Sir David, 'but that's not what I've observed.'

I felt my cheeks flush and it was not from the wind. 'You refer to my behaviour at the blacksmith's house in Langholm, I presume. I can explain. The blacksmith's mother was a pious woman, and while you were seeing to the horses she was telling us – my father and myself – a lively story of the travellers she turned away last week. A lady and two male companions. An unmarried lady,' I said.

'Ah,' Sir David said.

'Exactly that. The blacksmith's mother had most strong opinions on the morals of unmarried women who did travel in the company of men. And so you see why I behaved the way I did with Logan.'

'Yes, of course. And he did not deny you. That was very gallant.'

I supposed it was. 'Yes.' I had not foreseen the blacksmith's offer of the bed, and Logan could have made that difficult as well, but he had not.

Sir David asked, 'This long history you share – where did it have its start?'

His tone was conversational, not prying, and for that I did not mind trying to sift back through my memories for the answer.

'The first summer that the king came down from Scotland.'

'So ten years ago. You both would have been young.'

'I was fourteen. Logan was two years older. We disliked each other at first sight.'

But even as I spoke the words, they didn't have the ring of truth. He had intrigued me at the first – the tall and quiet Scottish boy who'd stood apart from all of us within the Close; who'd nodded so politely to me when I'd passed, and who had seemed a different person when I'd seen him laughing with his sisters. In honesty, I'd been more than intrigued.

How *had* we gone from that beginning to our current state?

Sir David said, 'No doubt he did you some great injury.'

I tried, but while I could recall a number of our arguments, I couldn't think of what began them, other than, 'He did insult a friend of mine at their first meeting.'

'Naturally, to witness such a thing would stir your loyalty.'

'I wasn't there,' I said, 'but I was told . . .' My voice trailed off, as it occurred to me I'd never actually seen Logan being insolent to Valentine, I'd only ever heard about it, and believed the tales. If they weren't true, then I'd done Logan an injustice.

For an instant I felt touched by guilt, but I quickly recovered when I realized Valentine had little cause to tell me lies, while Andrew Logan had been insolent to *me* on more than one occasion.

'Anyway,' I told Sir David, 'you're wrong to think Logan would care if I fell.'

'If you say so,' he said. 'Only I am much older than you. And I'm never wrong.'

We did not have to test the point. I stayed awake, or nearly so, for the remainder of the day. Sir David did not even have to sing.

At length we came into a little town set on the heights, with views of the surrounding hills. The road wound uphill past plain houses shouldered round a church whose steeple rose above them all, a spear of stone against the sky of gathered cloud.

I felt uneasy here, aware of all the eyes that watched us from the shuttered windows, and the woman standing in a doorway further up the street from where she stared at us more openly. It made me feel exposed.

For once, when Logan stopped outside a proper inn, I did not think it a particularly good idea.

When he came to lift me from the mare, I asked, 'Where are we?'

'Alston.'

I clung tightly to the handle of the pillion. 'Perhaps we should go further on, and try to find a farmhouse?'

Logan studied me. 'Your father needs the rest.' His hands closed firmly round my waist, and I had no choice but to let him lift me down, or look a fool. 'And so do you. Ye barely slept, last night.'

It surprised me that he'd noticed. With my feet on the ground, I was forced to look up at him, robbing me of any air of authority. And it had started to rain, lightly. None of my efforts to gather the plaid in the form of a hood helped to keep my face dry, with my chin tilted upwards, though Logan did block a good part of the wind.

He was too close. The woman who stood in her doorway was frowning.

Which were the only reasons I could think of later why I lost my reason altogether. 'I've decided it would serve me well to have you as my husband,' I told Logan.

He looked at me in that impassive way that let me know he thought I'd lost my mind.

I stammered, 'I do mean that we should play the parts of man and wife, not that we should be truly married.' And I summarized the explanation that I'd given to Sir David of why I'd behaved the way I had when we'd stayed with the blacksmith, ending with, 'There may be others who will harbour the same prejudices when it comes to maidens travelling with men.'

He said, 'Ye may be right.'

And then he did a thing I found astonishing – with both his hands, he carefully unwrapped the plaid I'd tangled round my head and shoulders, and re-wrapped it deftly so it shielded me from both the wind and rain, and tucked its folds in expertly so that the whole stayed fastened.

When he met the question in my eyes, he said, 'No Scotsman would neglect his wife's well-being in such weather.'

Then he turned and, just like always, Logan took the last word with him, while I stood and watched his back and couldn't find one thing to say.

I hadn't expected his touch to be gentle. It was so at odds with his size and his rough nature and with the force with which we'd always clashed, and it caught me so unawares and off my guard that I still felt off balance that night after supper. My father, who'd taken the chair at the small table next to me close to the fireplace of our lodgings' parlour, guessed the cause of my silence.

'What has he done this time?' he asked.

'Who?'

My father glanced up once, but meaningfully, from his work on his papers. 'Young Logan. Or should I more properly say, your new husband? I must confess, I did not think to have gained a new son on this journey, and all of it done with no need of a dowry.'

'I'm glad that you find it amusing.'

'I do. I agree with your purpose, of course, in the pretence, but watching the two of you carry it out can be quite entertaining. You've had your first newlywed argument, have you?'

'No.' I didn't choose to enlighten him further. Instead I leaned closer to study the pages that he'd started work upon. 'What are you writing?'

'Sir David's account of his meeting with Prince Henry at Stirling Castle. The one he related to us at the Roman wall.'

'Surely,' I said, 'he was telling that story to Hector? That can't be of interest to anyone else.'

But my father did not cease his writing. 'My orders, directly from my lord Northampton, are to keep a record of whatever Sir David says on our journey to London. It isn't for me to decide what parts might be of interest to those who will judge him.'

'But don't you think that—?'

'Phoebe.'

There would be no further argument, I knew. I left it there and went to bed. Our lodgings in the inn consisted of two separate bedchambers connected by this parlour, so that, as in Leith, I had a room unto myself for sleeping, while the men all shared the other.

The day had been a long one and my thoughts were tossed and troubled, so I knew the dream would find me, and it did.

I rose, as I had done in Leith, and went into the parlour, wanting only to be free of the confinement of the bedchamber. And, as in Leith, I found that I was not alone.

This time, Logan was not lurking in the shadows. He had left a candle burning and was standing by the window, looking out.

Surprised, I asked, 'Are not you worried Patrick Graeme and his men will see you?'

He shook his head slowly, without turning round. 'No. He isn't behind us the now.'

'But you said—'

'Aye, I ken what I said. He was nearly on top of us, so if he chose not to follow us down from the Roman wall, he had a strategy.' Logan turned then, and I saw the frustration writ plain on his features. 'He's cunning, the Laird of Inchbrakie. He couldn't have missed our trail. Not with the five of us riding, he couldn't have. He thinks to cut us off.' I'd never heard this tone in Logan's voice. It sounded almost like defeat. 'He thinks to get ahead of us and lie in wait and cut us off. And I've lost the advantage.'

I suspected he was talking more to himself than to me, and that my presence in the room made little difference to him, but I felt the strangest need to try to reassure him.

'Were I to place a wager, I'd still place it upon you to bring us safely through whatever bars our path,' I said. 'You are a match for any cunning laird.'

His eyebrows lifted slightly, and he took so long to answer that I braced myself for something mocking, but he only told me, 'Thank you, Phoebe.' Then he paused and turned the subject as though setting a clock's hands to a new time. He asked, 'Was Nicholas one of your brothers?'

Startled, I met Logan's eyes. Behind their grey impassiveness

I saw a kind of cautious curiosity. I nodded. 'Yes. My younger brother.'

Logan said, 'I thought he must be. You did call to him when you were dreaming.'

I nearly disputed this by telling him I never cried out when I dreamt – that I'd been told so many times by my Aunt Agnes and my father, who would know. But then I faltered in my certainty, remembering Aunt Agnes slept most soundly, and my father snored, and Logan, for his faults, was not a liar.

'Did I say aught else?' I asked.

'No.' When he saw my great relief, he added, 'Have no fear, you're not the only one among us plagued by dreams. At least ye only have to see yours when you're sleeping.'

I didn't understand. 'What does that mean?'

'Nothing.' He rubbed the back of his neck with one hand, and turned away again. 'It will be dawn soon. You should try to sleep another hour if you're able to. I'll see nothing disturbs ye.'

He was as good as his word.

When I awoke I discovered the day was a Sunday, and so we could not travel anywhere but the few steps to church.

At home, Great St Bartholomew's Church in our Close saw visitors so often from its placement near the hospital and markets and the fair that it was possible for strangers to both come and leave unnoticed. Here, there was no chance of that. We entered quietly and kept well to the back, yet from the stares and whispers we attracted, I feared that the minister himself might stop his sermon to remark upon our presence. I was grateful for the steady shield of Logan at my side, his back so broad that nothing harmful could get by him, and the instant that the service ended and we stepped outside and once more freely breathed the non-judgemental air, I felt a rush of pure relief.

'If the woman standing just behind you was a witch,' Sir David said to Logan later in the parlour of our lodgings, as we ate the dinner of cold meat and bread sent up to us by the inn's landlord, 'then the both of us are done for. She did stare at us so fiercely that her eyes were bulging, and – no, Hector, don't be frightened. I am not in earnest. She was not a witch. But it does almost make me wish I'd still been in my fetters, for that might have proved so scandalous she would have fallen in a faint.'

I saw the twitch of Logan's mouth. He said, 'If ever ye find yourself missing your fetters, just tell me, and I'll gladly put them back on.'

'You needn't bother. If I feel the need to escape, I'll be certain to give you fair warning.'

He spoke the words lightly, but Hector looked troubled. 'But ye wouldnae try to escape, would ye?'

Sir David gave the boy his whole attention. 'No. I gave my word as a gentleman that I would not, and that means something.'

Hector considered this. 'Do ye have to be a gentleman to give your word?'

Sir David shook his head, and would have answered him, had Logan not stepped in with, 'No, lad. Anyone can do it. But once done, ye have to honour it.'

Sir David seemed to be in full agreement, but his eyes were very calm as they met Logan's cool and wintry gaze, and I thought I glimpsed something at the back of them that made me wonder if Sir David might be thinking, as I was, about his cousin, Patrick Graeme of Inchbrakie, who with all his men was even now somewhere behind us or ahead of us, and riding to the rescue. And I wondered whether gentlemen who gave their word and honoured it considered being rescued to be different from escaping.

Andrew

County Durham, 11th May 1613

THE MARE WAS BEGINNING to favour her near hind leg. Only a little, and had she been human I would have suspected she sought to disguise it, not wishing to show any weakness, for though she was soft she was stubborn.

It was hard work, carrying two people over such hills, and I'd hoped that our Sabbath at Alston would give her some rest. She had travelled well yesterday, and she'd been sound when we'd set forth this morning from Stanhope, but now she was showing this change in her gait.

I'd had hopes we'd reach Durham by evening, but I wouldn't ruin a good horse to do it. Besides, in the few hours since midday the clouds had been darkening over our heads, and the wind bore the scent of a coming storm.

Westaway, who had been riding at my side the past few miles, must have observed some change in my expression, for he said, 'You needn't stop on my behalf. I am not tired.'

I smiled. 'I see that ye are not. But that is gaining strength.' I nodded to the mass of deep grey clouds in the northeast. 'We should seek shelter. Brancepeth Castle lies not far beyond those trees.'

'And will its owner give us entry?'

'Aye,' I said. 'Its owner is the king, and I am one of the king's Messengers.'

Westaway appeared confused. 'But I thought you were trying to conceal that fact. For surely, Patrick Graeme—'

'—has not been this way,' I finished for him. 'Graeme has

gone round another way, and seeks to cut us off, but that does mean he'll not have spread his lies here, and there's none who will be looking for a fugitive who's dressing as a Messenger.'

'You hope.'

'There's but one way to test my faith.' Dismounting, I undid the straps of my portmanteau and retrieved my scarlet livery.

Sir David drew the mare to a smooth halt a few feet distant. 'What *are* you doing?'

'What does it look like?' To Phoebe, I added, 'Ye'll want to turn that way, and watch those hills. Aye, like that.'

Sir David said, 'Yes, I see what you're doing, but why?'

'There's a storm coming. Your cousin Patrick is still on the hunt for us. We need a place we can stop that is safe and defensible, and Brancepeth Castle is both. But they'll not be admitting us without the proper authority.' I'd only worn the blacksmith's father's jerkin for five days, but already it felt strange to take it off and don my scarlet doublet, and in truth I wasn't sure which suit of clothing felt more natural.

Hector asked, 'Should I wear my red shirt, too?'

'No,' I told him, then, seeing his face fall, I cushioned that with, 'Best to wait first and see how we're welcomed.'

I'd not been to Brancepeth for years. The castle was well situated, flanked by wooded game parks where the bluebells were still making an impressive show beneath the trees. Its builders had wisely set it on the edge of a plateau, where the land fell away to the south and a broad stream – or beck, as they called it in this part of England – provided a natural moat on two sides, meaning no one could access it simply except through the village, which had been laid out in two straight rows of cottages facing each another like sentinels, all down the road to the castle.

Imposing behind its high stone wall and gate, Brancepeth

Castle revealed little more than the tops of its staggered rectangular towers upon first approach, leaden roofs and pale stone blending well with the grey, inhospitable skies. At its back, the square tower of an old church rose from the trees as a rearguard.

The Graemes would not find it easy to come at us here.

First, though, we'd have to gain entry – a privilege the guard at the portcullis gate seemed reluctant to grant.

He was near to my own age, a half a head shorter, and rougher in manners and speech. I'd met countless versions of him in my lifetime, most often in taverns and alleys, all men long accustomed to being the biggest and strongest wherever they went, and in using that to their advantage. They didn't like having the tables turned, found it unsettling, and struck back however they could.

This guard, who apparently had the sense not to try striking me physically, launched an attack on my patience. He asked for my name, and the name of the town we'd just come from, and whether all five of us came from the court of King James – and, though I'd heard it said many times God hates a liar, I thought it would speed things along if I telt the guard aye, we all came from the court. And so that was my answer.

But when the guard drew himself up, high and mighty, and said, 'I'll be seeing your warrant, then,' I wasn't having it.

Leaning in close to the portcullis bars, I tapped once, firmly, on the royal coat of arms embroidered on my chest in gold. '*This* is my warrant, lad,' I told him. 'When ye see that, ye open this gate, ye hear? Else ye will have the king to reckon with, and he's not such an even-tempered man as me.'

My sisters often told me when I spoke like that, when I went calm, I could be more intimidating than if I had raised my voice. I'd not have thought this guard could be intimidated, but he raised the gate.

He lowered his eyes, too, as we passed, but not before I'd seen in them a flash of fear. That, too, was unexpected. I'd allow my tone of voice and words might make the guard feel irritated. Apprehensive, even. But afraid? No. Something else lay at the back of that.

Nor was it confined to the guard. We came through the portcullis into a broad courtyard in the shape of a great octagon, with extra angles where the castle's southern towers faced us, shielded by the high stone curtain wall to one side and the lesser towers and stables on the other. And as one of the grooms came across to help us with the horses, I could see the same fear touch his features, too.

The groom looked quickly to the guard for reassurance, but the guard spoke sharply to him. 'Give our guests assistance. See their horses are well stabled. I must go,' he said, 'to fetch the constable.'

Westaway, at least, seemed pleased with our new situation. At the stable door, he eased himself down from the gelding's saddle with a sigh of satisfaction, looking round the spacious courtyard. 'Well,' he said, and scanned the sky, 'at least we will be safe here from the storm.'

I suspected we had stumbled unawares into a different sort of tempest, so I sent him a tight smile but said nothing, for I couldn't have in honesty agreed with him. And God *does* hate a liar.

DAVID

Brancepeth Castle, County Durham, 11th May 1613

ONE NEVER GOT USED to the cold. While the wind outdoors had a raw bite to it, still when he ducked through the door of the castle and entered the stone world beyond, the chill cut through him instantly, straight to his bones.

Phoebe Westaway was evidently feeling the effects of it that evening when they gathered downstairs for their meal. She wore her plaid wrapped round her – she had learned to fold it properly, he noticed – and in spite of that, she shivered. She wasn't a creature of court, he recalled. She was used to more homely surroundings. He sent her a brief smile of sympathy.

'Old walls,' he explained. 'They do keep out invaders, but also the sunlight.'

If her chamber was like theirs upstairs, it very likely had high ceilings and tall windows but a most indifferent fire, which hardly helped. The Messenger watched her in silence for a moment before rising from his seat to heap more coals upon the fire at the far end of this dining room. It would have no effect but was a gallant gesture, all the same. David wondered if she noticed.

They were waiting for the constable who kept this castle for the king. His servants made apologies. He'd been delayed, they said, but he had ordered that his guests be given every comfort in his absence. No, they couldn't say exactly when he might appear ... but, just upon the bye, *how* long did David and his friends intend to stay?

It amused him, while they spoke, to watch the Messenger. The big man was no fool, though either from his time at court or simply from his nature he had learned the way to keep his thoughts well shuttered while he took the details that he needed and gave none away.

To that last question, the Messenger merely said, 'I cannot speak of the king's business.'

And the servant who had asked retreated with, 'Of course not, no, 'twould not be proper. Do forgive me.'

'But,' the Messenger said, lowering his voice, 'my orders are to take the time I need.'

The servant, looking troubled, nearly dropped the plate he carried, and the Messenger took note of this before returning calmly to his meal. He must have felt David's gaze upon him for he met it, all in innocence.

David let him know he knew his game, and turned instead to Phoebe Westaway. 'My dear, you're looking every inch a Highland lass this evening, in your plaid.'

She smiled ruefully. 'I fear that it is not the height of fashion.'

'Nonsense. It becomes you well. And anyway, what use is fashion if it lets you freeze?' He helped himself to bread and passed the plate. 'My grandmother was the daughter of the Earl of Montrose, and even she wasn't too proud to wear her plaid when she felt cold. She'd certainly have worn it in here.'

Phoebe thought that very wise. 'I do not envy those who live their lives in castles.'

In surprise, her father looked up from his food. 'But one day, you will live in one yourself. You'll learn to like it, I assure you.'

Hector said, '*I* like it. If I lived in such a place, I'd never leave.'

He'll never let me leave.

In David's memory those words rang as clearly as they had the day the prince first spoke them, and the boy seemed to be facing him again, if briefly, with that stubborn stance, his chin held high, the sadness in his eyes a thing that pierced the heart. Prince Henry had been younger, on that day, than Hector – barely nine years old, but already grown used to disappointment.

You'll see. He'll find a way to keep me here for ever.

David angled his gaze down so he'd not have to hold those phantom eyes, and answered Hector in an idle tone, 'You may feel differently, in time. Would not you wish to see the world?'

'I see it every day,' said Hector.

'Ah, but if you never left this castle, then you'd have to be content to view things only through your window, and not live them for yourself,' he pointed out. 'You'd nevermore be free to wander through the hills, nor ride your horse along the road, nor see the ships sail out of Leith to places far beyond the sea.'

He clearly hadn't thought of that. He frowned. 'Well,' Hector said, 'I'd leave the castle *sometimes*.'

Westaway, across the table, looked at David keenly. 'Did Prince Henry ever feel the castles he was living in were cages?'

He was careful with his answer, mindful always of the fact that all he said was being written down. 'I could not tell you.'

'But it must have been a grand adventure for him to leave Stirling, finally, when the Queen of England died and King James brought his family south to claim the throne.'

'A great adventure, aye.'

Undaunted, Westaway tried prodding David into telling more. 'His mother came to fetch him for the journey, did she not?'

That detail was no secret. In some circles, it was infamous. 'She did.'

He might have carried on indefinitely in this manner, had not Hector asked, 'Did ye travel with him?'

Because then it was a simple thing to tell him truthfully, 'Aye, lad, I did.' And David found that he could steer the conversation to the rush of preparations for that royal progress south ten years ago, and find the small and funny things to tell him, and the grand ones, and he didn't have to mention all the tense and bitter days of conflict leading to the moment of their leaving.

Those were private memories, not for sharing. Of the people who'd been party to them, two were in their graves. And one would hold their conversations secret till she was in hers. So he could do no less.

But he remembered, every word.

Stirling Castle, Scotland, 7th May 1603

The hazards of having his pallet bed placed on the floor at the foot of the prince's bed were sharply brought into focus at first light when two energetic feet landed in a running leap close beside his head.

'David!' Prince Henry was already past him and pressed to the window that looked to the east. 'Do you hear that?'

Fully awake, David rolled to his back. Rubbed his eyes with one hand in an effort to focus. He heard nothing, but, 'Is it a choir of angels? Have I died?'

'No.'

'Ah. Did Master Newton finally fire a cannon so you'd not sleep late and miss your lessons?'

'No, David, come and *see.*' A lad nine years of age could have surprising strength, he'd learned. While the prince didn't exactly haul him upright, he did make it impossible for David to remain abed. Obligingly, David stood and joined the prince at the window. He did hear it now, far off as yet, but growing nearer, sounding very like . . .

Prince Henry said, excited, 'It's my mother.'

David thought that most unlikely, since the queen had not been here for . . . was it four years, now, or five? Not only had she been denied the keeping of her son but the king's rules for how she might have access to him, even for brief visits, made her feel unwelcome here, and even a queen's pride had limits.

Still, the sound he heard now of a multitude of wheels and riders on the road did have the chaos – and the grandeur – of a royal progress.

From the door that gave into the presence chamber came an urgent knock, and the prince's tutor, Adam Newton, slipped into the room and closed the door with care behind him. He looked agitated. 'It's the queen.'

Prince Henry sent David such a look of royal vindication, even standing in nightclothes, that David could not keep from smiling through his worry.

'Aye,' David told him, 'you were right, you're very clever.'

Newton glanced from one face to the other, and a light of understanding crossed his features as he focused on his pupil. 'Pray, what did you tell your mother in your letter?'

This was news to David. He asked the prince, 'You wrote to her?'

'He did indeed,' said Newton. 'To congratulate her, so he claimed, and I allowed it, since he'd also written such a letter to his father.'

That letter David had read, just as he'd read the letter the prince had received from the king. A month ago, this had been – at the beginning of April, not long after news had come north of the death of the English queen, and with it an invitation from the English parliament for King James to come south to sit upon the English throne and rule the whole of Britain.

It had fair broken David's heart to watch the prince's face

then as he'd read his father's letter and discovered that the king had gone, and had not even come to say farewell.

King James had enclosed a book he'd written, entitled the *Basilikon Doron* – meaning 'royal gift', in Greek – and styled as a letter instructing his son how to best be a king. The fact that he'd just had it printed, and in common English, not Latin, inclined David to think the king was aiming his words at a much wider audience, hoping to gain the approval of his newest subjects.

Adam Newton was including it with Henry's lessons, else it might have gone unread on Henry's shelves.

The young prince faced them both now with defiance. 'I may write to whom I please.'

His tutor said, ''Tis true, you may. But when you are a prince of Scotland, you must mind the company you keep, for your own safety. In the past two hundred years, this country hasn't crowned a king – or queen – who wasn't still a child, and then those children lived in constant danger. Ask your father,' he suggested. 'He was one of them. He suffered through the intrigues and the kidnappings by men who'd stop at nothing for a chance to be the regent and to rule the country till he came of age. The king would spare you that.'

'By keeping me a prisoner.'

The tutor sighed. 'Your Highness, you are not—'

'I know the history of my country, Master Newton,' said the prince. 'You've taught me well. How many of those children gained the throne because their fathers died by violence?' Newton did not give the answer, so the prince supplied it. 'All but one. My father knows this, too, I can assure you.' Looking from the tutor's face to David's, he asked, 'And in that book of kind advice he sent me, do you think he warns that when a king has children, they should be locked up so that they can't be used by those who seek to overthrow the father?'

He was speaking wisdom far beyond his tender years, and yet the pain that David saw within his eyes was still a young lad's pain – the loneliness of one who craved a parent's love, and family.

David could not fill that void, but neither could he stand and watch the prince in pain and not give comfort. Reaching out, he placed his hand upon the prince's shoulder, reassuring.

'He does love you,' David said.

'Perhaps,' the prince said. 'But he'll never let me leave. You'll see. He'll find a way to keep me here.'

And then he crumpled altogether, no longer the prince, but just a lad with all the world against him, and screwed his eyes tight shut and briefly leaned his head on David's heart, as he had done when he was small, before he straightened once again.

'I must get dressed,' he said, 'to greet my mother.'

They'd reached an impasse. Outside Stirling Castle's walls, the queen and her attendants held their ground and waited and would not retreat, while David's cousin's wife and her supporters, who'd been left to guard the castle, kept their own position just as firmly.

Since the death of David's aunt at the beginning of the year, his cousin's wife was now the sole Countess of Mar, and she'd assumed that mantle with its full authority. Her husband, being earl, was riding south now with the king to London, but he'd left her strict instructions.

'You were there,' the countess said to David. 'He was very clear. The prince must bide here and must not be given to his mother. That is what the king decrees. We cannot disobey the king.' She looked to David for agreement. David, walking at her side in the small gallery that joined the prince's presence chamber to the great hall, answered with a noncommittal noise that seemed to satisfy her, for she told him, 'Yet the queen demands that we deliver her the prince, and she will not stir until we bring him to her.' With a sigh, the countess held a pale hand to her forehead. 'She's with child, you know. This makes me seem the villain.'

David offered, 'Shall I speak to her? I realize I have not your rank, but she has sometimes shown me favour.'

'At this point, I'm ready to send out the gardener,' the countess admitted. 'I'm weary of playing the diplomat.'

David was not sure his efforts would yield any greater return than the gardener's might have, but he had his own reasons for wishing to see the queen.

She looked more tired than he remembered, which might simply have been from her ride, or from the fact she was with child, or from the sheer frustration of her present situation. While the queen was younger than he was by seven years, today she looked a good deal older, and David felt sorry for her. Even so, she held herself with dignity and grace upon the high seat of her coach as he approached across the grass.

He bowed. 'Your Majesty.'

She didn't miss the significance of his black serge doublet. 'It suits you,' she said, 'this . . . you'll forgive me, I forget the word you Scots use for your mourning clothes.'

'A dulle.'

'Just so. Black does become you.'

David faintly smiled. 'I'm told I have a melancholy face.'

'But not around the eyes,' the queen said, almost absently. Then, 'This is for your aunt, yes? The old countess.'

'Aye, Your Majesty.' He didn't expect the queen to offer

condolences. Her dislike for his aunt had been open and mutual.

'You are well bound by blood to these people here at Stirling,' she remarked. Not wasting words, she added, 'They refuse to give my son to me.'

'So I am told, Your Majesty. I'm also told he wrote to you.'

'He did.' Her downward gaze was keen. 'You didn't know.'

He shook his head. 'He kept it secret.'

'I'm surprised,' Queen Anna said. 'I thought you knew his inner heart.'

'There are some corners of the prince's heart that he keeps private,' David said.

'Good.' Anna looked away. 'Let's hope he manages to shield them well. It takes a little piece of you, this life.'

How many pieces of the queen had been surrendered to her royal duties, David couldn't know. She'd borne the king four other children since Prince Henry, all of whom had been removed from her and placed in separate households in the care of others. Two had lived but short lives, breathed their last breaths and been buried. Henry often worried for the health of his surviving brother, Charles, who was reportedly not strong, and of Elizabeth, his sister, whom he longed to know.

The queen was studying him, silently, and seemed to come to a decision. 'Shall I tell you what Prince Henry wrote to me?' Meeting David's eyes, she said, 'He told me, since the king would not be coming any more to see him, he hoped I'd supply that lack with visits of my own, which he did greatly crave because he'd wanted them so long. And that he hoped perhaps by seeing him, I might have greater cause,' she added, quietly, 'to love him.'

David, looking at her, saw her eyes begin to fill. She blinked, and cleared them, and concluded with, 'As if I needed any further reason.'

David took a moment to control his own emotions.

The queen asked him, 'Is he happy?'

David couldn't lie. He simply could not do it. Drawing breath, he told the queen, 'They will not bring Prince Henry out to you, because the king forbids it. They will never disobey the king. But neither can they disobey their queen.'

She frowned. 'You speak in riddles. Be plain.'

'They may not agree to deliver the prince to your keeping, but they can't deny you if you should demand they allow you to enter the castle.'

She stared at him, and he could see hope beginning to chase away some of the weary lines marking her features. She drew herself up straighter on the coach seat, and looked down at him.

'The Earl of Mar is your cousin.'

It wasn't a question, but David replied, 'Aye, Your Majesty.'

'And on whose side are your loyalties?'

Of all the questions the queen could ask David, he found that the simplest to answer. 'I serve your son, Your Majesty.'

Queen Anna looked at him long, then she gave a brief nod and she turned from him, and he was thus dismissed.

What happened after that was widely known, though rarely told without embellishment. Queen Anna had demanded entry to the castle, and of course they'd had to let her in, and once within its walls, she had refused to leave without her son.

There had been arguments, and tears. It had been terrible. The queen had lost the child she carried. Many claimed she played some part in that, as though the strain of the conflict itself were not lethal enough to a bairn in the womb. The king had sent the Earl of Mar himself back north to deal with things. Queen Anna would not treat with him, and in the end, after a flock of letters had flown back and forth by express between queen, king and earl, the whole matter was settled. The prince was by a convoluted chain of hands surrendered to the queen, and they prepared to head to Edinburgh, together with their entourage.

'Everything that happens, happens as it should,' Prince Henry said, the morning they made ready to depart. 'That's what the Emperor Marcus Aurelius says.'

Climbing gingerly onto her seat beside him in the coach, the queen smiled. 'You are studying Marcus Aurelius?'

'Not in the classroom,' he told her. 'But David did find me this book.' From his pocket, he drew the small, leather-bound book that he treasured. 'He says it's a good way to study my Latin, and also to learn ways of living a purposeful life.'

David, working to hold his horse quietly in position beside the coach while they waited for the whole procession to assemble, felt the queen's gaze fall upon him, and he turned his head to meet it, saying, 'He also has the king's book of instruction, Your Majesty.'

'Yes, of course,' Queen Anna said. 'Though this does seem a very special book.'

The prince told her, 'It's very plain. Not like the one that David carries. That one's exceedingly fine. You must see it.'

The queen looked at David expectantly. 'May I?'

There was no refusing the queen, as he'd said. David reached with reluctance into his own pocket and held out the book to her. It was a small volume, tightly bound in red Morocco with gilt decoration, but its true value lay within.

Queen Anna turned the pages with delight, and marvelled at the book's perfection – the Quatrains of Guy de Faur, in

French, but written all by hand, in diverse lettering that rivalled any printer's press. 'Amazing,' she proclaimed it. 'Such a work of art.'

Prince Henry proudly said, 'It is by Esther Inglis. David knows her. He did meet her when he lived in Edinburgh. She came here once, to visit us at Stirling, and she showed me how she shaped her letters so small and so finely, but I could not do them half so well. She said it does take patience.'

With her eyes upon her son, the queen said gently, 'Most things do.' She held the book within her hands and looked at David. 'I would keep this.'

There was nothing he could say to that but, 'It would be my honour.' But he felt the twist of losing something he had valued.

They were nearly ready to depart. All up and down the line of riders there was more activity. The wind caught at an edge of David's cloak and made his horse dance with impatience.

'David!' From the coach, Prince Henry looked at him with glee. 'We're truly going.'

David found a smile. 'Aye, we are.'

Queen Anna turned her head and studied David once again, and he felt sure she knew all the thoughts he was seeking to hide. She said, 'This Esther Inglis, she still lives in Edinburgh?'

David replied, 'Aye, Your Majesty.'

'Such a woman would be welcome at my court in London. I shall see that she does join us there.' She made it clear, from how she spoke, that she did not expect an answer. But as they began their progress, setting Stirling Castle at their backs, Queen Anna, who had lost an unborn bairn and gained a living son, caught David's eyes one final time. 'It takes a little piece of you, this life,' was her reminder. 'Take what happiness you can.'

ANDREW

Brancepeth Castle, County Durham, 12th May 1613

'I REALIZE I'VE SAID THIS already,' Sir David remarked from his seat on the bench in the stables, 'but you truly are in the wrong business.'

I was bent low to the mare's hind leg, with my hands smeared in a sticky blend of dark brown pitch and resin and warm, melted mastic that I was applying as a poultice. She did not yet have the windgalls, but I'd felt the first beginnings of the swellings just above her fetlock that would cause her trouble if I did not give her care.

Absorbed in this, I did not look around. 'Aye, so ye've telt me.'

'You are very good at what you do, but it is clear to anyone with eyes that you are happier with horses than you are when apprehending fugitives like me.'

He was not wrong, but I would not have told him so. Instead I answered him, 'I'm grateful for my place at court.'

'I didn't say you weren't. But if you had the freedom to choose your profession, I doubt you'd choose to wear that scarlet livery.'

I straightened from the mare's leg, reaching for the little jug of oil to cleanse my hands while I looked down the stables' length – the clean and homely warmth of it, with all the horses huddled close. The storm had finally struck this morning, starting with a heavy rain an hour ago, and only a few minutes past, the thunder and the lightning rolled through with a vengeance, but they were now moving off and leaving only wicked wind that battered at the windows, making all within these stables feel even more sheltered. More secure.

This *was* my element. The sort of place where I could very happily begin my every morning, but, 'Which one of us is free?' I asked Sir David.

'A fair point,' he told me. 'Certainly not me.' He watched me while I took the oil jug in hand and, with a rag, bent once again to oil the mare's hooves, then he said, 'Nor yet my brother. His heart's always been within the stables, too.' He smiled. 'I did spend many mornings just like this one, as a lad, at home at Abercairney, watching William with our grooms. He always had opinions on how best to see the horses cared for.'

'He still does,' I told him, and allowed myself to share the smile, if briefly. I had long experience of being on the end of lectures from Sir William Moray.

I'd never heard Sir David laugh. He sounded like his brother. And being here, among the horses, talking lightly and relaxed, it was an easy thing for my mind to turn backwards to the days when I'd worked in the stables at Somerset House, for Sir William.

'Instinct,' he'd told me once, when I was facing a problem with one of the foals, 'is your best guide. The Lord gave you that for a reason, so use it.'

Sir David was saying, 'It got him in trouble, though.'

I must have looked blank, because he explained, 'Sharing his opinion. On our way down from Scotland, the year the king came to the throne. William was the Master of the Queen's Horse then, but there was an Englishman who also wished to have the post, and interfered in how the horses should be managed. William would not hold his tongue, he gave his own opinion, and it came to blows between them, and my brother lost his place.'

I'd heard this tale, and told him so. 'It was unfair. At least the queen did let Sir William have the keeping of her stables, for I'd wager he was right in his opinion.'

'William's always right,' Sir David said.

I heard the echo of his brother's voice then – not from years ago, but from the last time I had faced Sir William, on the day I'd learned I would be heading north to Edinburgh.

'He has done nothing wrong,' he'd told me on that day, his tone as steady as his eyes. 'You'll bring my brother here to London and they'll force him to stand trial for the prince's murder, and they'll judge him as they please, but he is innocent.'

The worst thing was, I *knew* that he was right. I felt it in my bones, but I was caught between my duty and my conscience just as surely as I would be trapped against this stable wall should the mare choose to lean her weight against me now and pin me there.

She did not lean. She arched her head to nudge my shoulder with her nose. She was a Turkish mare, coal black and beautiful, with an elegant head like a Barbary horse and soft eyes that by turn could be stubborn or gentle, and now seemed to hold quiet sympathy.

Straightening once again, I set the oil jug down and asked, irritably, 'Where is Hector? The kitchens aren't that far. It shouldn't take this long to fetch back a bucket of ale.'

Sir David said he did not know. 'Perhaps the servants in the kitchen aren't being cooperative. He's but a lad, he'd not know how to deal with that.'

'I do.' I'd hung my hat upon a peg beside the stable door. I put it on now, so my uniform would have its full effect. Brutus, on the far side of the mare, looked round and glared at me, but I assured him, 'Bide your time, I'll get to ye. And you,' I told Sir David, 'wait here.'

He sat back obligingly, arms folded, but his eyebrows lifted. 'Aren't you worried I'll escape?' It was an idle dare; he didn't mean it. Or at least, I hoped he didn't.

'No,' I said. 'Besides, there's nowhere ye can go that I won't find ye.' As I drew my cloak around me, I looked back. ''Tis as ye said. I'm good at what I do.'

Hector wasn't in the kitchens. No one there had seen him. Half concerned and half ill-tempered, I went back into the rain and sought him in the chamber we'd been given on the first floor of the central tower, but he was not there either. Nor had he been seen by Westaway, who was, as always, busy with his writing.

I was crossing through the hall when I heard voices. They were coming from the old stone stairs that had been carved much like a tunnel through the thickness of the tower's walls, descending from this level to the floor below.

I will admit that when I recognized one voice as Phoebe's, I moved quietly – more quietly, perhaps, than I had cause to. But I did not seek to spy upon them. When I reached the open archway at the stairhead, I made no attempt to hide my presence, and by simply standing there I blocked a good part of the light, yet neither of them noticed.

They sat several steps below me, unaware. The lad was huddled close against the wall, his shoulders hunched, his head supported by his hands, the picture of pure misery.

Phoebe said, 'And anyhow, it won't last long. Storms never do. You'll see. It will be over soon, and you can fetch your – ale, was it?' When Hector nodded, Phoebe asked, 'Is this for you or for the horse?'

She meant that as a quip, to cheer the lad, but Hector was

past being cheered. 'The horses.' And he told her it was for my cordial, and explained how we were going to give it to the mare, and why.

'You do know a great deal about horses, Hector. I'm sure Logan thinks you are invaluable.'

The way he shook his head fair broke my heart. 'He'll think that I'm a coward.'

'Nonsense. Many men fear thunderstorms. You cannot live and not fear something.' Phoebe paused a moment, then as if she wished to prove that point, she said, 'I was once so frightened of the plague I shrank from touching any stranger who might carry it.'

Her words struck deep. I thought of how she had reacted when I had first offered her my hand to try to help her, all those years ago. How she'd recoiled from me, and how I had taken it as personal rejection.

Hector asked, 'How did ye learn tae not be feart?'

She shrugged. 'I grew a little older and I learned that ladies could wear gloves. And then I grew a little braver and I laid the gloves aside. We rarely lose our fears completely, Hector, but you'll find all people have them. They do simply move beyond them.'

Hector thought about this. Then he said, 'Not Logan, though. He isnae feart of anything.'

From where I stood, I couldn't see their faces, but there was a smile in Phoebe's voice when she replied, 'Perhaps not Logan. But he is exceptional.'

For all that it felt wrong to stand and watch them, it yet gave me a warm feeling to hear Phoebe speak of me in such a way. And that warm feeling grew when I saw Phoebe lay an arm of comfort over Hector's shoulder, so the lad could be a child for just that moment.

'You're a brave boy, Hector, honestly,' she told him, with a fond hug, 'to come all this way with us, and on your own. You needn't worry you're not brave. And Logan knows it.'

Stepping back, I made a second entry to the room, and made it loudly, so they'd hear my boots upon the floor. This time, when I reached the arched stairhead, they'd both turned where they were sitting, and were looking up towards me.

'Well done, lad,' I said to Hector. 'I was hoping that ye might have had a minute to look in on Mistress Westaway, to see she was not frightened by the storm.'

Phoebe was quick of mind, and did not need to catch my eyes to understand what I was doing. 'Yes,' she told me, 'Hector did suggest these stairs because they're very quiet, aren't they, Hector?'

Hector, to his credit, though confused at first, was not the sort of lad to tell a total lie. He told me only, 'I was glad tae keep your lady company.'

The stairs were dim, but I could see a tinge of red spread over Phoebe's features and I gathered she was less amused than I was by the choice of Hector's words. I said, 'And I am grateful for it. Though ye might have chosen some place less confined.' I looked at the stone walls with open doubt. 'Are not ye feart of spiders?'

Hector looked astonished. 'No. Are you?'

'I cannot bide the creatures.' Which was partly truth. 'Wee, nasty, crawling beasties.'

Hector looked at Phoebe, whose return glance seemed to say, *You see? What did I tell you?* But when her dark eyes met my own, they shone with quiet gratitude.

I cleared my throat. 'The storm is passing now, so if ye care to come with me and fetch that ale, we'll finish with the horses. I could use an expert pair of hands,' I said, 'to help me.'

'Aye, I'm ready.' Hector rose as though his legs were set on springs, and bounded up the stairs towards me.

As he pushed by me, I asked, 'And will ye be all right now, Mistress Westaway, if we do leave ye here alone?'

Her smile, all on its own, would have cleared off the clouds and made space for the sun, and had I been a lad of Hector's age, it could not have had more of an effect upon me, though I tried to keep that fact well hidden.

She said, 'Thank you, I believe I will.'

Old ghosts are stubborn things, sometimes. They like to linger, and to cling, and cloud our senses. Ducking low, I eased myself down the first few stone stairs so I could hold my hand outstretched to her, to help her to her feet.

I held my breath, I don't know why.

And then, quite naturally, she raised her own hand and I felt it fit warmly into mine, and with great care, as though she had been made of glass, I laid my thumb across her fingers.

Phoebe stood, and as she did, the old ghost fell away from us.

I let it fall, and for the first time in a long time, I had no last words to speak. I helped her to the stairhead, then I nodded and, with Hector at my side and still in silence, took my leave.

The sun was indeed shining when we set out the next morning. The mare's gait was normal, her hind leg improved, but to keep it protected I'd put on a new poultice and wrapped it well with a hose made of woollen cloth.

As I fastened the pillion onto the back of my saddle, Sir David examined the mare with concern. 'Will she carry me still?'

'Aye,' I promised him. 'We'll keep our journeys short for the next few days, and she'll be fine.'

He tilted his head. 'Will that not slow our progress to London?'

Adjusting a strap, I asked, 'And are ye in such a hurry to get there?'

Sir David said nothing at first, but I felt him observing me. Then he said, in a faintly amused tone, 'No. No, I am not.'

I wasn't, either, for various reasons. One of them was seated close behind me as we rode out through the castle gate and made our way along the village street, between the facing rows of houses. And another one was riding to my left.

I cast a sidelong look at Laurence Westaway and wished, not for the first time, that I didn't have the Sight. He looked his own self now, but when he'd greeted me at break of day, I'd seen him in his winding sheet. It had been gathered at his throat.

When it has reached his neck, I heard again my mother telling me, *ye'll ken his time is very close and can be counted then in days.*

He saw me watching him, and smiled. 'A fair day.'

'Aye, it is.'

He said, '"This castle hath a pleasant seat." That's from a play I saw last spring at the Globe Theatre, by the King's Men. They were speaking of a Scottish castle, but it aptly describes Brancepeth.'

I agreed. 'A pity that the constable was not at home.'

'Oh, but he was.' His eyes were sly. 'Did not you know? He was the whole time in his tower chamber, hiding from us. Yes, indeed,' he told me, when I looked at him in disbelief. 'I had it from his servant.'

'And ye did not think to tell me?'

'There seemed little point. The reason we were being fed so

well,' he said, 'was to distract us. I had no desire to lose such a delicious distraction.' He looked smug. 'And anyway, the constable was never going to show himself until we left. He thought the king had sent you to arrest him.'

I could feel my thoughts revolving. 'Why would he think that?'

''Tis difficult to fathom,' agreed Westaway. 'Although his servant told me that the constable is not well liked by many of the villagers, nor by the keepers of the deer parks, who have all accused him of mismanaging the castle for the profit of his friends and of himself. There is apparently some stained glass that was sold without the knowledge of the king, and many deer were shot and taken from the parks. And there were other issues. Letters have been written.' With a face that was all innocence, he added, 'That was how his servant came to speak to me, in fact. He noticed I was writing, and he wondered whether it was a report, you see, intended for the king.'

He looked so virtuous I could not help but be suspicious. 'And what did ye tell him?'

Westaway said calmly, 'Well, my boy, you know I do not like to tell a lie. I told him yes, it was.' His mask slipped briefly when his eyes met mine. They showed their mischief. 'That was quite a tender leg of mutton they did serve us yesterday at dinner, was it not? And that French claret was impeccable.'

Of course I laughed, but it was laughter tempered with a sense of loss, for Westaway would not be coming home with us, and I knew that without him, home would never be the same.

A little beyond Brancepeth, in the shelter of the forest, I once more took off my scarlet doublet and put on the blacksmith's father's clothes.

Sir David said, 'It's like being back at court, with all the masques and costume changes.'

From Brutus's saddle, I sent him a dry look. 'Ye may blame your cousin Patrick for the spectacle. We'll be upon a more well-travelled road, and he may well have gone ahead of us and spread his lies. 'Tis safer for us all if I'm not seen to be a Messenger.'

Behind me, Phoebe took a firm hold of my belt. 'And are we then . . . are you and I . . . ?'

I knew what she was asking me, and told her, 'Aye, we're married.' Which was not, perhaps, the gallant way to say it, but she knew exactly what I meant, as did the others.

Still, Sir David drily commented, 'A rare and easy way to win a bride.'

'Indeed,' said Westaway. 'I had to woo my wife for years before she finally married me.'

I'd never heard him speak of Phoebe's mother and he didn't say more now, but he stayed in good spirits all the day. To give him rest, I kept my word, and kept our journey short. We came to Darlington by dinnertime, and stopped there, and we took our time in starting the next morning.

This day's ride was not overlong, either. I took them south by the old road that for time out of mind had carried merchants, travellers, and Messengers like me from London through York into Scotland, or the other way around.

It was a busy road and showed the wear of it. We passed three people heading north, and were ourselves passed by a merchant's wagon heading south that left deep wheel ruts in the softened ground when it had gone from view. The rain we'd had two days ago at Brancepeth must have fallen here as well, because the ground was muddy still in places, and I had to veer the horses off the road from time to time so they could find a solid footing.

From the sky and wind, I felt convinced we'd have more rain that afternoon, for it was low and full of cloud and threatening. Sir David turned the hood of his dark cloak up in anticipation of it, but beside me, Westaway stayed cheerful.

'You're both worrying for nothing,' he assured us. 'I consulted with my almanac, and it assures me that the weather will continue clear and fine now until after Whitsuntide.'

I put less faith in what the movements of the stars and planets might foretell, but just then I was more concerned with the lone rider coming for us at a reckless gallop.

I'd not let my guard down that completely, and my hand was at the holster of my pistol on the saddle afore I saw that the rider wore the clothing of an age long past, and that his jacket and his horse were streaked in blood.

Afore I saw his eyes.

'Turn back!' the wraith implored me as he went by, heading for the north. 'Turn back! The battle has been lost.'

His voice was Scottish, meaning we most likely were a few miles to the north now of Northallerton, where anciently the Battle of the Standard had resulted in a great loss of my countrymen. I glanced behind. The wraith was gone, his horse's hooves leaving no imprints on the ground to mark their passing.

But my momentary lapse of concentration meant that Brutus lost his footing for an instant and he stumbled on the muddy road, and Phoebe's hands on instinct quickly let go of my belt and caught hold of my body, clinging firmly to my sides. I offered no complaint, although I reassured both her and Brutus as we walked on.

'There. I see a patch of blue.' Westaway, scanning the sky with its swift-running clouds, smiled and looked at me. 'Did I not say you were worried for nothing?'

But I wasn't looking at him. Past his shoulder, across the wide slope of the field to the side of the road, I saw several more riders on horseback approaching at speed. These were wraiths, too – their clothes were the same as the one who'd just passed us, their hair just as wild, and their weapons as heavy. I knew they would fade, just as he had.

But Phoebe pressed close at my back, her hands gripping my waist, and she asked in an urgent voice, 'Can we outrun them?'

And I realized this was my vision – the one I had Seen in the stables at home. Except Phoebe was Seeing the wraiths, just as I was.

I'd heard of this happening. My mother told me that those in the Western Isles who had the Sight could share their visions by their touch. That my own grandfather – her father – sometimes shared with her the things that he was Seeing. But I'd never tried to do it. This was new to my experience.

The wraiths, still half a field from us, lost substance and were taken by the wind.

'Outrun who?' I asked her, calmly, although inside I felt anything but calm.

It was unkind of me, I knew, to make her doubt what she'd just seen with her own eyes, but better that than having to explain the truth in front of everyone, and thus expose myself to all the penalties of witchcraft.

She fell quiet with confusion. Then, 'Forgive me, my mind shows me phantoms.'

'There are no such things,' said her father. 'You must have been sleeping.'

She didn't answer him, and seeking to atone for my denial of the truth, I said, 'Well, if there were such things as phantoms, they'd be thick upon the ground here, for this is a battlefield of note.'

Phoebe sounded encouraged. 'Is it?'

'Oh, aye. No doubt Sir David kens the history better than myself.'

He did, and kept us all regaled with a brave telling of the Battle of the Standard for the last few miles as we came to Northallerton. It was a vibrant market town, and well laid out for travellers. I stopped where I had lodged the last time I'd been here – the house owned by the Metcalfe family, opposite the church, since being cousins to the king, they could be counted on to lend support and loyalty.

The one great advantage to being my size was that people, once meeting me, didn't forget me.

'Young Logan! Well met,' Metcalfe greeted me warmly. 'And this beautiful lady is . . . ?'

'My wife,' I said, not thinking how that might complicate things on my travels this way in the future. 'Her father, and two of our friends. We are on the king's business. We'll need to have lodging the night, and the use of your stables.'

'Of course.'

Mistress Metcalfe's cook was excellent, and she herself was as attentive a hostess as her husband was an indulgent host. In such a home, warmed by the talk and the food and the company, with the clean, lime-washed ceiling and walls and the perfectly swept, polished floors and the windows that sent back the gleams of the candlelight, it would be easy for me to relax.

But a part of me stayed on alert, and I heard the sharp fall of the footsteps outside in the street afore the first knock came at the door.

Metcalfe rose to investigate. Coming back into the dining room, he told me, 'Logan, it is Granville, landlord of the Fleece, one of our local inns. He begs your leave to have a word with you.'

'Then ask him in.'

'He'd rather not,' said Metcalfe.

Not a sign that promised well. I stood and went to meet my mystery caller.

Granville of the Fleece was a congenial man who looked as though he'd rather have been anywhere just now than on this doorstep giving me his message.

'Beg your pardon, sir, but I've a gentleman who's staying with me, who has lately come with several members of his family.' Here he paused, and coughed. 'They are most keen to see their cousin.'

Graeme, damn him. My hand itched to lay itself upon my sword, and I tried not to look into the semi-darkness that was settling now upon the street, for I felt sure that he'd be watching from a window.

Granville said, 'This gentleman requests that you allow his cousin to come join them.'

'And if I refuse?'

The landlord of the Fleece appeared uneasy. 'Then he'll come and pay his compliments himself, sir, though he fears that you may find his tone too rough.'

A peal of laughter sounded from the dining room within the house, and I heard Hector's boyish tones rise over all, delighted.

Granville asked, 'What answer shall I give him, sir?'

From just behind my shoulder in the dimness of the entryway, Sir David said, 'Tell him I'll come.'

I half turned, and he parried my cold stare with his impassive one.

'Ye'll tell him no such thing,' I said to Granville.

Calm, Sir David held my gaze. 'I know my cousin. You do not. Think of the lad,' he told me. 'And the others. Think of her.'

I hesitated, and he took advantage of that moment, looking past me once again to Granville.

'Tell him I will come,' Sir David told the landlord of the Fleece, with full conviction.

Granville nodded. 'Very good, sir.' And with obvious relief, he turned and hurried off along the road towards his inn.

Sir David's glance was meant to signify that I still blocked the door. He said, 'I've given you my word that I will not escape.'

'Ye didn't give your word ye'd not be kidnapped. D'ye think he'll let ye stroll out of the Fleece once he has got ye safely in his hands?'

'It isn't up to Patrick what I do. Do you not trust me?'

'No.'

He fixed his hat more firmly on his head and said, 'I'll try not to be wounded by your scathing lack of confidence.' He tilted his head a fraction. 'Do you truly have a scar above your heart thanks to a gentleman who did betray your trust?'

It was a question I had not expected. 'Where did ye hear that?'

He shrugged. 'We did a lot of talking, Mistress Westaway and I, while we were riding. She seemed very keen to make sure that I understood it was no idle thing that you removed my fetters.' With his hat brim properly adjusted, his gaze levelled once more on my own. 'But I already knew that.'

I felt that I was frowning, but I only said, 'I show my scars to no man.'

'Nor do I.' His voice was mild, but there was something of an undertone within it that decided things.

I stepped aside.

'One hour,' I told him, 'or I'm coming after ye.'

'One hour,' he said, and stepped into the street. 'You have my word.'

DAVID

Northallerton, Yorkshire, 15th May 1613

PATRICK GRAEME OF INCHBRAKIE was neither tall nor fierce of feature, but men overlooked him at their peril. At the Fleece, he'd settled in an alcove to the side of the great fireplace, with the low-beamed ceiling overhead, a window to his shoulder, and his booted feet stretched out and crossed before him, drinking wine as one who might, at any moment, start to drowse amid the drifting smoke and conversation. But when he rose to welcome David, six men turned their heads and one half stood, so watchful were they of his moods and movements.

'Easy,' he advised them. 'All is well.' He folded David into a swift, hard embrace. ''Tis good to see ye've not been harmed. Ye had me worried.'

David let his eyes close for the space of half a heartbeat. He'd forgotten, in the time he'd been away, and in these stressful past few days, how good it felt to have the loving touch of family. He allowed himself to lean into the hug before he straightened.

'Granville!' Patrick called the landlord over. 'Drinks all round. My cousin is returned to us.'

One of the men whom David didn't recognize looked disapproving. 'Should we not be on our way now that we have him?'

Patrick held a chair for David. 'There's no rush,' he told the man. 'The Messenger has none to help him but an old man and a lass and a wee lad still wet behind the ears. He kens we have him in the corner. He'll not fight.'

The laughter that met that remark stirred something within

David that he'd not expected. Something that surprised him – an instinctive urge to rise to the defence. He took the cup of wine that Granville gave him and cut through the laughter with, 'That is no common Messenger. That's Andrew Logan.'

Patrick raised his eyebrows slightly. 'The one William speaks of?'

'Aye, the very same.'

'Well, that explains much,' Patrick said. 'I expected to have ye in hand long afore this, but he was fair sharp, for a Messenger. It was like chasing a clever stag who seeks to tire the hounds.' He glanced at David like a man who, having finished with a game, desired to replay its moves. 'How close were we to you at Langholm?'

'Very close.'

'I had a sense we were.'

'Aye.' David smiled briefly at the recollection. 'So did Logan.'

Patrick eyed him strangely. 'Anyway, we'll rest here the night, then at first light we'll ride to the coast. I've a ship that will carry us both to the continent.'

'Patrick.'

'It can't be France, of course. They have their spies there. But William thought Italy might—'

'Patrick,' David said, quietly.

'Aye?'

'I must go back.'

'Back to Scotland?' Patrick shot down the suggestion. 'There's no safety there for ye, not even to the north.'

'Not back to Scotland.' Looking steadily at Patrick, David sought to make his meaning clear. 'I gave my word.'

'To a Messenger?' Patrick scoffed. 'No man is bound by the promise he makes at the point of a blade.'

'I was not forced. I gave my word freely.'

His cousin, tight-lipped, exhaled the brief sigh that had always betrayed his frustration with hard knots and difficult puzzles and stubborn men. David knew Patrick was gathering patience.

'And what,' Patrick asked, 'did ye promise?'

'The first time? That I'd not escape.'

'But ye're not escaping, are ye?' Patrick said. 'Ye're being rescued. So ye can rest easy in your mind.'

David smiled faintly. If they'd found him several days ago, if they had come upon him at the Roman wall, he likely would have gone with them, and used that very reasoning to ease his conscience.

But that had been before his rides with Phoebe Westaway, when he'd learned more of herself and of her father; and before he'd started looking forward to the daily stream of Hector's questions, which reminded him of . . . well, it was familiar.

David said, ''Tis not that easy, Patrick, for tonight I also gave my word that I'd return within the hour.'

His cousin thought a moment, then he gave a nod. 'And so ye shall. With me and all my men behind ye.'

David shook his head. 'I cannot let you do that.' He knew in strength he'd never been a match for Patrick, nor in cunning, and there was a chance that Patrick might yet simply knock him senseless and be done with the debate, but they had always shared a bond of deep respect and love for one another, and he trusted that it would survive this test.

His cousin stared at him. 'Ye've lost your mind. Ye ken that it's a trap the king has laid for ye in London?'

David nodded.

'And he does not mean to let ye live.'

'I know it.'

'But because ye gave your word to one who is not worthy of it, ye would choose to walk into that trap.'

'I didn't say that.' David drank his wine. 'I'm not in London yet.' He set his cup down, adding as an afterthought, 'And Logan's worthy.'

Patrick shook his head. 'My brother George was right.'

'Pray, what did George say that was wise?'

'He said I should be careful, for ye might not have the will for living now the prince was dead, and we would both end up without our heads.'

For all it had been fired from a friendly bow, it was a sharper arrowhead that found its mark. 'And what do you think?'

'I begin to think that he was right.' Patrick's frown fell part-way between contemplation and concern, but then it cleared. 'Ah, well,' he said, 'ye've always had a melancholy face. Your head will look well on a pike above the Tower Bridge.' He grinned.

'And yours?' asked David.

'Why?' Patrick raised his eyebrows, all in innocence. 'What wrong have I done?'

'Tried to aid a fugitive from the king's justice.'

'Well.' His cousin shrugged. 'They'll have to catch me first, and I don't wish them luck with that. Have ye time for one more drink within the hour ye've been allotted?'

'I believe so.'

'Good.' As Patrick summoned Granville to refill their cups, he said, ''Tis not the king's men that do worry me. It is your brother William, when he learns I've left ye on the road alone.'

'I'm not alone,' said David.

'Maybe not entirely, but ye've none to guard your back.'

David sat back in his chair and disagreed. 'I have an old man and a lass and a wee lad still wet behind the ears.' He faintly smiled. 'And I have Andrew Logan.'

PHOEBE

Northallerton, Yorkshire, the same night

I KNEW WHAT I HAD seen.

There had been riders in that field – men who'd been galloping towards us with their swords in hand, as though they meant us harm.

The fact that no one else had seen them, and that they had vanished on the wind, did not make them the products of my mind. I knew I'd been awake, I'd not been dreaming. Which meant they'd been, as Logan had suggested, ghosts of men who'd lived in ages past, who'd fought upon that ground and fallen there. And that thought was disturbing.

For if ghosts could haunt a field by day, then where else might they walk?

Alone within my bedchamber, I drew the blankets to my chin and watched the squares of moonlight angling through the room's small window slowly creep across the floor. This was not an old house, it was near to my own age, and yet to-night it seemed as full of creaks and groans as an old woman settling in her bed, and each new noise, however slight, stirred my imagination and chased off all hope of sleep.

The mouse that scuttled in the corner became a phantom skirt. The branch that scraped against the roof tiles was a blade drawn from its scabbard. My own hair against my neck felt like the touch of someone's hand.

'You're too easy to fool, there's no sport in it,' Valentine teased me once.

He was right, I *was* too credulous.

Easing my grip on the blankets, I folded my hands on the top of them, forcing myself to be calm. I'd not thought about Valentine for ... well, for more days than I could remember. I tried to recall his face, but it was like chasing chickens. I couldn't quite grasp it, and others would get in my way.

And when I tried imagining what Valentine might do if he were in my place, that, too, was useless, because I could not imagine Valentine in any of the places where I'd been since leaving London, doing any of the things I'd done.

He was too fond of luxury to eat his meals outdoors and sleep with nothing but a woollen blanket on the cold, rough ground, beneath the stars. And he would have viewed Hector as a servant, and not sat with him upon the stairs to see he was not frightened by a storm.

Which left me wondering if Valentine and I were as alike as I'd always believed we were. When my mind was this full of thoughts, I could do nothing for it but to give it focus. Had we not been in a private home, with our hosts and their family sleeping only walls away, I might have risen from my bed and done as I was wont to do and gone downstairs and walked awhile, or paced within my chamber.

There was something very calming about pacing. Even Logan had surprised me by indulging in it in the hour after supper when Sir David had gone out.

I wasn't certain of all that had happened there. I knew the landlord of the local inn had come to speak with Logan, and Sir David had excused himself and gone to follow them, and Logan had returned alone.

My father, startled, had told Logan, 'But your orders ...' No doubt meant as a reminder of the fact that Logan had instructions not to leave Sir David unattended.

Logan had said, 'All is well,' and his tone had left no more room for argument, but while the rest of us had talked after our meal, he'd walked the room, arranging all the items on the mantelpiece, and straightening the pictures, setting things in order.

He was usually so self-contained and in control, I'd wondered at his restlessness. I'd watched him until he had caught me watching him, and then I'd looked away, perhaps too sharply.

Then Sir David had returned.

He greeted all of us, but his gaze went to Logan first when Mistress Metcalfe asked him if he'd like a glass of sherris sack.

'I thank you,' he said, 'but I have drunk too much wine already.'

Metcalfe asked him, 'Is your business at the Fleece all settled?'

'Aye,' Sir David said, his eyes still locked with Logan's. 'It is finished.' Then he looked at Hector, and at me. 'Sleep well,' he told us. And he went to bed.

Close by the window, Logan had not changed his stance nor his expression, but I'd thought he drew a freer breath than he had drawn since supper. He told Mistress Metcalfe, 'I will take that sack, if it's on offer.'

I should have done likewise. Sherris sack was strong, and made me sleepy. If I'd joined the others in a glass of it, I'd not be here now staring at my ceiling, with each one of my attempts to conjure Valentine erased by the remembrance of a larger man with steel-grey eyes who stood upon the stairs and held his hand outstretched towards me.

I finally took his hand and let my eyes close. He was smiling. 'I'll not let ye fall,' he promised.

And I slept.

Something had altered in the interplay between the men. I felt it the next morning, and I could not help but notice it as we continued heading south the next few days through Yorkshire. I would not have said that Logan had relaxed, but where once he'd clearly been Sir David's jailor, he behaved now more as a custodian, as though the mission weren't to hold the older man a prisoner but simply to safeguard his welfare.

The change was not entirely one-sided.

Five days after that evening in Northallerton, as we were making ready to depart our inn, the Black Bull, in the market square of Doncaster, the landlord offered to pack us a dinner we could take and eat upon the road.

Sir David said, 'That sounds an excellent idea, and most kind. What say you, Logan?'

Logan thought it excellent as well, and paid the landlord, and with Hector, went to make space in the portmanteaus.

But I looked at Sir David.

Quizzically, he asked, 'Is something wrong?'

'You called him by his name, not merely "Messenger".'

'Did I? I must be getting soft.' But he continued to do it. Midway through our journey that day, when the sun sat high overhead, Sir David drew the mare close alongside us and commented, 'Logan, I wonder that you are still wearing your borrowed clothes. Surely, now that we're not being followed, you can wear your own?'

I'd not yet heard this news. I asked, 'We are not being followed?'

Sir David nodded. 'My cousin called off the chase in Northallerton.'

I nudged my hand into Logan's broad back. 'Were you not going to tell us?'

He half turned his head. 'Let's just say I've less faith in his cousin than he does.'

Sir David smiled. 'I think,' he said, 'you like wearing the clothes. They allow you to sample the life of an ordinary man.'

Logan asked, 'Is that right?'

'Aye. The life you gave up when you put on the scarlet.'

This time Logan's head did not bother to turn. 'I'm not sure that I'd call working in the queen's stables an ordinary life.'

'A more settled life, then.'

'Ye think what ye like.'

I knew Logan's tones well enough to know he'd drawn a sharp line under that column of conversation.

My father's voice came from behind us. 'Logan, you will want to feed my daughter soon. She tends to grow short-tempered if she does not get her dinner.'

Logan called back, 'Aye, I've noticed.'

I assured them both that I was fine, and did not need their management. 'I am not hungry yet,' I lied.

'Nevertheless,' said Logan, 'that does look a likely place to stop and have our dinner, there, do not ye think?'

I could not see where he was pointing. 'Where?'

'Just there, ahead of us.'

Sighing, I came back with, 'How I could I possibly see what's ahead? You are built like a tree.'

Logan half turned again, and I saw his raised eyebrow and – so I imagined – the edge of his smile. 'Aye,' he said calmly, ''tis past time we stopped.'

He *did* choose a good place, beneath a spreading sycamore that cast its shade in dappled patterns on the grass and caught the murmur of the wind within its leaves so it became a softly whispered song.

The horses were tethered close by and could graze and converse with each other the way horses do, with their snorts and soft whinneys and shakes of their manes, plainly glad to be able to rest for a short while from carrying us in the warmth of midday.

And in spite of my earlier protest, I felt better, too, after eating. I'd not have admitted as much, though, to Logan. It might have made him feel yet more superior.

He watched me idly for a moment before asking me, 'What kind of tree?'

'I'm sorry?'

'If I'm built like one, there must be some variety ye have in mind.'

My father, smiling, called upon Sir David, who sat leaning with his back against the sycamore, absorbed in the small book that once had been Prince Henry's. 'Does Marcus Aurelius Antoninus have aught to say about trees?'

Glancing up from his reading, Sir David replied, 'He is very fond of fig trees.'

Logan grimaced. 'I've no wish to be a fig tree.'

I know I rolled my eyes. 'I can't imagine that a busy Roman emperor would place any importance upon what tree you – or he – might be like.'

Focused once more on his book, Sir David told us, 'No, indeed. Marcus Aurelius felt that what mattered in life was to keep your words true, your thoughts honourable, and your actions good.' Then he paused, and set his book aside, and looked at Hector. 'That's a maxim you should mark, my lad, for it will serve you well in life, as it did serve the prince.'

Hector was finishing the food that we had left unfinished. 'What's a maxim?'

'Well . . .' Sir David sought a simple definition with the ease of someone who had once been well accustomed to explaining things to children. Or one child, in particular. 'A maxim is a truth. A rule to live by.'

Hector promised he would do his best to live by it. 'But I'm no prince.'

Sir David told him kindly, 'True words, honourable thoughts and good actions aren't the sole domain of those with noble blood, my lad.' For a moment, sitting there against the tree, he seemed to be considering something. 'Let me tell you a story,' he said.

Hector was fond of Sir David's tales. 'Is it another one about the prince?'

'No, not about the prince this time. About a stable lad, a little older than yourself. I've heard it often. It's a tale my brother never tires of telling.'

Logan glanced at him, but didn't interfere.

Sir David said, 'This stable lad, he had a gift with horses. He could tame those none could ride. He knew what ailed them as if they had told him in their language, and he knew the way to cure them. One day, in my brother's view, he might have been a stable master. Maybe even Master of the Horse, as once my brother was. But fate decided differently.'

'What happened?' Hector asked.

'His father died.' Sir David said it plainly, without sentiment but not without compassion.

When I looked at Logan's face, I saw no sign of a reaction there. And yet I knew – of course I knew – the stable lad was him.

Sir David continued, 'His father had been a King's Messenger, one of the best. And he'd asked that his son might be given his place when he died. So the stable lad overnight found his world changed for the worse.'

Hector didn't see how that was possible. 'He was a Messenger.' His tone implied that was surely enough to solve all of life's problems.

'But now he was fatherless,' Sir David said, 'and the head of his family. And shunned by the Messengers with whom he worked, who believed that he did not deserve his position. 'Tis true, that was unfair of them,' he added, when he saw Hector's expression, 'but then life is rarely fair. Nor was it fair that the first mission he was sent on was so dangerous.' He settled his back against the sycamore, gazing out across the fields for a moment as though he were seeking the safe path between Hector's impatience to hear the tale and Logan's tolerance of having it told. Then he said, 'There was no hint of danger, mind, when he was sent. It was only a road, and a bag with a letter and jewel that the king wanted sent to the queen in her progress. Except on this day, there were thieves on that road.'

Hector's eyes grew wide. 'Thieves?'

Sir David assured him, 'Aye. Three hardened brigands, with a fourth friend in the palace who had told them of the jewel, so they knew what road it would travel by, and that it would be carried by a Messenger alone, just twenty-one, and inexperienced. They lay in wait, and ambushed him.'

I tried to close my mind against the picture of the fight that must have taken place upon that road – the three men against Logan, unsuspecting. I had selfishly forgotten many details of that summer. I remembered, though, his mother's face when he'd been carried home. And how the Logans' house had stayed so dark and silent for weeks afterwards.

My father had tried telling me what happened, but I'd had no patience then to hear of anything concerning Logan. Valentine had told me, 'Watch, they'll make a hero of him now. Such men fall upwards through their lives.' And I'd agreed that it was shameful.

Now the only shame I felt was that I'd ever been that person. Had those thoughts.

Sir David told Hector, 'Some people say he was shot by eight pistol balls.'

Logan smiled thinly. 'Some people exaggerate.'

Sir David turned. 'You're familiar with the tale then. Good. How many shots was it?'

I wasn't sure Logan would answer. He measured Sir David for a moment with his quiet gaze. 'I heard it was five.'

My indrawn breath could not be helped, although my hand flew swiftly to my mouth to cover any sound.

Hector was speaking for me, anyway. '*Five* pistol shots!'

Sir David said, 'I do agree that would kill most men, but our stable lad was . . .'

'Built like a tree?' Logan offered.

Sir David was drily amused. 'Am I telling this story?'

'Ye're taking your time with it,' Logan said.

'Our stable lad was determined and brave, and he fought back against those three brigands. He fought for his life. He killed one, overpowered the other two, tied them all three to their horses and, even while wounded so badly, he brought them the rest of the way to the town where the queen was. Delivered the jewel and the king's message, and gave a very poetical speech . . .'

Logan scoffed. 'He said nothing at all. He was all but delirious by then, and couldn't put two words together.'

Sir David said, 'Well, in *my* version, he gave a poetical speech. After he bowed to the queen.'

'Ye must surely mean after he fell from his horse in the marketplace, for that's the last thing that he does recall.'

Hector, who had been watching the two men with growing understanding, finally closed the circle. 'He speaks of you!' he said to Logan. 'You were once a stable lad, like me.'

'I telt ye that already, did I not?'

'Aye, but . . .' He was still trying to make sense of all he'd heard. 'Five pistol shots! Where are they? Can I see the scars?'

Sir David reached a hand to tousle the boy's hair and said, 'I fear, young Hector, that you must die disappointed, for he shows his scars to no man.'

Logan's mouth held its firm line, but I could see his eyes had softened. 'For you, Hector,' he said, 'I'll make an exception. If Mistress Westaway will turn around.'

I turned, not meeting his gaze, more because I had no wish for him to see just how affected I was by the things I'd heard. I could hear him unfasten his doublet and take off his shirt, and I heard Hector counting.

'Five! Just as ye said,' Hector told him, in awe.

'Did ye think I would lie?'

'But what is that one, there?'

Sir David answered, 'That was from a gentleman who broke his word.'

'That,' said Logan, contradicting him, 'is from a lass.'

Hector was horrified. 'She stabbed ye?'

'No, lad. Cupid's arrow struck me hard, in just that spot, the first time I did see her smile. A man will never heal,' said Logan, 'from that kind of wound.'

My father said, 'A pretty tale. Pray, what might be the lady's name?'

'Nay,' Logan said, 'that would be telling.' He was done with the display. I heard the rustle of his shirt, and then he told me I could turn around.

He had his doublet fastened. Still, I did not look above the level of his chin, not even when we'd finished with the dinner and he'd fetched the horse and came to lift me to the pillion, for I did not trust that my emotions would not show.

But as we started south again upon the road I told him, quietly, 'An oak.'

He leaned back slightly in the saddle, angling his head down to hear me better. 'What?'

I cleared my throat. 'You asked what sort of tree you were,' I said, and raised my chin so that my voice would be more sure. 'You are an oak.'

He turned his head a fraction further so that I could almost see his profile, but otherwise he stayed so still I might have thought he held his breath. And then, accepting what I'd said with a short nod I took for thanks, he faced the road again and we rode on.

When we reached our inn that evening at the town of Tuxford, I kept to my chamber, pleading that I had a headache, which was partly true. The perfume of the handkerchief that I still kept within my bodice had been bothering me all the afternoon.

Sitting at the small, round table near the window in my chamber, I drew out the handkerchief and spread it smooth – a square of white lawn edged in ivory silk, with the initials V and F embroidered at one corner in a thread of silver gilt. A token of a man's professed affection. I recalled how lovely I had thought it was when Valentine had placed it in my hand. Now, I only noticed that the scent of it had faded. In a week or two, no more, it would smell unremarkable. Sometimes expensive things were like that – potent, and yet passing.

It was curious, but I found that I could not clearly see his face within my memory. I could hear his words, though. And they did not paint a fetching portrait, for beneath their charm they sounded selfish and unkind.

I turned my thoughts back through the years and saw how I'd allowed those words to colour my own view of Logan, when in truth, if I unravelled everything, like pulling on a thread, I found that at the very start of things he'd done me no true injury, nor offered me an insult, and I could not think where our dispute began.

'Why does he deserve your thoughts?' That was what Valentine had asked me on the morning I'd met Logan at the conduit and we had argued.

Why does he deserve your thoughts?

Because, I wished I'd told him then. *He is the better man.*

Somebody knocked upon my door. I went to answer it. The landlord's daughter, all of seventeen, entered with bread and ale.

'Beg pardon, mistress,' she said, 'but your husband thought you might be hungry.'

It was just like Logan to do something that would prove my point. I had to swallow hard to find my voice. 'I thank you.'

As she moved to set my meal upon the table at the window, her gaze fell upon the handkerchief. 'Oh! That is very beautiful. I've never seen its equal.'

I smiled faintly. 'Would you like it?'

'Me?' She looked astonished. 'I could never—'

'Truly, I insist.' I took the handkerchief and folded it and placed it in her hand, closing her fingers round it just as Valentine had done with mine. 'Take it,' I told her, 'as a gift.'

Take it, he'd said to me. *Mayhap when you come home, I'll have a gift for you of greater worth.*

Except I had discovered that, much like the man who gave it to me, it had very little worth at all.

As a little girl, I had looked forward to Whitsunday for, to me, it always marked the start of summer, with a whole week of festivities to follow. There would be a fair, and brand new clothes to wear, and singing and processions. For adults, it might simply be a holiday. For children, it was magical.

I saw that magic now reflected in the way that Hector stared so longingly at all the decorations that were being set up in the market square outside our lodgings. Having now arrived in Nottinghamshire, we were taking rooms at the White Hart at Newark. If one could believe its landlord, the White Hart had ruled its corner of the marketplace for some two centuries or more – its timbers straight despite their age, three storeys tall beneath a smartly tiled roof. At ground level, a square-walled, covered passageway cut through the building, leading to the cobbled courtyard just behind that serviced the inn's stables. And above the passageway, a small army of plasterwork figures set in separate niches stood along the bottom of the gallery, watched over by the inn's bright, painted sign.

Hector liked that sign, and said so while we stood beneath it in the doorway of the inn, waiting for Logan and the landlord to conclude their business. 'But,' Hector asked, squinting upwards, 'why does the deer wear a gold crown round its neck?'

My father said it showed the creature's connection to royalty. 'King Richard the Second, who ruled many years ago, chose the white hart as his badge – as his personal emblem.'

'Why?'

'The white hart means peace,' said my father. 'And King Richard wanted his people to know that his reign would be peaceful. He was the son of a very great soldier, the Black Prince, well known for his wars, but King Richard had no wish to be like his father.'

Sir David, passing just behind them with a portmanteau,

remarked, 'All sons would rather chart their own course in this life, I think.'

I thought at first he might be speaking of Prince Henry, for it had been widely noted and remarked upon within my social circle that King James and the prince often disagreed. But then I noticed that Sir David was looking at Logan, who appeared not to have heard.

Logan's attention was entirely upon my father, and his gaze assumed that odd, unfocused quality that came and went so quickly no one else seemed to observe it. I was even more inclined to think it meant that he was worried, for my father *did* look tired.

'We'll stay here the week,' Logan said. He left no space for it to be discussed. 'It's Whitsun week all over. We were fortunate to find our lodgings here, but in the next town all the inns and houses might be full, and I'll not take that risk.' He turned to smile at Hector. 'Anyway, they'll have the fair on Tuesday. Ye'll not wish to miss that.'

Hector's look of joy was dampened only slightly when my father clapped a hand upon his shoulder and reminded him that boys who sought to kick their heels up at the fair must first attend their souls at the Whitsunday sermon.

Which we all did. I'd been spoilt, admittedly, by being raised within the Close at St Bartholomew's, because the church there was so beautiful. Still, this church here at Newark, but a stone's throw from our inn, was most impressive. It was very large, with soaring ceilings painted in exquisite patterns, full of darkly polished wood, pale stone, and high, arched windows filled with stained glass in bright colours, letting in the light.

The minister kept his words true to the spirit of the day, taking his sermon from the Book of John, when Jesus, knowing that his time was growing short, assembled his disciples and reminded them to honour his commandments. 'If a man love me, he will keep my words, and my Father will love him,' the minister read from the text, and I saw my father's head nod in agreement at my side. But then the minister read through the Ten Commandments, giving them notations of his own, and midway through the reading, my father went very still, and bowed his head, and after that was silent with his thoughts.

'No, I am well, there is no need to fuss,' he told me later on that afternoon, when I expressed concern. 'It is no more than a slight aching of my head.'

But on Monday he kept his own company and after dinner he went for a walk by himself. Or at least, that's what he believed, for he most likely would not have seen Logan, who quietly slipped out to follow him, leaving young Hector in charge of Sir David.

Sir David very dutifully played the part of prisoner and did not stray from Hector's sight. And Hector, to his credit, did a fine job as a Messenger. He eyed Sir David with suspicion.

'I would have your word ye'll not escape,' he said.

Sir David raised his eyebrows slightly. 'I've already given it.'

'Tae Logan, aye, but not tae me.'

The corner of Sir David's mouth quirked upwards, but he straightened it so that he, too, looked serious. 'You have my word,' he said. 'I'll not escape.'

Hector relaxed somewhat. He drew his chair so that he sat between Sir David and the door. But he still craved his stories. 'Did Prince Henry favour war or peace?' he wondered, clearly thinking of the White Stag's sign.

Sir David gave this thought. 'That is a question with no simple answer, and depends much upon circumstance. I will say, though, that more than any conflict or the lack of it, the prince did love the prospect of adventure.'

And he shared a few tales of Prince Henry's first encounter with his much-loved master shipbuilder, and of his visits to the dockyards, and the great ships that were built for him. He told us of the prince's friendship with Sir Walter Raleigh, that great favourite of the late Queen Elizabeth and hero of England's war against the Spanish Armada, who had himself sailed on so many adventures and now was kept locked in the Tower by King James for what the prince felt was a misunderstanding. Sir David told us, too, about the prince's determined support of the quest to find the Northwest Passage, and his dream to strengthen the colony at Virginia while founding new ones on more distant shores.

'He had a great desire to sail to the far reaches of the world, and wished to venture off the edges of the map, to see what he'd discover there.' Sir David looked towards the window, and his smile was brief. 'He did have many dreams.'

I'd watched my father grieve for all my life. I knew the signs of it. I would have let Sir David sit in silence with his memories, but Hector asked, 'Where did he sail to?'

'Nowhere. In the end,' Sir David said, 'there wasn't time.' His gaze came back to Hector's, gently. 'But he did have plans. I'd tell you what they were, but I fear it would leave poor Master Westaway with a cramped hand from all the writing he would have to do to note them down in his report.' And then he smiled again, this time directed to the open doorway of our lodgings.

I'd been so involved in what he had been telling us that I'd not seen my father coming in, but there he stood. The walk had done him good, it seemed. The wind at least had brought some colour to his face. But he did not yet look himself.

'I am too tired to write this evening,' he assured Sir David, and not waiting for his evening meal, he took his leave of us and simply went to bed.

Logan, returning not long afterwards with a flat, paper-wrapped parcel that he set down near the door, suggested Hector might want to do likewise once our supper was eaten and the horses seen to. 'The fair is tomorrow,' he said. 'An important day, and ye'll be wishing to look your best.'

Hector looked down at the jerkin and shirt he'd been wearing since Langholm and wrinkled his nose. 'I'll be looking like this.'

'Will ye, now? Then I've wasted my money on *that,*' Logan said, giving a nod to the parcel beside the door, 'haven't I?'

Hector's face lit up. 'What is it?'

'Ye'd best open it,' Logan advised, 'and find out.'

In a scramble of paper and string, Hector tore through the wrapping and pulled out a new shirt of white linen, clean and unworn, fitted hose, and a plain, dark blue doublet with shining brass buttons. His mouth fell open and his eyes began to fill. 'Is this for me?' He stared at Logan. 'Truly?'

'Aye.' There seemed to be a certain tone of Logan's voice reserved for Hector and the horses only. ''Tis tradition.'

I think we all were touched by Hector's innocent and genuine reaction to the gift that might have been the first new suit of clothes he'd ever had for Whitsuntide. So much so that when he expressed dismay that we did not have any new clothes of our own, we did our best to reassure him.

Logan could do little more than promise he would wear a clean shirt on the morrow, 'Which is nearly the same thing,' he said, to Hector's doubting face.

Sir David offered, 'And I have a second doublet I shall wear.'

All I could tell the boy was, 'I have a brown petticoat to wear in place of this one.'

Hector said, 'That will look bonny, for your eyes are brown.'

Logan laughed. 'With compliments like those, wee man, ye'll fit in well at court.' He reached into the pocket of his doublet and took out a folded piece of fabric, which he passed to me. 'Ye'll have this also, if ye wish it.'

Speechless yet again, I took the handkerchief, unfolding it and smoothing it upon my knees. It was a simple square of Holland linen, very soft and simply edged in small white stitches that exactly matched the cloth. It had one small decoration only, in one corner, wrought in fine black thread – an acorn on a curling stem beneath the stout protection of an oak leaf.

'It seemed fitting for ye,' Logan said. 'And I have noticed that ye've not been carrying your other.'

'No.' I was still looking at the oak leaf, tracing it with idle fingers. 'No, I gave that to our landlord's daughter, when we were at Tuxford.' Why I told him that I wasn't sure, except it was a thing I felt that he should know. 'Its scent did not agree with me.'

Logan made no reply at first, and so I raised my eyes and found that he was watching me. And then he spoke, and I discovered I was wrong. That tone of voice was not reserved for only Hector and the horses. Logan said, 'This one is plain and has no scent.'

'That makes it much more practical,' I told him. 'Thank you.'

I could feel Sir David's eyes upon us, so I chose that moment to excuse myself and go to bed, but I spread my new handkerchief upon the pillow underneath my cheek, and for that night at least, the dream passed by me. Mayhap it could see that, like the little blackwork acorn, I was too well guarded.

Awakening on Tuesday morning, I found that the market square had been transformed into a place of wonder for the Whitsun fair. I'd seen the stalls and booths while they'd been building them, but nothing had prepared me for the swirl of life and colour and the wild chaotic glory of it all. I rose and dressed and barely touched my breakfast, eager to be out there in the midst of it.

My father smiled. 'You are a child, yet. You should see your eyes.'

I didn't need to. I could feel my own excitement, and was sure it would be showing. 'Then you'll have to come and dance with me, the way you always used to at the Whitsun fairs.'

My father touched my face and told me, 'I would rest awhile longer. I will come and find you later.'

Kissing his cheek, I made him turn that to a promise before I went outside with the others. As we stepped over the inn's threshold, just for a moment, I saw Logan pause as though weighing the wisdom of bringing Sir David into such a crowd, where a prisoner might disappear with the ease and the speed of a scarf in the hands of the conjurer who stood performing his tricks now a few steps away.

But then Logan firmly walked forwards and set down the rules of the day. 'We keep out of the drinking booths. We stay together. And we must stay out until we win at least one prize.'

'You're our best hope of doing that,' Sir David said. 'I see there's wrestling.'

But Logan did not wish to wrestle. 'Hector,' he called his apprentice to his side, 'where will we start?'

Predictably, Hector chose a small booth selling sugar candy, comfits, and all manner of sweetmeats, and once fortified with some of these, he dragged us off to see the players in the furthest corner of the market who were acting out the tale of Robin Hood. It was a spirited, rousing retelling, with much laughter from the crowd, and having won his Maid Marian, Robin urged all of us watching to join in the races and games, while with all of his men and his fair lady he strolled the marketplace, cheerfully lending encouragement.

It was Sir David who first saw me watching the dancers. The second time they started forming a circle, he casually said, 'Do you know, Hector, Messengers really should know how to dance.'

'Why?' asked Hector.

'They just should.'

And the next thing I knew, there the four of us were in the large circle, standing and waiting while the small troupe of musicians started playing 'Three Poor Mariners'.

Sir David told Hector, 'Now, this is an easy one. See, they're choosing a few people now, and soon they'll start to dance around inside the circle while we sing the words together, and then when the music stops, each dancer must stop, too, and face the person they have stopped in front of, get down on one knee, and kiss that person's hand, and bring them thus into the dance. It's great fun, you'll enjoy it.'

I nearly laughed aloud at Hector's sideways frown. He asked, 'How can a kissing dance be fun?'

Sir David said, 'You'll see.'

It was fun. And it wasn't long till Hector's was one of the loudest voices singing:

'We be three poor Mariners,
Newly come from the seas,
We spend our lives in jeopardy,
Whilst others live at ease,
Shall we go dance the round, the round the round?

And shall we go dance the round?
And he that is a bully boy,
Come pledge me on the ground.'

Hector fairly shouted the word 'ground!' every time, then laughed to see the growing field of dancers dropping to their knees to kiss the hands of whomever they'd ended up across from in the circle. I was so amused by Hector that I nearly missed the moment when a young lady with golden hair bent to her knee in front of Logan and, with a quick shrug and grin, he was swept off into the dance.

I'd lost my place within the tune. I sought to get it back again. 'We spend our lives in jeopardy, whilst others live at ease . . .'

It should have been an easy thing to spot a man as tall as Logan in the field of dancers, but I'd somehow lost him, too. I tried to focus past the blur of spinning bodies.

'. . . pledge me on the *ground*!' sang Hector, as Logan stepped in front of me and smoothly knelt. He took my hand in his and kissed it, and then kept possession of it, hauling me into the moving circle. There were other people dancing with us, and I knew it, but I did not see them. I saw only Andrew Logan, and the grey eyes I'd once thought were cold.

Too soon we came around again to where we'd started, and the singing stopped, and I brought Hector in to join us. I feared this might leave Sir David on his own, but he'd already been invited by an older woman, so we were the four of us again, and dancing faster, ever faster, as the music picked up speed with every step, until there was no one remaining on the outside of the circle, and the rest of us could not keep up the pace to sing the words.

When we all stumbled out of the dance flushed and

laughing, Robin Hood himself was waiting for us. Or, more properly, for Logan.

'Come, sir, you must try your luck,' he said, 'at wrestling.'

Logan shook his head. 'I thank ye, no.'

'The prize is very large this year.'

That caught Hector's attention. 'Logan,' he whispered, but loudly. 'A prize.'

Robin Hood – or, the actor who played that part – nodded. 'Indeed. And there's pride at stake, because our champion is undefeated.' Here he motioned towards the raised platform where a man waited who was nearly Logan's size, standing in his shirt because of the day's heat, ready to take on all those brave enough to pay their pennies for the chance to grapple with him. 'Thomas Hobson, Ironmonger, Alderman', the sign beside him read, so this was evidently being done to aid his business and political career as much as to raise money for the church. He'd been bantering with everybody passing by, good-naturedly, but when he saw that Robin Hood was talking now with Logan, he looked apprehensive.

Hector pushed at Logan's arm. 'Ye must!' he said. 'A prize!'

I'd seen men face the gallows with a fair sight more enthusiasm. Teasing, I told Logan, 'I thought you liked fighting.'

'Why would ye think that?'

I didn't know how the impression had been formed, or when, but I knew, 'You fought Valentine.'

His downward look was dry. 'I warrant God himself would come to blows with Valentine. But truthfully, I've never laid a hand on him.' He turned, in answer to the constant prodding at his side. 'All right,' he said to Hector. 'Hold my doublet, then.'

They drew a crowd, because they were so well matched in their height and size. Yet Logan was so clearly younger, fitter, and more skilled at wrestling that it seemed there was but one way that the match would end.

I knew the very moment he decided not to win. I saw the change of his expression, and the dropping of his shoulders, and the way his stance relaxed. He let himself be taken down.

When Thomas Hobson was declared the winner, Hector was incredulous.

'The ironmonger must have cheated.'

'Now, then,' said Sir David, 'you can't lay a charge so serious at someone's feet before you have the facts.'

The wrestling platform was still thickly crowded round with people reaching to congratulate the winner, and praise Logan for his effort. Robin Hood had joined them, and had launched into a lusty speech while someone who looked very like the landlord of our inn held up two tankards for the wrestlers, and the crowd cheered.

Hector paid it all no heed. Arms crossed, he faced Sir David. 'Was the tale ye telt me about Logan and the brigands true?'

'It was,' Sir David said.

'Well, if Logan was too strong for three men to defeat him when he was sae badly wounded, how could one man do it now?' asked Hector, sceptical. 'He couldn't, that's what. Not unless he cheated.'

I kept silent, not revealing what I'd noticed. Toasts were being drunk now on the platform, and the tankards were refilled.

Sir David smiled. 'I must say, Hector, you do argue with the logic of a lawyer. And you're right to think that Logan's much too strong to be defeated. Yet he fell. And why was that?' He waited for an answer for a moment, then he gently said, 'Because he is a good man, and the ironmonger also is an alderman – a man of some importance in this town, who has to live here and command respect, and Logan would not take that from him.'

The ironmonger certainly looked pleased with the result. He was now making speeches also, and the tankards had been drained and filled a third time. Logan had stepped back, as though attempting to remove himself.

Sir David said, 'It takes a man of strength to let another man be strong. To stand aside and let him claim his moment. I've known men of high estate who could not do so.'

Hector granted that. 'But Logan didnae win a prize.'

Sir David turned his gaze across the bright confusion of the marketplace. 'I do not wrestle,' he confessed, 'but in my youth, I did well when I played at quoits. I noticed that there was a little pitch set up across the way. Shall we go try our luck? Yes? Good. Oh, Mistress Westaway will take that.'

Hector gave me Logan's doublet, and Sir David said as he was being dragged away, 'If you would kindly let my large guard know my smaller guard's removing me to a new corner of the fair, but I am well secured and he'll have iron rings to hit me with if I should give him trouble.'

I knew that everything was fine, but I still watched to see exactly where they went before I turned and started pushing my way closer to the wrestling platform. Logan was no longer there. I found him at the back of it, between two booths in what had the appearance of an alleyway. He put a warning finger to his lips. 'Ye don't want Robin Hood to hear ye, else he'll have me up to do it all again, and once is plenty.'

'It was thoughtful, what you did,' I said.

'What did I do?'

But he knew, and I let him know that I did, too. I told him how Sir David had explained it very tidily to Hector.

'Aye, well,' Logan said, dismissively, 'he seemed a decent

man. It cost me nothing but a piece of pride, and ye should ken I have more than my share of that to spare.'

It struck me just how little I *did* know him in this mood, when he was smiling and at ease, upending all my preconceptions of his nature. I'd been led to think he'd fight all men because he was a brute, but now I saw he turned his temper only against someone like the guard at Brancepeth Castle gate, who'd been rude and belligerent, and even then he'd only shown its blunted edge.

It made me wonder all the more what Valentine had done that night at the Star Tavern in our Close that had drawn Logan into such a tumult. But I did not ask. Instead, I simply passed along Sir David's message, and the doublet.

Logan, with a nod, accepted both. Slipping his arms into the sleeves of the doublet, he made as if to shrug it on, but that motion stretched the linen of the shirt across his chest and caused its opening to gape. I saw the scar above his heart.

The blade – it must have been a blade – appeared to have been twisted, for the scar was not a clean, straight line, but jagged at its edges. And he'd told one bit of truth to Hector – though it was an older scar, it stood out red against his skin as though it were determined not to heal.

I wasn't sure what impulse made me reach my hand to touch it, but at any rate I didn't get the chance. Logan caught my fingers gently and prevented it.

He told me, 'That would be unwise.' Although his words were light, I thought they seemed less of a warning than a challenge. 'Especially after they served me three pints of whatever that witches' brew was.'

His eyes were definitely brighter, but I reassured him, 'I don't think it's robbed you of your reason.'

'No, my reason is intact. 'Tis my restraint that's lacking. I do fear I might forget myself and . . .'

'And?'

'And do what I've wished to do since first I saw ye.'

I was not kissed against my will.

His grey eyes, as his head descended, sought and found permission in my own. Nor did he hold me fast and pinion me as other men had done when social gatherings gave them the licence for such contact. He didn't hold me at all. All the touch I felt from Logan was his kiss, and that was warmth enough.

I was twenty-four, of course I had been kissed before, but never with such tenderness, or thoroughness. Or care.

I found my voice and told him, 'Had you done that when you first saw me, you'd have spared us a great many arguments.'

He laughed, and I believe he might have kissed me for a second time, except his eyes, which had been warm on mine, lost focus briefly, and his whole expression changed. He straightened, drawing back.

I didn't understand. I'm sure I showed that plainly. 'Logan?'

Lightly his hand lifted to brush my cheek and then fell from my face and he forced a smile. 'Forgive me, Phoebe. I meant ye no disrespect. The drink was very strong.' But Logan wasn't drunk, I knew. His hands were sure and steady as he finished fastening his doublet. Then, as if he hadn't just changed everything about my world, he said, 'Let's go and find the others.' And he led me from our sheltered place back into the confusion of the fair.

David

Newark-upon-Trent, Nottinghamshire, still 25th May 1613

NEWARK'S CASTLE, FRONTING ON the river, was of warmly golden stone with glittering, large windows that the bishop of a bygone age had built to bring light to his dining hall, amongst the other chambers.

Hector had not let go of the prize they'd won at quoits – a hollow toy horse cast in pewter. Being silver grey, he'd named it Brutus after Logan's horse, and to be honest, it did hold an echo of that great beast's haughty curve of neck and noble head. As they passed the castle wall now, Hector held the toy horse up so that the sun would throw its shadow larger on the stones, and asked David, 'Are ye certain we'll not get in trouble?'

'Very certain,' David said. 'I know the owner well. He would not mind us walking through the castle grounds.' It was perhaps as well the owner was just then abroad, for it would not have been an easy thing explaining Logan's presence, nor the reason they were travelling to London.

'It's a bonny castle,' Hector gave it his approval. 'Did ye come here often with the prince?'

'Not often, no. We stopped here on that first procession south from Edinburgh, to join the king at his new English court. And then again . . .' The sunlight on the river seemed too bright. He looked away from it, and cleared his throat. 'And then again in summer, when the prince was some years older.'

Hector raced his shadow horse across the glowing stones. 'Look, Logan! Look at Brutus running!' With the brief attention of the young, he ran ahead across the grass and down towards the smoothly gliding water, eager to explore.

David saw a different shadow running with him, looking back and beckoning. A taller lad, with hair of reddish gold and eyes that could by turns be full of wit or fire or watchfulness.

That August, though, they'd been impatient.

'If it will not stop,' the prince had said, 'I'm going to cut it off, and that will be the end of it.'

David had supplied the prince with yet another handkerchief and pointed out that noses were essential to the face.

'Not mine,' Prince Henry said. 'Not when it bleeds. It never used to do this, David.'

That was true. The nosebleeds had not started until earlier that year. 'The doctors will take care of it.'

'The doctors tell me I should stop my swimming, and not ride so often in the heat. I fear to think what they'd prescribe to cure my headaches.'

David had glanced up. 'You're having headaches?'

'Only sometimes. Why?' Prince Henry knew his tones of voice, and frowned. 'You are concerned. You do not think that it could be the new disease?'

He'd meant the fever that had suddenly seemed everywhere that summer, creeping into people's homes and stealing lives.

'I do not,' David had assured him, though he hadn't told the prince what he *did* fear that it might be, because those fears of poison seemed too terrible to think of, then.

Too terrible to bear the weight of, now.

The river idled by, and David pushed the memories back with firmness, for he did not want to think about that final summer. It was still too hard, a wound unhealed.

But still, that shadow ran ahead of him, and summoned him

back with it to another stately residence, beside another river, in another time.

Whitehall Palace, London, New Year's, 1608

Celia's husband was a good man and not easy to dislike, but David tried. They'd been standing in a weighted silence now for several minutes beside one of the long windows that looked out towards the frozen Thames.

Not far away, the prince was still receiving those who wished to give him presents. Celia, lovely in a gown of midnight blue, was fifth in line.

For her sake, David tried to think of something neutral and polite that he could raise in conversation, but before he managed it, a figure all in black slipped from the milling crowd of guests to stand between them.

Celia's husband looked relieved. 'My lord Northampton. Happy New Year.'

David didn't trust Northampton, who seemed always on the cusp of being genuine, but never quite achieving it – the end result, no doubt, of a long life spent navigating the uncertain tides of court on a ship rigged with sails of ever-changing fortune.

With a smile, Northampton shook their hands and said, 'I've not seen such a violent frost upon the Thames since I was young. The bargemen will be out of business soon if there is not a thaw.' He turned to Celia's husband. 'How are you enjoying life in your new parish?'

'Very well, my lord, I thank you.'

'And your wife? Does she miss being here at court?'

The glance at David might have been imagined. Celia's husband said, 'A little, I expect.'

Northampton nodded understanding. 'Women are more social creatures, by their natures. Consider my niece, for example.'

They all looked at the vibrant young woman – no more than a girl, really – holding a very small court of her own near the end of the room. Frances Howard, Northampton's niece, was still in essence a newlywed, having not long ago married the young Earl of Essex, one of Prince Henry's best friends.

'She belongs here at court,' said Northampton. 'She'd wither away in the countryside.'

David privately agreed that Frances Howard was not withering. She'd collected a string of admirers, from what he could see.

'It is a pity,' said Northampton, 'that her husband is so serious.'

'He's young,' was all that David could say in the boy's defence while still remaining diplomatic, though he *wished* to add that families like the Howards would perhaps do better not to marry off their children young for their own profit. But he knew the words were pointless, for Northampton, like the others of his family, could not help but keep manoeuvring his chair a little closer to the king's in an attempt to regain influence and power.

Celia's husband looked more closely at the group. 'But surely that is not her husband who does hold her hand?'

'No,' David told him. 'That is Robert Carr. Sir Robert Carr, I ought to call him, for the king did knight him Christmas Eve. He is a gentleman of the king's bedchamber.'

A woman's voice, familiar to them all, joined in. 'His Majesty's most valued friend, of late.' Queen Anna, passing by, had caught them unawares. She paused and waited while they bowed and wished her a good New Year.

Northampton said, 'I hear we are to have a wondrous masque from you and all your ladies for Twelfth Night, Your Majesty.'

The queen confirmed this. 'Master Jonson has created something special, I'll not spoil it.'

Celia joined them, with a low and perfect curtsey, and the queen remarked, 'If you were still at court, my dear, I'd find a role for you within my masque.'

'I would be honoured,' Celia told her. 'But we must return home.' She was standing near David. She turned to him. 'I have a gift for you, also,' she said.

He could feel what it was, through the wrapping: a small book.

Celia smiled. 'To take the place of that which you … mislaid.'

She knew full well the first one had been taken from him by the queen, but it would be impolitic to say so. David closed his hand around the gift without unwrapping it, and slipped it deep into his pocket.

''Tis a thoughtful present. I shall treasure it,' he told her.

She looked pleased. Her husband said, 'I do not wish to interrupt, but it is time that we were on the road. We will be two days in our journey as it is.'

She nodded. Looked at David. 'It was good to see you.'

'Aye. And you.' He smiled, but kept his guard raised so she would not see his feelings. She was happy in her life, he knew, and he would not upset her, though his own heart had remained unchanged. He'd written sonnets to that upturned face.

Dear, once you told me that you dream'd my death
Was past, and that your eyes beheld my grave …

Ah 'twas no dream! If you will but perceive
How in effect for you I hourly die . . .

'A happy New Year,' Celia wished him.

Then her husband took her arm, and then they were gone.

Northampton followed in their wake, with some excuse. But not the queen.

'She loves you still,' Queen Anna said to David, standing there beside the window, while the gathering moved on around them.

David said, 'She loves her husband. He's a good man.'

The queen did not dispute this. But, 'They say you wished to marry her. Why did you not?'

'He asked her first, Your Majesty.'

'So then you are a fool.'

'I'll not deny it.' David looked again across the room at Frances Howard, with her minor court of men, Sir Robert Carr their favoured leader, and her husband not among them. 'But then marriage does not always make men happy.'

'No,' the queen agreed. And then she asked, 'Is my son happy?' It was something she asked often. David always tried to give an honest answer.

'I believe he is, Your Majesty.'

'I worry for him. I have but three children left,' Queen Anna said. She'd lost another daughter a few months ago, the little Princess Mary, who had suffered from a devastating fever and been taken by it. David had seen firsthand the effects that loss had wrought upon the queen, who had sent men to view the opening of the child's body, demanding she be told the certain cause of death. 'I'm not allowed to grieve,' she'd told him once, when she had come to pay a visit to the prince in the days afterwards, 'but this would not have happened if my daughter had been in my care.' For, like the other children, at the king's insistence Princess Mary was removed at birth and placed within a different household to be raised.

Queen Anna followed David's gaze across the room of revellers, and said, 'My son should take care not to make an enemy of Robert Carr.'

He said, 'It is an easy thing to do.'

He noticed she'd not called the king's new favourite 'Sir'. Perhaps it had not yet become a habit, for the knighthood was a new one, though he'd never known the queen to do a thing that had not been intentional.

She smiled. 'I'll grant you that. But he does have the king's whole trust. And worse, he will do all he must,' she said, 'to hold the king's affection.' A pause. 'I will be blunt with you, Sir David, for I know you are a man of honour and will not repeat my words.'

He waited.

After what appeared to be a brief attempt to frame the words, she simply said, 'The king has never been a trusting man.'

'That is a product of his childhood, I'd expect,' said David.

'Yes, I know. He often was betrayed by those who should have loved him more. But that was long ago. These are his children. I'm his wife.' She did not state what duties they were owed by him, but merely said, 'In his view we're no more than weapons that another hand might wield against him. That is sad,' she said, 'and dangerous.'

The prince had seen them, and was crossing now towards them with a broad smile.

'Guard him well, Sir David,' was Queen Anna's final comment, before turning to embrace her son.

She wasn't wrong, thought David as he stood and watched them talk. The king did look upon his family with distrust. And since the failed treasonous powder-plot, three winters past, which had been aimed at killing both the princes and the king and setting wee Princess Elizabeth upon the throne to rule as a new, Catholic queen, the king had grown yet more suspicious of those who might use his children as pawns in a game against him.

Not that anyone could use Prince Henry as a pawn, thought David. Henry was becoming more and more his own man, every day. But that, too, held its dangers.

There were already some within the kingdom – and among their foreign allies on the continent – who made no secret of their view that this bold, energetic prince, with his modern ideas, would make an exceptional king, and that his time to rule could not come soon enough.

'Hide your New Year's present well, David,' the prince advised him, laughing, 'for my mother has just tried to steal mine.'

'Slander,' claimed Queen Anna, with a smile. 'I but admired it. Esther Inglis does such rare and lovely work.'

'It is inscribed to me,' Prince Henry told her, holding up the little book bound in red velvet and embroidered in both gold and silver threads, adorned exquisitely with seed pearls so the whole effect was of a jewel. He said, 'You shall not have it.'

'I have you,' she told him. 'You are all the New Year's gift I need.' And with a kiss upon his cheek, she took her leave of them and moved on to attend to other guests.

Prince Henry squared his shoulders. 'We should find my father,' he told David. 'I've not given him my present.'

'Very well.'

As they drew near to Frances Howard and her entourage, the prince frowned. 'She is shameless. She forgets that she is married, to so disrespect my friend.' He glanced at David. 'They are sending him on tour, were you aware of that?'

'I heard a rumour.'

'Two years on the continent. I argued with my father, but of course he didn't listen. No doubt Carr put the idea in his head.' Prince Henry aimed his frown this time at the sleek Scotsman holding Frances Howard's hand. 'Just as King David in the Bible sent Bathsheba's husband off to war in hopes he might be killed, because he wanted her himself.'

David sought to reassure him. 'I don't think Sir Robert hopes young Essex will be killed while on his tour.'

But as they passed the little group, Sir Robert Carr looked up.

Marcus Aurelius had written that you could tell a man's character by looking in his eyes, and David saw more than he cared to see when his gaze met Sir Robert's.

The crowd shifted, making room as King James came towards them. Outwardly, he made a great show of affection, folding the prince into a warm, fatherly embrace, though David knew that it was partly for their audience of onlookers. There were many new faces here at court this evening, come from Scotland and elsewhere to celebrate. The king was doing what he loved best – putting on a show.

'My son! A happy New Year.'

'Father. And to you.' Prince Henry had been diligently working on his father's gift for weeks. He looked to David now, who drew it safely from his pocket and passed it across so that the prince could properly present it. This, too, was a small, bound book, handwritten. 'I've been giving you these literary offerings at New Year's these past seven years,' the prince explained, 'and now that I am older, I did think it fitting to attempt one more important. 'Tis a thesis on a sentence of the ancient Greek poet Menander, writ in Latin.'

The king's eyebrows rose. 'My clever son.' He took the book and turned the first page, curious. 'What sentence did ye choose?'

Prince Henry spoke so that his voice would carry clearly to the party sitting but a mere stone's throw away, and knowing all who heard him would place their interpretation on the reason for his choice.

He told his father, evenly, 'Evil companions corrupt good manners.'

The king looked up. Sir Robert stood, as though he had been challenged, but the king glanced sharply at him and he sat again, if restlessly.

As with Sir Robert, David read the king's whole character within his eyes, and wished that he had not.

'My clever son,' the king said, for a second time, and leaning close, he brushed the prince's cheek with a light kiss, although to David, both the king's tone and the kiss were colder than the ice upon the Thames. 'A thoughtful gift. I thank you.'

Then he passed from them, with all his train in tow, and Frances Howard and Sir Robert and their clique fell in behind.

'Well,' said David, seeking to make light of things, 'you always had a rare, fine gift for making friends.'

The prince had laughed.

His laughter was one thing about Prince Henry that did not change as he grew. Another was his sense of justice.

A year passed.

New Year's came, and went, and February brought a thaw, and David tallied the accounts and made an inventory of the prince's holdings. In the wardrobe, he discovered a fine saddle, richly made and beautifully embroidered, that had been a present to the prince from King James some eighteen months earlier. 'What would you do with this?' he asked.

Prince Henry told him, 'Nothing, till my father pays the man who made it.'

David sighed. 'Your Highness . . .'

'It is not right, David. I'll not use a thing that's not been paid for. Write again and tell my father that the saddler must be paid. And put that back into my wardrobe.'

That the prince was resolute made David proud, but he did not imagine that the king approved of his son's moral views, nor of his growing independence.

One more year passed.

And Prince Henry turned sixteen, and came to manhood. His creation as the Prince of Wales, a formal grand event, was a rare spectacle that bridged the final days of May and the first days of June. In London, people swarmed to see the prince's barge upon the Thames, flanked by two fanciful sea monsters that bobbed floating on the water. There were trumpeters and oboe-players making lively music, and processions of all sorts of dignitaries. Later came the solemn ceremony that was held in Parliament, and the grand dinner afterwards at which the prince was served together with his beloved sister, Elizabeth, and younger brother, Charles, in Westminster Hall, shoulder to shoulder with the greatest and most influential lords in all of Parliament.

Had David been Prince Henry's father, he could not have been more proud. The prince had gone through all the day in perfect step, and shown himself to be the very image of a king in waiting.

But while that delighted all the common people watching, and most of the men in Parliament, it had not pleased all.

David had been quick to note those men who felt the threat of young Prince Henry's popularity.

And he had watched the king.

He'd watched the king as well, the New Year's night that followed. They had been at Whitehall once again, this time in the grand banqueting house that the king had lately built, and David had been one of twelve men taking part in a new masque Ben Jonson had created for the prince, in which the prince had played the leading role of Oberon.

David always wondered how these things went off as well as they did, for it was pure chaos in the sidewings. The wrong men wore the wrong hats, and the scenery threatened to collapse, and the two tame arctic white bears who'd been hired to pull the chariot for the prince's grand entrance proved to be a challenge for their keeper, and required constant treats to keep them well contented.

'Have some faith,' Ben Jonson murmured, standing next to David in the darkness as the masque began. 'It always works.'

The two were friends, and David knew that Ben was right. And yet, 'I wish you had not praised him quite so fervently within this play,' he said.

'How could I not?' asked Ben, and both men looked together at the prince, who stood across from them, the candlelight reflecting on the armour of his costume – a bold recreation by Inigo Jones of the battle dress of ancient Roman emperors, complete with cape and feathered helmet. 'Just look at him, and answer me. How could I not praise such a prince?'

Of course, there was no answer to be given. Henry had been made to shine.

And when he finally made his entrance in his chariot, drawn

by the bears, the song that Ben had written for the other players to sing had seemed fitting:

'Seek you Majesty, to strike?
Bid the World produce his like.
Seek you glory, to amaze?
Here, let all Eyes stand at gaze.
Seek you Wisdom, to inspire?
Touch, then, at no other's Fire.
Seek you knowledge, to direct?
Trust to his without suspect.
Seek you Piety, to lead?
In his Footsteps, only, tread.
Every Virtue of a King,
And of all, in him, we sing.'

The final two lines had been turned into a chorus and some in the audience had joined the players in the bright refrain, and the men had danced, and then Prince Henry held his hand out to the queen and drew her into a fine dance, the pair of them together. David thought he'd never seen Queen Anna look so happy.

But one member of the audience had not been pleased. And at King James's side, Sir Robert Carr had taken note of that, and turned it to his own advantage.

Within a few months, he was no longer simply the knight Sir Robert Carr, but had been raised with honours to be Viscount Rochester, a man with even greater powers than before, and more entrenched in his position at the king's right hand.

And there would nevermore be room there for Prince Henry.

Hector had Logan running races in the grounds of Newark Castle. It was not a fair match, at first glance, but David noted with a small smile how Logan checked his speed so that the lad could run alongside without making it appear that he was holding himself back. Towards the end, Logan most artfully lost energy, allowing Hector to surge forwards in that all-or-nothing and determined way that young lads had when they still held some innocence. And hope.

Falling in feigned exhaustion on the grass, Logan exclaimed, 'Ye beat me fairly, lad. Ye could outrun a greyhound, so ye could.'

The sound of Hector's laughter twisted David's heart a little. He was seeing shadows, still.

Another time. Another lad, who had been born to shine as brightly as the sun.

It took a certain kind of man to stand aside and let another shine. And David knew – he'd always known – King James could never be that man.

PHOEBE

Newark-upon-Trent, Nottinghamshire, the same day

MY FATHER, THOUGH THE day was warm, had lit the fire in his room. I told him lightly, 'Logan will not thank you for that. He worked hard at wrestling.'

'Did he?' Turning as I came into the bedchamber, my father smiled. 'And where is he now?'

'With Sir David and Hector. They went to have a walk around the castle grounds. The owner is an old friend of Sir David's who is travelling in Italy, I do believe. Sir David said he would not mind.'

'And why are you not with them?'

I could not explain that properly. Not to my father. I said only, 'I was tired. Besides, I wished to spend some time with you.'

His eyes weren't fooled. 'You worried for me. That's not the same thing.'

'You said you'd come to find me.'

'Yes, I'm sorry. I had business to do.'

I frowned. 'What business?'

'It's finished, now.' He drew a chair beside the window for me. 'Come sit with me. There are things I would say to you.'

He looked so tired. I shook my head. 'You need to rest.'

'It is important.'

'What could be of more importance than your health?'

'My soul,' he told me. 'My eternal soul.'

It was strange to see him reflect upon something so serious while through the window the sounds of the fair drifted in – mingled laughter and music and snatches of brief conversation as people walked past in the square below.

'Phoebe,' he said to me. 'Sit.'

Trying not to show concern, I sat, and turned my chair to face him.

'I've been thinking,' he began, 'of Sunday's sermon. It has been a heavy weight upon my mind these past few days.'

I didn't understand, and would have said as much except he held his hand up in a plea for silence before he went on.

'When Mary, Queen of Scots was held in prison here in England, she kept up a secret correspondence with her Catholic friends. It was a simple thing to intercept their letters and discover their conspiracies,' he told me, 'but the spymasters of our late Queen Elizabeth desired to draw as many flies as possible into the web. They already had people with the skills to open all the letters to and from Queen Mary and reseal them so they could be read before they were delivered. What they wanted was a person who could take those unsealed letters and so alter them, by adding postscripts, say, and in a hand like the original, to lure more traitors to the light.'

I frowned. 'I don't see how—?'

'Suppose we intercepted a letter in which Queen Mary instructed a man to be somewhere at seven of the clock on Friday evening, to receive information. I might add a postscript telling him to bring along five of his friends, whomever he should choose, so long as they be well affected to the cause. No more than that.' He looked away. 'No more than that. Except, of those five friends, I doubt that all of them had treason in their heart. And none would have been there at all if not for me.' He rubbed his forehead. 'Anyway. I did the job that I'd been hired to do. I did it well, and men were drawn into the trap and hanged. And my reward for aiding in their downfall was our house at St Bartholomew's.'

I heard the shame within his voice, and felt some measure of it, too. It was no easy thing to learn, to know my father, who had always taught me that it was a sinful thing to tell a lie, had been a part of such an underhanded venture.

With a sigh, he carried on, 'My lord Northampton knew, of course, what I'd done in the late queen's time. He told King James.'

I was not sure I followed. 'Was the king then angry that you'd so deceived his mother?'

My father shook his head. 'This king has not the sentiments of ordinary men,' he said, without explaining further. 'No, he was not angry. He was interested.'

Then I was still at sea. 'But what does any of this have to do with Sunday's sermon?'

'The sermon turned upon the Lord's commandments, and how we must follow them to find our way to heaven. And what is the ninth commandment?'

'" Thou shalt not bear false witness against thy neighbour".' Even as I spoke the words, I saw my father's eyes begin to water, and my own mind cleared. I leaned to grasp his hand in both of mine. 'But what you did was very long ago, and you've long since repented, and . . .'

'It isn't what I did, my dear.' My father laid his free hand over mine, and pressed it lightly, as though I were the one seeking comfort. 'It is what I'm doing now.' He did not let go of my hands, but he sat back into his chair and turned his focus to the fire. 'Why do you think my lord Northampton sent me north with Logan?'

'Why, to write down . . .' Then I began to understand. I said, more slowly now, 'To write down what Sir David says.'

'Except that's not what they did truly send me here to do. It's not what I've been writing. I've been crafting a confession of how he did kill Prince Henry, as my secret orders told me to.' The shame shone still more brightly in his eyes. 'I wove some of Sir David's tales in, to be sure, but most of it was mine.'

I pulled my hands back, shattered. 'No.'

'I'm sorry, Phoebe. Please forgive me.'

'No, you cannot do this. They will execute him. It's not right, you—' Breaking off, I looked towards the fire, then at my father's face, and realized what he'd done. 'You cannot do this,' I repeated, with the certainty of one who knows the limits of the conscience of a person they do love.

He shook his head. 'No, I cannot bear false witness against any man, much less a good man like Sir David. I have burned it all.'

I flung myself against him as though I had been a little girl, and sank into the reassurance of his warm embrace. 'I'm glad,' I told him, as he stroked my hair. 'But why agree to such a terrible arrangement in the first place?'

'Why, for you, of course. You are the thing I hold most dear, most precious, so what else could make me strike the Devil's bargain?'

I felt certain I would not like what came next. 'What was this bargain?'

'I compose Sir David's false confession, and my lord Northampton will arrange for you to marry Valentine.'

That brought me upright, and my father said again, 'I'm sorry, Phoebe. But I cannot do my part, and so the bargain will be broken. We shall have to find another way for you to have your life of ease at court.'

I told him, 'I don't mind, believe me. I don't wish to marry Valentine.'

He viewed me with new interest. 'No? When did your heart change course?' And then, 'On second thought, there are some things a father need not know. It is enough for me to know your heart will not be broken, and that I've not lost your love.'

'You never could lose that,' I promised, and settled myself once again in my own chair. My father looked content, but there was still one thing that troubled me. I asked, 'Did Logan know what you were doing?'

'No.' He seemed surprised I would suggest it.

'How can you be sure he did not read what you were writing?'

'I am sure.'

'But, how . . . ?'

'He cannot read.' He said it bluntly, in the manner of a man who knows that nothing less will stop the questions, but who doesn't like divulging a friend's secret.

'Oh.' I was taken by surprise. I'd just assumed, for all these years, that Logan was an educated man. I said so to my father, and he set me straight.

'He is. He came to me for lessons, and I taught him all in private. He's as educated as the finest merchants' sons in London. But he holds the lessons all in memory, here.' My father tapped his temple. 'For he cannot read. He says the letters dance and shift upon the page, when he attempts it. I have seen it happen thus for some. It is a sad affliction.'

'Oh,' I said again, because there seemed so little else to say. I could not think what my world might have been, if I'd not had my writing and my books.

'He mustn't know I've told you. He's a proud young man, is Logan.'

I said absently, 'He is a Leither.'

'I do beg your pardon?'

'He's a man of Leith, you do remember? Stubborn, proud and . . .' I could still not think of that third quality.

My father sent me an indulgent smile, and said, 'At any rate, he shares his private life with but a precious few. My lord Northampton knows, of course. He was a friend to Logan's father, and he is a help to Logan now. When Logan's sent on an assignment that requires any writing, he's provided with a scribe. Most often me.'

'That's thoughtful of my lord Northampton.'

'Sometimes. Though I do suspect the reason he chose Logan for this mission was precisely because Logan cannot read.' His gaze touched mine with certainty that I would take his meaning, and I did.

If Logan could not read, then he'd not know what was in the 'report' my father wrote each evening. He'd not understand the depth of the deceit, nor yet its danger to Sir David.

My father warned me, 'Logan must not learn that, either. It would wound him terribly, and I would not hurt Logan for the world.' He made me promise, then he nodded, and said, 'Anyway, it's naught but theory. Nobody can know the workings of my lord Northampton's mind.'

The fire had begun to die, the low flames only showing with reluctance now and then amongst the ashes.

Watching them, my father said, 'It's just as well you've changed your view of Valentine. I do confess I've had my doubts about him, although I did overlook his failings because you were fond of him, and closed my ears to all that people said.'

'What did they say?'

He raised a shoulder in a half shrug and replied, 'The talk in the Close when we left was that Valentine debauched a young lady, and that her brother, who was even younger, called Valentine out in the Star. They said her brother struck Valentine, who then turned his friends upon the boy like dogs in a pit, and had Logan not stepped in to be his defender, the boy surely would have been killed.'

This was a day of revelations. I stayed silent for a moment, thinking now I finally understood why Logan, on that morning at the conduit in the Close, had told me that I had his pity if I stood in Valentine's defence. And that he felt no shame for having done what needed doing.

'One never knows,' my father said, 'if all the tales one hears are true, but it is best to pay them mind.'

I nodded. 'Mayhap I'm not meant to have a life of ease at court.'

'You can't escape it,' he assured me. 'It's your destiny.'

I'd lived too long with destiny to try to win this argument.

My father said, 'But there are other men at court. Some are mere scribes, like me. And some are Messengers.' He met my startled glance and smiled. 'You'll find the path you're meant to take. You'll have a good life, you will see. Your stars may have concealed themselves when you were born, but they were most auspicious stars. They marked you well for happiness.' He reached one hand as he had often done when I was small, and smoothed the hair behind my ear. 'You will be loved,' he said, 'as you deserve to be.'

Something was wrong. When I rose and dressed and came out of my bedchamber on the next morning, Hector and Sir David were already at the stairhead, going down. They did not turn to say good morrow.

And before I'd taken two more steps, the door to the men's

chamber opened. Logan moved into the corridor, where just by standing there he blocked my progress and my view.

He did not say good morrow, either. He said, 'Phoebe.'

And I knew.

Before I saw his eyes, I knew.

I felt as though someone had dropped a stone upon my chest, and pressed out all my breath and feeling. Logan gently took hold of my arms and told me, 'It was peaceful. In the night. He didn't waken.'

I was glad of that, at least. There was a tiny, frayed spot near the second button down on Logan's doublet, and I could not look beyond it. Each imperfect, broken thread was seared into my mind.

I said, 'I wish to see him.'

Logan seemed about to argue. Then he nodded. Stood aside.

My father lay upon his bed as though he were still sleeping. I might almost think he was, until I touched his hand, and found it cold. I slipped my fingers into his. They did not hold mine back. 'Could not you wait?' I asked him in a whisper when I bent to kiss his forehead, knowing I'd receive no kiss in answer. But I knew that, even had he waited until we were home in London, there would never have been any time that I would have been ready to let go my father's hand and say farewell. I couldn't bring myself to do it now.

And Logan didn't force me to.

He simply went on standing there, a solid presence at my back that radiated comfort.

Though I had no certain memory of the order of events in the few days that followed, I remembered Logan being often close behind me.

He'd retreated from me since the fair, and all the passion that he'd shown me in his kiss was gone now from his manner, which in all ways was deliberately polite. But he was there. He did not leave.

There were so many things that needed to be dealt with and arranged. My father had not brought much with him north from London. It was tactfully suggested to me by the local minister that I might wish to give his clothing to the poor, and I allowed it, though I kept the gilded clip he always wore upon his hat – the one shaped like a rose. I kept his almanac, with Mr Parker's forecasts and advice. And I kept all my father's writing instruments.

It seemed to me impossible that he should never hold his pens again. I laid them carefully like fallen soldiers in the little wooden box he carried when he travelled, with the pouncet-box and ink.

Logan, watching from my shoulder, asked, 'Where are his papers? I should take those now and keep them safe.'

I hesitated, wanting to be truthful, and yet wanting to preserve my father's honour. He did not deserve to have his failings and his past mistakes forever colour how he was remembered, like a drop of ink will stain a glass of water.

I didn't know if God himself had so arranged things that my father might be gifted with the chance to ask forgiveness for what he had done, and for what he was doing to Sir David; or if it had been my father's stars, as he so fancied, which had brought him to this place and let him hear that sermon in the days before he died. But in the end, it did not matter. He'd repented and he'd set things right, and I felt certain he *had* been forgiven, and had gone now to his peace, and I'd not break it.

All I said to Logan of the papers was, 'He burned them.'

'Burned them? When was this?'

I told him, 'Yesterday. He wished to play no part in what

you're doing to Sir David.' Which was true, but I had phrased it poorly. 'I am sorry. What I meant to say was—'

'I ken what ye meant.' When Logan turned away from me, I could not see his face but from his voice I knew my words had touched too sharply where I hadn't meant to do him harm.

It likely was because of this that I did something highly out of character.

On Thursday afternoon, while I was passing by the dining room, the landlord hailed me. 'Beg your pardon, Mistress, as I know you're busy with all the arrangements for your father, may he rest in peace, but as your lad's off fetching ale just at the moment, I do wonder whether I might give you this to take out to your husband? He was wanting it directly.'

'This' was a sizeable mortar and pestle of bronze, holding a small bag of what looked to be sugar candy. I knew that Sir David and Logan had gone to the stables to see to the horses, and normally only necessity made me go anywhere within ten feet of a stables, but I felt I owed it to Logan, and anyway, I wanted company.

That was a brave enough start. By the time I reached the stable door, I was rethinking my decision. I could smell the beasts, and breathing in the scents of horse and hay, I felt a moment's panic. Stepping back to one side of the open doorway, I drew deeper breaths and sought to calm myself.

From here, I heard Sir David's voice.

'The simple thing to do,' he said, 'is to send Hector back to Leith together with the mare.'

'Except,' said Logan, 'I'm not sending Hector back. Not on his own. He's but a lad, it's far too dangerous.'

'Well, naturally. I said it was the simple thing to do,' Sir David told him. 'Not the best thing.'

'No,' said Logan. 'I'll hire someone else to take the mare,

and put it on account. They can be paid by Lady Lindsay when they get there. They can take their time in doing it, and give the mare some rest. And ye can ride the gelding.'

'Or,' Sir David said, 'we keep the mare, and Mistress Westaway can ride her.'

'No,' said Logan.

'Why not? Brutus would welcome a lighter load. I know she's nervous of horses, but surely, with one or two lessons—'

'No,' Logan said, more strongly. 'She is more than nervous.'

'Frightened, then. But all fears can be conquered.'

'Can they?' Logan's tone was harsher than I'd ever heard it. 'What would ye ken of Phoebe's fears? She lost her family, all except her father, to the plague when she was small. And when the dead cart came to take her mother and her brothers, she ran after it to stop them, and another cart horse knocked her down. A lass but four years old,' he said, 'against a horse the size of Brutus. Picture that. And when ye've done that, toss in all the feelings she'd have felt upon that morn, and ye'll come close to understanding why she can't abide the sight of horses.' He fell silent for a moment, and I heard the scraping of a brush against one of the horses, rhythmic and with purpose. 'That's a fear ye cannot conquer,' Logan said, 'with a few lessons.'

I was frozen where I stood, in total shock. I hadn't known that Logan knew. It never once had crossed my mind to think that—

'Do forgive me,' said Sir David. 'I had no idea. I thought . . .'

'Aye, I ken what ye thought. But ye're never to suggest it to her, else she'll think she's weak, and I'll not have that. I'll not have that,' he repeated as the scraping stopped. I heard a rustling sound as though he'd turned upon the hay where he was standing so he faced Sir David. 'Are we clear?'

'Aye,' said Sir David. 'We are very clear.'

I could not stand forever in the shadows of the doorway like a coward. Someone soon would come along and I'd be noticed, and then everyone would know that I'd been standing here and listening. Much better if they thought I'd just arrived.

I drew a breath and set my shoulders and walked briskly through the door.

Logan stood beside the gelding, and as I approached he set his back to me and went on with his grooming of the horse. He always moved that way, now that I thought of it, whenever we were near a horse together. I'd just thought that he was being rude. But now I saw the move for what it truly was – not an attempt to shut me out, but an attempt to shield me, standing squarely between me and what I feared.

To his back, I said, 'The landlord sends you sugar candy and this pestle.'

Standing at my other side, Sir David swept in charmingly. 'Ah! For your secret cordial powder, Logan. Now I'll finally see how it is made.'

Logan turned his head and looked at me over his shoulder. 'Thank ye, Phoebe.'

'It was nothing.' With a quick nod of my head, I turned and left them before I betrayed the depth of the emotion I was feeling.

I'd have given much that week to have passed one hour without tears.

But grief did not allow me that. It found me without warning, rising suddenly in surges for which I was unprepared. They always brought an unexpected rush of tears that filled my eyes and, even if they didn't quite spill over, made me sharply turn my head or even stop and close my eyes, until the surge had passed and I was once more in control.

I wanted sleep, but could not find it. Wanted food, but could not eat it. Wanted a distraction, but could take no interest in the world beyond my chamber door.

My father's funeral was on Friday of that Whitsun-week. They buried him near to the yew tree in the corner of the churchyard. He would have approved of that spot, from which a living man might gaze up at the steeple of the grand and lovely church against the summer sky, or watch the fledgling birds a-flutter in the branches of the trees.

I must confess I did not listen to the solemn words said by the minister, but after it was done and the few other mourners – there were very few – had gone, Sir David stood beside the grave, in his black doublet, looking down at where my father lay.

'Though thou be dead in part, all cannot die,' he said. 'Thy mind's brave conquest shall survive thy breath.'

I said, 'That's beautiful. Who wrote it?'

'I did.'

I'd forgotten that Sir David was a poet. I could feel my eyes begin to swim again with tears. I blinked them back and told him, 'Thank you.'

He was such a gallant man. A good man, as my father called him. In these short weeks, I'd become accustomed to his company.

But it was strange to see him riding on the gelding as we headed out of Newark on Monday morning.

The black mare had been entrusted to a local groom who'd see her safely north to Leith. The groom had met us in the courtyard of our inn, where Logan gave him the instructions for her care, and stroked the mare's sleek neck, and told her calmly, reassuringly, 'Ye will be fine now, lassie. Ye were bred to walk a gentler road than this one, were ye not?' She'd nuzzled at his sleeve and he had given her a final pat and said,

'Ye will be well.' Yet I could tell he hadn't wished to leave her. Logan truly did care deeply for the horses, and I had the sense that part of him would always be a stable lad.

As we left the town, we passed a gallows at the roadside. It was empty, much to Hector's disappointment, though Sir David told him to be cautious what he wished for.

'When I first came down from Scotland with the prince,' Sir David said, 'there was a man yet hanging from this gallows.'

Hector's mood improved. 'What was his crime? Was he a murderer?'

'A cutpurse, who, appearing like a gentleman, had travelled down from Berwick with the court and robbed them all that way.'

'From which ye should take note,' Logan told Hector, 'that not every gentleman is what he seems to be, beneath his fine and fancy clothes. Nor is he to be trusted.'

Hector looked towards Sir David, who by changing his expression and adjusting his cloak round his shoulders, tried to look untrustworthy.

Hector ignored him, keen to know more about the cutpurse. 'How did they catch him?'

'I'm afraid I do not know, I was not there,' Sir David said. 'I only know they brought him to King James, who ordered he be hanged. There was no trial.'

I frowned. 'No trial? But that is not in keeping with the law.'

'Whose law?' Sir David asked. 'The law of common men? Or kings? Because I can assure you, King James does acknowledge only one of those.'

Logan warned him, quietly, 'Be careful with your words, because your talk does sound like treason.'

'Does it? Well, it may be I'm not thinking clearly. I am tired.' Sir David did look weary as he said, 'At any rate, some people thought it was a poor way for King James to start his reign in England.'

'Why?' asked Hector.

'Well,' Sir David said, 'if that was how the wind would blow with King James on the throne, if he would hang a man before that man was brought to trial, why then would he not bring a man to trial before that man had done aught wrong?'

He left that question there, for us to ponder, as we carried on towards the south, where London lay; but for some distance I could feel that empty gallows waiting, ever watchful, at our backs.

Anna, Queen of Britain

Bath, Somerset, 29th May 1613

A bird of prey was circling high above, against the sun. From time to time, it would be lost from view behind the high walls that enclosed this bath, the one they called the King's Bath, with its healing pool of sea-green water bubbling from an ancient spring.

Her doctor had been moving her according to his regimen – one day the great bath, then the small, and then no bath at all, a purge, and now again the King's Bath, which was largest of them all and fully open to the sky.

From where she was sitting, on the stone seat in its arched niche set within the wall, with the water rising warmly past her chest, Queen Anna had a broad view of the bath with all the windows overlooking it, the ornamented stonework and the several ladies who'd been tasked to wait upon her in attendance, wearing, like her, canvas shifts designed to mask the body's shape more artfully than linen.

But Anna had grown tired of watching water and the women, so instead she leaned her head back and looked up. And so she saw the bird.

She didn't know what kind it was – mayhap an eagle. James would know. It was a bird of prey, which meant it had to do with hunting, and if it had aught to do with hunting, James would know.

'He loves his hawks and hounds more than he ever will love us,' Henry complained once, and although she had corrected him, she'd known that he was right.

She still recalled the evening, not even two months after the death of their little Mary, when James had come into her chamber, distraught.

'She is gone,' he'd said, as though the loss had just struck him. 'She's gone, Anna. What shall I do?'

And she'd reached for him, giving him comfort, relieved that he'd finally permitted himself to grieve for their daughter. Anna had been finding it so difficult to stumble through this time alone, with everyone insisting she should show a brave face to the world.

'I thought you didn't care,' she'd said.

'Not care! Do you know just how rare a white gyrfalcon is?' James asked. 'To have one fly away and not return is . . . well, the loss is more than I can bear.' He'd slumped into a chair, head in his hands, and she had looked at him in silence for a moment.

Then she'd quietly gone out and closed the door.

Above her now, against the sunlit sky, the bird of prey made one more circle, full of purpose. Henry, too, might have been able to identify the bird, not because he loved hunting over-much, but because he took such an interest in all things, and had such a wide scope of knowledge.

He'd lost much of his taste for hunting in the year that he turned seventeen, when he and James had gone to Royston with a hunting party from the court, as they had done before. Only Rochester had been there, too, and things were always infinitely worse whenever Rochester was there.

She hadn't been there riding with them, hadn't seen what happened, hadn't heard their words; but she'd been told that James had reprimanded Henry, there in front of everyone, and Henry hadn't stood for that – he'd straightened in his saddle and replied in cutting tones that brought his father's temper to the boil. James raised his whip as though to strike, and Henry wheeled his horse and galloped off, leaving the other hunters with a choice: stay with the king or follow Henry. Most had followed Henry.

'You apologized, I hope,' Anna said to Henry when she had been told about the incident. She'd gone to visit him at Richmond, and they'd walked in the Long Gallery, where Henry kept his paintings and the other works of art and curiosities he was collecting.

'I made a very nice apology,' said Henry, 'though it earned me little but an insult. He forgave me but he also told me I was a poor huntsman. Which I might have given answer to, but David trod upon my foot.'

'Entirely by accident,' Sir David Moray said. He was, as always, walking a few paces just behind them.

'Yes, of course,' said Henry, with a smile that showed how little he believed it. That was the year he set aside French fashions and began to dress in the more modest, plain Italian style. It made him look more manly. 'It's just as well you stopped me, though. I should not so demean myself. And anyway, he is not wrong. I never have much cared to hunt, and Father cares for little else.' His tone, though light, held bitterness. 'He loves his hawks and hounds more than he ever will love us.'

Anna reassured him he was wrong. 'Your father loves you.'

'Does he? If the stables were aflame, and Jewel and I were trapped inside' – he named his father's favourite hound, a brutish and ill-tempered beast – 'and Father could choose to save only one of us, then I'd be lost.' But Henry smiled again, as if to show he didn't care. He slipped his hand in Anna's, as he'd done when he was small. 'You are the only one he does respect. One day, you'll have to share the secret,' Henry said, 'of how you manage it.'

It's not respect, she could have told him then. *It's done by finding something strong enough to bargain with, and using that as leverage.*

Sitting in the King's Bath now, Queen Anna realized, from that memory, how she might still help Sir David Moray.

Word had reached her earlier this week that he had been arrested, and was on the road to London with the Messenger. But perhaps all hope was not yet lost.

For, after all, James had spared Lord Balmerino's life, not because he loved her, but because he feared the truth that she might otherwise reveal.

Sir David knew the truth about what happened to her son. She felt convinced of this. The old blind man had told her so.

And once Sir David shared that truth with her, then she could save *his* life, as she had saved Lord Balmerino's. She would have to take events into her own hands, and return to London.

The bird of prey passed lower, and its shadow chased across the waters.

Suddenly, a narrow column of pure fire, like the flame of some great candle, swiftly rose straight through the water of the bath, not eight feet from where Anna sat. As it reached the surface of the water, it spread instantly into a burning circle that flared sharply and was just as suddenly blown out, the way a life might be extinguished by a greater hand.

The ladies let out a wild, collective shrieking, but Queen Anna did not move, nor did she make a sound. Her heart raced in her throat and she had one thought only: *Henry.*

She saw again the blind man's upturned face, and heard his voice: *He said to tell you that he kept his promise. That his flames of truth and justice are yet burning, as you wished.*

He kept his promise.

And she would not fail him.

She looked up. The bird of prey had ceased its circling and was soaring in a straight line, heading eastward.

Anna stood, and bid her ladies find their courage. 'It is time for us to leave.'

Andrew

Huntingdon, Huntingdonshire, 2nd June 1613

HECTOR WOULDN'T FALL ASLEEP.

I thought at first he feared the dark, as he'd done at the Roman Wall, for he was just a lad who had been thrown too soon onto his road alone, and had a right to see more shadows than the rest of us. But it was not the dark.

Even when I had lit a candle with some vague excuse of needing one to find some item in my pack, the lad stayed sitting upright on his pallet bed, eyes fixed and wide with fierce determination.

In the proper bed, Sir David slept and lightly snored. I'd given him that comfort knowing he'd likely have little of it once we got to London, and because he was the oldest of us, now that Westaway was gone.

I kept my voice low, so I did not waken him, and said to Hector, 'Messengers must get their sleep, lad.'

He sent me a glance that was pure misery. 'I can't. They'll come and get me then.'

'Who will?'

He said, 'The minister said Master Westaway was carried up tae heaven by the angels. And they came while he was sleeping.'

I began to see the problem.

Hector told me, 'I don't wish tae go tae heaven.'

'Well, of course ye do. But not the now, I'll grant ye.' My heart softened, for he looked so small against the darkness. 'Never fear, lad. Did I not already promise ye that ye've no chance of dying while I'm guarding ye?'

He hadn't yet forgotten what I'd told him in the Tarras Moss, because he nodded. 'But . . . what if the angels come tae carry me tae heaven while ye're sleeping, too?'

So many worries for such a wee lad. 'Hector,' I said, 'if anyone, angel or no, tries to take ye to heaven, I'll break the damn'd gates down and bring ye right back.'

'Truly?'

'Ye have my word.'

Which was all the assurance he needed to lay down his head on the pallet at last. He was sleeping within a few minutes. I would have been, too, had I not heard the sounds from the chamber beside our own.

Phoebe's terrible dreams seemed to find her most nights, and although she made nearly no noise, I was always aware when she had them. The pattern was always the same: she would toss, and then stop, and then toss yet more violently. And then she'd waken, and fall still, or rise and walk restlessly over the floor.

But tonight, she did something she'd never done. She called out, 'Logan!'

Sir David and Hector kept sleeping, but I answered that call so quickly I scarce touched the floorboards as I went into the corridor and into Phoebe's room, bringing the candle with me.

She was still asleep, but in a terror, her eyes wide and staring. Moving cautiously towards the bed, I said, low, 'Phoebe? Waken up, now.' But she didn't waken properly until I touched her shoulder. 'Ye've been dreaming,' I explained, when she looked up at me.

She blinked and told me, 'You were gone,' as if that revealed everything. And when I would have drawn away, she grabbed my arm and told me, 'No. Don't leave me, Logan. Please don't go.'

All men have limits. She was testing mine. Her hair was loose and long about her shoulders. She was in her shift. The room was full of moonlight. And she drew me down to sit with her upon the bed.

But Phoebe wasn't meant to be my lass. I'd Seen that when I'd kissed her, at the fair. I'd raised my head to look at her and all the world had wavered and begun to blur, and suddenly I'd Seen her, not at Newark, but against a sunlit wall, and Valentine had stood beside her with a smug expression, holding to her hand. He'd told me, 'Give us your congratulations, Logan. Phoebe has agreed to be my wife.'

I'd felt the pain of that as though I had been shot through with a bullet. I could feel it now. But whatever I Saw would surely happen, and could not be wished away. I could do no more than to protect my heart – and hers – by keeping things between us honourable and cordial and no more.

But Phoebe looked at me and asked, 'Will you please hold me?'

'Phoebe . . .'

'Please.'

And so I pushed my limits just a little further. Sitting back upon the bed, and keeping carefully outside the quilts, I gathered Phoebe in my arms so she would feel secure, and not be frightened of whatever demons chased her in her dreams.

She leaned against me, gratefully. After a while she said, 'They shut you in, you know, when you have plague. They lock the house and no one can come in or leave.'

She spoke for the first time to me about her mother and her brothers, and what she remembered of them. Sometimes there were warmer memories. Always there was sadness.

Then she asked, 'How did you know about the horse?'

So she *had* overheard us. I'd suspected it, from how she'd

looked at me when she had come into the stables on that day at Newark. I told her, 'My mother telt me, years ago. She likely heard it from your aunt. They talk.'

'I see.'

''Tis not a fault to be ashamed of, fearing horses,' I assured her. 'I've seen grown men who'd not stand within arm's length of Brutus, and ye show more courage every day than them.'

'I'm not so brave, not really. I think often of the phantoms that I saw when we were coming to Northallerton,' she said to me, 'and wonder just how many might be walking in these rooms with us.'

I glanced around the chamber. 'None.'

The smile in her voice was meant to chide me for what she believed was my attempt to soothe her with a lie. 'You cannot know for certain.'

'Aye, I can, in fact.' If I was not to have her, I at least would have full truth between us where I could. I paused, then took a leap of faith. 'Those riders that ye saw above Northallerton,' I said. 'I saw them, too.' And I described them, so she'd not have any doubt.

She went completely still against my chest. 'How is that possible?'

'Among my mother's people of the Western Isles of Scotland, there's a gift, or curse more like, we call the Sight – the Second Sight. It gives us glimpses of what is to come. The Sight is passed along in families through the blood. My mother's father had it strongly,' I said. 'As do I.'

She turned her head and stared at me and said, 'You are not serious.'

'I wish that I were not.'

'You can see things that haven't happened yet?'

I nodded, and she seemed to be struck by a realization.

'When your eyes ... when you do this' – she did a striking imitation of what I must look like to those watching – 'are you Seeing then?'

'Aye.'

Phoebe looked away again and thought on this a moment. 'Can you do it when you wish?'

'No.'

'When we Saw the riders, how was it that I ... how could I See them?'

'You were touching me.' I told her how it worked among the people of the Western Isles when they desired to share the things they Saw.

'But if you cannot do it when you wish,' she asked me, 'how then can you ever share your visions?'

I admitted that I did not know.

'Mayhap I'll have to hold you always,' Phoebe said, and drew my arms more tightly round her, leaning back against my chest. She could not know how deep an ache that drove into my heart.

I felt her head grow heavy as she drifted, but her mind was busy and she still had questions. 'Logan?'

'Aye?' I brought my head down closer.

'Did you See my father? Did you know when he would die?'

This part was difficult, but still I told the truth. 'I knew his time was short. I Saw no more than that.'

The minutes passed, and then she asked, 'Logan?'

'Aye?'

'Have you Seen me?'

My mother always held it was unkind to tell a person what you'd Seen about their future, and I used that now as an excuse to set aside the truth for this one time.

I told her, 'No.'

'Good. For I would not wish to know.'

She did not speak again, but settled her head warm beneath my shoulder, with her cheek turned softly to the solid beating of my heart. I kept my arms around her long after her breathing told me that she was asleep. I stayed there, sitting in that same position, holding her. After a while I let my head rest back against the panelled wall, and I slept, too, but I did not let go of Phoebe. Not this night.

Soon enough, the time would come when I would have to. Not this night.

Valentine would have her for a lifetime.

But this night was hers and mine.

PHOEBE

Royston, Hertfordshire, 4th June 1613

ROYSTON WAS A MARKET town that formerly depended on the business of its corn-traders, until the king had chanced to stop here on his first long journey down from Scotland, and had fallen so enamoured of it that he'd built his hunting-lodge here. Now, most of the buildings on the town's main streets were given to the king's use, as Sir David had pointed out when we'd arrived early yesterday evening.

'There, just past the hunting lodge, that's where the equerries stay,' he had told me, 'while opposite, in all those houses, are the other servants and the stable lads. To this side of the lodge, that is the buttery, and then this building houses the king's guard.'

The narrow street, and that which crossed it, seemed a court unto itself, complete with kennels for the hunting dogs, a cockpit, and a bowling green.

'Where did the prince stay?' Hector asked Sir David.

He had only hesitated slightly, no doubt fighting memories. 'Here.' The regal house upon the corner, but we'd turned the horses then, and with our backs towards it we had travelled up the street a little distance to our inn.

Our chambers shared a private parlour that had but one access from outside. It led to the first floor gallery that overlooked the courtyard and the stables just behind the inn, so we were well secured. But still, I didn't sleep well. Maybe it was from the noise below us in the street, for Royston was a busy town. Or maybe it was because I was overtired from our day's ride, which had been long. Or maybe it was simply that I kept remembering the feel of Logan holding me, at Huntingdon.

He'd still been there when I'd awakened, which surprised me. He had been awake himself, and looking at the window, thinking. But the minute that I'd moved, his focus shifted and his eyes met mine.

'Good morrow,' he had told me.

Things felt different in the daylight. I'd been suddenly self-conscious and had gathered up the quilts with both my hands. 'Good morrow.'

'Are ye well, now?'

'Yes,' I said. And, 'Thank you.' And then, because it had seemed important he should know, 'I won't ... that is, the things you said last night, about how you can See what is to come. I won't tell anybody else.'

His eyes had done that trick again, where they did gather warmer colour. Mayhap it was something grey eyes did. 'If I thought that ye might,' he said, 'I never would have telt ye.'

And then he had sat upright, and he'd let me go, and before I could think of anything to say to keep him there, he'd touched my shoulder lightly with one hand, and stood, and left me.

Had that truly been just yesterday? I'd replayed it now so many times within my mind it seemed much longer since it happened. So no, I did not sleep well last night, and this morning I rose early and, while waiting for our breakfast, sought distraction in my father's well-loved copy of Mr Parker's almanac.

The weather, Mr Parker promised, would hold fair for this day and the next. The moon tomorrow would be new – a time of changes. But against today's date, Mr Parker had marked one of his red 'D's for 'Danger', warning that the day would hold misfortune.

I had never taken almanacs and their predictions seriously, but today, that 'D' made me uneasy.

'What does Mr Parker say?' Sir David asked me, as he came into the parlour.

I looked up, and closed the almanac. 'The weather will be fine.'

'Good.' He turned to Logan, who had just come in with Hector as his ever-present shadow. 'Mistress Westaway assures us we'll have sunshine all the day. Where are you leading us?'

Before he answered, Logan greeted me and said, 'Ye should have stayed in bed, it looks like. Ye've had two long days of riding, and two nights with little sleep.'

He might have put that last more gallantly, but fortunately Hector was too young to draw the wrong conclusions and Sir David was a perfect gentleman who didn't bat an eye.

I said, 'I'm well enough to travel.'

'Nonetheless, ye'll have some space to rest the day,' said Logan. To Sir David, he went on, 'We're heading to the Falcon next, at Puckeridge, but it's not safe to travel in the daylight. If we leave an hour afore the sunset, we'll be there by midnight.'

I stared at him across the table. 'There'll hardly be a moon tonight.'

He told me, 'All the better. In the meantime, Hector, after breakfast, I need ye to run down to the house where the king's equerries stay, past the hunting lodge, and fetch a bridle for me.'

Hector looked uncertain. 'Me?'

'Aye. I had rather not be strolling down the street if I can help it. Tis the king's town, and the walls have eyes, and I'm too recognizable.'

I frowned, because he usually seemed more relaxed when he was close to men who served the king. At Brancepeth, he had even worn his scarlet. 'But you were known and recognized,' I pointed out, 'when we were in Northallerton. And there, you did not seem to mind.'

Logan said, 'Royston is nothing like Northallerton. This is the court in miniature. There may be men with secret orders lying here in wait to stop Sir David and myself.' He put it in plain words. 'The prince is dead. If he *was* murdered, those who did it wish to hide that truth, not have it come to light at trial.'

I saw a flash of deep emotion cross Sir David's face. 'You cannot think that I would be in league with those who—'

'Killed the prince? Of course not,' Logan told him. 'But I think ye might hold evidence that can condemn the ones who did.' He waited, but Sir David did not choose to meet his challenge. Logan turned his head and met my eyes. 'Your father burned his papers, which does tell me there was something going on within our mission that he did not trust. We would be wise to follow his example.'

Logan once again instructed Hector how to find the house of the king's equerries, and gave a name to ask for, and a second name in case the first man was not there. 'Tell him that ye need a Northern bridle, red if he does have it, and well oiled. Tell him who it's for,' he said, 'but do it very quietly.'

I saw the war of thoughts and worries wage on Hector's features. On the one hand, he was desperate to win Logan's praise, but on the other, he had just heard Logan talk about how Royston was so dangerously unsafe.

And he was just a boy.

I smiled brightly at him. 'Would you mind if I came, too?'

'What?' Hector asked.

'What?' Logan asked.

I faced them both with innocence. 'It would be nice to get

some air, and exercise my legs. It isn't far. Just down the road. We will be there and back before you know it,' I told Logan. 'Hector will take care of me.'

'That's right,' said Hector, straightening. 'I'll guard your lady. You can guard Sir David.'

I reflected that, had anybody told me just a month ago I'd like to be called Logan's lady, I'd have thought them mad. Completely. Irretrievably. Today, I only felt my face grow warmer as I caught the edge of Logan's glance and looked away again before he read my thoughts.

Sir David said, 'That's very thoughtful of you, Hector. But perhaps I'll come along with you two. You can guard me, also.'

'No,' said Logan. 'Ye'll stay here and help me with the horses.' There was private meaning in the firm look that he sent Sir David. 'That is not a risk ye need to take.'

If I had felt the change in Logan's attitude after Northallerton, I felt it even stronger now – he was not Sir David's jailor anymore, but his protector. I couldn't help but wonder how he'd cope with being thrust again into that former, harder role when he was forced to bring Sir David to the king.

'From Puckeridge,' Sir David mused, as though his thoughts had followed the same path, 'we will be only one day's ride from London.'

'Aye,' said Logan.

And we said no more about it over breakfast, because we all realized what that meant, and none of us were ready for it.

Hector would make a good Messenger. He grew nervous when we passed the great brick-fronted hunting lodge that jutted out into the road, with its gables and tiled roof and two tall chimneys, and approached the smaller house not far beyond. But he knocked bravely at the door, and asked by name for the first equerry whom Logan had requested, and delivered him the message as discreetly as if he'd already been in the king's service.

'You did that perfectly,' I praised him when the bridle was delivered. 'Logan will be proud.'

Hector beamed. With the bridle slung over his shoulder, he continued to take his duties seriously, walking between me and the street to protect me from anyone passing on foot or on horseback. But this time, when we passed the king's great hunting lodge, a man stepped from the doorway and grabbed my hand.

Hector cried out. If the boy had been wearing a sword, he'd have run the man through, but it happened so quickly that neither of us had much time to react. And, in the end, the man did nothing threatening – only raised my hand and kissed it.

'Phoebe! I'm so glad we found you.'

Still in shock, I blinked and stared at Valentine. 'Whatever are you doing here?'

'We are on the king's business.'

That was the second time he'd used the plural. I asked, 'We?'

He turned to the tall man who lounged a little distance off against a nearby wall, resplendent in a suit of slashed pale blue with trim of braided gold. 'Lord Rochester,' he said, 'may I present my neighbour, Phoebe Westaway.'

'I am enchanted.'

I had seen Lord Rochester before, but from a distance. Then, he'd seemed a paragon – his curling auburn hair, his perfect beard, his dashing earring, and his walk that seemed to tell the world here was a man to reckon with. Now, close at hand, I only noticed that he wore the same expensive, cloying scent as Valentine, and that they both seemed weighted down with finery, and that their hair must take them a long time each morning to arrange.

Not so with men like Logan, who more often smelled of horses and of honest sweat and soap, and owned but simple clothing, and wore their hair close-cropped against their heads, and spent their coins and time in ways of more importance.

Valentine had not let go of my hand, but I lowered my eyes with respect and curtseyed.

Rochester's gaze moved to Hector. 'And this must be Hector . . . Reid, is it? Well met, young man.'

Hector bowed and stammered out a greeting in reply. He seemed to take pride in the fact that a man of obvious importance would already know his name. It made me apprehensive.

We were standing in a public street with people all around us, I could hear their cheerful talk and laughter, and the day was bright. The sky was brilliant blue above the rooftops of the houses, and the sunlight fell with warmth upon my face. But I felt suddenly alone, and very cold.

Valentine chided me, 'You did not write, as you promised to do.'

That was an easy thing to answer. 'You surely must have known,' I said, 'it would not be permitted.'

With a smile, Valentine looked again to Rochester. 'I told you, did I not? I told you he would not allow it.'

'Aye, you did.'

They clearly spoke of Logan, so I raised my chin and said in his defence, 'I could not write to you by the king's orders. It was in the warrant, Valentine.'

He searched my face with interested eyes, and then he shrugged. 'No matter. We did manage to keep track of you, although you didn't make it easy. Our men lost sight of you for some days between Hawick and Brancepeth. I did fear the worst.'

The knowledge other men besides the Graemes had been following us brought a chill into my veins but I tried not to let it show. I told him, 'There was no need. I was being well looked after.'

'So I see. But I am sorry,' he said, 'to learn of your father's death.' He said it in a tone that dripped of sympathy, and had this been a month ago, I'm sure I'd have believed him.

Now, I felt that growing sense of unease deep within my belly, and knew well enough to pay it heed. The perfumed scent of both men, standing close to me combined, was almost stifling, and not thinking, I drew out my handkerchief to shield my nose and mouth so I could breathe some cleaner air.

Valentine said, 'I do agree, the wood fires have too strong a smell this morning. We should get you off the street. Where are you staying?'

Hector said, before I thought to warn him, 'At the Bull, just up the road.'

'Then we will walk you back,' said Valentine.

I said, 'That is not necessary.'

Rochester slipped smoothly into step with us, reminding me of nothing so much as the adder that had crossed our path within the Tarras Moss. Except the adder had not meant us harm. 'I do insist,' he said.

I waited till we'd passed the guardhouse, then touched Hector on his shoulder. 'You should run ahead,' I said, as cheerfully as possible, 'for Logan needs that bridle.'

But as Hector nodded, Rochester reached down to rest a

hand on the boy's shoulder, so he stayed with us. 'Oh, I think he can wait.'

None of the people we passed understood what was happening, and there was nothing they could have done. This was the king's town, and Rochester was the king's favourite, so who was to cross him?

Still holding my hand, Valentine sent a curious look down towards me. 'That isn't the handkerchief I gave you.'

'No. I'm afraid I misplaced that one.'

Once again I was an object of study. 'No matter. I'll buy you a new one,' he said, 'for a wedding gift.'

I nearly choked. 'A what?'

'My lord Northampton lately did inform me that he made arrangements with your father for us to be married. I'll admit, it caught me somewhat unawares, but it will greatly please *my* father. He has long been keen to see me settled.'

'Valentine . . .'

'And then, of course, *my* prize in the arrangement is a baronetcy. Would you not be pleased to be the lady of a baronet?'

'But, Valentine . . .'

'Ah, here we are.'

My head was whirling as we passed beneath the archway leading to the courtyard of the inn, and when we came into the cobbled space I stood a moment with my back turned to the sunlit wall and tried to sort my thoughts enough to make a firm reply.

Ahead of us, the stables stretched in a long line, washed white with lime beneath a slanting tiled roof. And in the open doorway Logan stood, eyes wary, watching us.

He looked as though I'd struck him, and I wanted to assure him that it wasn't what it seemed, but Valentine spoke first.

He raised my hand, held firmly in his own, and called out,

'Give us your congratulations, Logan. Phoebe has agreed to be my wife.'

I tore my fingers from his grasp. 'I have done no such thing.' I stepped away, and brushed my hand upon my skirt as though to cleanse it, and then I told Hector, 'Come now, Hector, bring the bridle.'

Logan's face cleared, and his shoulders rose and fell as though he'd taken a deep breath of pure relief, and with a nod he motioned we should get behind him, though he spared a smile for us as we came near. 'Ye took your time,' he told me.

'We had company.'

'Aye, so I see.' He took a step into the sunshine. Logan could bow gracefully, when he had cause. 'Good morrow, my lord Rochester.'

He was granted a nod in return. 'Logan.' Rochester's gaze swept him, archly. 'I see you're not wearing your livery.'

'No, my lord. I thought it safer, considering who was my prisoner, not to draw too much attention.'

'I see. No doubt it's been a great burden,' said Rochester, 'but I am here to relieve you of that.'

Logan frowned. 'My lord?'

'I will be taking Sir David to London. The king has requested it. 'Tis why I'm here. We were sent to await your arrival.' Rochester smiled narrowly. 'Clearly our guardsmen weren't keeping a close enough eye on the streets. Or the inns.'

'Aye, well, I'd not be too hard on them,' Logan said. 'We did arrive at the hour when they commonly do eat their supper, they most likely missed us.'

I hadn't heard anyone moving behind us, but Rochester said, 'Ah, good morrow, Sir David. A pleasure to see you again.' And he made a slight, mocking bow.

Sir David stood to the side, just behind me, and neither replied nor moved.

Valentine said, 'He's not fettered. Is that wise?'

Ignoring him, Logan told Rochester, 'I'll see your warrant, then.'

'I beg your pardon?'

'I'll not hand Sir David to anyone without the king's own authority.'

Rochester's hand touched the hilt of his sword as he straightened, indignantly. 'I *am* the king's own authority.'

'Nevertheless.'

How could Logan keep calm? I was quaking inside, but his eyes and his voice were like ice, and I sought to draw strength from them, looking instead towards Rochester. That was how I saw the change of expression, like wheels turning in a machine, in the instant before he reached into his pocket.

'All right, then. If you do insist upon reading the warrant, I have it here.'

He held it out for Logan, but I knew, with utter certainty, from looking at his face, that he knew Logan could not read.

Logan hesitated. Set his jaw.

And I stepped in between them. Looking up at Logan I said, 'Wait, your hands are dirty from the horses. Let me read it for you.' And I boldly took the paper that Lord Rochester was offering before he could retract it.

In the courtyard, no one spoke while I read through the paper silently.

'My lord,' I said to Rochester, 'I'm sorry, but I fear you've laid your hand upon the wrong item mistakenly, for this is not your warrant. It's a letter from your tailor.'

His eyes met mine with deep impatience. 'Is it?' Snatching

back the letter, he examined it and rammed it once more deep into his pocket. 'So it is. The warrant must be in my chamber, still. Come, Fox.' He looked past me to Logan. 'Wait here till we do return.'

'Of course.'

But once they'd vanished through the archway, Logan turned to us and told us, 'Right. No time to waste. We're leaving. Up and get your things.'

I would have followed Hector and Sir David, only Logan held me back a moment. Tipping up my face with one hand, he looked closely at my features and then asked, 'How did ye ken I couldn't read?'

At first, my father's voice spoke up: *He mustn't know I've told you.* So I quickly spun a tale that sounded true enough.

'I guessed,' I said. 'You never read things for yourself, you always have them read to you, and when you need to write something, you always use a scribe.'

Logan was too clever, though, and when his eyes met mine, I knew he knew he'd caught me in a lie.

I sighed. 'My father told me,' I confessed, 'in Newark, but he told me all in secret, and he made me promise not to let you know. He did not wish to hurt you.'

'Nothing that your father did could hurt me,' Logan said. 'He was a good man. Though I'm sorry that I made ye break your word to him.' His smile was rueful. 'And I'm sorry that ye ever learned.'

It bruised my soul to know this big, strong man could think so little of himself he'd worry such a thing would make me think the less of him. Recalling what he'd told me of my fear of horses when he'd sought to give me comfort, I turned his own words back upon him now.

''Tis not a fault to be ashamed of,' I assured him. 'I've known men who read and write with ease who have not half of your intelligence, nor yet a quarter of your heart.'

He looked at me. His touch stayed gentle on my chin, but lowering his head he kissed me briefly. Kissed me hard.

There was not time for more.

Upstairs, we quickly gathered our belongings and repacked them in the portmanteaus. I was so focused on that task that later, I could not explain exactly how things happened. Only that one minute, all was well.

And then it wasn't.

Without warning, I was yanked back roughly by my arm, and found my back against a man's chest, with a knife point pressing just enough against the tender skin beneath my jawline that I felt the coldness of its steel.

I froze, and did not move. Except my eyes searched wildly for Logan, who stood several feet away against the far wall of the parlour, beside Hector and Sir David.

Logan's whole attention was on me, and on the man who held me captive. At my ear, Lord Rochester's voice said, in smooth tones, 'Let's forget the warrant, shall we? Let me have Sir David.'

Logan told him, 'If ye harm her, there'll be no place ye can hide.'

'I thank you for the warning. If he moves,' said Rochester to Valentine, who stood beside us, 'put a bullet in him.'

I could not turn my head, but from the corner of my eye I saw the pistol Valentine was aiming at the others, and my heart sank.

Hector kept looking from one person to the next with the expression of somebody watching a play on the stage, as if all of this didn't seem real. But when Rochester mentioned shooting Logan, Hector reacted with fear, and Sir David put one hand upon his shoulder, reassuringly.

'Don't worry, lad,' he said. 'It will be fine.'

Rochester said, 'Yes, Hector, be a good lad and fetch me Master Westaway's papers.'

I spoke up then, mindful of the blade beneath my chin: 'My father burned his papers when we were at Newark. They are gone.'

Rochester tensed. 'What, all?'

Sir David looked at him. 'A wrinkle in the plan?'

Logan frowned. 'What plan?'

Sir David, in his measured way, was striving not to set fire to the fuse. He calmly said, 'The king no doubt was hoping for a hasty trial, to put me in the Tower, so he could publish my "confession" and then I would die by … suicide?' He looked to Rochester for confirmation, and appeared to find it, for he nodded and went on, 'A fittingly ignoble end. And all would be resolved. But then,' he asked, 'why go through all the effort of this journey, when I could have been dispatched with ease in Paris or at Abercairney, and a false confession published anyway?'

I felt Rochester shrug. He said, 'Because the king desires a trial to lay the rumours all to rest and satisfy the people.'

''Tis a new thing for the king to give a care for what the people want,' Sir David said. 'You have your place at court still, after all.'

'Insult me all you like,' invited Rochester. 'It changes nothing.'

'But it gives me satisfaction.'

Logan said, to Rochester, 'Ye will not take my prisoner. I'll not allow it.'

'Then she dies.' Beneath my chin, the knife point moved. I felt a fierce prick, and the trickling warmth that meant that I was bleeding. Only slightly, but enough to bring a flare of rage and dark concern to Logan's eyes.

Beside us, Valentine reacted, too. 'You cannot kill her,' he protested. 'You did give your word. There is the matter of my baronetcy . . .'

'Lad,' Sir David told him, 'he cares nothing for your baronetcy, nor for you.'

'Ignore him, Fox,' said Rochester.

Sir David said, 'He's pure ambition, wrapped in silk.' He looked again at Rochester. 'Did you procure the poison, or was it my lady Essex?'

The pause was slight. 'I don't know what you mean.'

'Of course you do.' Sir David held Rochester's gaze with cold disdain, and said again, 'Of course you do.' Another pause, and then Sir David asked, 'Did the king know?'

Rochester didn't answer, but Sir David, as though reading something in the courtier's eyes, asked, 'Did he give his blessing?' And then his expression altered and he asked, more slowly, as though fearing the reply might be too dreadful, 'Did he play a part?'

Rochester held his silence, and Sir David looked away.

'God help us all,' he said.

Rochester gripped my arm more tightly and the knife dug in a second time. 'Enough of this. Sir David, come with us.'

Sir David patted Hector's shoulder, told him once again that everything would be all right, and started to step forwards.

'No!' In mingled disbelief and pure defiance, Hector said, 'Did not ye hear what Logan said? Ye will not take him!' And with that, he threw himself at Valentine.

The pistol shot rang out so loudly in that confined space that I felt certain it had stopped my heart. I watched – we all watched – Hector fall.

I never was quite sure who moved the fastest. With the acrid-smelling powder smoke still drifting through the air, obscuring some of what was happening, I caught a glimpse of Valentine and saw his stunned expression. I saw Sir David swiftly use that moment of confusion, as he left his place, to take Valentine's sword.

And then Sir David became someone I had never seen. At first, I wasn't sure why Rochester had flung me to the side and let me go, until I saw the speed and skill and fury of Sir David's fighting. Why I'd thought he was a docile man, I didn't know – perhaps it suited him to let us view him in that way, and he was grieving. But he'd spent his every hour for years beside a prince who loved to joust and run at rings and ride and fight, and, after all, Sir David was a knight.

I ran to Hector. He still breathed, but it was laboured. Under his jerkin, a red stain had spread on the shirt at his shoulder, and I saw the tear where the bullet had entered. I pressed at the place with my hand as I gathered him into my arms, with his head on my lap.

Logan, too, was no longer against the far wall. He was busy with Valentine. I didn't look, and I tried not to hear. I rocked Hector.

'Hold on. Please hold on, Hector,' I whispered.

Even with his own sword and the dagger he had held against me, Rochester was no match for Sir David, who had backed him up against the wall beside the door. Sir David, breathing heavily, touched Rochester with his sword's point beneath his chin, in the same place where Rochester hurt me, and pushed the blade in just enough to make him bleed.

'You would do well to run,' was his advice, 'before I kill you.'

He did not need to say it twice. He motioned towards Valentine and added, 'Take your dog.'

The two men slunk away, but still the room did not feel safe.

Not even after Logan came to crouch beside me, all his worry showing in his eyes.

'How is he?'

'Breathing. But it's bad.'

Sir David joined us. He was no longer the warrior, but only a man who'd lost a boy he cared for, and who plainly feared that he might lose another now.

I said, 'He needs a doctor.'

But Sir David shook his head. 'Not here. This is the king's town. I will trust no doctor here.'

I didn't see a way around it. 'We can't let him die.'

'I've no intention of letting him die.' Sir David's face, when he looked up at Logan, was determined. 'Ready the horses as quick as you can,' he said. 'I'll carry Hector. I know where to go.'

It was the longest ride I could remember.

'Hold tightly to me,' had been Logan's warning as we'd left the courtyard. 'We'll be moving fast.' And so we had.

Sir David had held Hector closely in his arms, before him on the saddle, and the Garron, secured to the gelding, kept pace alongside us as we left the main road south and moved through darker woods and over fields and marshy ground.

We stopped but once, at a small town where Sir David pounded at the door of an apothecary's and procured a handful of ingredients – I could recall the scents of turpentine and rose oil – and urgently applied these to the wound at Hector's shoulder.

'This is the French way,' he said, 'for treating gunshot.'

Logan frowned and asked, 'How did ye learn that?'

Without looking up, Sir David said, ''Tis better, sometimes, not to know all that there is to know about a man.'

At nightfall, by the last edge of the dying moon, we came to a small village where two churches stood close by each other in the darkness, and beside the smallest of them stood a house where candles burned within a window warmly, and Sir David said to Logan, 'Here.'

Things happened quickly, after that.

The door was opened to us by a man who knew Sir David, and his wife came just behind him, with their children peeping through from the half-opened door of their own chamber to discover what the cause was of this strange disturbance.

Hector, very carefully, was laid upon the kitchen pallet, near the fire. The man ran for the doctor, while his wife stood by Sir David as he cared for Hector's wound.

I'd never felt so helpless.

'Sit,' said Logan. He had taken water in a basin and a cloth and knelt before me as I crumpled to a leather-seated chair beside the door. 'Now, breathe.' And with the same sure, gentle touch he used when dealing with the horses, he began to wipe my throat, where I had bled.

I met his eyes.

'Brave lass,' he called me. Then he lightly kissed my forehead, and he stood.

I didn't feel brave. But I wanted to be brave for Logan. Drawing a deep breath, I looked around at this new room. Beside me was a table where somebody had been writing. There were fine, expensive papers stacked with care in one neat corner, a variety of pens and inks, and to my great amazement a small page ruled out in miniature, with penmanship far more exquisite than I'd ever seen.

No, that was not quite true. I'd seen its equal only recently, with my own eyes. At Leith.

I looked up quickly, staring at the woman who was standing by Sir David, holding up a candle for him while he saw to Hector.

I caught at Logan's sleeve when he would have walked off. 'Where are we?'

'I couldn't tell you.'

Sir David said, 'Willingale Spain.' When he glanced round, he noticed the way I was watching the woman and smiled slightly. 'I've been a poor friend and not introduced you. Madame Kello, may I present Mistress Westaway.'

I knew my face altered, because to all those who loved writing, the wife of the minister of Willingale Spain was known for more than her husband's accomplishments.

Sir David told her, 'See? Your fame does reach this younger generation. She knows who you are.'

She smiled, and said in a voice that still held a French accent, 'I'm honoured.'

I stood, only to drop into an awkward curtsey. It is a strange thing to meet our idols. But, 'The honour is all mine,' I said, to Esther Inglis.

DAVID

Willingale Spain, Essex, 9th June 1613

PHOEBE WESTAWAY KNEW. HE was certain of that. She was clever, she'd figured it out on their third morning there. She had found Esther's book of his poems – the one he had published two years ago, and she'd been reading the sonnets. The fifth one, in particular, had captured her attention. Curled into her chair, she'd read the lines aloud, from when he'd written of his need to tell his 'soul's felt-pain unto my fairest-fair', until the couplet that did end the poem, wistfully berating his reluctant tongue that could not speak the words he wished to say but had instead betrayed him one more time: 'Beat back with sighs, yet it returned again, but spake of pleasure when it should of pain.'

And Phoebe lay one hand against her heart as though it pained her, as she raised her head and looked at David. 'This is very sad.'

'I was a young man when I wrote it. My emotions ruled my reason.'

'But she broke your heart, this Celia.'

Esther's husband had been washing the face of their middle son, a boy who might be six or seven years of age and who had taken a great liking to Hector, and could rarely be persuaded to stray too far from the pallet bed in case his new friend should need something while he was healing, or in case the doctor, while on that day's visit, should want something fetched.

With a smile at Phoebe, Esther's husband had remarked, 'If

David ever tells you who she was, you must inform me. I did think I had it figured out once, but I've been reliably informed that I was wrong.'

Phoebe had looked startled. 'Was her name not truly Celia?'

Esther's husband shook his head. 'That is only a device. Every poet has his Celia. It is how he masks his true love's name, and guards his private life from prying eyes.'

David had, in that small moment, done something unwise. He'd looked at Esther. She'd been looking at him, too. Their eyes had briefly met, and held, and glanced away.

Her husband had not noticed. Had not seen.

But Phoebe had.

So now she knew.

If she had asked him outright, he'd have told her: Yes, I've only ever loved one woman in my life, and that is Esther Inglis. Yes, I lied and called her Celia in my tales because I feared your father's writings would expose her to great danger from the king. And yes, I love her still.

But Phoebe did not ask.

She let him guard his private life, for which David was grateful. Not that he'd had any private life to guard, of late. He had been fully occupied the first few days with Hector, till the lad's fever had broken and the doctor had allowed that he would live. Hector had each day seemed stronger then, and eaten more, and talked more brightly, leaving David more relaxed and more able to breathe.

The danger was, though, that left space for other feelings.

Which was why he'd come today to stand alone within the quiet church, where no one else could see him. Logan didn't seem to mind it any longer when they weren't in the same room. Perhaps some part of Logan wished that David would forget his oath and seek escape, so Logan would be spared the burden of conveying him to London. But they both knew such a wish would be impossible.

Impossible, Prince Henry's voice said in his mind. *He's asking the impossible. I'll not be bought and sold.*

His presence seemed so close that David felt for certain if he turned, he'd see the prince within the wide arch of the Norman doorway, striding forwards with that confidence that he'd been gaining daily . . .

But the doorway remained empty.

David closed his eyes, and filled the emptiness with moving figures. And remembered.

Whitehall, London, Twelfth Night, 6th January 1612

'He is in love.' Ben Jonson, standing next to David in the semi-darkness of the banqueting hall, watched the prince with knowing eyes. 'You see the way he looks at her.'

'Aye,' David said. 'But it will never be allowed, because the girl is not of royal blood and brings no money to the table, nothing of value to the king.'

The pressure had been growing as the prince approached his eighteenth birthday. Italy, Savoy and France, and others, all had daughters whom they wished to marry to this prince who would, one day, be king of Britain, and King James was keen to turn that fact to his advantage, playing every suitor off against the other in a test to see who would produce the greatest prize.

But Prince Henry had looked keenly at his parents' marriage, with its clouds and arguments, and at the marriage of his young friend Essex, which had foundered on the rocks of infidelity and seemed now past recovery.

'I'll not be rushed,' he'd said to David. 'I will take a bride, but she must be of my own choosing. Not a Catholic, either, for the people never will accept her. I will choose a woman I do love – a British woman, for then I'll not have to take a mistress.'

David knew Sir Walter Raleigh had advised the prince to keep his own path for a while, because the world was changing and the prince and his young friends would be the rulers of it one day. Raleigh also told the prince his eighteenth year would be momentous, and there were few people whom the prince admired as much as he did Raleigh.

But before the prince had spoken with his father, he'd asked David, 'What do *you* think of the matches they propose?'

'Honestly?'

'We're always honest.'

'I don't think that any of them,' David said, 'will make you happy.'

With a flash of his broad smile, the prince had thrown his arm round David's shoulders in a quick embrace, and passed into the presence chamber of the king.

The interview had not gone well. Prince Henry had emerged a half hour later with a fierce expression, muttering, 'Impossible. He's asking the impossible. I'll not be bought and sold.'

That had been midway through December.

Now, as David stood beside Ben Jonson, waiting for the masque to start, he watched the prince's face and felt a surge of nerves.

This masque was, in all ways, not normal. It had been composed at the last minute, on a paltry budget. Inigo Jones had not been hired to make the costumes, nor was there elaborate scenery. And the only actors were the King's Men, with support from a few members of the court. Prince Henry was himself not taking part.

Instead, the prince sat watching in the audience, near to his father.

David felt the tension settle deeply in between them.

He asked, 'Ben, what did you write?'

'What he did ask me to. No more.'

The masque had started, then, and there was nothing David could do to prevent it. He watched Cupid take the stage to make complaints about the frivolous and fleeting pleasures of such things as masques. At least, the audience was meant to think that it was Cupid, until another actor entered and, after a lively exchange, revealed him to be an imposter.

'Does any take this for Cupid? The Love in court?' the audience was asked, and they were then assured that he was not – that it was only Plutus, god of money, who had stolen Love's place. The actor explained how tyrannical Plutus held Cupid confined in the cold while performing the functions that Love had once done in the world, such as friendships. And marriages.

David watched the prince, who was steadfastly looking at his father. And the king was furious. They all could see it.

'Come, follow me,' the actor said. 'I'll bring you where you shall find Love.'

And Cupid – the true Cupid this time – entered in his chariot, and sang a song of triumph to show he'd regained his power.

'Ben,' said David, 'this was a mistake.'

'Away with that cold cloud, that dims my light!' sang Cupid loudly.

Ben was looking at Prince Henry, too. 'You may be right,' he murmured.

As the song built to its final lines, the king's head slowly turned. His eyes held steady on the prince's, but Prince Henry did not look away as Cupid sang, 'Thou hast too long usurp'd my rites, I am now lord of my own nights.'

If they had both been holding swords, the challenge of that moment could not be more clear.

Prince Henry's nosebleeds had begun not long after that night.

David noticed through the last part of that summer, that the prince's headaches and his faintness seemed to worsen after he'd dined with his father and the Viscount Rochester, but David pushed those dark suspicions back, and put his faith and hope into the prince's doctors, who were seeking different remedies.

In mid-September, Esther sent the prince a special copy of the Psalms of David as a gift to cheer him, in her own fine hand that was admired greatly by Prince Henry's mother.

'She has such great talent,' said the queen, as she leafed through the pages of the book, 'and I approve this dedication, for I do agree you are admired by the whole universe, and shine more brightly than all other princes of the Christian world.'

The king had frowned. 'Is that what she has written? Give it here.' He'd grabbed the book, and read the dedication for himself, and snorted, before handing it back to the queen. And then he had looked darkly at Prince Henry. 'Will ye bury me, I wonder?'

David hadn't liked the jealous tone in which he'd said that, but again he'd pushed his apprehensions to the side, because the king was yet his king.

And still Prince Henry sickened. Three weeks later, he'd been struck with his last illness.

David never would forget. It had been swift. It had been terrible. It had been hard to watch. And in the end, it stole from him the only son he'd ever known.

He'd done all that Henry asked him, at the last, and all the things that Henry could no longer ask. He'd burned the papers Henry wanted burned. He'd sent the necessary updates to the queen, who broken-hearted, had removed to her own residence to wait for the sad word she knew would come. He'd sat in silence for those final hours with Henry's head against his heart. He'd closed the eyes that had not ceased to hold his own from that first night at Stirling.

But he never would forgive them. And he'd not forget.

The little church at Willingale was ancient, and its nave was straight and plain. It had no aisles, no chapels, and no sheltered corner where a man could kneel and pray in private.

'David?'

Turning, he saw Esther standing in the open doorway. There was light behind her, and her shadow stretched towards him.

'David? Are you well?'

He nearly told her that he was. He'd got through these past months that way – by lying, telling everybody he was fine, that he was coping with the loss, that he was learning to get on with life. That it was God's will, after all.

Instead he said, 'My lad is gone.'

He felt the quick and sudden rush of warmth within his eyes, and then the tears spilled over and he could no longer see her clearly anymore.

'They killed my lad,' he said. 'My lad is gone.'

She'd reached him, then. Her arms came round him, giving comfort, and he took it, and his head came down to rest against her hair as he surrendered to the sorrow that had sought him for so long.

David couldn't remember the name of the small lad now standing with Esther – they all had names out of the Bible, it seemed like. This one had come out of the house a few minutes ago and was watching the sun set now over the fields.

It was late for a lad of his age to be out. Esther told him so, but he was stubbornly waiting to see the colours of the sunset. He found it disappointing.

Esther smiled. 'But wait. For when the sun has disappeared, its dying gift, on leaving us, is to make all that it has touched more beautiful than it had been before, that we may know the sun was here, and hold its memory till we meet with it again.'

And as she promised him, a moment later all the clouds caught fire along their edges in a glorious display that spread across the sky until it seemed there was no corner of it that had not been painted with the glowing light.

Esther told her son, 'You see? It is not gone.' And looking over her son's head at David, softly said, '*He* is not gone.'

He let his walls down once again, and let his eyes show her all that was in his heart, and told her, 'Thank you.'

David stood a little longer in the field after Esther took her son into the house to ready him for bed. He was still standing in the field when Logan wandered out to join him.

'How is Hector?' David asked.

'Awake.'

'He shouldn't be, this late.'

'Aye, well, ye tell him that,' invited Logan, looking upwards at the sky. 'Are ye developing an interest in astrology?'

David smiled. 'No, but I do wonder if Phoebe's father might be somewhere up there now, in some auspicious constellation, gazing down upon us. That is what the ancient

Romans thought the stars were, after all. The lights of those we've lost.'

'I thought they did believe the stars were gods,' said Logan.

'Not all of them. When Marcus Aurelius lost his wife, he had a special coin cast to let all of Rome know their beloved empress had become a new star in the sky.'

'Then,' Logan said, 'I've no doubt Phoebe's father will be up there, too.'

'He cannot care for her too well, though, from that distance.' David kept looking up, even when he felt Logan's gaze lower to study him. ''Twould be a shame if she were left alone.'

'I will not leave her undefended,' Logan said, 'but neither will I hurry her. She has just lost her father.'

David nodded. 'I do understand. I thought I had time, once. I loved a woman, much as you love Phoebe, and I wished to marry her, but . . .' David nearly said, 'Another man did ask her first', but no, it was not ever quite that simple. Looking at the stars, he merely said, 'I missed my chance to ask her. We have but a little time upon this earth, Marcus Aurelius reminds us. If we do not take the chances we are given, they will go, and we will go, and not return.'

The silence stretched, and David could not tell if he'd offended. He hoped not. Then Logan said, in a mild tone, 'Marcus Aurelius has a lot to say, for a dead man.'

'Aye.' David smiled. 'He does. But he speaks truth. And should we live three thousand years, he tells us – nay, ten thousand – still a man cannot lose any life but that he is now living, nor indeed can he live any life but that which he must lose.' It was the simplest, best advice that he could offer in that moment. It had grown colder. Turning from the field, he set his steps towards the house and clapped the younger man encouragingly on the shoulder. 'Live it wisely, Logan. Live it well.'

ANDREW

Willingale Spain, Essex, 10th June 1613

THE ONLY ROOM WITHIN this house that could be counted private was the small room that the minister, our host, used as his study. It had barely space to keep his chair and books and one small table. Phoebe, sitting in the chair, looked up at me with patience.

I'd rehearsed the words on wakening this morning, in my mind. They'd sounded well enough, then. Now, they sounded painfully inadequate for such a woman.

'We have had our difficulties,' I began again, 'but I would like to think we've overcome them. I'd like to think ye ken my feelings have . . . my feelings are . . .'

I stumbled on the order of the words, and drew a breath, prepared to start again, but in her upturned face I saw a tiny gleam of hope that sparked a deep response within me, and I threw aside my mental script.

'The Devil take it, Phoebe. I do love ye.' The confession came out in a rush, but honestly. 'Ye took my heart the moment I first saw ye, and no other lass will have it.'

She looked astonished, as well she might be, but then she did a thing that gave *me* hope – for the first time, she called me by my name, and in a tone that gave me courage to continue. 'Andrew?'

Kneeling so my face was on a level with her own, I said, 'I'm not a wealthy man, but I do promise I'll provide for ye. I'm not a pious man, but ye will never come to harm. God kens I'm not an easy man to love, but Phoebe, if ye'll be my lass, I swear I'll make ye happy.'

Incredibly, she took my face in her two hands and looked directly in my eyes, and her own eyes were welling up with unshed tears. 'You're asking... are you asking if I'll marry you?'

'Aye.'

Then she kissed me, and I found my answer there.

Since it would be a few days while the licence was arranged, I saddled Brutus the next morning and rode into nearby Chelmsford to the market there, and bought a ring.

It took a while. I made the merchant spread his wares across his booth, to his frustration, and asked him to read each ring's inscription to me, claiming it was best for me, that way, to judge the poetry.

Some of the mottoes leaned too far towards religion; others sounded too much like a pledge you'd offer to a friend. But then he showed to me a heavy band of silver gilt, inscribed with Roman lettering around its inner surface, and he read aloud the words: 'My heart you have.'

And I knew then I'd found the one.

On the Wednesday morning following, I placed that ring on Phoebe's finger, and the minister at Willingale pronounced us married.

We were not in church, but in the front room of the house, so Hector, sitting up now in a chair but still in need of rest, would not miss out on all the joy and ceremony. I believed I heard him cheer the loudest when we kissed.

I was relieved to see him looking so recovered. He'd be well enough to ride in a few days, but he'd come close to dying when we'd first arrived. So close, in fact, that while I'd held the lad's small hand, the minister had come to sit near Hector's head, to say the prayers for preparation of the dying.

Then he'd asked Hector, 'Son, do you believe in God?'

The lad's voice had been weak, but carried the indignant tone he'd showed us at the Roman wall. 'Of course I do,' he'd said. 'I'm not a fool.'

The minister had let that pass as being from the fever. 'Good. And do you know what happens when God's angels carry you to heaven?'

'Aye.' Hector's eyes had closed, confident. 'Logan will break the damn'd gates down, and bring me right back.'

I had squeezed his hand tightly. I hadn't let go of it all that night, and in the morning the fever had broken, so mayhap I truly had beaten the angels who wanted to carry him off. Either way, he was with us yet, even if he was dismayed today that I'd not dressed in my Messenger's scarlet for my wedding.

I lied. 'I didn't think of it.'

Hector forgave me with a shrug. His mind had turned to other things. 'Logan, d'ye think King James will let me be a Messenger?'

'We'll have to wait and see,' I said.

He frowned, and called upon Sir David, standing near us, for assistance. 'But I've proven that I'm strong though, haven't I? That I can fight?'

Sir David said, 'Aye, lad, we always knew that you were brave. Though sometimes, it does take more strength to know when to avoid the battle.'

There he paused, and glanced at me, and might have looked away had I not caught his eye and tipped my head to motion him to join me in the corner for a quiet word.

Once there, I said, 'Ye've thought of something. Tell me.'

'You are newly married, Logan. You should think of nothing more today except your wedding night.'

I let my glance dismiss that notion. 'Where would ye suggest we go, in this house, for a wedding night? The bairns are hanging from the rafters. No, we'll let that wait for London – and if your dead Roman has his thoughts on *that*, he'll have to keep them to himself,' I added, as I saw him drawing breath.

Sir David closed his mouth obligingly.

I asked, 'What's on your mind?'

He said, 'The way I see it, you were charged to bring me south to be examined, yes? And Westaway was charged to write down a report.'

'And?'

'Well, you can still complete your mission. There is paper here.' He nodded to the table near us. 'I can write my own report. I know the things I saw. The things that happened. I was there.'

'And what will that accomplish?' I asked. 'Ye'll be dead if I do bring ye to the king.'

Sir David's eyes held private knowledge. 'But the king,' he said, 'was not the only one who sent for me.' He smiled. 'I have a plan.'

The great palace at Greenwich was built in the form of a square, with the king's lodgings stretched out along the green bank of the River Thames, and the queen's lodgings facing the gardens and hills to the south, and a courtyard between them.

Just now, all that showed of that palace's grandeur were the glittering reflections cast upon the night-dark river through the myriad windows behind which the lamps yet burned.

My friend Roger, having met us in the stables near the waterfront, looked back and whispered, 'Mind your step. The guards are near.'

I bent as low as possible, and waited. We'd left Hector in the stables with instructions to watch Brutus, and a trusted friend of Roger's who had strict instructions to watch Hector, for his shoulder still was not yet healed enough for prowling in the dark.

I was beginning to wish I'd left Phoebe in the stables, too, although I doubted she'd have stayed there. She was close behind me now, and keeping silent, with Sir David at her back.

At last the guards moved on. Their shadows passed. When Roger stood, we followed him.

The hills looked down upon us as we slipped between the porticos and through the entrance. Started up the stairs.

'You must be brief,' said Roger. 'You'll not have much time.'

We'd reached a long, arched gallery with paintings hung to either side. We moved along it swiftly, but not fast enough, for at its end, a guard stepped in to block our way.

He told us, 'State your business.'

'It is private,' Roger said. 'I am her groom.'

'I know who you are, Moor,' he said. 'But who are they?'

I saw the set of Roger's jaw, and knew it well. He pointed at me. 'That is Andrew Logan, the King's Messenger,' he told the guard. 'And you will let us through.'

The guard's expression changed. He stood aside. We entered a large hall, where at the farther end a group of women in fine gowns were sitting round a table, playing at a game of cards.

They turned as we came in.

I knelt then, so I only saw a wide, embroidered skirt sweep gracefully towards us, in my downcast field of view.

Queen Anna said, 'Sir David,' in a voice that sounded genuinely moved. 'I'm very glad to see you safe.'

Sir David, kneeling at my side, replied, 'Your Majesty. For that, you may thank this man, Andrew Logan, who did guard me well.'

The queen acknowledged me, but warily, no doubt because I served the king.

And then she touched Sir David on his shoulder. 'Come,' she told him. 'Walk with me.'

DAVID

Greenwich Palace, Kent, 20th June 1613

HE KNEW THEY DID not have much time. The king would shortly hear that he had come, and he'd be silenced.

David took the folded papers he had carried close within his coat from Willingale, and gave them to the queen. 'I've written all I can remember of the last year of the prince's life,' he said. 'His habits and his health, and where he went.' He paused. 'And where he dined.'

Her gaze was keen. She didn't ask him, not directly, but he knew she shared his fears.

He said, 'When you've read that, then you will know all that I know.'

Queen Anna held the papers close. 'I thank you for your trouble.'

'It was nothing. It . . .' He searched for words. 'I thank you for your son.'

She gave a short nod, as though holding back emotion. Then she asked him, 'Do you know why I did write to you?' When David shook his head, she said, 'A blind man spoke to me. He was some kind of necromancer, I suppose, who heard the voices of the dead. He told me Henry wanted me to find you.'

David stared at her. 'A necromancer?'

'Yes, I know. It sounds unlikely. But he did nearly quote Marcus Aurelius,' said Queen Anna, with a twisting smile. She told him what the blind man said, and how it so closely matched what Henry told her in private, and that seemed so remarkable that David couldn't properly absorb it in his mind.

And yet, he found it reassuring, thinking Henry wasn't altogether lost and gone. That he could still reach out and speak to them.

'What happened to the book?' Queen Anna asked. 'The one that Henry always carried?'

David could not lie. 'I have it now, Your Majesty.'

She looked at him expectantly. 'May I?'

There was no refusing the queen. David reached with reluctance into his pocket and held out the book to her.

Anna turned the pages, her eyes filling slowly as she saw the prince's writing in the margins. 'This was always special to him.' For an achingly long moment, she held onto it. Then she passed it back to David. 'I am sure it's special to you, now.'

He closed his hand around it tightly. 'Aye, it is, Your Majesty.'

'Be sure you take good care of it,' she told him, 'on your journey home to Scotland.'

David felt sure it could not be such an easy thing to be dismissed. 'The king may not be pleased,' he said, 'if I return to Scotland so soon after my arrival here.'

Queen Anna, with her head high, let him see why she'd been made a queen. 'I will deal with the king, Sir David.'

'Your Majesty.'

He bowed, and was about to take his leave, when she stopped him, in a voice that sounded like a mother's, not a queen's. 'Sir David?'

'Aye, Your Majesty?'

'I'm glad he did have you.'

And then she turned in a grand, regal swirl of skirts, and went back to her game.

In the stables of the palace, they discovered Hector sitting perched against the rail of Brutus's head-stall and chattering to David's brother William.

William greeted them with outward cheer, although his eyes raked David with concern until he satisfied himself his younger brother was unharmed. 'I've made a friend in this young lad,' he said, to David. 'He's been telling me the tale of how he got his scar.'

'Ah, yes. It was most bravely earned.'

His brother looked at Logan. 'From what I've heard thus far, it seems that I do owe ye thanks,' he said, 'for all ye did to keep my brother safe.'

'I did my job,' said Logan.

'Rather more than that, I think.' With interest, William looked beyond him to where Phoebe stood within the stable doorway, keeping well back from the horses. 'And that is your wife?'

'Aye.'

'She must be as brave as Hector, to have bound her life to yours.' He smiled, and turned again to David. 'Where will ye be staying? I can make room at my lodgings.'

David shook his head. 'I have been given leave to travel home, to Scotland.'

William said, 'But I've proposed ye for a place within Prince Charles's household. Come, ye must at least stay till the council has decided. If they choose ye, it will grant ye some protection.'

David said, 'I thank you for the effort, but you know as well as I do that it was a pointless thing to do. It won't succeed, you know. One of Rochester's creatures will be given the place, and the king will oppose me and never allow it. Besides, there was only one prince for me.'

'What will ye do?' William asked.

'I've a gelding to return to Leith. And then I was thinking of Gorthy,' said David, his mind on the Perthshire estate near where both of them had spent the years of their childhood. 'It is a lovely place, and peaceful, and I will be free to live there as I will. And it is close to cousin Patrick, who will no doubt be glad not to have to chase over the countryside trying to rescue me.'

His brother laughed. 'He may not be chasing all over the countryside, but I daresay you'll find that he's over that river the now,' William told him, 'and waiting to give you an escort back home.'

David thought it possible, but privately he hoped not. He was ready to be done with escorts for a while.

He'd never liked goodbyes. With William, it was never truly a goodbye, for they would always see each other for the hunting in the Highlands come the summer's end.

With Hector, it was harder. But he steeled himself and fixed the smile upon his face and let the lad believe they'd meet again, although in David's long experience, such partings were most often final.

'No more scars, now,' he told Hector. 'One is all you need.'

'Logan has more.'

'Logan's a bigger man, and has the size to bear them.'

Phoebe, waiting at the stable door, had wished him a safe journey. Having watched him say farewell to Hector, she'd made sure that David knew, 'We'll take good care of Hector. He will always have a home with us.'

'I'm grateful for it.'

Phoebe had embraced him warmly. 'I will miss you.'

'And I you.'

But when he'd come to Logan, David had not known what words to say. He turned some over in his mind but then discarded them because they did not fit the way that he was feeling.

As the silence lengthened, David finally held his hand outstretched, and Logan shook it. It was not enough. But nothing ever would be.

William came with him to make certain he got safely to the road. 'Be careful, now,' he cautioned David, always the big brother. 'You're alone, and it's a long road back to Scotland.'

David took hold of the gelding's reins. The moon was very bright tonight. The sky was filled with stars. He looked up, as he'd always done, and heard a hopeful voice within his memory.

Then you will be with me all the time?

He smiled, and said to William, 'I'll not be alone.'

Phoebe

Great St Bartholomew's, London, 21st June 1613

It felt strange to be standing in this house without my father here. The rooms all had a different feel, and echoes sang where I could not remember ever hearing them. The floorboards creaked behind me.

Andrew asked, 'D'ye have everything ye need?'

I smiled faintly, for that question had a double meaning in my view. I turned, and leaned into the arms he offered me, my head against the shelter of his chest. 'I do.'

He meant my clothing, and the few belongings that we'd come to gather so that I could have them at his family's house. My house, now, too. Aunt Agnes had been living there since we'd been gone, and had already settled in. This morning, in the small hours, when we'd straggled in exhausted after our ride here from Greenwich, I'd expected that the Logan house would be shuttered and dark.

Instead I'd found Aunt Agnes sitting up with Andrew's mother, waiting for us. 'I just had a feeling,' Andrew's mother said, which left me wondering about this Second Sight and how it might be passed down in the blood.

'Can women have it?' I'd asked Andrew, as I'd tried to keep my eyes from drifting closed.

He had been busy dressing Hector's shoulder while the boy was sleeping. 'I don't know.'

'Well, does your mother have it?'

Andrew's pause told me he'd never entertained the thought. 'I don't know.'

'Mayhap you should ask her.'

That was all I could remember of our conversation. I had slept, and when I woke it was already afternoon. Andrew was busy, and the day was full.

But now, we had this moment to ourselves, while Hector and Aunt Agnes and his mother were yet in the Logans' house, with Brutus and the Garron stabled safely in the stalls below.

Evening was drawing in. The shadows slanted long across the walls, and touched the portrait of King James my father once had been so proud of, gifted to him by my lord Northampton. Perhaps it, too, had been a reward for some business my father did that had been less than kind.

I knew I'd not feel sad to let this house go, when the lease ran out, because it felt wrong living in a home that had been gained by such deception.

Something curious was happening. The whole room wavered, for an instant. Then it faded at its edges, and became another chamber, in another place.

King James, instead of standing stiffly in his portrait, turned – a living, breathing man – and said, 'Our choices, Logan, can have unforeseen effects.'

I found those words unsettling, as much from the way he said them as from what was said, but even as I registered the tone in which he spoke, the room regained its proper form.

I looked at Andrew. He'd been gazing at the portrait of King James, and I could see his eyes just now were losing their unfocused stare.

'All is well,' he reassured me, when he saw my worry and he realized that I'd Seen what he was Seeing. 'I don't always See the whole of things. And anyway, whatever is yet coming, we will weather it.' He turned me in his arms so he could look me in the face, and lightly traced my cheek. 'I am an oak, remember? I do stand against all dangers.'

He kissed me, and the room began to fade for reasons other than the Second Sight, and when he raised his head he said, 'We've not yet had our wedding night.'

His breathing was, I noticed, as uneven as my own.

I said, 'I know.'

'Which of these chambers does belong to ye?'

So then I finally saw the scars he'd shown to but a few, and in return he saw the heart I'd never shown a man at all. I'd known already that he could be fierce and tender all at once, but I'd not known the half of it. And afterwards, he wrapped me in the blankets and his body, and we closed the world away from us, and for that moment – just that moment – all was truly well.

Andrew

Whitehall Palace, London, 8th July 1613

NORTHAMPTON, IN HIS HABITUAL black, had been watching me now for some minutes with sympathy.

We were again waiting in the small room where the king kept his books and his writing things, and where the diamond-paned windows were letting in light of an uncertain quality.

I had been summoned to court for the first time since my return, so I was wearing my livery, but I was finding it hard to get comfortable. Neither my livery nor I had changed our size, and yet my clothes felt as though they no longer fit, nor did I feel that they became me well. The gold seemed somehow tarnished and the scarlet not so bright.

As I fidgeted to get the collar settled right, Northampton told me, 'I don't think he will behead you just yet, but he is angry. And rightly so. How could you disobey your orders?'

I could stand in silence against most things, but a false charge wasn't one of them. 'I disobeyed nothing. My warrant said I was to bring Sir David "hither", which I took to mean that I should bring him to where the king was,' I told him. 'And the king was then at Greenwich.'

'But you did not bring him to the king.'

I pointed out that it was not my place to navigate the marital arrangements of the king. 'The queen wished to see Sir David. I cannot refuse the queen.'

The king's voice, speaking from behind us, said, 'In faith, I can appreciate your problem.'

As he entered, both Northampton and I knelt. He bade us rise. He outwardly looked pleasant, but his eyes held fire, like coals banked deep and waiting to be fanned to flame. Northampton had been right. The king was angry.

'I myself do find it very difficult,' he told me, 'to refuse the queen. 'Tis why Sir David Moray is at home in Scotland now, and not in the Tower awaiting his trial.' His smile was tight. 'But then, the queen does have it in her mind that he is of no use to our enquiries, and the queen is often right. It is a shame he could not stay in London, but the council did not think Sir David worthy of a place within Prince Charles's chamber. They were convinced he'd been a poor advisor to Prince Henry.'

I suspected that the council had been more convinced the king would think ill of them if they showed Sir David any favour, but I did not say so. I'd caught only an edge of the darkness Sir David described at the court that had taken the life of the prince, and I could not have said whether King James had truthfully played any part in it, but it seemed more and more likely to me that those close to him had, and there was often truth in that old saying that to know a man's companions was to know the man.

The king said, 'He was always filling my son's head with wild thoughts, and turning him against me. 'Tis much better that I choose more wisely for my younger son. Our choices, Logan, can have unforeseen effects.'

And there it was, the phrase I'd Seen. No threat to me, although he plainly was displeased.

'The queen,' he said, 'has made one more demand of me. It touches you.'

'Your Majesty?'

'She asks that I dismiss you from my service.'

I'd not heard that right. 'Your Majesty?'

'Apparently, her stables grow so large she has need of another stable master to attend her business there. Sir William Moray, my old friend, whose judgement I'll allow is better than his brother's, recommended you.' The king, still irritated with this new turn of events, presented me with this as though there were no choice involved on my part. Which, of course, there wasn't. 'You may give your livery tomorrow to my lord Northampton, when you start your service to the queen. The lease upon your house will stand as long as you do serve her. I do thank you, Logan, for your time. And for the Garron you delivered to me. It will suit me well for my next hunt.'

And that was all. I was dismissed.

Five years, five bullets and a sword slash, countless miles ridden in all weathers, men who'd cursed me, men who'd praised me, and a lad who'd left his home in Leith to follow me.

I was no longer a King's Messenger.

I'd lost my father's legacy, and gained my own.

And finally, I felt free.

Anna, Queen of Britain

Theobalds, Hertfordshire, 16th July 1613

She set the arrow to her bow, and moved with care between the trees.

The men were not far off, beside her. Anna heard them talking in low tones, so they'd not frighten off the deer. James was among them.

This was the first day that he'd felt well enough to rise from bed and join them, having been struck suddenly by some intestinal complaint that brought him twisting agony, much like the purge her doctor had prescribed for her when she was last at Bath, when she'd misjudged the dose.

She hadn't shared that piece of information, though, with James. She'd only tucked the empty bottle deep among her linens, and gone to his chamber to see how he was managing.

His face had shone with perspiration, and his eyes were overbright. She saw his pain, and was indifferent. It was but a fraction of the pain their son had suffered, at the end.

'Sometimes the things we eat,' she said, 'do not agree with us.' James met her eyes. In innocence, she'd told him, 'I am sure that it will pass.'

Alone, within her chamber, she had taken up the papers that Sir David Moray handed to her. Smoothed them with her hands, and read them. He'd been very circumspect. 'I cannot absolutely know,' he'd written, and, 'I cannot with certainty accuse . . .'

But it was all there – all the damning evidence. The dates, the names, the places. There could be no more denying it. And though she had no means to seek true justice for her son, she could seek vengeance where she could.

James might not feel remorse. But she would make him feel.

The men were moving past her now. James had the hounds with him. He called to Jewel, his favourite hound, and Anna saw the dog leap up.

He loves his hawks and hounds more than he ever will love us.

She felt a single tear begin its path down her hot face. 'For you, Henry,' she whispered. Then she raised her bow, and took her aim. And let the arrow fly.

PHOEBE

Great St Bartholomew's, London, 27th April (St George's Eve) 1614

THE STARS WERE HIDDEN at my birth. There was no moon. And yet my father was assured my future would be fortunate. My stars, although unseen, would serve me well.

'Whatever happens in your life,' he'd often tell me, 'you'll be guided by the planets and their motions. They will lead you to your destiny.'

I'd once believed that to be purely fancy.

But this morning as I walked across the grass still wet with dew, I could not help but wonder whether that old doctor of astrology had read my stars correctly after all. Although we still lived here within the Close at St Bartholomew's, it could be said I had the comfort of a life at court, for Logan served the queen and she was quick to show him favour in return, as she showed favour to his sisters, who had married this December past, and lived not far away.

The sun was rising, touching all the highest leaves on the tall tree beside the church and turning them bright green and gold with promise, and the breeze was blowing lightly and a solitary bird was singing as though it would tell me that the morning would be fine.

Across the Close, the Foxes' house stood empty. They had gone, nobody knew to where, and no one cared.

I knew where Andrew would be, though. I found him in our stables, getting Brutus ready for the day. Hector, who had grown a foot at least within the past year, wore clothes that were, as ever, just like Andrew's – only now those clothes were not merely a copy, but the true thing, since he also served the queen.

He looked exasperated. 'All I'm saying is, if I *did* have my ain horse, I could ride it every day tae the queen's stables, and I'd be there that much earlier tae do my work.'

Andrew only told him, 'I will think on it.' He stood within the nearer stall, his back towards me. 'In the meantime, take that bucket, lad, and fetch some water from the conduit.'

Hector did as he was told, but rolled his eyes at me, with feeling.

'And I see that,' Andrew said. 'Don't think I can't.' He turned as Hector left us, and his gaze angled down to greet me.

I asked, 'Are you being difficult?'

'Maybe just a little.'

It was in his nature, I supposed. He'd always been a most infuriating man.

I said, 'He'll like you better in a week, I'll warrant.'

Andrew said, 'Two weeks. By then I'll have the last bit of the money saved. The gelding that I've chosen isn't near the size of Brutus, but he *is* a dapple grey.'

That would please Hector.

Brutus heard his name, and stretched his neck out, carefully, and I reached just as gingerly to pat his velvet nose. I'd learned to almost like the way he blew his breath against my fingers. It was small, but a beginning.

I looked at Andrew, handsome in Queen Anna's livery of rich, deep orange velvet over gold. He slanted me a sideways glance. 'Ye miss the scarlet?'

'Not at all. This suits you well.'

'What's in your thoughts, then?'

I said, 'I've been pondering the qualities of Leithers.'

'Have ye?' Andrew grinned. 'Faith, ye've been in my debt a

year now, all for want of telling me the third part of my nature as a man of Leith. What were the first two?'

'Stubborn,' I reminded him.

'Well, aye, I'm fairly that.'

'And proud,' I said.

'It's been suggested. And . . . ?'

I set my back to Brutus, and reached up to link my arms around my husband's neck. 'And mine.'

'Now that,' he said, his grey eyes warm, 'I'll grant ye without argument.'

He offered me a kiss to seal the bargain, and I took it with a smile. There would be arguments enough to come, I knew, as with all those who, by their stars or by their wills, had bound their lives together.

But on this day, I felt I'd won enough to share the victory, so I gave him that last word, and let him keep it.

About The Characters

Every book has its beginning. This one began on a wintry late afternoon in a second-hand bookshop when, enticed by a sign reading: 'More Books Downstairs', I left the offerings on the main floor and descended into a quiet haven of overstuffed shelves. There, gathering dust in a back corner, I discovered *The History of the King's Messengers*, by V. Wheeler-Holohan, published in New York in 1935. The cover was plain, only text and a crest, but the dust jacket promised, 'The colorful and most secret story of a famous English institution that has always piqued the curiosity of novelists, playwrights and readers is here told authoritatively and fully for the first time.'

Intrigued, I bought the book, brought it home and added it to my own overstuffed shelves of Books That May One Day Prove Useful for Research.

And there it sat, gathering dust.

Until, as ideas do, mine started shaping themselves into something approaching a story.

I'd just learned about the connection between young Prince Henry and Sir David Moray, and thought there might be something there to explore. But I'd need some adventure, I thought. Some excitement.

So I made tea (which is how all adventures begin, surely?), and I finally sat down to read the book I'd bought and set aside those years ago.

Before this, I'd known nothing of the King's Messengers, but Captain Vincent Wheeler-Holohan – who'd served during the Great War in the 12th (The Rangers) Battalion, London Regiment – had been appointed a King's Messenger on 15th

March 1920, and by the time he wrote his history of that branch of royal service, he was intimately acquainted with it, able not only to speak of its history, but of its ongoing practices.

Captain Wheeler-Holohan had been able to trace 'the appointment of a King's Messenger simply *as* a "King's Messenger" and nothing else' with certainty to 1485, in the reign of Richard III. Others, including today's Royal Messengers via their website, claim an older history 'dating back to at least the reign of King John' in the 12th century.

Whatever their beginnings, the service evolved and Captain Wheeler-Holohan was able to find, in 1641, the first mention in the records of the 'Forty Messengers of the Great Chamber in Ordinary' (there could be only forty, and men waited years for a vacancy) although he suspected they'd existed in this form for a long time before this, and my research tends to prove him right.

One of the more colourful aspects of the Messengers' history involves the silver greyhound that serves as their identifying badge. One theory is that the greyhound was chosen because it featured in the coat of arms of the House of Lancaster, and that the Lancastrian Duke of Somerset granted its use to the Messengers at their creation in the 14th century. A second, more romantic legend puts the silver greyhounds in the hands of young King Charles II when, in exile during Cromwell's rule, he needed some way for his four hand-picked Messengers to recognize each other and be recognized as carrying his word. The legend says Charles took a silver dish that had four running greyhounds on its lid as decorations, broke the greyhounds off, and gave one to each Messenger to carry as their private proof of loyal service.

Romanticism aside, this legend actually seems more likely to me, if only because there is no greyhound on the detailed uniform of the memorial effigy of Mr Thomas Davis, Gentleman, in Llandegfan Church, Anglesey, in Wales, 'SERVANT TO Y^{E} TWO MOST ILLUSTRIOUS PRINCES HENRY & CHARLES BOTH PRINCES OF WALES AND NOW TO KING CHARLES Y^{E} FIRST MESSENGER IN ORDINARY OF HIS M^{TIES} CHAMBER', who died in 1649, before the Restoration of Charles II.

Because of this, I did not make a greyhound part of Andrew Logan's uniform, since he would have been serving at the same time as Mr Thomas Davis, Gentleman.

From their creation until the early 19th century, the Royal Messengers received both their orders and their pay from within the Royal Household, but modernisation requires bureaucracy. In 1824, during the reign of King George IV, control of the Messengers was transferred to the Foreign Office, and in 2020 became the responsibility of the Foreign, Commonwealth and Development Office (FCDO Services), on whose website you can find more details of their modern operations.

Captain Wheeler-Holohan's book sent me down a wonderful research rabbit hole of articles and interviews and memoirs, and backwards from there into the original court documents where they still existed.

In the *Issues of the Exchequer; being payments made out of His Majesty's Revenue during the reign of King James I. Extracted from the original records belonging to the ancient Pell Office ...* more commonly called the *Pell Records*, compiled by Frederick Devon and published at London in 1836, I found a treasure trove of payments made to Messengers, with details of their missions.

I'd already known from my research for previous books that Messengers were sometimes called upon to arrest people, but in the Pell Records I learned much more about this aspect of their service, from the days they spent upon the road, to troubles they encountered and the wording of their warrants.

And the character of Andrew Logan came to life.

All writers work in different ways. When it comes to my fictional characters – those who aren't based on real people from history – I've learned through the years that it's best for me not to waste any time trying to plan them before they turn up on the page, but to trust my subconscious and meet them as they arrive, much as I'd meet any stranger.

Thus my characters will frequently turn up with names and surnames, and with traits and quirks and secrets they reveal to me in stages through the writing of the book. That Andrew chose to be a Logan wasn't too surprising, since I'd already created a fictional family of Scottish Logans in my earlier book *The Winter Sea*. I knew their descendants would probably feature in some of the story ideas I had for the future. It seemed only natural one of their ancestors would turn up now.

But I was less prepared for him to have the Second Sight. That meant more research. Fortunately, we know a great deal about the Second Sight in Scotland in the 1600s, thanks largely to Robert Boyle, famous British scientist and one of the founders of the Royal Society, who in 1678 interviewed Lord Tarbat, soon to be appointed Lord Chief Justice of Scotland, seeking 'to receive some credible information' on the phenomenon that so many Scots apparently accepted as genuine.

Lord Tarbat obliged with detailed information and a letter giving several examples of which he himself had been a witness. 'I heard very much, but believed very little, of the Second Sight,' Lord Tarbat wrote, 'yet its being assumed by several of great Veracity, I was induced to make Inquiry after it in the Year 1652, being then confin'd to abide in the North of Scotland by the English Usurpers.'

I have my own idea as to why Lord Tarbat might have gained new interest in the Second Sight that year.

Two months before he headed north, he'd been at Edinburgh, together with a group of fellow soldiers and acquaintances, including a good friend of his whose wife was very pregnant. Lady Anne Halkett, in her *Autobiography*, writes a detailed account of these days, including the meal at which a woman 'who they say had the Second Sight' predicted there would be great sadness in the house within the week. And indeed, within the week Lord Tarbat's friend's wife died in childbirth, with her newborn.

This tragedy, so strangely foretold and touching Lord Tarbat so personally, would likely have been on his mind as he went north into the Highlands, where he 'was induced to make Inquiry after' the practice of the Second Sight.

And in one of those strange twists of interconnected fate, his unfortunate friend was one of Robert Boyle's former Fellows of the Royal Society: Sir Robert Moray – celebrated soldier, statesman, philosopher and spy – and the nephew of Sir David Moray, of this story.

Robert Boyle doubtless intended to publish the results of his investigations into Second Sight. He never did. Instead, Lord Tarbat's letter circulated privately among Boyle's friends and associates, and coming from a scientific source, it lent an air of new legitimacy to the subject, and inspired others to begin their own investigations.

Many of these, like the notes and correspondence of the diarists John Evelyn and Samuel Pepys, or Scottish minister Robert Kirk's comprehensive work *The Secret Commonwealth*, weren't published until the 19th century. But they give us a fascinating and useful overview of Second Sight as it was practiced and observed (and sometimes feared) in Andrew Logan's lifetime.

All these varied sources gave me a wealth of common traits and features – among them the fixed gaze, the winding sheet, and the ability to share visions through touch – that I could then pass to Logan to make sure his Second Sight functioned by the known rules of those times.

Finding a home for my fictional Messenger in a city as lively as 1613 London was simple enough, in the end: I gave him the house that had once belonged to a former King's Messenger, Thomas Tyrrell, at the end of King Henry VIII's reign, in Great St Bartholomew's Close.

With the exception of the church itself and its famously picturesque gatehouse, few of the buildings currently in Bartholomew's Close and the Cloth Fair would be familiar to my characters (although there's still a pub on the site of the Star Tavern – at the writing of this book, it was called the Rising Sun, and served a cracking Sunday lunch). But it has somehow managed to retain its atmosphere, and at the centre of the Close, beneath the trees, exactly where the conduit once stood, water still flows beneath the ground, now capped by a brass plate marked 'Fire Hydrant'.

Nearby you'll find a modern building on the corner that was occupied in 1613 by a little house whose history was bound, through its ownership, with the history of Mary, Queen of Scots and her trial for treason. I thought this a fitting home for Phoebe and her father Laurence, who, while fictional, is modelled on the real-life writing master Peter Bales, whose own writing school was located 'at the upper end of the Old Bailey', a stone's throw from Great St Bartholomew's Close.

I 'met' Peter Bales while researching scriveners, as background for Laurence's character. In the *Biographia Britannica: or, the Lives of the Most Eminent Persons Who Have Flourished in Great Britain and Ireland, etc.*, published in London in 1747,

I learned how Bales had been recruited by Queen Elizabeth I's spymaster for the team of men intercepting 'disguised correspondence' passing between Mary, Queen of Scots and her supporters. The team had one man who could open letters and reseal them, undetected, and another man who could decipher any code. Bales, being 'expert in the imitation of hands', was employed to 'add, according to instruction, any postscript, or continuation of one . . . to draw out such further intelligence as was wanted for a compleat discovery, from the traytors themselves, of their treasonable intercourse.' And another piece of my story's puzzle fell into place.

Whether Peter Bales ever received the reward he desired for his clandestine work, I don't know. The *Biographia Brittanica* says 'he was several years after in quest of a place at Court, though we cannot find that he ever obtained it'.

A place at Court could bring uncertain fortune, and few understood that better than the many real-life characters I chose to leave out of this book – who played their parts, but who would make the pages of this story far too crowded and confusing.

Patrick Graeme, the real-life 3rd Laird of Inchbrakie, managed to shoulder his way in, as Graemes will do in my novels. I've learned to keep out of their way, for they usually make the books better whenever they turn up.

And naturally, whenever there's an Abercairney Moray, I make space for them, as well.

I should mention that my choice of spelling of the Moray surname for this novel was deliberate. I've no doubt that some historian will write to me and tell me that I've got it all wrong. They will tell me David and his brother William signed their last name 'Murray'. They'll be right.

But the spelling of the family surname varied in those days.

In the marriage contract of David's parents in 1560 it's spelled 'Moray', and in private family papers he's 'Sir David Moray'. David's brother's children – notably Sir Robert Moray of the Royal Society, already mentioned – used the Moray variation. Why David and his brothers used the 'Murray' spelling, I don't know, because they're not around for me to ask them. I can only speculate they found it easier to anglicize their surname at a time and in a place when being Scottish – whether you were king or commoner – meant facing English prejudice.

While I'd usually defer to David's preference, in this case I had to take into account the fact that all the other people from this family who have found their way into my books have spelled their surname Moray.

So, for consistency, and to avoid confusion for my readers, I used the Moray spelling here, as well.

I trust that David will forgive me.

He has suffered worse injustices. The chief one being, in my view, that as with many of the Morays of Abercairney, he's been half erased from history, leaving the faint imprint of a man who, in his day, would have been widely known and recognized by everyone at Court.

Most biographies of Prince Henry only mention David in the prince's final days, telling how Henry, in pain and delirious, called out to David repeatedly, and David came. They *might* note how David sat in grief, a solitary guardian on the chariot that carried Henry's effigy during the long funeral procession. But otherwise, he's mostly left unmentioned while the prince's other household members – Henry's tutor, for example – get the larger share of limelight.

But when you go back to the documents written while David was still alive, you get some sense of his importance. His name turns up regularly in the reports of foreign ambassadors who have business with the prince, in the correspondence of other courtiers and in the accounts of payments made to and from Henry, which David clearly helped to organize.

The Life and Death of Our Late Most Incomparable and Heroique Prince Henry, Prince of Wales, previously attributed to Sir Charles Cornwallis, Prince Henry's Treasurer, but now believed to have been written by a courtier named John Hawkins, provides a useful and contemporary view of Henry and the men around him.

Writing from his personal experience, Hawkins makes it very clear that David Moray was not just 'the first and onely Gentleman of his Highnesse Bed-chamber . . . (continuing so alwaies untill his death)' but that David also was 'the onely man in whom [Prince Henry] had put choise trust'.

Historians throughout the years have borrowed many details from this one account of Henry's life and death, but no historian I've found has bothered to include Hawkins's observation that Sir David 'in this one death, suffered many'.

And so, year by year, David has faded to the shadows, and his place at Henry's side has been reduced to a mere after-thought, while other men who did not have the prince's 'choise trust' have been given an inflated role in Henry's life.

David's poetry has largely been forgotten, too. He mingled with many of the leading poets of his day – Michael Drayton called him 'my kinde friend' and contributed a dedicatory verse to David's first book of published poetry.

All the excerpts that I've quoted in my novel from the poetry of David have been taken from that book, of which I'm fortunate enough to own a copy (as it was reprinted by the Bannatyne Club in 1823, together with his poetical 'Paraphrase' of the 104th Psalm).

I've lightly modernised the spelling of the poetry, since the original contains lines like 'A yeelding flaue vnto thy mercy flees', which not only irritate my copyeditors but would throw my readers out of the flow of their reading.

This book contains the sonnets to David's 'Cælia' – the mistress whose true name remains unknown. That David was once deeply in love with someone is very plain from these sonnets, which also hold the evidence of his heartbreak.

But that, or so he claims in his first sonnet, was when both he and his unsettled Muse were young, before:

'. . . she grew more grave, and I more old,
Under protection of a royall name'.

With Prince Henry's death in November 1612, that protection fell away from David. As one courtier wrote to a friend, Henry's household was 'brake up the last of December, and his Servants sent to seek their Fortune'.

David's name was put forward for a place in Prince Charles's household the following summer. A personal letter from one gentleman to another at the time relates that another applicant was accepted 'by my Lord Rochester's means. Sir David Murray was not only rejected, but taxed openly at the council-table, for having suggested none of the best councils to the late prince deceased.'

David turned his back on London and retired to Scotland, where he settled on his new estate at Gorthy, close by his family's estate of Abercairney in Perthshire. He died there in 1629, leaving his property to his brother John.

According to the Moray family's private papers, David never married.

But his sonnets, and the love they spoke of, stayed within my memory. So, in the writing of this novel, I took some poetic licence of my own, and gave him a romance with Esther Inglis.

They were definitely friends.

And it is possible they met through friends in common in the years when Esther first lived and began to work in Edinburgh. She was a Huguenot – a French Protestant – the daughter of refugees fleeing Catholic violence against Protestants in France. Settling in Edinburgh, her parents found work there – Esther's father as the master of a French school, and her mother as a skilled calligrapher.

Esther learned the art of calligraphy from her mother, and surpassed her in skill. She mastered more than forty forms of hand lettering, creating little books that were illustrated masterpieces, bound in velvet and embroidered silk, sometimes with stitched designs of pearls. These books were dedicated to and presented to people of worth at the Scottish and English Courts, in hopes of obtaining their patronage. After her marriage in 1596 to Bartholomew Kello, who served King James as Clerk of Passports and foreign correspondence, Esther's books also became useful tools for her husband's diplomatic efforts on behalf of the king – in 1599, while James was working to secure his path to the English throne, Queen Elizabeth I and a few of her closest followers were given books by Esther Inglis as gifts.

Because she produced the books first and then offered them, rather than working on commission, she relied upon the generosity of those who received them, and her income was always uncertain. She gave several books to Prince Henry, who paid her handsomely for them, but her husband's appointment as minister of the church of St Andrew's at Willingale Spain (now Willingale Ongar) in Essex, in late December 1607, for all it took the family farther from the Court, must have brought them, for the moment, some stability.

It also brought them tragedy. In 1614, a year after the events of this story take place, Esther lost two of her three sons, reportedly to scarlet fever – nine-year-old Isaac in July, and thirteen-year-old Joseph in September. Their brass memorial plaques are still preserved in St Andrew's Church in Willingale today, bearing witness to their short lives and their parents' grief.

Not long afterwards, in 1615, Esther, Bartholomew, and their surviving children returned to Scotland. Esther died at Leith in August 1624, having been forced to borrow so much money that she had nothing to leave her husband, daughters and son except a debt of more than £150 Scots.

But she left the world a most exquisite legacy.

Some fifty of her books survive. A few are held in private hands, while others are preserved in public collections like those of the Royal Libraries of Copenhagen, Stockholm and Windsor, the Bibliotheque Nationale in Paris, the National Library of Scotland and the British Library.

And while she died in her mid-fifties and lost two young sons to illness, I've no reason to think Esther wasn't happy in her life. Being a religious woman and a proper Calvinist, I doubt she would ever be unfaithful to her husband.

Still, a writer's mind takes note, sometimes, of those intriguing puzzle pieces that don't seem to fit.

The dedications Esther wrote within the books she gave as gifts were worded in the humble language common to the Court and, long or short, remained respectfully impersonal. Except for one.

On New Year's Day, a year after moving to Willingale Spain, Esther gave a special gift to David Moray – an advance copy, as it were, of her husband's translation of A TREATISE OF PREPARATION TO THE HOLY SUPPER OF OUR ONLY SAVIOUR AND REDEEMER JESUS CHRIST.

She had given David books before, but this was unlike any of the other books that she'd created – it was plain, made to look like a printed book, with no illustrations. Nor was its dedication like her others. It began ordinarily enough, with Biblical references to the various gifts God bestows upon men. And then the dedication became, for Esther, very personal indeed.

'I writ this Sir to yow, esteeming you in my hart most happy on whome God hes multiplied many good guifts and graces not only of the body, but lykewaise hath giuen you a beautyfull soule: So that truly it may be said to you which our Saviour sayes to the faythfull soule Behold thou art fair my love.'

In all the books of Esther's that contain a dedication, I'd never seen another one in which she quoted from the Song of Solomon – the Song of Songs. A love poem.

Nor had I seen her twice praise a man's beautiful soul, let alone repeatedly mention his 'temporal beauty and many gifts of the body', and the romantic in me couldn't help but wonder . . .

So, I put the plain but special gift that Esther made for David into David's pocket in my novel. And their story in this book is the result.

But it is only that – a story, and my own invention.

Whatever the true nature might have been of their relationship, they likely were the only ones who ever fully knew it, and it seems they left no proof of it behind for us to find. A rare achievement in a Court that did not lightly keep its secrets.

Among the other courtiers well acquainted with the secrets of King James's court was one man who deserved more space within this book than I could give him, since he greatly influenced Prince Henry's life, and Henry thought the world of him. But it is not possible to summarize Sir Walter Raleigh – he demands too large a canvas – and if once you let him on the page, he will command it, as he once commanded ships and men on voyages of grand adventure. So, I'll leave you to discover Raleigh for yourselves, and where he fits into the prince's life. But I can share, at least, these words of wisdom that he wrote to guide the work of those who followed him:

'Historians desiring to write the Actions of Men, ought to set down the simple Truth.'

As much as I agree with him, I found this very difficult to do when I approached King James.

Posterity can't even settle on a single number to assign him in the list of British monarchs, so depending on the angle of your viewpoint, he's King James VI of Scotland, or King James I of England, or King James VI and I of all Great Britain. That he comes to us already with this changeable identity is actually in keeping with his character.

To know the truth of James's nature, I feel you'd have had to know him when he was a small child, before he realized that most of the men – and women – he encountered viewed him as a playing piece upon the game board of their own ambitions. As the son of Mary, Queen of Scots, the infant James had been crowned king while his mother – who'd been driven from her throne – was still alive, and from that moment, every ruthless, warring faction in his country sought control of him. They kidnapped him, they lied to him, they terrified and terrorized him. And he learned that it was safer not to show his true face or his feelings, or to give his trust.

This comes through clearly in accounts of him, and in the documents he left behind. His letters, books and poetry were written with an audience in mind, and when you study everything together, sometimes you can see where he said one thing to one person while the next day telling someone else the opposite. His spoken words, as they've come down to us, have been filtered through third parties, some of whom were his passionate supporters, others of whom were his enemies, all of whom had their agendas.

While I allowed James to speak some of his 'own words' in this book – most notably in the scene of his first meeting with Andrew at Whitehall, where James's references to the Scottish Seers who foretold his mother's death and to his own interest in the phenomenon are drawn entirely from a letter by Sir John Harrington describing his first meeting with King James in 1603 – I tried, for the most part, to shape his character not by his words, but his actions, and by how his immediate family interacted with him.

Some of *their* letters also survive, and by reading those that passed between Prince Henry, Anna, and King James, the family dynamic I observed was one that struck me personally as toxic, with James alternately loving and cold, and the others seeking to appease him. For example, when Anna replied too slowly to one of James's letters, James refused to send her 'a token' by Henry, who was instructed to make sure the queen knew why she was being punished. Henry, who was fifteen at the time, replied with a letter that tries to defend his mother, calm his father, and explain his own desire not to be 'a peace breaker'.

Of course, I did not know King James. I did not live within that household, so I cannot say with certainty that he was a controlling and emotionally abusive person. But if a man raises his whip in anger to his nearly-grown son and heir in public, and then several years afterwards actually strikes another son and heir (Charles) also in public – those actions tell me much about that man. And if my own interpretation of this complicated king is different from the way some others view him, that perhaps is how James might himself have wished it, for he seemed to strive to show a different face to everyone he met.

Queen Anna likely knew his nature well. She was fifteen when she left her happy home in Denmark to become his wife. From all accounts, their marriage started well enough, and with affection. That affection might have lasted all their lives, I cannot say, but I *can* say with a fair bit of certainty, from all I've read, that James was not an easy man to live with, and their marriage had its difficulties.

And I can promise you that, if one more historian holds up the fact that Anna bore children on a regular basis as proof that their marriage was happy, I'm going to personally call them and give them the number of their local rape crisis centre. I lost count of the number of times a book or article would promise me that Anna and James must have reconciled their differences because Anna was pregnant again. Women, then as now, were subjected to rape and coercive sex within marriage, and queens who are very unhappily married can still produce children, which proves nothing more than a person's fertility.

Whatever the state of her marriage, Anna found solace in her friendships, and her family.

She was especially close to her younger brother Christian, King of Denmark. On 1st August 1614, Christian arrived unannounced in London, having travelled incognito from Denmark 'without any of his people knowing his purpose'. He went straight to see his sister at her palace. King James, sixty miles away on progress, had to turn back for London, while everyone there scrambled to learn the reason for this unexpected visit.

Was there a possible war brewing? Secret negotiations on some matter of state? Worried, the Venetian ambassador sought out everyone involved, and in a week he had his answer – the conflict that had drawn the Danish king to London wasn't international, but intimate. 'The queen wrote to him about some small dispute with the king and asked him to come and find a remedy.'

Some historians maintain that this wasn't the true cause, but I'm prepared to believe it, and the fact that Christian came so quickly to Anna's side leads me to believe the dispute might not have been so small.

Anna has, in my opinion, been greatly underestimated by many of the people who, in writing of her, chose to merely copy and perpetuate the same (and often second-hand) accounts that came down through the centuries and claimed she was hysterical, or frivolous, or foolish.

The Anna I encountered in her letters and the documents available was someone very different. She was clever, full of life, a loyal friend, a loving mother, and more patient in her strategies than people gave her credit for. And she was a skilled huntress.

So when I learned she'd shot King James's favourite hound by 'accident', the summer after Henry's death, it made me wonder. Because having learned much about Anna, that did not seem like the sort of thing that she would do by accident.

I might be wrong, of course. But I'm a writer, and because it happened at the same time that King James was stricken with his sudden and mysterious digestive illness, I could not resist placing my own interpretation on the source of those events.

Anna's own health, unfortunately, proved to be a continuing problem for her, and her visits to Bath in 1613 did not produce the hoped-for cure. (The episode of the flames rising in the King's Bath during Anna's visit there that year is anecdotal, and appears to have been published for the first time in the Reverend Richard Warner's 1801 book, *The History of Bath*, without attribution.)

She took a turn for the worse on 22nd February 1619, three days after what would have been Prince Henry's twenty-fifth birthday. One of her attendants, in an eyewitness account of Anna's final days and death, claimed that she signed a will before dying 'to leave all to the Prince [Charles], and withal her servants to be rewarded.'

In the end, though, this will either vanished or was simply disregarded. Prince Charles only got a small portion of income, while James kept the larger part of Anna's property himself, and shared it with his current favourite.

Anna died on 2nd March, 1619, and James went 'to the races within three weeks of her death, even before the funeral had taken place', but he did at least write her a poem, that ends:

She is changed, not dead, for sure no good prince dies,
But, like the sun, sets only for to rise.

He might have written similar lines for Prince Henry, but it was left to others to eulogize the young man who had been, for eighteen years, a nation's greatest hope.

The Earl of Dorset, two weeks after Henry's death, wrote to a friend: 'To tell you that our Rising Sun is set ere scarce he shone, and that all our glory lies buried, you know and do lament as well as we, and better than some do, and more truly, or else you were not a man, and sensible of this Kingdome's loss.'

Henry was mourned abroad as well – in the Colony of Virginia, where the city of Henricus or Henrico had just been named in his honour, and on the continent – his appeal was international. The always-observant Venetian ambassador described him shortly after his death in this manner:

'Many predictions centred round his person, and he seemed marked out for great events. His whole talk was of arms and war. His authority was great, and he was obeyed and lauded by the military party. He protected the colony of Virginia, and under his auspices the ships sailed for the north-west passage to the Indies. He had begun to put the navy in order . . . He was hostile to Spain and had claims in France . . . his designs were vast.'

We don't know all Henry's designs because, from his deathbed, he ordered Sir David Moray to burn 'a number of Letters in a certaine cabinet in his closet', but we do know that Henry planned to accompany his sister Elizabeth and her new husband, the Prince Palatine, back to Germany after their wedding – whether to find his own Protestant bride among the princesses there (he'd discussed the possibility with Raleigh), or to fulfill his lifelong dream of travel and adventure, or to lead a Protestant crusade against some Catholic force upon the continent, as some of his followers urged him to do, and as people in France feared might happen.

That his death ended those plans just when they would have come to fruition was seen by some as evidence of foul play, and the rumours that he'd been murdered rose immediately.

Those rumours did not spare King James, whose disagreements with his son were widely known and openly observed. In the summer of 1607, when Henry was thirteen, the Venetian ambassador had written to his government of a tangle of wills between Henry and James, reporting that James 'took it in no good part; nor is he overpleased to see his son so beloved and of such promise that his subjects place all their hopes in him; and it would almost seem, to speak quite frankly, that the King was growing jealous; and so the Prince has great need of a wise counsellor to guide his steps.'

Even then, people could see the danger that might come of the king's envy and mistrust of Henry's growing popularity.

The belief that Henry had been poisoned was shared even by members of his own family. Queen Anna was reportedly convinced of it. And Bishop Burnet, in his *History of His Own Time*, writes 'Colonel Titus [one of King Charles I's most loyal men] assured me that he had from king Charles the first's own mouth, that he was well assured [Prince Henry] was poisoned by the earl of Somerset's [i.e.Viscount Rochester's] means.'

Rochester, the king's favourite, was a logical suspect, since he and Henry strongly disliked one another. In the history books, you'll more often see Rochester referred to as the 1st Earl of Somerset, the title he was given later on in 1613, the year in which this book is set, together with the title Baron Brancepeth – making him the lord of the same Brancepeth Castle where my characters spend time, in County Durham. But to keep things less confusing, I'll just call him Viscount Rochester.

He did, in fact, marry Frances Howard in 1613, after she scandalously divorced her husband, the young Earl of Essex, with the active assistance of King James. But Rochester and Frances then found themselves at the centre of an even greater scandal two years later. That affair is too complex for me to deal with properly within these pages, but it involved the murder – by poisoning – of Rochester's best friend and close advisor, Sir Thomas Overbury, a crime for which Rochester and his new wife were arrested and brought to trial.

The similarity between this poisoning and the death of Prince Henry did not go unnoticed. Sir Thomas Overbury had been poisoned by means of various foods and medicines, like those given to the prince. Many of the same people were involved in both cases. It caused a sensation, and Rochester's fall was swift.

He and his wife were found guilty and imprisoned in the Tower, but eventually they were pardoned and set free, although others involved in the poisoning were executed.

Perhaps what saved Rochester's life was his fierce warning to the king that, if James pushed him too far, Rochester would tell a secret that James did not want to have told.

James was frightened by this threat, from all accounts. Rochester kept his life, and gained a pension, and the secret was not revealed. But James moved on to his next favourite.

When Sir Edward Coke, the Lord Chief Justice who presided over the first trials of Rochester and his wife, cast his net too widely in his search for conspirators, and said, too loudly, in the open court, 'God knows what became of that sweet Babe Prince Henry (but I know somewhat)', James relieved him of his position.

This, Sir Anthony Weldon writes in his 1689 book *The Court and Character of K[ing] James,* 'stopt the breath of that discovery, of that so foul a murder, which, I fear, cryes still for vengeance'.

Two centuries years later, in 1882, an English doctor named Sir Norman Moore smothered things further by publishing a paper titled: *The Illness and Death of Henry Prince of Wales in 1612: A Historical Case of Typhoid Fever.*

Dr Moore's study is imperfect. He discards details that don't fit his theory, and assumes facts that aren't proven, but based upon his single paper, the historical record has gradually shifted over the years from allowing that Henry might have died from a fever, to stating categorically that he died of typhoid.

I may be an outlier, but I object.

I stand with the historian J. W. Williamson, who in his 1944 book *The Myth of the Conqueror: Prince Henry Stuart, a Study in 17th Century Personation,* gives Dr Moore some credit for going back to the original autopsy record, but then writes: 'though the physicians of 1612 had no knowledge whatsoever of pathology, they were generally accurate describers of what their eyes beheld. And what they saw when Henry's body was opened on the day after his death, and what they wrote into their report, does considerably less than prove either the absence of poison or the presence of Sir Norman's typhoid . . . the symptoms of heavy metal poisoning (arsenic, for example) frequently and successfully mimic the symptoms of typhoid and other fulminating diseases (which is precisely the reason so many poisonings in the past could go camouflaged as other dire infections).'

No one, in my mind, can say with any certainty what caused Prince Henry's death – if it was natural, or not, or if some person had a hand in it, and who that might have been. We are four hundred years too late, and we can do no more than speculate.

Prince Henry once commented that men often took great care to provide themselves with expensive stone monuments to ensure they'd be remembered after death, but they'd do better to pay attention to the choice of who would write their history, for no monument was as lasting or as fair 'as that which is framed by a fortunate penne'.

That his own life is so often overlooked and forgotten strikes me as sadly ironic, because to me his death provides one of the more intriguing 'what ifs' of history.

How different might the world have been, if he'd survived? If, instead of King Charles I, who believed a king answered to nobody but God, there had been a King Henry IX, who believed a king should serve his subjects? Would Britain still have been divided by the Civil Wars?

But then, perhaps, I would have had no Jacobites to write about in other books, so maybe I should let those 'what ifs' lie.

Besides, this is not truly Henry's book, nor Queen Anna's, nor James VI and I's.

Their lives run through it, but the story belongs properly to ordinary people – real people, like the nameless Black groom who was painted by artist Paul van Somer holding the bridle of Queen Anna's horse at the Palace of Oatlands in 1617, and who inspired my character of Roger Peters; or the Armstrongs of Langholm, the Metcalfes of Northallerton, the constable of Brancepeth Castle, and the Alderman and Ironmonger Thomas Hobson, whose memorial brass plaque hangs in the crypt of the church at Newark upon Trent, beside the marketplace.

Years ago, while researching another book, I chanced upon a Jacobite chaplain's report from the Battle of Preston, in 1715. 'There were taken at Preston seven Lords,' he wrote, 'besides 1490 others . . .'

He stated this so casually, seeming to dismiss the deaths of those more than a thousand men in favour of the noble lords, and I couldn't help but think of Shakespeare's Henry V, and the scene in which King Henry, just after the Battle of Agincourt, asks his herald: 'Where is the number of our English dead?' The herald hands the king the list, and Henry reads aloud the names of two nobles, a knight, and a gentleman, and then announces in relief: 'None else of name.'

We are, most of us, 'none else of name'. When we're gone, few of us will end up in the history books. But I like to believe each life matters; and just as our lives are important to somebody, people who lived in the past were important to somebody, too.

So, where I find them, I do what I can to give them back their voices, and give them back their places in the history they helped shape.

And where they've been erased, then I create them, as I did with Phoebe, and with Hector, and the women of the Close.

And sometimes, when they've been reduced to lists of names and numbers with their warrants in the records of a royal household, as with all those brave King's Messengers who left their trace behind in James's annual accounts . . .well, then I weave them all together into one man, and create an Andrew Logan – one King's Messenger, to be the voice for all of them, and bring them all to life.

'None else of name', but not forgotten, with a story to be told.

A Note of Thanks

I owe thanks, as ever, to Anna and Daniel Moray Parker and their children, who always welcome me so warmly to their home and give me the freedom to wander round Abercairny and Inchbrakie, letting me dive as deeply as I like into the history of their family for the next story.

Anna is directly descended from the Sir William Moray in this story, whose portrait still hangs in the family home, not far from David's. It's an honour and a privilege to be able to bring both of them to life.

I'm thankful also to their cousin and our friend, Alex Graeme, award-winning owner of Unique Devon Tours, who's directly descended from Sir David's cousin Patrick Graeme, 4th Laird of Inchbrakie, in this story.

Alex very kindly put his skills to work on my behalf and was my guide on a bespoke tour through the Scottish Borders and across the north of England, tracing the exact route by which his ancestor pursues my fictional characters in this novel. We parted at Northallerton, as Patrick and Sir David do, with good wine and good wishes, and the book would not be half of what it was without his help.

And I'm very grateful to award-winning Perthshire storyteller and activist Jess Smith, who in the first year of King Charles III's reign was honoured with a British Empire Medal (BEM) for so brilliantly advocating for and breaking down barriers on behalf of her community of the travelling people of Scotland, and who, with her husband Davie, took time to walk over the old Inchbrakie Castle site with us, and brought the past to life with song and story.

My thanks to the Mackie family of Ross and Gorthy, for letting me walk where Sir David once walked, and climb the hill to stand where his house once stood, so that I could look across his lands at Gorthy and feel a connection to him.

Thank you to Kat Mayer, Education and Engagement Officer at the Tarras Valley Nature Reserve at Langholm, who drove Alex and me around for the afternoon and brought the moss to life – and who happened to mention the adder she'd seen there, a short while before . . .

Thank you to the woman who sold us our entrance tickets at the Roman Army Museum near Greenhead, Northumberland, and, learning we had little time to tour that day, suggested we might want to drive a little further on and go to Cawfields, where we could properly wander round Hadrian's Wall at the milecastle.

Thank you to the Reverend Alison Hobbs, one of the owners of Brancepeth Castle, who took time to show us around and through that wonderful place, and then left us to explore, which was when we discovered the staircase in the wall that plays a part in the story.

Thank you to Christine and Charles Flood, owners of the Porch House of Northallerton (formerly owned by the Metcalfe family). The Floods hosted me during my stay there and gave me the full tour of their beautiful, historic home, down to the original staircase and a surviving section of the old wattle-and-daub wall.

While at the Porch House I also met Mr Granville Smith, who, besides being an amiable breakfast companion, graciously gave me the use of his name for 'my' landlord of the Fleece at Northallerton, for which I owe him thanks.

Alison Lindsay, the Head of the Legal and Historical Search

Rooms at the National Records of Scotland, was, as ever, beyond helpful in finding any stray fact that needed finding, and her friendship is something I value.

I value, too, the friendship and support of my writing companions: Elizabeth Boyle, Kathy Chung, Eileen Cook, Crystal Hunt, Mary Robinette Kowal, Liza Palmer and Nephele Tempest, who are always at my back, as are my own close friends and family – especially my mother, who has long been my first reader and first editor, and helps me find my way through the most challenging of stories.

My agents, Felicity Blunt, Rosie Pierce and Shawna McCarthy, mean more to me than they can know.

And thanks seem insufficient for my editing team: Clare Hey at Simon & Schuster UK, Brittany Lavery at Simon & Schuster Canada and Deb Werksman at Sourcebooks in the USA, who together made this the best book it could be.

Thank you to Cassandra Rigg and Clare Wallis for their thoughtful and meticulous copyediting and proofreading, to Judith Long for shepherding the book through all its stages of production, to Pip Watkins for designing the amazing cover and restyling the 1612 map, and to the sales team, publicists, and all the other staff at Simon & Schuster who work so tirelessly behind the scenes to bring my books to life. Your efforts may not always be seen, but I promise you they're very much appreciated.

To the booksellers who help my books find their readers, a special thank you from the little girl who helped my mother in *her* bookshop and is always very grateful for the work you do on my behalf.

And thank you so much, as ever, to all the librarians, who with reviewers, bloggers, and so many others are responsible for helping my stories connect with the people who want them.

To those who gave me help whose names I didn't think to ask, and those who helped but whom I've forgotten to thank here (a growing list, as I get older), please know I'm in your debt.

My final thanks are personal.

When I did the research for this book at Abercairny, I spent a lovely day with Anna's uncle, David Drummond Moray, and his wife Iona. Since this novel tells the story of his relation – an earlier David Moray of Abercairny – I was looking forward, when I went to Scotland next, to bringing a draft copy of the book with me, to give to David and Iona in return for their generosity.

Sadly, he won't ever get to read it.

David Drummond Moray passed away on 21st January 2024, and he will be greatly missed. But like so many others, I am grateful to have met him, and I'd like to offer these few lines of poetry Sir David Moray wrote four hundred years ago, in memory of his cousin – yet another David Moray – since to me they speak so perfectly about the man we've lost.

For David Maurice Stirling Home Drummond Moray (1945–2024):

In nothing more thy virtue proved her power,
Than in thy friendships well advised choice:
Who lov'd thee once, still loves thee to this hour,
The grave their sight, but not their love doth close

Sir David Moray – *'Epitaph on the death of his deare cousin, M. David Murray'*

1. Leith
2. Hawick
3. Langholm
4. Cawfields
5. Alston
6. Brancepeth Castle
7. Northallerton
8. Newark Upon Trent
9. Royston
10. Willingale Spain
11. Greenwich
12. London